PERFECT UNION

CODY GOODFELLOW

Ghoulish Books
an imprint of Perpetual Motion Machine Publishing
Cibolo, Texas

Perfect Union
Copyright © 2022 Cody Goodfellow
Original Copyright © 2010

www.GhoulishBooks.com
www.PerpetualPublishing.com

Cover by Frank Walls

NATURE (the Art whereby God hath made and governes the world) is by the Art of man, as in many other things, so in this also imitated, that it can make an Artificial Animal . . . For by Art is created that great LEVIATHAN called a COMMON-WEALTH, or STATE, which is but an Artificial Man . . .

—Thomas Hobbes, *Leviathan*

"I ask you: what did people—from their very infancy—pray for, dream about, long for? They longed for some one to tell them, once and for all, the meaning of happiness, and then to bind them to it with a chain. What are we doing now, if not this very thing?"

—Yevgeny Zamyatin, "We"

RATURE (the Art whereby God hath made and governs the world) is by the Art of man, as in many other things, so in this also imitated, that it can make an Artificial Animal . . . For by Art is created that great LEVIATHAN called a COMMON-WEALTH, or STATE, which is but an Artificial Man . . .

—Thomas Hobbes, *Leviathan*

"I ask you: what did people—from their very infancy—pray for, dream about, long for? They longed for some one to tell them, once and for all, the meaning of happiness, and then to bind them to it with a chain. What are we doing now, if not this very thing?"

—Yevgeny Zamyatin, *We*

FOREWORD

Either I mistake your
Shape and making quite
Or else you are that
Shrewd and knavish sprite
Call'd Robin Goodfellow:
are not you he
That frights the maidens of the villagery . . .
—*Midsummer Night's Dream, Act 2*

A LITERARY CHE GUEVARA with a sardonic sense of humor; a John the Baptist whose head has so far eluded the silver platter; the lonely voice crying in the suburban wilderness; an artist of incantatory prose and a writer of disturbingly American *anime*, of sorts, the 'toons' playing on the screen of the reader's mind; a master of streetwise characterization; a Puck of genre mischievousness; a Loki of locution . . .

Cody Goodfellow.

This poet of prodigal sons is several slashing cuts above the flailing, japing ruck of "bizarro fiction" writers; he's a kind of undiscovered John Kennedy Toole, but unlike Toole is not a man to give up on this viper-venomous world. *Cody Goodfellow never gives up.* Nor do his protagonists, his antiheroes and underheroes, his working class mythopoetic archetypes—they claw and burn and furiously love and simply *insist*, as they play out the Goodfellow themes: psychedelic augury, visions of tragic revolution; the underclass search for existential meaning;

the just-missed-it loves; the magic that simmers just under the surface of the tatty quotidian.

Oh, Cody Goodfellow is *known*—by the cognoscenti, and the hipper critics; take for example this remark from *Publisher's Weekly* as to his epochal novel *Unamerica*: "Goodfellow satirizes the excesses of capitalism, religion, and drug culture in this macabre dystopian fantasy . . . a wild, trippy journey through a horrifying nightmare version of America."

Yes indeed.

And now we have what may be his magnum opus, *Perfect Union*. This novel might well bring Goodfellow a vast new readership. Hungry readers seeking the *frisson* of Chuck Palahniuk's best, or a more-readable rush of William Burroughs, will get satisfaction at last from *Perfect Union*.

Because the novel is a most potent metaphor. I mean—what the hell *is* going on, in our world? So desperate are we to find a society that fully *functions*, that understands the wild variety of human possibility, it seems we will go to any wild extreme. From Transcendentalist communes in the mid 19th century, to the later freethinker abandonment of conventional mores; from the self-deceptive glimmer of the Christian Scientists, on to Marxism and anarcho-syndicalism, to Pol Pot and the Killing field; to religion-rigid communities—televangelical denials of science, and Islamic State murderous hardliners; oh, don't forget the Kruel Kool-aid of Jonestown; don't forget those who can be talked into cutting off their own testicles and drinking death for a ride on the Hale-Bopp Comet; and we never lose the Armageddon fanciers, smugly waiting to be raptured up before the Lake of Fire swallows everyone else. What does all that stink of? Desperation, ladies and gentlemen. Sheer desperation. Humanity is desperate to make sense of its dilemma; its thrownness, the *Geworfenheit* of Heidegger. We are bilious in Sartre's *La Nausée*, we are stuck in his Bouville,

FOREWORD

his 'mud town'. The real coming of age isn't in a boy fighting to be a man; it's an adult's realization that life is nothing like it's cracked up to be and most of us die as failures trying to keep a little dignity in our passing. We give up hope, and we settle. And all this leads, for the more stubborn of us— the rebels, the rowdies, the Cody Goodfellows—into some level of search! Where's the damn treasure map?

We become desperate. Perhaps so desperate that we willingly sign on for the drowsy transcendence of a bee colony . . .

Goodfellow's characters! Homemade intelligence; the self-starting intelligentsia of the demimonde. Strange heroes, more heroic than the trained, the deeply "educated", because they have to fight class wars as well as wars of social revolution. His writing evokes character and description as one interlocked thing, in sentence after ringing sentence:

May led him on a secret trail through the woods after the sun set behind the mountains, and the limpid pools of shadow swelled and drowned the trail. Night fell like the dimming of the house lights in a theater. He stopped once, thinking he'd heard a crash and a wailing siren, somewhere down the valley, but it was hard to say what it was, let alone how close. Another time, she'd stopped and he'd almost walked into her. Almost lost in the chirping of the insects, he thought he might have heard a muffled pop like gunfire. He looked at the nape of her neck, stole a grazing touch on her shoulder, dabbing his fingers in the clammy sweat that he could smell over the tang of pine pollen and sun-roasted soil.

In *Perfect Union* we are swept along on a picaresque search, a weird fusing of desperation and sublimity, on a quest for the real revolution. The inner revolution. The lost revolution. And at last we find . . . poetically charged irony.

In short—Cody Goodfellow.

John Shirley

CHAPTER 1

THE COUNTRY WAS supposed to be quiet at night.

Chester turned down the radio so he could focus on the road, which meandered between huddled pines and over broken mountain terrain like the trail of a drunken bloodhound. Few and far between, gravel driveways and mailboxes with no numbers jumped out of the dense undergrowth and just as quickly vanished. His tired eyes searched every patch of shadow, but none of them hid the overgrown dirt road to the big house.

Even in daylight, the turnoff was hard to spot. The trees camouflaged and damn near choked it off, but he'd planted a Budweiser can on a stick on the shoulder. Someone must have moved it . . .

He kept his ears cocked for the smothered thud and squeal of Ruth's blasted-out car stereo speakers, but he could barely hear even the gurgling growl of his old Mazda pickup's four-cylinder engine over the dental-drill symphony of the insects, and the chattering of his own teeth. Controlling what he could, he took them out and put them in his pocket.

The country was not quiet at all, tonight, adding to a list of shattered illusions, chief among which was that making and dealing drugs was not easier than honest work.

He'd cleaned out every pharmacy and convenience store in four towns, and a couple gas stations where friendly cashiers who were also customers let him bag way

1

over the state-mandated limit of pseudoephedrine. Milk crates filled with boxes and bottles of cold medicine rattled around on the seat beside him.

The whole operation had been planned down to the last detail, but Bo burned down the trailer they were using in Oroville, so they'd had to improvise a new place to cook. As the only one in their troika with no outstanding warrants, it fell to Chester to resupply. It always fell to him, because he was the only one who could cope. There were no partners, only parasites.

He wanted to get off the road and get fucked up. He wanted Ruth and Bo to cook the shit so he could get back to Sacramento and sell it, buy himself some proper dentures that fit. Something flashy, with his initials in tiny diamonds or blinking LEDs. When they pulled all his meth-rotted teeth in juvie, they guilt-tripped him hard about not taking care of them, but once they were out so he couldn't grind them, and never had to brush, he didn't see what all the fuss was about.

Chester leaned over the wheel, peering hard into the cavernous darkness for any kind of landmark. His phone couldn't get a signal, he recognized nothing, and weren't there signs on the fucking road, before?

Right then, he saw the only thing he didn't want to see. Headlights chopped through the trees and carved up his dark-adapted sight with careening blades of blinding white fire. The shakes came over him so bad, he had to fight the urge to jump out of the truck and run into the woods.

Chester looked for a place to flip a bitch, but both shoulders dropped into ruts clogged with brush. Nobody would be poking around the woods at this hour with their brights on, except cops. Jesus, he was cooked.

He prayed and pumped the brakes and tried to get his teeth out of his breast pocket all at the same time, and that's when he saw the Bud can on the stick.

"Fortune favors the prepared," he crowed, as he

steered the Mazda down the narrow, rutted dirt track. Learned that from wrestling in high school. Only went to one practice, but that slogan on the wall (next to the one on the ceiling: IF YOU CAN READ THIS, YOU'VE BEEN PINNED) had done him more good than anything else in school, except, of course, chemistry.

The road whipsawed hither and yon down a steep slope, then up another and into a grove of oaks. Pine saplings and sagebrush clumps clawed at the truck's undercarriage.

He'd begun to think he'd made another wrong turn when the black forest curtain rolled back to admit him to a huge open meadow. The road waded through tall brown grass, passing some skeletal sheds and a tumbledown barn, looping and slurring over level ground like it was dizzy, but eventually, it ended at the steps of the big house.

He held his breath, killed the lights and the engine. His tweaked vision crawled with twisty purple hallucinations; the forest and sheltering mountains seemed to drift around his axis, towering shadowy shapes that couldn't sit still.

The throbbing song of the forest closed in on him, mocking his panic. A million little live things—crickets, mosquitoes, moths, cicadas, beetles and stranger bugs—strummed his nerves with their eternal song of invisible dominion. Sitting in the dark, swimming in rancid crank-sweat, cringing at hallucinated sirens, trying to keep the shrieking susurrus of the insect kingdom from driving him insane, Chester let the wild horses of his fear run themselves ragged until, after a hundred deep breaths, they stopped dragging him.

No accusing headlights followed him out of the woods. He let the stale breath out, shocked by its tainted fecal aroma, the rot in his teeth settled into his heart and lungs.

The place was just like Ruth said, when she came back from finding it. It wasn't on any maps, and nobody knew it, or at least nobody talked. You went looking for it, you'd never find it in a hundred years, but if you needed it—or if it needed you—there it fucking was.

Chester whistled through his bloodless gums. Though by nature an incurious man, his overstimulated brain stuck to the riddle of the house like flypaper.

The big house sprawled out forever and loomed over him like a brownstone tidal wave. Two giant-sized stories, with squinting slit windows and a single impaling tower in the center, reminded Chester of old prison movies. The plain façade of stained brown brick reared up against the starry sky as if enraged by its abandonment, defiantly giving the finger to the insane terrain that hid it from the world.

Yes, they'd finally struck lucky.

Chester unloaded the cargo, stacking the milk crates at the foot of the porch. Let Bo carry it in.

A splintering crack, like a branch torn from a tree, echoed across the open space. Nothing moved that his manically roving eyes could catch.

The tall double doors stood half-open. The dark behind them might have been a wall of coal. An old police flashlight in his shaky grip, Chester skipped up the steps and hollered, "Rise and shine, bitches, Time to work!"

Where the fuck was everybody?

Outside, the stars glowed like cocaine under a blacklight, so bright he almost cast a shadow. Inside, the darkness was so thick you rubbed your eyes for fear you'd gone blind.

The flashlight beam led him into an empty room bigger than a bowling alley. The slap and shuffle of his sneakers echoed off the distant walls and came back as a monster stalking him in hobnailed boots. He chased after splashes of human-shaped color that flitted through his weakening light.

A mural of farmers and woodworkers and other country bullshit covered the far wall. It was the same brand of boring artwork you'd see in any government building from the Depression, but the angular workers creeped him out with their naked but sexless bodies, and the sunbursts of mustard-yellow crap someone had splattered over it to blot out their faces.

Chester tried one of the oddly narrow corridors that fed off the common room. There were no breadcrumbs, but they'd left a trail of beer cans. Bo had set up his chemistry kit in a windowless kitchen somewhere on the ground floor. When Chester left, nobody wanted to explore the cellar or the upstairs, but they could have done anything if they got bored. He hoped they'd just fucked and passed out, and hadn't started another fire.

Fucking idiots. He switched off the flashlight and listened for redneck pillow talk. He heard only his blood beating in his ears, and a humming emptiness like a live telephone line. Bo said all the wiring was trashed, but in the stifling silence, Chester felt a weird resonance in his bones, a muzzled rush of caged energy like a power line transformer.

He clutched his chest as if to squeeze his heart back to a slower pulse. *Slow down, player . . . letting your mind run all off on you. Get it under control—*

He took out his snuff box and did a quick key-bump into each nostril to straighten out his jangled nerves.

And that was when he heard her.

She sounded like a cat in heat, low and breathless moans ratcheting up to an endless, ululating squeal that made him shiver.

All his anxiety over the spookiness of this gigantic old ruin got filed away. He had to see them before they saw him, and stopped. If they were high enough and he played his cards right, maybe he could join in.

The corridor got much wider, but the ceiling was so low, he had to duck, peering into rows of tiny cells cramped with smothering heat and the earthy stench of livestock.

The geeks who lived here must've kept pigs and cattle indoors, but the more he smelled it—and the scent must've been strong indeed, to register with Chester's perforated scent receptors—the more it reminded him of the pickled, spicy tang of a women's locker room.

The sounds of feminine pleasure died out. They must have cracked Bo's nitrous oxide tank. It was the only safe way to get high while you were cooking crystal, because it scorched your brain and atomized you, then burned off in a few golden, infinite moments, leaving a mellow afterglow that wouldn't interfere with the handling of volatile chemicals . . . unless you were a hardcore burnout like Bo. Once, back in Sacto, he and Ruth left the tank wide open in his car with the windows rolled up, and almost died drooling through rictuses of braindead joy.

His heart still raced, but the empty hum crowded it out of his ears. So low and deep he heard it in his colon, and the wall vibrated under his hand. Earthquake? Unless he was tripping, the whole house throbbed like an engine going a million rpm in first gear.

Whatever they were up to, Chester didn't want to catch them, anymore.

His shaky hands slid over blistered plaster and into an open doorway lit by the deep red glow from an exhausted battery lamp. "Get decent, bitches," he hissed, but he still caught them red-handed, though just what the hell he'd caught them doing completely eluded him.

Dig big, beer-gutted Bo with his bib overalls around his ankles, slithering slickly atop Ruth's bony, swaybacked ironing board of a body. A tornado of bees swirled furiously around the room, spewing out of cracks in the brick walls. Both coated with viscous, golden slime that softened their forms into lumps like bugs trapped in amber, melting them together so Bo's slobbering mouth and clumsy tongue seemed to penetrate the reedy cords of her throat and probe around under her skin, causing her half-lidded eyes to bug out, her scrawny claws to rake his back and plow divots out of it like saturated clay. Slatted ribs and fat rolls mingled and meshed, bones popped out of sockets and slashing around in the mess like driftwood in a storm drain.

Bo thrust into her languidly, yet so deeply, his cock should have jutted out of her mouth. She let out that bubbling cat-sound again, and her glazed eyes opened and rooted Chester even more tightly to the spot.

She twisted and slid halfway out from under her erstwhile partner to reach for Chester while her hindquarters, casually bent at a spine-snapping angle, continued to milk the spunk out of Bo. Her face was puffy under its coating of slime, cheeks ballooned like she was holding in the mother of all nitrous hits, and wanted to pass to him.

Chester cursorily weighed the torrent of angry insects, the melting flesh and the sloppy, boneless nature of his partners' coupling, against Bo's stupor and the invitation to put his mouth on Ruth, something she had never, in the deepest depths of drugged disgrace, been willing to offer. None of this was real, he told himself, but that kiss. All he had to decide was whether to put his dentures in or not, and in the end, he knelt down and locked his toothless mouth over hers.

Sensations gushed in and swamped each other, and his mind a little paper boat on the crest of it, with no compass or sight of shore. His lips solved the mystery of the slime, at least. They were smothered in honey.

Jesus, he was died and gone to Heaven. With one eye fixed on Bo's warped, humping form, he relaxed and sucked in what Ruth had to offer.

It wasn't nitrous, but it sure as hell did get him high.

Honey flooded his palate with such force it clogged his sinuses, squirted out his nostrils, and blocked his windpipe. His body tingled all over with desperate pleas for oxygen. He tried to break free, but her arm wound round his neck once, twice, a third time, and drew him closer.

Fighting to breathe, he watched Bo buckle and subside into the viscous pool of Ruth's concave bosom. Bo's teeth clamped on her nipple and tore it free, but her honey-glutted flesh streamed out between his teeth and reformed. His face dribbled off his head, skull deflating like an old basketball, eyes rolling and nostrils flaring as they smeared off on her belly and sank out of sight.

Spots danced before Chester's eyes. He could see nothing more, when he finally took the flashlight and smashed it into her head, which closed over it and sucked it out of his grip. He backed away from Ruth, her arm stretching out like taffy until it tore off.

He found the door somehow, gagging and crabbing backwards with gooey streamers of honey and liquid Ruth dangling from his mouth, her boneless arm still draped around his neck. His partners dragged their fused bodies out into the hall after him, mutely begging him to join them for good. He rolled over and found the strength to crawl, but he had no idea which direction he was headed. All was unbroken darkness, and that insidious vibration grew louder and more insistent.

From slots in the moldings along the floor and ceiling, they poured out in such dense clouds that they blocked out the distant rectangle of silver starlight that marked the front door. They buffeted his honey-slick face with their tiny bodies and beating wings, stuck fast and stinging, killing themselves to prick him, tearing out their own guts by the hundreds, the thousands, stinging him all over and driving him down to the floorboards under their onslaught.

Chester forged ahead, bearded in scuttling bees. Crunching underfoot, swarming his face, dive-bombing down his throat with each involuntary gasp for air and gout of honey-vomit. The droning pounded at him even after the bees swelled his eyes shut and stopped up his ears with their dead.

Seemingly driven mad by the honey smeared on Chester, they buried him alive, but he still crawled to the doorway and, fueled by the last dregs of crank and adrenaline, found his feet.

With a hoarse war-whoop, Chester lurched towards the cool evening breeze wafting through the open double doors. He saw his crappy old Mazda and the woods beyond, and he reached out for them, feeling, of all unlikely things, incredibly lucky, just as the doors slammed shut in his face.

The curtain of bees lifted off him all at once. He slumped against the heavy oak doors, then turned as the air stirred and thrummed with a whole new kind of tension.

Through one surviving eye, Chester saw Bo's Coleman stove and all the glass and metal cooking implements, and an armada of silverware and nails and broken glass and splintered wooden beams, and all of it in flight as if shot from a cannon, all of it coming, at supersonic speed, for his face.

CHAPTER 2

"**PUT THAT SHIT** away, before I take it away."

Andrew looked up from the text message screen on his phone and saw he'd steered the pickup truck across the double yellow line again. An oncoming semi blared its air horn and swerved onto the shoulder as Andrew righted the truck.

"Shit, I'm sorry," Andrew said. "Did I wake you up?"

"Your driving kept me awake. The road goes straight, Andy. Why can't you?"

Andrew tried to think of a clever retort, but it was beyond him. His brothers-in-law formed an inscrutable bundle of blanket on the bench seat beside him. The voice was so thick from sleep, he couldn't tell which one was speaking. He wondered if coming from a big family would have made him sharper, or just given him multiple neuroses and a facial tic.

He typed, *Gotta go—Love U*, hit SEND and pocketed the phone.

He was dying for a smoke. If his brothers caught him smoking, they'd tell Laura. He peeled a piece of Nicorette gum out of the blister pack in his breast pocket and began the laborious task of chewing the miserable peppery nicotine juice out of it.

Beyond the two-lane blacktop rolling under them, the night was jet-black infinity, with only distant, guttering pinpoints of isolated light. He hadn't noticed a sign anywhere, but by the rancid manure stench clogging the air, he guessed they were somewhere downwind of Harris Ranch. Just over halfway there.

"You want to drive?" he asked after a while.

A whisper, sibilant, under the blanket, then, "No, but watch the fucking road, won't you?"

He watched it, still trying to think of something to say. The jumbled, woolen mountain range of Dean and Dominic stirred and subsided beside him, but with each breath, they seemed to grow larger, pushing him against the driver's side door.

By dawn, if they didn't kill each other, they would be in Sacramento. There'd be more space. One of the twins would drive the U-Haul truck they'd rent, and they'd caravan up to Grass Valley. Everything that would come after—the intervention, the move, the ride back—he preferred to think of as something someone else would do, though with his body. There would be lost tempers and fights, and as the only non-blood relation on the scene, most of it would heap on him. If only he could sleep through it and wake up back in San Diego . . .

The phone chirped in his breast pocket, but he didn't dare take it out. He reached for the travel mug in the cupholder and killed the cold, chalky dregs of his coffee.

He looked over at Dean and Dom. The blanket had ridden up so Dom's leg was exposed. An arm lay across it, lightly tanned with no tattoo sleeves, so he knew it was Dean's.

The twins were raised separately before puberty, Dean by his father, Dominic with his mother. Dean entered the Navy as an officer, while Dom joined the Army long enough to piss Dad off, then got a discharge and became a meatcutter and part-time tattoo artist. Dean had a wife and two sons, while Dom got more pussy than an animal shelter. Everything they did and said was to distinguish himself from his twin, or to piss the other off. Yet, when, as now, they lay closer together than man and wife, as if, in sleep, they returned to the womb and tried to become one.

Two miles down the road, he snuck the phone out and read the message. *Love U too—Nite.* He bit his lip and put away the phone. More he wanted to say, and if he did nothing else all night, he might find the right words.

He was actually very good at that, finding the right words, the perfect comeback, when it was too late.

It was a dry, ionized day when he climbed into this truck, leaned out and kissed his wife, and a static shock arced between their lips. His brain shorted out and he hugged her, delivering multiple tiny shocks wherever he touched her. She jerked away and his last glimpse of her as the truck pulled away was her wary eyes blinking above her hand shielding her static-stung lips, asking, "What the hell did you do that for?"

She didn't answer the phone, and he worried. Dean and Dom picked on him mercilessly. When they stopped for gas at an Arco station in Shafter, he was thinking only about how he could sneak off and smoke a cigarette, when he got another text message. *Miss me yet?*

He jammed the gas pump nozzle into the tank, typed *U know I do,* and sent it off.

A reply came immediately. *What would u do to me if u were here now?*

Excitedly, he'd typed an inspired response. Dom's braying laughter came out of the cab, but he sent off the message, and only then noticed that he wasn't texting his wife.

"Nice one, assholes," he said as he climbed in, but Dom and Dean just stared at him like they'd both swallowed chewing tobacco, his wife's hooded eyes in the same face doubled, until he looked away and shut up.

Any sense of camaraderie that might have been building since he married into the family melted away on the road. The twins bickered silently when he was around, and in hushed but violent tones when he was out of earshot; but to his face, they were a united front, and he little more than a hitchhiker. What they were coming up here to do was family business, and he, those identical eyes seemed to say, would never be family.

He watched for the signs that announced his progress every seven miles, the agonizing crawl protracted without music or conversation as a distraction. He told himself not to think, not to worry, just drive. Avenal, Coalinga, Mendota, Firebaugh; bleak farm—and prison-towns and half-abandoned gas stations, populated by pump jerks, waitresses and cashiers who must be under some kind of house arrest, or why would they live out here? People who couldn't handle the real world of cities and people, broken-brained loners and simpletons, exhausted migrants ditched here by coyotes fleeing *la migra*, and dangerous lunatics like the woman they were going to see.

He thought of an old, dumb riddle. *Why did it take three Boy Scouts to help the old lady across the street?*

Because she didn't want to go.

If he thought any more about her mother, he was going to start getting pissed. Speaking of, he felt like he had a medicine ball sitting on his bladder. Los Banos—almost, literally, "the bathroom." He flipped the turn signal and turned down the lazy loop of offramp to a short strip of drive-thru restaurants and gas stations.

When he rolled up to the pumps and over the rubber strip, the bell clanged and Dean and Dom disentangled and slid wordlessly out of the truck. Andrew started to explain, then thought, *Fuck it*, dug his lighter out of his backpack and went in to the gas station.

The clerk was an old redneck woman cured in menthol smoke. She rang up and bagged his root beer, turkey jerky and Camel Ultra Lights, and made change without giving any hint that she was actually awake. He took the restroom key, which had a badminton racquet attached to it so it would be hard to misplace.

As soon as he rounded the corner, he lit up.

"Hey buddy, you think you could help me out?"

Andrew guiltily tossed the cigarette before he realized it wasn't one of the twins. He saw the man peel off the wall of the gas station and shuffle into his way before he could recover it. Under the snot-green fluorescent lamps, his flannel shirt looked like something scraped off the ocean floor. A grimy meshback Snap-On Tools cap cast his face into shadow, but Andrew could see that, in the middle of the night, in the middle of nowhere, this guy was wearing sunglasses.

"I—me and my wife, I mean—we ran out of gas? We're on our way to Sacramento for a job interview—fresh start, an' you know, I got stuck, could you help me out with a few bucks?"

Andrew needed to piss in the worst way, and was about to. He fished a couple dollars out of his front pocket, change from the snacks, and handed it over.

Grubby fingers snatched the cash out of his hand as if he might change his mind, but when he sorted through the tiny wad, the man got up close. "Come on, man, we're in the middle of fuckin' nowhere, this won't even get me to the next gas station—"

"Sorry, it's all I have, man." Andrew tucked his head down and feinted right, then tried to duck around on the left, but the panhandler brushed him back with his shoulder. He pocketed Andrew's money and pushed him with the other hand. "How about a couple smokes, and something to eat, for starters?"

Andrew dropped his bag and backpedaled to keep the hand off him, told himself to go back to the truck, he didn't need to piss that bad, anyway—

Suddenly, the panhandler jerked sideways and slammed into the wall with one hand still trapped in his pocket. Dominic cross-checked him with a hockey brawler's total disregard for life and limb, brawny shoulder and huge biceps laid across the back of his neck, smashed nose and crooked teeth taking a bite of the aluminum siding.

Andrew moved to stop them, but Dom elbowed him out of the way and, in the same motion, whipped the panhandler around and punched him in the throat.

His eyes bugged out like deviled eggs, his mouth working breathlessly. A front tooth dangled by a shred of sinew, and blood bubbles spurted out of his nose. His legs betrayed him, pants darkening at the crotch, and he would've collapsed, if not for Dominic's hand on his collar.

"Go piss," Dom said.

Andrew let himself into the men's room and stood there, trying to catch his breath, unable to get a squirt out. After a minute, he flushed anyway and let himself out. Dom dragged the panhandler, who wheezed like a broken recorder, into the single stall, kicked him in the balls, dropped him facedown on the scummy tile and unbuttoned his jeans. As Andrew walked back to the truck, he heard Dom bark, "You fuck with my brother, you fucked with me, and when you fuck with me . . . "

Dean sat behind the wheel with a phone to his ear. His fingers did some kind of intricate mnemonic device dance on the dashboard, or maybe a ritual to stay calm.

"Calling your mom?" Andrew asked.

Dean nodded irritably, then hung up. "She's not home."

"So? I thought this was supposed to be a surprise."

"She's always home."

"You think something happened to her?"

Dominic came around the gas station and climbed into the pickup bed, where he nestled among their bedrolls and duffel bags and seemed to fall instantly asleep.

"No," Dean said. "But I *hope* something happened to her. Get in the fucking truck."

CHAPTER 3

THEY WERE FINALLY coming for her.

After all this time, all those years of ingratitude and neglect, they were finally coming back.

She cursed the dietetic fig snacks that were all she could reach from the bed. Goddamned empty things were like food from the land of the dead, you had to eat two whole pounds of the shit to feel anything.

To *feel*—

How did she feel, right now? Did she dare to look at herself? So often, the truth was more than she could accept, the worst of it the realization that all this was wrought by her own hand, or by the weakness in that hand, and whose fault was that?

She counted her fingers, studying them blearily until she spotted the glowing ember at the end of the extra one, and sucked it, let the smoke drool out between her lips.

She felt drunk, to tell the truth. Which was strange, because she hadn't touched alcohol in almost two years, because of the side effects off her meds. And she'd stopped taking those, when the voices assured her she no longer needed them.

She flexed the knotted muscles of her back, rolled out of bed, and looked at herself in the mirror: a big, tired woman in a frayed flannel nightgown; bloated, overripe pumpkin head, shaggy with graying hair; wide, crumb-caked mouth and sad, glassy eyes blinking back baggy rolls of fat and blobs of smeared mascara.

In spite of it all, she felt pretty good today, in a way so long lost to her that it felt new, and almost remade her in its strange healing light. Today, she had something to look forward to.

They hadn't called ahead, but she could feel them coming. The voices told her. It was supposed to be a surprise, so she didn't want to spoil it, didn't want to do anything that might wake her up, if this was another dream.

The first white-gold rays of sunrise broke through the gauntlet of pine-bristled peaks that framed the view from her bedroom window. A promise made and broken every day, before now.

She got up and dressed herself, warmed some soup. The little prefabricated shack was already stifling. The wind chimes outside were still, and not a needle stirred on the pines that crowded the edge of her yard. She fired up the big air conditioner, a huge refrigeration unit she'd bought at a government auction. Built to cool an Army battalion headquarters, it made the vinyl windows bow and ice crystals start to spread up the wall with its first bellowing, arctic breath.

No sign of the dogs. Chuck, her old Yorkie terrier, usually curled up at her feet all night, his arthritis so bad he seldom left the house. None of them came running when she tapped the kibble scoop against the edge of the padlocked trashcan with the food in it. The house was still and silent, but for the roar of the air conditioner.

Come to think of it, she hadn't seen any of them yesterday, either, but the bowls from last night were all empty. Her feet were sore, and now she remembered looking for them, wandering down the road and even into the woods.

She clutched at her heart as an ugly notion struck her. The county might have come again, and taken the last of her family away. She was a good mother to them, ten dogs and a fluid but healthy population of cats; but that old, psychotic pervert who lived down the road had sicced the sheriff on her once before. She was in a fog from her meds then, and made a bad case for herself. They left her only a handful of cats and Chuck and Dewey the dachshund, because they were too old to cause trouble—and Toshiro, but only because he ran off into the woods when they came.

Her mind was still so cloudy, but with a real focused effort, she recalled that she gave up and went into the house because that was when she heard the voices, and knew that they were coming.

"Chuck? Come here, boy . . . " He was an old, old dog, and might well have gone off to die. She still had Dewey and Toshiro to look after, though she wouldn't weep if the other dog never came back.

Toshiro was Dominic's dog, a Husky-Samoyed mix on paper, with more wolf in him than anything else. Too wild for the city, he got left on her doorstep when Dom joined the army. He only showed up every other day or so, to eat, mark his turf and maybe kill a couple of her chickens, then disappear into the woods.

He'd killed a whole litter of kittens once, ate them up like a Christmas *hors d'oeuvre* platter, so she wouldn't put it past him to do something to the cats. She went around back to the chicken coop. She made her legs carry her bulk at an unaccustomed jog, though there was nothing to be done.

Clumps of bloody feathers wafted up around her boots in the yard beyond the plywood chicken coop.

"Bad dog!" she shouted, in case he was out there. She put a bell on him once, but he slipped it in minutes. Given the trouble he caused all up and down the valley—almost legendary accounts of the "devil-dog" burned her ears at the supermarket, and had even begun to show up in the paper—she'd decided it would be better not to tag him at all, for fear they'd track him to her door.

She stomped around the side of the coop and bit her tongue in shock. Toshiro was suddenly and completely off the hook.

The back wall of the coop lay on the ground outside the yard where something had thrown it after ripping it clean off. Inside, guano and straw and trampled eggs and shoals of drying blood, but no carcasses. Toshiro always feasted on a few choice morsels and left the rest, but there was not a bone or a beak in sight. Something that walked on its hind legs had left deep, broad prints in the muck.

Bears?

"Toshiro? Come, boy!" she called out and clapped her hands. Slipping on the mud, she caught the ragged wire wall of the coop and climbed out over the breach in the fence. The tracks were shallow to invisible on the thin alpine topsoil, but she could see by the stray droplets of chicken blood that they led off into the woods. Where the wild brown grass gave way to pines and poison oak, she found a scrap of black fur like a lost toupee, stiff with blood and dander.

She went staggering back into the house and found the cooking sherry in the back of the cupboard, shotgunned a hearty salvo of swallows before gagging and throwing up in the sink.

Her head ached from stringing so many thoughts together in a row while staving off unreasoning fear. Her heart throbbed with artery-clogging guilt and remorse. More little things entrusted to her care, and she loved them without limit and lived for them, and still failed them. All she'd ever wanted to do was to give life, to nurture and protect it and send it out into the world, and every time, it all went so wrong. She was weak, she was unfit, she was damned—

She had nothing left to lose.

She was *free*.

It was time to go. They were here.

She wiped her mouth and went outside without shutting the door. As she passed the mantel shrine to her favorite four-legged children and the row of framed pictures of her kids arrayed like a jury, she felt her eyes brimming with tears. If only *they* would have come for her, if only they cared. If only they could forgive her—

But now, she had somewhere to go, someone who needed her. A new family. The voices told her so.

And then she saw the one she was waiting for, a soft silhouette in the blue shadows at the edge of the woods.

She walked calmly into the trees until her eyes adjusted to the sudden gloom. There was only the one out there now, but there were more inside the big house, and they needed her. They needed a mother.

He was a short, scrawny man, but beyond that, she could tell very little about him, because he was swollen up like a sausage and blue-black all over with welts and wounds. Bits of glass and chrome and even some silverware stuck out of him here and there like he'd been caught in a tornado in a greasy spoon. His eyes were closed over with blisters of venom and pus. He trembled with strain and barely contained agony, but a Queen's beefeater never stood so ramrod straight as he did, when he opened his mouth to speak.

She came closer. She barely heard a whispering static buzz from deep down inside him; but wrapped up in it, she heard a tiny voice and parts of words, but his cracked lips didn't form them. He was like a radio feeding her a signal from a distant transmitter. Closer still, she tipped her ear to the buzzing mouth. And she heard the voices coming out of it.

"We need you . . . save us . . . our family . . . needs you . . . "

She knew what to do. Ever since that day when the bee swarm got into the air conditioner and stung her all over, she'd known what to do.

PERFECT UNION

That was the day she first heard the voices. At first, she figured they were like the old voices her meds were supposed to repress, the ones that told her she was worthless, that made her hurt her children and everyone who loved her. But these ones were kind, soft and fuzzy with unconditional love, and they needed *her*.

She took the little man in her arms and pressed his broken head to her bountiful bosom, cooing, "There, there," and the moment, the gesture, was so right, that she almost fell asleep on her feet, and barely flinched when the bees came out of his mouth and stung her again.

When her face was pocked with stingers, she knew where to go. With her arm around the little man's shoulders, she walked into the woods to find her new family.

CHAPTER 4

THEIR LITTLE CONVOY had been lost for nearly an hour when Dom turned down Fear's "More Beer" on the stereo, popped the bottlecap off his third Miller Light on the steering wheel, looked at Andrew and asked, "How much do you really know about our mom?"

Andrew tried not to freak out or grab the wheel, but the road disappeared behind a boulder with pines perched atop it just ahead, and they were going way too fast. At least there was room to freak out, now that Dean was driving the U-Haul truck behind them. And small comfort it was, with Tailgunner Dean pushing them on like a broom pushes dirt as he bobbed his head in indignant agreement with everything Rush said on the AM radio.

Dom's wraparound shades gave no clue as to where his eyes were. Andrew made himself turn off the anxiety, because this was just another test. "Next to nothing. Laura's not her biggest fan." He'd actually heard quite a lot of it, at marriage counseling.

"She used to hit us in her sleep." He turned to watch the road again, but Andrew's sphincter clenched tighter than the security at a Dianetics Celebrity Closet Cleansing. "No shit, she used to get up in the middle of the night, sleepwalk into our room, and whale on us. When we had a room."

"I'm sorry, man," Andrew tried, but the effort sputtered and died. What did he want, a hug?

But this was important. Dom's voice went low, like he was afraid his brother would overhear. "Her boyfriends beat us, and we hit each other all the time. It was the only way we knew how to treat each other. She dragged us from town to town when one of her boyfriends was running from the cops, or when he got locked up. Once, this shithead car thief she was fucking broke Dean's collarbone, and she told the doctors I did it to him, to keep the shithead out of jail. I got put in a reform school and then foster homes for a year, before she got me back. I was lucky."

Dom killed the Bud tallboy and chucked it over his shoulder into the truck's bed. "Shit was bad, so bad Dean and Laura don't remember half of it. We don't owe her a goddamned thing. But here we are . . . ."

Andrew wanted to ask him why he was coming up to help her move. When Laura heard of her mother's run-in with the law, she'd been terrified that Mom would move downstate to be close to them. In a rare proactive move, Andrew recruited the twins to intervene and set her up somewhere safe and cheap in Sacramento, so she wouldn't end up around their necks. He'd figured Dom felt the same as Laura did about her, but the waves of loathing rolling off him like solar flares spoke to something deeper, to which Andrew could only be a mute witness, or an accomplice.

Finally, Andrew said, "I know it wasn't what she meant to do, but she made you guys strong. You turned out pretty good." Wow, that sounded lame.

Dom smiled and cocked his head like a dog hearing its own bark coming out of a stereo speaker. "Now that's *good* bullshit. Really, why'd you come, though? Laura made you?"

A host of answers crowded in on him, but each stank worse than the last. "I wanted to help the family. That's what family does, right? Growing up, I just had my mom, no brothers or sisters, and—"

With one hand on the wheel, Dom plugged one nostril and honked snot explosively out the other. Andrew moaned, "Jesus, man. Let me get you a Kleenex."

"Can't blow this into a Kleenex."

"But the truck—"

"My truck." He blew again, dislodging something green with the heft and wingspan of a fruit bat. It hit the floorboard between Andrew's sneakers.

"Hey, you wanna smoke?"

Andrew looked around, tried to laugh. Dom's black shades locked on him. The road was going into convulsions on the jagged mountainside. Dom's hands clenched the wheel so tight it squeaked. "No, not really . . . "

"Good, just testing you."

"Oh, okay. Are we close to her house?"

"Yeah, we're almost there," Dom replied, and lit up a joint.

Andrew sucked in a breath to change the subject, when Dom coughed, "There," and turned off the road.

The truck's wheels skipped in and out of ruts in the dirt drive, the engine fussing and howling as it fought for traction. The driveway wound up a steep hillside and squeezed between two stands of looming pines like huge praying hands, passed a mailbox ventilated by shotgun blasts, a lonely tire swing twisting in the faintest of midmorning breezes.

"Oh shit," Dom grumbled. Waving his arm out the window, he honked and shouted, "Stop! Dean, hold up—"

Claws scraping on metal and snapping limbs as the trees tried to pry the roof off the rental truck. Dom stopped and threw the parking brake. Dean gunned the accelerator and bulled through the low-hanging curtain of branches. He stopped just short of Dom's bumper, huge in the rearview mirror.

Dom pinched out and pocketed the joint. "Slide over and drive the truck up," he mumbled. "Don't fuck up my clutch." Then he jumped out to go scream at his twin. "There goes the deposit, asswipe!"

Andrew reluctantly unbuckled his seatbelt and climbed over the stick shift. He drove an automatic at home and could manage on the highway, but he couldn't shift without stalling to save his life on a steep grade.

The wheel was slick with sweat. He paused Fear so he could think, but Dom shouted, "Fuck!" and punched Dean's door, then screamed at Andrew to get the pickup out of the way.

Andrew shoved the stick shift into first and made the pickup shiver with the utterly *wrong* sound of gears eating each other. He crushed the clutch to the floor and popped it.

The truck bucked and shot up the drive, over the rise and onto a terrace. The back bumper of a dusty whale of a luxury sedan took up half of the horizon. Andrew swerved around it, the steering going all mushy as the wheels sank into a quicksand pit of gravel. He let the truck stall out.

Andrew looked at the big car he'd almost smashed up. A black Cadillac Fleetwood, maybe ten years old, stickers plastered all over the bumper, trunk and window, so haphazardly that he couldn't read any of them, let alone see inside. A crust of pine needles, pollen and bird and bee shit on the windshield was several weeks deep. Ridiculous— yuppies in the city who never braved any terrain rougher than the speed bumps in their gated burbclaves drove monster Hummers, while Mom got around out here in a pimpmobile with shot shocks. Andrew got out and walked around the Cadillac to check out the house.

It was quiet, but not the quiet of a big open space like the desert or the open sea. A row of oak trees soaked up the sounds of the big rental truck inching up the driveway, so it sounded half a mile away. Birds twittered and warbled in the trees, and a chromatic threnody of chimes stirred from the eaves of the house.

It was a prefab three-bedroom cabin with a two-car garage so stuffed with junk there was no room for a car. The white plastic siding had been hosed down recently, but it was coming off the walls, and soggy pink fiberglass insulation peeked out everywhere. Barbie's alpine Unabomber shack comes with everything you see here!

A row of kennels ran alongside the garage, but they were all empty, the gates wide open. A Roughneck trashcan overturned at his feet, a few pebbles of dog food and ribbons of a generic kibble bag strewn across the yellow lawn.

Andrew was a long way from home, where a raccoon or a possum in the dumpster corral could pass for a wildlife encounter. What the hell lived up here? Foxes? Coyotes? Wolves? Mountain lions? Bears? Oh, my.

Suddenly, he had to pee.

He went to the front door and looked for a doorbell. He almost knocked, but then thought better of it, because it finally set in that maybe this silence wasn't normal, even for this place, and the missing woman was his mother-in-law.

He opened the door, but damned if his feet were going to carry him right in. The smell of it washed over him, and now it was with a sense of dread that he assured himself that maybe this *was* normal.

"Hey, dingus, you see my dog?"

Andrew jumped and spun in place with his hands out in surrender.

Dom stood there, flushed, sweaty but amused by the startled look on Andrew's face.

"I . . . don't . . . I didn't see any dogs."

"Shit, that's weird." Dom turned and walked back down the driveway. Over the edge of this terrace, the yellow box of the rental truck crested and hove into view. The roof was badly scratched up, and one of the corner turn signals was gone.

Dean climbed down and crossed the lawn under full sail, like a flag officer delivering surrender terms. Andrew got tired just watching him. "Where is she?" Dean asked.

Andrew looked around before he answered. "I didn't see her."

"Who *did* you see?"

"I didn't see anybody."

"Then say that the first time." He went in the front door without replying to Andrew's lame parting shot, "What, no salute?"

Andrew waited on the porch. Now and then, Dom shouted, "Shiro! Hey, shithead, Daddy's back!" sending terrorized woodland creatures stampeding out into the open. He heard Dean methodically search the house, slamming doors and making the Tupperware windows quiver.

He knew better than to offer to help either of them. The thought of sitting in the truck for another minute made his ass throb, but he didn't want to go inside. He checked his watch and decided he'd earned a smoke and a phone call.

His cell phone bleeped No Signal, though he waved it around like a tricorder on *Star Trek*. Now, he had to go inside.

Pussy, his brain called him, already using Dom's voice. *You came all this way, and you're gonna wait on the porch in the heat.* He finally girded his loins and tugged the heavy screen door open, if only because he definitely, desperately had to pee.

It was cold inside.

Stepping over the threshold was like breaking through a membrane and passing into Russian winter. Andrew gagged on the stench of dog musk, dander, sour potpourri and the rancid residue of a million microwaved meals and overcooked stews. The rooms were dim, shades drawn, so that only the humped shapes of too much furniture could be made out. Every surface was caked with a patina of dust and dog hair; he stirred big, sneeze-inducing clouds of it just moving through the murky living room towards the yellow light seeping through the dining room curtains.

Pausing, waiting for his eyes to adjust, he called out, "Hey, Dean? Ms. D'Amato?" She'd reverted to her maiden name as a declaration of independence, Laura told him once; silly, really, since the revived surname was her father's, and only suggested a regression, a call for a do-over that the world never deigned to acknowledge. When they got married, Laura took Andrew's name to get away from her father's, but she had flirted with trying to convince him to adopt a new, third surname of their own invention.

No answer.

This trip was my idea. Why do I feel like a little kid nobody wanted to bring along?

Andrew navigated the alleys between couches of clashing upholstery designs and found the darker rabbit-hole of a hallway. His eyes still adjusting from the dazzling sunlight, he stopped dead in mid-stride as he saw that he was surrounded by dogs.

They stood on the bookshelves and on a coffee table between the couch corral and the big dead eye of an old projection TV. He counted five, the smallest a scrappy cinnamon-haired terrier, the largest a silver-muzzled mutt with some border collie in it. They stood frozen, ogling him and poised to spring. He held his breath as he waited for them to react, hands open and dripping sweat. He wasn't phobic about dogs, but he was wary of them, especially when he was alone in their house, and they outnumbered him.

The moment stretched on and out until he could bear it no more, and he let out the breath, but they still didn't move.

An uneasy laugh leaked out. They didn't bark, bite or breathe, because they were all stuffed.

What an idiot he was, but how the hell should one react to something like this? Mom loved her dogs a little too much, he guessed, and couldn't let them go.

On the walls around the dogs, like devotionals at a shrine, were faded family snapshots. A bodacious, curvaceous woman with big red hair and a bright, intelligent smile stood beside a strapping guy with the mustache and sideburns of a 70s TV cop or a Steelers linebacker. Andrew recognized Laura's dad; the slightly pinched look around his eyes was there, but his smile must've blinded the photographer, and his hand on his wife's belly proudly testified that she was pregnant.

Andrew never heard anything about his in-laws' marriage, except that it ended before the kids were old enough for school, let alone a divorce.

Other pictures, of people and dogs and cats he didn't recognize, and then a few of the kids. The three of them on a playground at a rest stop. The highway transfixed the horizon, and the kids sagged in baggy thrift-store clothes. Dean's face crumpled in a pout, or maybe just a fat lip, twin to the bruise on Dom's knuckle. All of them had a weary, hunted look in their eyes as they dubiously tried to smile for the camera.

Dad remarried and became a lawyer, letting Mom have—or punishing her with—full custody, and never looked back. He took the kids in for a few critical years of junior and high school. He put Dean through Annapolis, but for Laura's graduation, he bought his daughter luggage and train tickets.

Dean took to the rigorous structure of Dad's house and excelled, while Dom acted out and fucked up at every opportunity, ran away when they wouldn't kick him out.

A school picture of each of them—Andrew marveled at these, because Laura had only a few pictures from childhood, and hated to look at them. Laura in corduroy overalls and Garanimals turtleneck, with her big green eyes focused right through the camera on a point in the next county; her lips, pursed and precociously full for a girl of seven or eight, in the best attempt at a smile one could expect of a child who has been beaten before breakfast.

Dean sported a damning caricature of his father's pinched look, the forked lines above his eyes more fitting on a beat cop with ulcers, than a first-grader.

Of them all, Dom's picture was the most childlike, but at the same time, the most unsettling. Maybe it was just because little Dom had yet to ink every inch of skin south of his face, but his smile was big and sunny, and nobody who didn't know the whole story would doubt its sincerity. But it was the same smile Dom wore today, when Andrew tried to spin some upside to his horrible childhood. The smile said, *It's all bullshit, suckers . . . suck it up.*

A crackling, whirring sound, like an asthmatic machine clearing its throat, came from the back of the house. Andrew went in search. The hall was even darker, all the doors closed, except for the master bedroom, whence came the odd noise.

"What are you doing?"

Andrew jumped and blurted, "Fuck! I'm just waiting for somebody to tell me what the hell's going on."

Dean came out of the bedroom with a phonebook in one hand and a cordless handset in the other.

"She's not here, and the phone's dead. Where's my brother?"

"Outside, looking for his dog." Andrew tried to shrug past Dean, who blocked him. "Where's the toilet?"

"She was here. She didn't leave in her car."

Was that Dean-humor, or was he not listening? "Maybe she went for a hike or something. Jesus, I really got to piss."

Dean leaned in close enough for Andrew to smell cinnamon gum and that dookie odor people's breath got when they hadn't eaten all day. "What's really going on, Andy?"

"What?"

"Whose side are you on?"

Andrew stood at attention and looked Dean in the eyes, at that fork of stress rising up out of his furrowed brow and spearing his brain. *Listen, Dean. I am not in your fucking Navy. I don't appreciate the fucking head games. I am on your sister's side, because she is my wife, and I love her. I know I can't kick my own ass, but if you don't stop pissing down my neck, I'm damned sure going to kick yours.* Why none of this came out of his mouth was a question better left unasked. "Dean, I don't know anything, alright? She's your mom, you know more about this than I do."

"Go find Dom. I want to start moving the furniture out of the living room before lunch."

Andrew looked around, at the piss-stained couches and cluttered coffee tables, and weighed the relative horrors of going back for a bigger truck, or making two trips. Most of it was useless shit; maybe they could leave some of it here. "Don't you think we ought to at least wait until she comes back?"

"Just go find my brother, alright?"

Andrew went outside. The sudden wash of heat made his brain swell. If he didn't get away from Dean, it was going to explode.

He saw Dom standing at the edge of the scorched lawn, talking to a girl—dishwater blonde, with upturned tits that brazenly, bralessly defied gravity, the heat of the day and an undersized tube top. The girl looked up at Dom like a silent movie ingénue as he described his dog.

It was a testament to the untapped superhuman powers of mutants living among us, that Dominic Kowalski could walk into a forest, and come out minutes later with a date on his arm. Andrew was in open awe of Dom's magnetism, with no envy, because it was as far beyond his comprehension as the intricacies of pro skateboarding or astronautics.

He wandered through the oak trees, their heat-warped limbs choked with parasitic mistletoe, down the drive and out onto the road. The twins wanted him to squire messages between them, they could fuck off and knock their heads together for a while.

Andrew couldn't see any signs of life in either direction on from the end of Mom's driveway, the neighbors' mailboxes and markers set back on the shoulder and camouflaged by pine and oak trees. Nobody who lived here wanted to be found.

He walked up the road, baking stolidly in the hot, arid, heavily pollinated air, and the syrupy, sleepy quiet. The road lost itself in the hills at his back, and connected a mile ahead to the two-lane highway that eventually led to the empty brown veldt of Sacramento, so there was no thru-traffic. Nothing manmade moved or made a noise at all. Gnats danced in the sun, curdled nodes of white light scribbling frenzied mating dances that climaxed with kamikaze runs into his eyes and ears.

Shit, he left his phone in Dom's truck. He should try to call Laura, but he knew it was still too soon. She hated it when he was desperate almost as much as he did.

No, he should be using this time to recharge his own sense of self, while letting her decompress and come to appreciate him in his absence. That's what the counselor said. Give her space. That was the problem, though, wasn't it? She wanted space—

She should be the one out here. Nothing but space, and the used-up chunks of it from people gone by. But he'd tried to show willing and lift her burdens for a change, had overcome her protests and assured her that she could forget about this problem, at least. Over and over, he'd said the words he'd read in a magazine somewhere were, to any woman's ears, the sexiest in the language: "I got this."

He passed a single-wide trailer half-engulfed by a blackberry thicket, blackened and gutted by fire, with scorched curtains flapping in the breeze through melted plastic windows. Shreds of yellow police tape peeked out of the impassable undergrowth. It was a miracle the fire didn't spread and eat up the whole forest. On the road from Sacramento, they'd seen Dept. of Forestry signs advising that the fire risk was extremely high. Inspired, he lit up a cig and kept walking.

Laura never flat-out nagged him to quit, but she had her methods. For his last birthday, she bought him a monogrammed Zippo lighter shaped like a tombstone. When she got especially pissed at him, she spiked one smoke in every pack he bought with an exploding cigarette load. Such low-grade terrorism was her way of showing she worried about him.

Until counseling, she never really opened up to anyone. It took weeks for them to recover from the flash flood of emotional sewage uncorked by that first session. He vowed he would fix what was wrong, but when she finally told him, it was like opening a can of novelty nuts and real snakes spilling out.

The only part he couldn't fix, it turned out, was that he disappointed her. He was what he was and she loved him, but when she thought of their future, it scared her. Her migraines, it turned out, were panic attacks. He wouldn't get a real job that would support a family, because he needed time and energy to chase his dream, yet he wouldn't get off his ass and catch it.

She didn't understand, and he couldn't show her without getting angry and blocking the channel of intimacy, as the counselor put it. She had no idea how hard it was, how much he'd already given up, how everything he'd done was not in the pursuit of some selfish dream, but to provide for his wife and start a family.

All his life, he'd loved music. Not just the loud, lousy crap that pissed off his parents, but any great music, from Beethoven to the Beasties, stirred in him a feeling deeper than he could describe. It felt like home.

All his life, he *knew* he would be a musician. Mom couldn't afford lessons, let alone an instrument, so it wasn't until junior high band that he was forced to discover that he couldn't play a kazoo for shit. He tried as hard as anyone could, and his love and energy were enough to see him through a shitpile of half-assed garage bands where his abysmal quitarwork hardly stood out. But every so often, jamming with a kid who possessed talent, he had to quit to keep from drowning in bile. What good was loving music, if he couldn't play it?

By college, he was already making deals with his future. He threw himself into the campus radio station, made music director before his junior year, and carried eighteen units while washing dishes in the dorms as part of his financial aid. Radio captured his imagination and salved the old scars of his failed first career, as he discovered he had a genius for picking and programming music.

He honed his turntable skills at frat parties and faculty mixers. He interned at the local alt-rock station. He interviewed and hung out with his idols and partied on record company expense accounts, because they were blissfully unaware that his station only broadcast to the student store, fewer than a hundred listeners on cable FM radio, and a couple dozen deeply troubled freshmen in the dorms. He came as close as he ever would get to popularity, and was happier than he ever thought he would be in his life.

Then he graduated. A BA in Communications Studies, with a minor in English Lit, and not even the Army wanted him. 91X was voracious for unpaid interns, but quite satisfied with the burnt-out, middle-aged lechers they already had for jocks, and his record company contacts all got fired or had no sage advice to help him move on.

His resume wilted. A couple offers for graveyard shifts at Christian Pop and country stations in Alaska and Arkansas were all he got. He went to work at Tower Records, where his erudition and uncanny passion for music earned him a plum berth as assistant manager. He'd found what he was good at, what he was clearly meant to do, yet the heavens selfishly refused to open up and shine their pearly light on the impassable tollroad of his destiny.

A lot of the small-time P2 stations he once could have worked at, in Fort Wayne, Spokane or Salt Lake City, now had DJs in larger markets tape their inane stop-set chatter and phone it in between blocks of automated musical pablum. The huge corporations that owned nearly every station in America were either shutting them down, cloning them into creepy robo-stations they disarmingly called Jack or Dave, or flipping them to sports and talk or Latino or Jesus-freak music.

Certification on the vaunted DJ2000 programming software and an insatiable appetite for corporate bullshit were essential, but engaging wit and intuitive genius for building a mood with esoteric album cuts, not so much. He had given up his dream and settled for something he merely enjoyed, but nobody would let him do it. But he would not give up. Not with Laura in his corner, egging him on . . .

Laura, bless her heart, just didn't get it. When he tried to describe the banquet table of the music industry, with a buffet for a handful of gluttons, and teeming legions fighting for crumbs, her tired, indulgent eyes would unglaze, seeing surrender, and she'd redouble her efforts to get him to try something else.

Dreaming and jamming badly in his studio in the garage on the odd day off was what he needed to stay alive, but his dream had somehow become an existential threat to his marriage.

Go back to school, get a teaching credential. Succumb to the family curse, like his mother and his grandmother, who dreamed of other careers. Grandma despised teaching; she knuckled under to the times and taught a high school because her hillbilly parents—hardbitten sharecroppers from the Alabama piney woods—wouldn't send her to a business school that took women seriously. She found a puppet husband through whom she could run a business, sitting up late balancing the hardware store's accounts while Grandpa puttered in the garage with his electric trains. Andrew had mingled at keggers with more than a few kids who got hounded out of high school because "Witch Hazel" Feeney disliked their hair.

Mom wanted to be a doctor, but the sexist professors at the university killed her ambition, and she dropped out of senior year three months pregnant. Maybe she let go too easily. Eventually, she went back for her credential and taught elementary school. Mom was a good teacher, a selfless martyr who poured her heart and soul into saving the most vulnerable kids in the worst neighborhoods; but it wore her down, and she watched medical shows like others watched football, second-guessing the TV doctors while she graded spelling tests.

Andrew couldn't do it. To give up would degrade his life into a broken promise. He tried to meet her halfway. He quit the record store—when it closed for good, thanks iTunes—and tracked down a job tailor-made for his unique skillset. He effortlessly pulled down fat commissions at Guitar Center because he knew all the bullshit a deluded wannabe rockstar needed to hear, to commit to spending wedding-ring money on an amplifier rig.

The money and schedule were good, and the freedom from suits and ties and piss tests was a godsend. But the prospects for advancement were slim to none, unless the store manager, a onetime rhythm guitarist for Eddie Money, either died or decided to promote him into the corporate sphere.

Andrew dropped the cigarette and thoroughly crushed it out on the pavement, *you're welcome, Smokey.*

A peeling silver church steeple glinted at him out of the woods, but when he went up the steps to the vestibule, he found the doors chained and barricaded with mounds of broken beer bottles. The windows were boarded up and all the signs stripped, as if whoever worshipped here got burned hard.

Out here, a weird mix of humanity had solidified in layers, the winners in the society game getting away from it all on long weekends at tricked-out vacation cabins, and running into the inbred descendants of the self-exiled failures their greatest-generation grandparents beat out of their slice of the incredible shrinking apple pie. The natives banged around against each other like knives in a drawer, until all the sharp edges were worn down, or until they were honed so sharp, they cut everything they touched.

Almost half a mile down the road, he found another driveway. A mailbox lay in the gutter beside its broken post. The plain tin receptacle had been stove in by the local softball team's batting practice, but Andrew could still read the bumper stickers stuck on it. U.S. OUT OF NORTH AMERICA, the decapitated mailbox declared, in lieu of a name, rank or serial number. THIS MAILBOX KILLS FASCISTS.

Erosion had hacked deep ruts into the unpaved driveway, and grass and sagebrush saplings had begun to take root and reclaim it for the woods. Andrew figured it only led to another abandoned property, so he was looking up at the crest of the ridge, where the drive disappeared between twin signs that said TRESPASSERS WILL BE EATEN, instead of watching his feet, when he tripped on the ankle-height wire stretched taut across the road.

Bells jingled in the bushes. Andrew jerked backwards with a girlish shriek, landed on his ass and had to grab at the crumbling drive to stop himself sliding backwards headfirst down the driveway.

"Just stay down," a harsh voice rasped at him from behind. He heard a click that sounded ominously firearm-related, and boots scraping the earth, getting closer. "I know what you're about."

Andrew's breakfast knocked at the back of his throat. He choked it down and tried to keep his voice level. "I'm just visiting your neighbor, sir. I didn't mean anything—"

"The one with the dogs."

"No—I mean, yes, sir. She's just my mother-in-law. I've never even met her."

"Well, she's a fat, crazy parasite, young man. Fat from sucking the life out of every poor bastard she comes across, and crazy from hunger for more of the same."

This, from a geezer who hides in his front yard, with a shotgun. "I'm not arguing with you, sir. Can I get up?"

"What do you want?"

"I was just looking for her, sir. We came to move her out—"

The gun clicked again, the hammers being released or the safety catch. "You're here to take her away?"

"Yeah."

"Get up. Slow. I don't know you from Adam, and we're a long way from anybody who'll care if you get blasted."

Andrew got up *very* slowly, eyes still on the ground. "I don't want any trouble, mister. I'll just go back and—"

"Hell no," the old man spat, raising the gun. "You're like as not a government spy . . . or a scab, and I don't much care for either."

"No, I'm just the parasite's son-in-law."

"You think I was born yesterday? You know who I am, son, you know I've been hunted since before you were born."

"But I *don't* know who you are!" he shouted, losing control, hoping Dom heard him. Somebody—

Andrew locked eyes with the man, with all four of his eyes; his gold-flecked, bloodshot brown ones and the beady black barrel-eyes of his shotgun. His parched, broken veldt of a face and straggly white beard, his moth-eaten black beret, his knurled, liver-spotted hands, took on mystical significance. "You want to sneak around and try to see what I'm up to, eh, laughing boy? It's your masters' lucky day. I'll show you."

It was dark inside.

Only half the light fixtures had bulbs in them, and labor, antiwar and animal liberation posters were tacked up over the windows. A huge red flag hung on the wall opposite the front door. Andrew had to screw up his eyes to recognize it. Ancient history for two hundred. A hammer and sickle on a red field. *What was the Evil Empire, Alex?*

The walls were covered in shelves and teetering towers of books and stapled manuscripts. A grubby dinette set huddled in a gloomy nook, an antique manual typewriter and a reel-to-reel tape recorder parked in a drift of crumpled foolscap amid the wreckage of a breakfast. A neat but used-up kitchen lay beyond it, and Andrew smelled insanely strong coffee brewing. A hall, screened by another Soviet flag, presumably led back to the bedrooms.

"Nice. Very nice. Do you have a phone?"

"Of course not. What in hell would I want with all of that jiggery-pokery?" The old man unloaded the shotgun, propped it by the door. He hissed as his shaking hands struggled to pull the shells out; broken blood vessels, gnarly, jutting knuckles and crooked fingers shuddering like spastic needles on a lie detector or a seismograph. He saw Andrew staring and grumbled, "Union busters tuned 'em up with a pipe wrench in '47," then hobbled into the kitchen.

Andrew scanned the room for mail or magazines,

anything with the old man's name on it. "My wife's mom's phone is dead, and we can't find her."

He came out of the kitchen with two chipped mugs and a pair of binoculars. "Is that white devil your dog?"

Andrew took a mug and sipped it, to be polite. The coffee was indeed strong and black, but oddly sweet. The opposite of how he took it, but as the first mug of the day, it was a godsend. "No, it's my brother-in-law's. He's taking it with us."

The old man spit coffee back into his mug. "That dog is a killer."

"He just kills rabbits and stuff, I heard."

"Never mind what you heard. He's like something from an allegory, that dog; the bestial impulses set loose to sabotage the great work."

Andrew got a sinking feeling he'd been had. The wild accusations had all been a ruse to trap him into a wellness visit. Normally, he was quite adept at shooting the breeze with old cranks. He earned a rep in high school as a sub sinker, because he could draw substitute teachers into aimless, tangential monologues, derailing the class and, in one sad case where a substitute English teacher got cozy enough to launch into an unhinged rant about the Jews, getting them fired.

But the old man's bitter paranoia wasn't an amusing goof right now. It was scary, and when Andrew imagined himself alone in a cabin at the end of his life, making chitchat with strangers at gunpoint, it made him sad. "Listen, we've got a lot of packing to do, and like I said, the dog's going—"

"Nobody's going anywhere." The old man slurped his coffee, set it down with a grimace, and went to the window.

Andrew drained the coffee down to the glob of resinous honey at the bottom, shot to his feet and walked to the door. "I'm going right now. My brothers are looking for me . . ."

The old man made no move to stop him. He rolled back

a corner of a poster with faded cameos of Lenin and Trotsky on it, and peeked out at the woods with the binoculars. "The great work's come too far to falter now, for want of able hands. He's getting desperate. Even that monstrous bitch has her uses, I guess."

Andrew stopped and looked at the shotgun. The old man took the shells out. "Who's desperate? If you know something about where she went, you'd better tell me." *You don't want to deal with Dean and Dom . . .*

"You really don't know?" The old man looked puzzled and gloomy. "No, they'd keep it all a secret, and then try to bury it, hide the truth from the masses, like they always have. But not this time. Events are in the saddle, and ride mankind."

Andrew's head itched like he had fleas. He went back over to the window. The old man seemed not to notice him, peering through the binoculars at something in the trees.

"Yeah, Emerson's great," Andrew snapped, "but where's our mom?" The word popped out of his mouth like food he didn't remember eating. He'd never even met the woman, had only spoken to her on the phone a few times, but in the face of this stranger, he claimed her as family.

"You read books? I didn't think anyone read, anymore. You might understand some isolated details, then, but it's impossible for the uninitiated mind to grasp the grand scheme."

Andrew came close enough to smell the Ben-Gay and creeping sickbed stink of the old man. "I don't want to grasp anything. I just want to know where she is, and my brothers want to know where she is, and they will put your ass in the hospital."

The old man looked at him, and Andrew saw a tear in his eye. "They were so *close*," he whispered, "so close to utopia. The first Leviathan colony, we never had a chance . . . but the new one, I thought they were different. They became the state. They went further than even Marx could have imagined. But something always goes wrong, doesn't it?"

"Who are you talking about?"

"There's two factions now, and no neutral parties. Zero against One, body against mind, labor against capital. It's simply not in human nature to take the final step, to let go of power. But that shouldn't have been a factor, this time."

Andrew tried on a pair of fists, but he didn't know how to grab the old man and shake him. He'd go get Dom and Dean, and they'd get to the bottom of this. He flashed on Dom beating the panhandler at the gas station, imagined the old man's bones snapping like soda crackers under those huge, tattooed hands. "Please, don't make me . . . "

"One side or the other took her in," the old man said in a rush, oblivious to Andrew's threat. "Scabs make a settlement less likely, but anything to break the siege."

Oh shit, was it ever medication time. Andrew went to the typewriter. A stack of neatly typed manuscript lay in a wire tray beside it, surrounded by wads of trash. CHRONICLE & MANIFESTO OF THE 2ND UTOPIAN STATE, read the title at the top, BY LEON SPRAGUE. The prose was set in unwieldy slabs of dense, academic jargon that turned to mush in his mind before he found the active verb in the first sentence. "You're part of this cult, too?"

"It's not a cult, it's a commune. And no, they wouldn't have me. 'I am for them, even though they are not for me.'" The old man took up the binoculars again and focused on something. "Richard Wright. You know Wright?"

Andrew rubbed his eyes. It was too early or too late for this shit. "Why . . . is he outside, right now?"

"If they fail, someone, somewhere, will learn from their mistakes. If they succeed, it will be the year zero, and the end of history."

A sketch in the manuscript stack caught Andrew's eye. He pulled it out. A human figure, elaborately scribbled over, stood on a hill, the sun and the moon on his shoulders. The tight whorls and dashes that made up the body were like one of those hidden pictures in kids' magazines. The man was made of countless tiny men, faces and flexing arms. It reminded Andrew of the frontispiece illustration of Hobbes' *Leviathan*, but this amalgamated man was headless.

"The end of war, the end of poverty and famine, the end of ignorance of the collective good, the end of avarice . . . " The old man's words became a hollow chant, a reflexive mumbling as empty of meaning as breath. Andrew turned to go.

Something thudded against the exterior wall of the cabin. The overloaded shelves groaned. Dust and termite shit sifted down from the exposed rafters.

"It's not safe, out there." The old man set down the binoculars and stepped away from the window. "You should go . . . "

Andrew looked around and around the cabin. "What the hell was that, a bear?"

It hit the wall again, scraping against the timbers and knocking books off the shelves. A framed certificate, yellowed and stained beyond legibility, crashed to the floor and spat glass.

"They're curious about you, son."

"Who is?"

"The broken Proletariat," he barked with an impatient snort. "The Headless State. You're a smart boy. They need smart boys . . . "

Andrew heard nothing more, but he could feel it in the soles of his feet. Something big, just on the other side of the wall, shuffled and probed the cabin like it was a box filled with treats. But what if it was Dom, out there? Then it was the old man, who should be scared. But he didn't want to risk his neck by sticking it out, just yet. "Listen, I'm just gonna go . . . "

A shadow passed by the window, blocking out the

filtered sunlight and plunging the room into blue darkness. "Go on, then," the old man snapped. He stalked over to the table, pinched a piece of fresh foolscap up in his arthritic claws and fed it into the typewriter.

Andrew ran for the door and threw it open before he could think about it, was already running outside, *don't stop, don't think—*

But he did stop at the top of the driveway, pulse roaring in his ears. He felt nothing coming up behind him and heard no sounds, but he made himself stand still, hands clutching his vitals, when he saw a wolf-dog cross the yard. The dog was white, where it was not red.

"Toshiro?" Andrew called, but the dog snuffled and disappeared into the woods.

Andrew went around the corner of the cabin, hoping to see which direction Toshiro went, but the dog was long gone. A shallow backyard of knee-high sedge grass ended in a steep slope, shaggy with gnarly live oaks and firs. Nothing in the yard but a row of huge galvanized steel tubs with scraps of fruit, vegetables, dog kibble and meat in them. Raw meat, crawling with flies. The tubs looked new, but were crushed and bent as if the local goon squad had gotten in some batting practice on them, as well.

Without looking back, Andrew walked down the driveway, careful to step over the tripwire. Everything the old man said started to unspool in his mind, and he willed it into the garbage. Leon Sprague was on his own trip, light years from anything that mattered, but his isolation and insanity steeled Andrew's resolve to do more than just ride along on this fool's errand. He was a part of this family, and he would do what family did. He would help to heal them, and bring them together.

CHAPTER 5

ANDREW REALLY BELIEVED he could get through to his brothers-in-law, until he ended up defending Communism.

They were sitting at a booth in a diner—Dom had closed his eyes and chanted, "Not Denny's, not Denny's," over and over as if the name itself was triggering an acid flashback.

"I don't think they have any vegetarian dishes here, Andy," Dean chided, and pulled into an unassuming dump with a crudely lettered sign—POND DINER—that proclaimed MOST AMERICAN FOOD!!!

They ate in relative silence, Andrew studiously not looking at them, because watching them eat would've cracked him up. Side by side, they looked like the comic and tragic masks. Dominic had dyed his hair black, while Dean's was sun-bleached. The sleeves of lurid ink on Dom's corded arms set them apart from Dean's leaner, tanned ones, but their hands described the exact same guarded gestures. They reflexively shielded their plates and fended each other off like hardened cons at chow hall. Dom tried to spear a sausage off Dean's plate, and Dean riposted his fork away with an exasperated sigh.

Dean was droning about how the war was not a mistake, and how the President, if he had any balls, would expand it to wipe out the rest of the trash, especially that senile tyrant, Castro.

To which, Andrew had unwittingly replied, "Why do

you have such a hard-on for Castro? Is he threatening you?"

"No, he's not *threatening* us," Dean sneered, "but he's a goddamned Communist."

"So? What's wrong with Communism is what's wrong with everything else. If people could actually make it work, it'd be the best thing for everybody. It's fair."

Dean took out a tiny plastic box and unspoiled a length of dental floss. Gripping it like a Thuggee assassin with a garrote, he began to throttle his teeth. "That's why it sucks."

"You're saying that capitalism works? It caters to people's basest instincts and encourages them to cheat and steal, and the top one-percent own half of everything, while millions of honest working people starve."

"Nobody ever said life was fair, Andy," Dean smirked.

"The Communist manifesto promises food and housing and work."

"Communism is a shitty idea, from top to bottom," Dom cut in. Andrew almost got whiplash. He hadn't expected Dom to agree with anything his brother said. "People cheat, people steal. Nobody can make it fair, so you just have to make it work. If everybody got paid the same, nobody would try, and they'd *still* cheat. And if everybody shared and earned their keep, they wouldn't be people. They'd be like ants, or some shit."

"Oh, bullshit!" Andrew's face flushed. "People can live together and take care of each other. You just don't know how to get along, because you . . . had to fight for everything. Nobody taught you—"

"Damned straight," Dom snorted.

Dean added, "And you're better off, growing up alone with a lot of stupid ideas about how the world works?"

Looking at them right now, both sporting the same superior scowl, the differences disappeared, and they were two alternate-universe takes on the same guy. Andrew expected them to start shouting him down in stereo. "Growing up alone," he said, "you learn to think for yourself, and when people are full of shit, you can just walk away."

"Well, if you want to talk shit about capitalism any more, maybe you better just walk away, right now."

"Maybe they'll let you wash dishes to pay for your meal, comrade," Dom put in.

He looked at them for a while, searching for a proper retort, when something too funny to say just popped into his head. Laura once told him that their mother, in one of her fabled cruel whims, said she named them as she did, when first she gazed upon that pruny, sour face in duplicate. Tweedle Dean and Tweedle Dom.

Andrew got up with root beer drizzling out his nose and flagged the waitress, who was refilling the saltshakers at the hospitality station. She was vampire-pale and quirkily pretty with bobbed, bottle-black hair, maybe all of eighteen. She smiled a bit too hard at Andrew when he asked for the restroom. "Right over there, hon. You here visiting?"

He stopped, taken aback by her high, forced gaiety. She had sleepwalked through serving them, and Dean wanted to stiff her. Now, she looked like he'd just asked her to a barn dance. "Sure, we're visiting my mother-in-law. Why do you ask?"

Her glossy green-gold eyes flicked at his brothers, then at his ring, losing not a scintilla of their desperate luster. "Nobody vacations up here. After the fires a couple years back, people think we're all gutted out, so nobody comes here but the tweakers from Sacto, and the hunters, during deer season. But it's a nice place to get away."

"Yeah, it's pretty great. Listen, I gotta—"

"So where's your wife?" Her too-red lips parted, long, nicotine-stained teeth and pink tongue peeking at him, clouding his mind.

"I—she didn't come . . . "

The waitress just smiled at him and tilted her head, giving him more rope.

"Listen, maybe you've seen—"

"Your wife? Is she lost?"

"No . . . no, my mother-in-law. She lives in a cabin up the road? She's kind of a big woman, with brown, curly hair—"

"And she has that dog!"

"White dog, eyes like the devil?"

"That's the one. No, I haven't seen her around, but she used to come in for breakfast like twice a week. Those her sons?" She pointed at Dom and Dean, busily looting and vandalizing his food.

"Yeah." He shrugged, trying to force a change in subject, but she kept right on noticing them.

"They look like her. They're assholes, aren't they?"

Andrew giggled. "What makes you say that?"

"They smeared the dictatorship of the proletariat. People like that ought to be lined up against a wall."

Andrew suddenly needed to pee again, really bad. "Right, well, I gotta—"

"Hey, I get off in a few minutes, do you think maybe you and your jackbooted lackeys could give me a ride into town?"

Andrew backed up. "Um, we weren't headed there—"

"But you could, right? I've been here since before sunrise, and my ride cancelled . . . I could make it worth your while."

"No, she could not." A big, rawboned bottle-blonde in a white smock with chili-stains down the front elbowed the waitress out of sight. "She's got to pull a double shift. And she don't need a ride from a stranger, no offense."

Andrew backed all the way to the men's room door with his hands up. "None taken, ma'am," he mumbled, and bumbled out of sight.

At the bottom of the little valley, just behind the aptly named Pond Diner, lay a modest lake or a massive pond, just large enough for a boat landing and an island in the center. A dense shock of pine trees crowned the rocky islet, and a rope swing, from which kids swung and plunged from a dizzying height, dumped an endless line of kids into the cool green water.

Dom ambled down to the picnic tables by the shore, dropped his pants and ripped off his tanktop. Peeking into his boxers, he called out, "Hey, suckers, is it normal for one of your nuts to be a whole lot larger than the other two?" He leapt into the shallows, a brilliant blur of tattoos and muscle and white, whipped water, and dropped into a furious freestyle stroke.

A few elderly rednecks gave them the stink-eye from their lawn chairs on the bank, where they lazily tended their fishing poles and toasted the afternoon with lukewarm Lucky Lager.

"You going in?" Dean interrogated.

"Naw," Andrew fretted, "not so soon. That burger's sitting in my gut like lead, and I know I'll get cramps."

Dean called him a pussy and started talking about Hell Week at Annapolis. Andrew dropped trou and ran for the water.

The shallows were red and cloudy with sediment. The irregular line of the shore and the density of the crowding pines made it impossible to judge any kind of shape. A few cabins peeked out of the woods here and there, and a lone sailboat tacked into the breeze across the water, but it felt like the middle of the wilderness.

Andrew dove in with a falsetto war-whoop. When his chest broke the water and the cold grabbed his package, he realized that he hadn't talked to his wife in over three hours, hadn't even tried.

Out past where he could touch bottom, the water got seriously chilly. It sucked the strength out of him, so he didn't have the wind to curse Dean when he backstroked past him, effortlessly dunking him with one hand.

The pond was not so tiny, now. He began to doubt if he could make it to the island, but when he looked over his shoulder, the shore seemed even further. He bobbed for a while, massaging sensation back into his arms and legs.

Dom shouted his name from the top of a sentinel oak on the shore of the island, then sprang out into space, howling like Tarzan. The heavy jute rope bowed the highest branch in the tree and flicked Dom high and far out over the lake, almost halfway out to where Andrew treaded water. He spun end over end in the air, weightlessly nailing three somersaults before gravity remembered to claim him. He threaded the needle of the water with a respectable splash, and didn't surface until he popped up on the steep, rootbound shore. Dean came out of the water beside him, said something ending in, "Andy," that made Dom laugh.

Andrew sucked it up and stroked the rest of the way out. A line of five shivering kids, the oldest maybe fourteen, waited at the foot of the oak, while a tomboy in cutoffs and a string bikini top scaled the mossy two-by-four rungs nailed to the trunk.

"Let this dude through," Dom barked. "Let him have cuts, he's a virgin."

The kids all stepped aside, more out of deference to Dom's imposing build and surreal tattoos than respect for Andrew. "Oh, I'm not a swinger, Dom," Andrew blurted. "Ask your sister."

"Ha fucking ha." All jocularity lost in a stormy glare. "Climb the fucking tree, Andy."

"No, seriously, man, I'm no diver. I just came out to cool off."

"Bullshit, you have to do it." Dom nudged him up the

ladder, then said, "Hey, wait, you need this," and passed him a cold, wet flask.

"No way."

"Drink up, chief."

Andrew took a tiny sip. It burned his mouth like Lysol and made his stomach spasm, but he had no idea what it was, and he'd consumed and thrown up pretty much every spirit known to humankind.

He passed the flask back and climbed halfway up, but Dom and Dean had all the kids chanting, "Andy, Andy, Andy," and pointing skyward. The giddy endorphin rush of the swim and the shot went to his head. He climbed to the top.

Andrew hated heights. He wasn't phobic about them, but whenever he stood at the edge of a great height, he felt the irresistible urge to fall, to throw himself over. Not to end his life—even he had too much to live for—but it was like some part of his brain wanted him dead.

Andrew clung to the top rung one-handed and reached out for the rope.

He looked out across the pond and saw the sun splashing off the water and the white sailboat and the green trees and mountains piled up forever, and he saw his mother-in-law's cabin halfway up the mountainside, near a valley where the trees crowded together and stood as tall as redwoods.

He felt like singing. It was one of those scenes he hoped to remember, really relive, in the moment before his death. He took one more look to psyche himself up to dive.

On the far shore, he saw a shaded cove with no sign of human habitation, but for the woman who came out of the trees. She wore some kind of tattered brown clinging garment, but when she waded in and dropped to her knees at the water's edge, it lifted off her like smoke, leaving her naked and red and raw.

Andrew almost lost his grip. "Hey, guys, look!" But

nobody could hear him over the chanting of his hated proper name.

He shaded his eyes and strained to see more detail. She was young and lean and had fiery red hair halfway down her back, but something about the way she knelt in the water and dipped her face into it disturbed Andrew. It was not the least bit self-conscious or dainty, but feral. People did indeed come out here to get away from it all.

Someone else came out of the woods behind her, at a dead run. A huge, gray man was all Andrew saw, a huge gray man with a big rock. If it looked bigger than a man, or had some bigger parts and other parts not so much or not at all, he could attribute it to the blur of speed. But the man definitely had a rock, and he smashed the red-headed woman's head in with it.

Andrew screamed, "No! What the hell—"

"Jump, sucker!" Dom shouted, and gave the rope a tug. Andrew clenched the rope like grim death and let it shift his center of balance ever so slightly, and slipped off the ladder.

The rope was slimy and slick, the huge woven strands of mossy jute frictionless between his fingers, sliding right through them. The tree was just out of reach and he was twenty feet above the bank, not the water. He kicked and twisted in the air, but gravity was not impressed at all, and rushed right in to collect him.

He saw the sun and the water and the faces of his brothers-in-law, mouths agape and eyes popping out, finally impressed by something he did.

And then the earth kicked his ass, and the water went in for the pin.

CHAPTER 6

IT WAS NOT always as great to be Dominic Kowalski as he made out, but it had its compensations. He was well aware that things just came his way, as if some badass guardian angel pulled double swing-shifts to make his life a legend for others to marvel at. So when the hot girl rang the doorbell and told him, "I think I know where your dog ran off to," he asked no questions. That was just his life.

Dean was hip-deep in packing up Mom's bedroom, and gave only a grunt when Dom told him he was going out to look for Toshiro. Andrew lay curled up on the bed, right where they'd left him. He'd been semi-conscious when they pulled him out of the water, and Dean's by-the-book examination had confirmed that he hadn't broken his neck or hit his head, but his breathing was shocky, and he didn't respond to his name. One of the kids on the island loaned them an inflatable raft to ferry Andrew back to shore, and Dom had run up to the diner to get his truck. They agreed there was no need to send for an ambulance, and left him to sleep it off.

The girl was still waiting on the porch when he came out, zipping up his leather jacket. He racked his brain for her name, and concluded that she hadn't told him, when she'd come up to the house earlier, to see the strangers.

She lived down the road, she'd said. He guessed she was at least eighteen, and had a good eye for such legally crucial anatomical detail. Her sandy blonde hair was done up in braids that bounced and taunted him like the flapping loose reins of a runaway horse. In a tube top and tiny denim cutoffs, she was hardly prepared to go out hiking in what would, in about an hour, be full dark, but she wore big clompy hiking boots, and the scratches and insect bites up and down her long, lean legs bore witness to her willingness to go off the trail. And if the glassy glint in her eye hinted that she was high or just a bit haywire, that was cool, too. He'd done crazier.

He got his big cop flashlight out of his truck, and they took a trail off Mom's property and up into a canyon between thickly forested ridges that blocked out all but the faintest corona of sunlight.

Girls usually couldn't stop chatting him up about his tattoos and muscles, fishing for compliments on their own physical allure. Their comments never surprised, but they were part of the game; by the syrupy density of their chatter, he could gauge whether he was minutes or hours from the payoff. They almost always thought they were using *him*.

But this one clammed up once they got into the hills, just looking him over now and again, like she was trying to guess how much she'd get for him at market.

He called out for Toshiro a few times, but felt like an idiot. For all the open space, the serried ranks of trees drank up his voice before it got very far at all. "What makes you think he'd be up here?"

She smiled over her shoulder at him, a little girl with a big secret. "Because there's food up here. Duh . . . "

She turned away and walked on. For a skinny girl, her ass was a meaty shelf that stuck out so far, the law ought to make her stuff a red marker rag in her hip pocket. Some subtle cue in the set of her back made him speed up and touch her shoulder, made his voice querulous and reedy. "Honey, Toshiro's a sharp dog. If he wants to come home, he knows the way. It's getting kind of dark. Why don't we—"

"You're afraid," she said, and when he protested, she cut him off. "It's okay to admit it, but I didn't think a big, strong guy like you would be scared."

This bitch's tricks had whiskers on them, but they were working. "Bullshit, I *love* being scared. What's there up here to be scared of?"

"Bears, mountain lions, snakes, tweakers, pot growers, and communists. And me." She flashed a knowing leer, but he shivered at the look in her eye, the unfiltered longing to possess him in some cruder way then he had planned for her. "You in the Army, or something?"

"Was once. How could you tell?"

"A soldier," she cooed, and stroked his arm. "Strong."

The compliment rubbed him the wrong way. Everything about this . . . "What about my dog? You said there was food."

"There's a big farm up here, an old one, but people still live there. You know, one of those communes?"

The trail broke away from the valley and followed a ridge that skewed up and down one of the framing mountains, but the trees thickened to block out any kind of view. Looking around, actually thinking of his dog for the first time, he growled, "You don't know my dog, girlie. Shiro begs when he can't steal, but he can steal anything. He wouldn't hang out with a bunch of hippies, anyway."

"He'd rather starve?"

"He's smarter than most people. He can live off the land, and when that gets old, my mom takes care of him."

She turned off the trail to go behind a big cluster of brush. "Maybe he's up there because your mom's up there."

"What about my mom?" Dom tried to follow, but she shoved him back onto the trail.

"I need to pee."

He started to protest that she had nothing he hadn't seen a thousand times, but shrugged it off. Country manners. And what was that shit about his mom? Some kind of cutdown? Or did she actually know something? He wanted to ask her right now, but he didn't want her to notice him crawling up to spy on her.

In many books, this would rate Dom as a creep, but he didn't read other people's books, except maybe Wilt Chamberlain's. It was the game. Girls drew lines and boys crossed them, always with a big smile and a wink. She might get mad but the game was never fun, unless they wanted it more than you.

Dom stooped down on all fours and peeked between the bare branches at the base of the bush. He stifled a groan of appreciation at the sight of her milky white ass splayed to its fullest effect by her squatting with her thighs akimbo and boots widely planted on the slope.

But she wasn't making, just yet. With her back turned, yet he could tell she was putting all the effort she could muster into it. Her back rippled and arched as if she was already picturing them together, but no waterworks.

He strained in the failing light to catch a glimpse of her beaver, for purely scientific reasons. You could tell a lot about a girl by the state of her treasure.

The purple light of the sunset through the trees illuminated a thick thatch of dark brown hair, less than a lunge away. She had to know he was watching. She strained harder than ever, raising her arms above her head and giving a single little grunt. Maybe this wasn't what he wanted to see, after all, and he started to avert his eyes, when he saw something come out of her.

It was tiny, and only because he was staring so intently in the first place did he notice it. It did not fall or squeeze out of her, but it came out, hanging upside down by the downy hairs of her pouting outer labia and busily fanning its wings dry.

It was a bee, and a big one. A bumblebee, or a yellowjacket, a huge, black and gold specimen freshly emerged as if from a flower it'd been pollinating, or from the honeycomb that hatched it.

He gasped, almost bursting out in braying laughter. She was in for one hell of a surprise, and would never believe him if he warned her, so why try?

But it hadn't just flown up and landed on her, had it? It was wet, preening its antennae through the scythes of its forelegs, waggling its fat abdomen in a final flight checklist, fresh and still wet from climbing out of her cootie catcher.

"I can't go when you're looking," she said.

He backed up, totally at a loss. "I'm just a nature lover, sweetie."

He turned and let his legs take him a ways up the trail until he could let out the laughter he'd bottled up. *Any second now, she ought to give a scream, and then we'll see what's what.*

The bush shook just then, and the girl did give a cry, but it was only a muted yeep, as if she'd lost her balance or peed on her boots. "You alright down there?"

She didn't answer.

He made a lot of noise coming back down the trail to the pee bush. "You okay, baby?"

He came around the bush, already grinning in anticipation of seeing her tumbling ass-over-teakettle with her shorts around her ankles.

But she wasn't there. A stream of piss, already sucked into the thirsty topsoil, trickled down the steep slope, straddled by a pair of footprints. He looked into the bush, dense with waxy leaves and blue shadows, and down at the jumble of granite boulders downhill, but saw no sign, and the light was failing all at once.

Dom held himself very still and called out, "Hey girlie? You out there?" No sound but something pecking at a tree trunk and the yawning creak of the trees leaning into the failing evening breeze.

If she ran off, he would've seen her. If she were hiding, she would come out. Or not, and the hell with her. "I don't play games, baby, so if you want to come out tonight, do it now."

No answer. Well, Dom thought, fuck her. These were her woods, and he'd only make a fool of himself, if she didn't want to be found. And if peeking at a strange woman making water in a bush was wrong, he had no use whatsoever for being right.

A little more than ten minutes passed by before Dom gave up trying to find the trail back to the cabin, and went wandering.

He thought back to his Army training, but nothing from the wilderness survival manual really helped. The trees here were too dry to have moss on any side, and he had no compass, let alone a map. He went downhill. Sooner or later, he'd cross a road or a stream, and end up by the lake where his idiot brother-in-law had dove in and missed the water. Wow, that was memorable . . .

He cracked up again when he thought of Andrew. Usually, dorks like him brought out the worst in Dom, but once you got past the stink of insecurity and *Dungeons & Dragons* bullshit, Andrew was almost an alright guy. He seemed genuinely devoted to Laura, which was a first. So long as he kept her happy, Dom would go along to get along. He recalled the panhandler at the gas station, and how Andrew almost pissed himself when Dom cut loose. Guy grew up with no brothers and no father, so he never learned how to dish it out, let alone take it. Well, he'd learn fast, in this family.

He slid down the slope and broke through a tight fence of trees into a big open meadow. This must be the hippie commune, but any and all expectations, of tie-dyed Eloi veggie nubiles picking beans and spreading the gospel of free love, immediately dried up faster than missing girl's piss.

For one, the place was totally deserted. Across the huge expanse of level acreage, he saw only a scarecrow, tipped over in the dirt, the shells of half-collapsed barns and sheds, all painted a deep, dark red, and a few shovels, hoes and other broken tools.

Dom could fit what he knew about farming into a thimble and still have room for a thumb, but he was pretty sure you harvested in fall, not late July, and you probably didn't rip everything out of the ground and tear it apart on the spot. It looked like a riot had wiped the place out. "Where were you," he asked the scarecrow, "when the shit went down?"

And then there was the house. It didn't look like any of the ashrams Mom was keen on in the seventies—ranch houses with tents, tepees and broken campers strewn out all around in a stunning display of New Age serfdom. It was a tall two-story workhouse of quarry granite blocks and gray timbers, with tall, narrow window-slits and big heavy iron-banded oak doors, and a peaked turret standing out from the roof, like a panopticon guardtower in an old prison.

It had to be some kind of abandoned penal experiment, or something. It was too solidly built and too damned ugly not to be a public project. The girl said people lived here now, but Dom doubted it.

He let the stillness into him a little at a time, mistrustful, and he was almost grateful to hear, behind the tuning orchestra of nocturnal insects and the screech of an early owl, the benign cosmic bubbling of the Percolator.

A lasting aftereffect of one his most revelatory acid trips was a mild auditory hallucination that was always there when it got quiet enough, like tinnitus, but soothing, the muted bassbin pulse of a totally sickass rave in a neighboring dimension. He could hear it quite clearly, now.

The Percolator was the sound of the universe doing its thing, of karma and causality creating the future. Far from freaking him out about having broken his brain, it reassured him. If it was not an objectively real phenomenon, it was still something he could count on, something he alone could hear as it made everything happen.

Silence grated on him. Solitude made him feel like he was shrinking. Without someone beside him to provide a sense of scale, he could disappear inside himself, and go to countries best left off the map. He cursed the girl for dangling exactly what he needed, then ditching him. He hated that about himself, how he had to go looking for his reflection in others, and couldn't stand by himself. Even the Dorian Gray dittohead funhouse image of Dean was a comfort, next to being alone. Mom put that in him.

Mom. If there was a place where people could get sucked into playing her games, she'd go there. And if they were as bad at judging people as they were about growing crops, they'd take her in.

The house stood back at the edge of the meadow, hard against a devil's postpile of boulders and straggly pines that twisted into a glowering peak of naked rock that seemed to scrape a hole in the sky. Behind it, the moon hung in the indigo firmament, bleached white in the crisp alpine air.

He crossed the field and ambled up the wide steps to the big double doors. Approaching them in the dying light, he saw jagged graffiti splashed across the doors in the same dull red paint that covered the flattened sheds. He had to climb up on the porch before he could read it: WOE TO THE SHEPHERDS WHO FEED . . .

A big crimson sunburst of pooled, dry paint on the flagstones beneath the last, hastily scrawled word, hinted at the scene when the vandal was caught red-handed, hyuk hyuk . . .

The doors were open just a crack, and glided apart with a well-oiled groan when he touched them. The dark inside was like a curtain of black velvet that parted grudgingly when he flicked the flashlight beam around inside. "Hey, anybody home?" he called out. "I'm your new neighbor, eh?"

The flagstones were rough-hewn local granite, and reminded him of the crowns of molars. As he stepped over the threshold, a gleam of reflected light off glass caught his eye, and he jumped aside and away from it. Shards of glass and twisted bits of metal jutted out of the inside panels of both doors, as if they'd been fired out of a cannon.

Figures, people up here would be making drugs, and laying traps to make intruders sorry. Backing away and pushing the doors to, he noticed something disquieting about the spacing of the junk embedded in the door. An elliptical space in the middle was clear of debris, so the junk formed a loose "O" shape, as if something, or someone, stopped a lot of it with their body.

Whoever tripped it, they were not here, so Dom tiptoed across the floor in shuffling, sweeping steps, like you'd take to ward off stingrays in Baja, alert for tripwires or trapdoors, all that D&D bullshit.

He went to Haiti in the Army, but he only faced a couple of short, inconclusive firefights. He knew what it was like to fear for his life, had even come to enjoy it a little more than a little. But when he was alone, with nobody to prove himself to or lord it over, he started, just a bit, to be afraid that he might be afraid. And not the extreme thrillseeker adrenaline rush kind of fear, either, but the old-school, bedwetting, *"Mama, there's a monster in my closet,"* kind of fear.

The room just kept going and going, featureless and unfurnished, to the far wall, which was draped in black muslin and probably in a different area code from the front door. Not that his cell phone worked out here . . .

He listened for the Percolator but couldn't hear it here, and that was bad. He thought he could hear that buzzing hush like the whisper of silence in old, old movies, instead. The Percolator was a rudderless cosmic machine, but this was something else. This was driven. It hummed like a voice, or a million little voices. Like a beehive.

God damn that girl . . .

He saw a couple of low, wide doorways in the back wall,

leading into deeper dark, and followed the wall around to the side, eventually coming to one flight of stairs going up, another down. Looking up the stairwell, he saw a bit of light from outside, faint but unmistakable in the gloom.

He listened, thought he heard a single cry from upstairs and far away, and without meaning to, he thought it might be a woman calling out, and it might just be his mom. He rushed up the wide stairs and slid a big door on rollers aside, and whistled.

Fuck, this wasn't a prison or a commune. It was an insane asylum. Or a zoo.

The corridor before him stretched the length of a football field to the far wall, intersecting with other corridors, which he could see throughout the house, because there were few interior walls, but many, many bars. The rooms were blocks of cells. Each cell had a bare pallet on the floor and a book or a cup beside it, and a few had chairs that were bolted to the floor of tarred railroad ties. There was no proper ceiling, but only more bars, open to the elements and the scrutiny of the tower.

When Dad took them up to the Bay Area for the infamous last great outing, they toured the Winchester Mystery House in San Jose, a freaky sprawl of a mansion built to bedevil the vengeful ghosts of all those killed by the Winchester repeating rifle, who would claim Sara Winchester, a batshit crazy dwarf and the widow of the last of the heirs to the fortune, on the day she finished the house.

But ghosts weren't the only enemies of Winchester's peace, for she contrived a cylindrical crow's nest of a room above the top floor to conduct her séances and spy on the rooms where the servants worked and slept. The ceilings of these rooms were glass, so Winchester could oversee every menial task and catch thieves, whom she feared almost as much as ghostly Indians.

When Dom looked up through the barred roof and saw

the moon and the ripening stars and the looming tower overlooking all the vast space, he was awestruck at the total control the place wielded over whoever was fucked up enough to live here. Did he not feel like a rat in a maze, and did he not feel as if someone in the tower watched him right now?

He kept looking up as he strolled the corridor, picked a cell at random and unzipped, pissed all over the floor while giving the finger to the tower.

This place sucked. Toshiro wasn't here, Mom wasn't here, and the strange country bitch wasn't here, so why was he still here? He turned back towards the stairs, but he got confused and walked into bars. When he followed them, he went round and round without finding a door.

He hadn't touched anything, he hadn't gone to sleep, he hadn't heard a door close, so where was the fucking exit?

He paced around the chair in the center of the cell. His flashlight beam went brown, then died. He shouted, "What the fuck, Chuck?" but there was only an echo. Was this a flashback, a real one, or was he just losing it?

He stopped and very suddenly sat down in the chair.

Behind him, he heard the door of the cell clang and slide open, and a shuffling of hobnailed boots on the floor. He tried to get up, and found that his mind was the only thing he could still control. His body just sat there, unable to so much as twitch, as that buzzing, million-voiced will, the furthest thing imaginable from the Percolator, grew louder and louder, until it came from his own mouth.

A gloved hand fell on his shoulder. He couldn't turn his head or open his mouth to speak. Close up to his ear, the buzzing became a tortured imitation of human speech. "Scab," the voice said, "or spy?"

Dom could only look where his eyes were pointed, at the dull, blue-gray bars and the rows and rows of empty cells beyond. The buzzing crawled around maddeningly in his skull. He could almost picture it, thousands of busy bees creeping among the soft gray folds of his brain, harvesting his thoughts like pollen and nectar, then flying out of his mouth in a cracked voice he could barely recognize as his own. "I'm looking for my dog."

"No lies."

"My mom . . . We came for my mom. My brothers and me . . . We came to move her . . . "

"You were a soldier."

The bees bored into his head and it itched so bad, he would have torn the lid off his skull and scratched his brain if he could, but all he could do was silently beg them to find what they wanted. At last, he said, "In the Army. I didn't like it, so I quit."

The glove tightened on his shoulder, and the interrogator shuffled into view. He saw a heavy canvas smock draped on a short, slumped figure, and a beekeeper's hood, a mesh screen that gave only a vague silhouette of a head within. "You will be our army."

Another hooded figure came around the chair. Much heavier and taller than the first, this one carried a huge ceramic mason jar and a ladle. He fought to get up, but couldn't blink, couldn't even look down at his powerful, musclebound body, dead as ground beef. Couldn't stop his mouth dropping open as the fat beekeeper unsnapped the lid of the jar and dipped the ladle into it.

"The head has been severed from the body," the interrogator buzzed. "The rebellion must be broken, the body restored."

The fat one held the ladle, brimming with viscous, golden honey, up to his lips. He watched his tongue slide out to catch a lazily dangling droplet.

"The Great Work cannot fail."

Above, an explosion of stone on metal that rang the cellblock like a tuning fork. A huge rock shattered against the barred roof of the cell. Shards of stone showered them, pinging off bars and lacerating his flesh. Another boulder hurtled overhead and slammed into the tower, and then a steady downpour of large and small stones and broken branches.

The buzzing ascended to a fever pitch, then it was suddenly so faint he could barely feel or hear it. Whatever was holding him down had its hands full elsewhere.

What he could feel doubled him over. His limbs tingled as if his whole body had gone to sleep for want of blood. He tried to make his hands massage sensation back into his legs, but he could barely make a fist.

The interrogator stood frozen, animated only by odd galvanic twitches, but the fat, matronly shape dropped the ladle into the jar and knelt before him. "Dominic," it whispered in a husky buzz.

Dom tried to lever himself up against the arms of the chair. He wobbled and fell back, gasping for breath. It was all too like being lost in the K-hole.

Another rock smashed itself to bits right above their heads. A baseball-sized chunk tore off the interrogator's hood—there was no head inside.

But there were bees. An enraged swarm took to the air as the hood was snatched away by the meteoric rock. The headless body tottered around the cell, a river of bees gushing out the neck and sleeves of the billowing smock, which sagged and lay flat on the floor as the swarm roared out into the night.

Dom rolled out of the chair and crawled across the cell to the still-open door. Behind him, the fat one rustled as it reached out and caught his leg.

"Bitch, back off!" He tried to break free, hating his weakness. When he lashed out with his arm, he only lost his balance and fell on his face. Dull gray fireworks sparkled in his eyes. Strong hands rolled him over, and a huge, heavy body pinned him flat. There was more than bees inside this one.

"Mom?"

She removed her hood and leaned in close so he could see her through his concussion and the bees crawling all over her face. She smiled. "Dominic, baby, I'm so happy you found us."

The bees rose up off her face like steam and dove into his eyes. They covered every exposed inch of him and plunged their stingers into him all at once.

"You're not my mom . . ." He screamed and screamed, even as he started to drown when she ladled gobbets of honey down his throat.

CHAPTER 7

ANDREW WAITED ON a street corner downtown for Laura to pick him up. He'd been waiting for a while, long enough to wonder if she hadn't gotten lost or had an accident, but he knew she'd be there. She always came. She was the reliable one.

The corner was at the end of the turnaround the buses used to service Horton Plaza, and the little skating rink was set up on the promenade opposite the mall entrance, and hordes of novice skaters whirled and tumbled like laundry in a washing machine. Night was falling, the faux-gaslamps all down the avenue adding their burnished golden glow to the lurid wash of head- and tail-lights and the neon from all the shops. He stood beside the Spreckels theater box office, out on the curb so he'd be easy to spot.

She always came, and she was always on time. If she was late, something was wrong . . . or she was punishing him.

And he knew just why.

He was always late.

It was a widely known rule of thumb that if you wanted Andrew to show up somewhere, you told him to meet you at the time he'd need to leave his house, because that was always how it worked out. Not his conscious decision or even pointed negligence, but just the way the universe had it fixed. If he successfully budgeted out grooming and other obligations, he got a long distance call, a dead battery, or a freak traffic jam. He wasn't a flake, but there was a lag time, an entropy bubble, that he could never quite breach. Everyone who liked or loved Andrew learned to make it work . . . everyone but Laura.

In her father's household, punctuality was a kind of mania in and of itself; to be late, no matter the excuse, was pure and simple disrespect.

He was half an hour late picking her up on his first date. So nervous, he locked his keys in his crappy old Volkswagen when he jumped out to get some breath mints at the AM/PM, and after failing to find a locksmith, had to bust the wind-wing to get in. She forgave him, but the look in her eyes told him he was already down in the count, even after the rest of the date went off without a hitch.

And right here, on this corner—

It was after they'd been living together for a few months, and she was still working in the mall. Her car was in the shop, and he was supposed to pick her up after she closed the store. He was at home, playing a game on the Playstation, when he looked at the clock and screamed. 10:30. He was supposed to be there right this instant. He could rush downtown in ten to fifteen minutes. It wasn't something he'd have sweated with anyone else in the world, but with Laura, it was death.

He got there in eleven minutes, but he knew from the instant he cut through the traffic to the curb, that he had never been so late in his life.

Police tape made a corral of traumatic street theater out of the stretch of sidewalk where he expected to see her leaning in front of the Levi's store. His heart hitched and fetched up in his throat, and he was already slipping out from behind the controls of his body, thinking, too late, too late, too late—

Downtown San Diego wasn't like Detroit or Baltimore, but it had its moments, and an unaccompanied woman waiting at the corner could only expect to draw trouble. She told him stories about the panhandlers and thugs that came onto her when she waited for him, but always with an amused contempt that made him think she got off on the attention. He'd never dreamed—

And there she was, standing just outside the tape, looking at him like she'd never been so disappointed in all her life, with one finger lazily tapping on the face of her watch like a clockwork toy running down.

He stopped and got out, ran around the car and reached for her, but her arms warded him off. "I'm only eleven minutes late, baby. I'm sorry, are you okay?"

Her big green eyes bored into his, unblinking; her face was as pale, smooth and hard as marble, except for the fresh spray of wet red freckles across one cheek. "If you were five minutes earlier," she said, "I never would have seen this."

He looked over and saw what the cops and the paramedics were trying to put back together again.

He saw the soles of Doc Marten boots, nine-holers, mighty orthopedic rubber soles chewed up by centuries' worth of shuffling through the mosh pit of life. Ragged, holey black jeans with band names and symbols doodled all over them in white correction fluid. A cheap imitation leather jacket, even more densely and ineptly ornamented with buttons, studs, patches and paint. Above that, hamburger.

A teenage runaway punker, the kind of kid who gathered around the Horton Plaza bus stop like pigeons, begging for spare change and hurling snide remarks at random passersby. He recognized the jacket, though he couldn't picture the kid's face, especially not now.

These kids always latched onto Laura because they figured since she wore corsets and stylish post-punk shoes, she must be a soft touch. She hated panhandlers almost as much as she hated truancy. "Change comes from within," she'd always say, and glide blithely away.

The cops looked up now and again, and Andrew saw an open alcove on the stairs that climbed the side of the five-story mall directly overhead. A woman looked down from there, explaining with hand gestures how the boy had jumped off.

"Out of the way! Out of the way!" Another punker kid, pipestem thin with a green mohawk, clothes stiff from sleeping on the street for weeks, pushed through the crowd and jumped the tape. The cops shoved him back but he kicked at them as he grabbed the dead kid by the sleeve. "He didn't mean it, Lord!" the kid screamed at the sky. "He didn't mean it! He fell . . . "

Andrew watched as the kid was dragged screaming off to a squad car. "Everybody pray for him, okay? Pray real hard, so God takes his soul, okay? One-Two-Three, Pray!"

He apologized all night, but all she said was, "You didn't push him." She never said another word about him being late. She had accepted it—but no. She had given up hope that he would, or she could, change it.

And now, here he was, waiting for her on the very same corner. He looked up and tensed, alert for falling punkers.

She would come.

He'd already been waiting so long, and he had no cell phone, and hated to wear a watch. There was a big clock above the skating rink, but he'd have to cross the street to see it, and if he was anywhere but right here when she arrived, she'd think he only just wandered up, and it would all be for nothing. As if waiting here would make them even. If it would balance their books, he'd wait for a year, but he knew he'd been too late too many times. This would not make them even, and it probably hurt her, who prided herself on her timely arrivals and was probably sitting around the corner, looking at her watch, suffering twice as much as he, but hell-bent on teaching him a lesson.

And as each minute swelled and broke like a fever, as

each set of headlights that swung into the turnaround proved a fresh disappointment, he learned.

And as the tide of the night turned, ejecting all the prosperous shoppers and broke strollers and reclaiming all the human flotsam who thought they might escape, he discovered just how sorry he could be, but even this transformation wasn't enough. He broke down as the lights went down block by block, as they guttered and died, and the cars sank into the bubbling tar of the street like sleepy mastodons, and the sidewalk beneath his feet melted away inch by inch like an ice floe. When there was no more room for both his feet, he tried to balance, but his will to wait was eroded, and even if the alternative was drowning, if it meant an end to always being lost and late and sorry, he would welcome it.

He sank.

As dazed when he woke up as he was when they laid him down, Andrew slowly, painfully came to remember that he'd fallen asleep in his mother-in-law's bed. He woke up in a warehouse. Boxes stacked high above the bed on three sides, and on the fourth, Dean had arranged a staging area for the final assault on his mother's worldly possessions. Flat boxes, shipping tape, markers, a coffee mug and a checklist were in regimented disarray on the floor, meaning he must be working somewhere else in the house. The air in the room was stagnant and gravid with recycled pet odors. Somewhere far off, he heard the modulated barking tones of a TV news show.

It was more than a little weird, coming up here to meet his wife's mother, only to find her gone, and wake up in her bed. In the D'Amato clan pantheon, Mom was a legend equal parts Bigfoot and Vlad the Impaler; a repulsive and cruel enigma whose worst excesses were arguably the heart of her charm. By comparison, Andrew's mother was a sweet, retiring lady who spent Andrew's childhood laid up with a migraine, so even Dom's most lurid tales of Ma D'Amato's wild oat-sowing nights left Andrew feeling as if he'd missed out on something.

He took all the stories with a bowling ball-sized grain of salt, because he'd spoken to her six or seven times on the phone. No way anyone could be as bad as they said; and the woman who periodically tried to wheedle her way past him to speak to Laura was indeed charming and bright as hell, but undeniably eccentric, if not certifiably batty.

The first time she called, Andrew was intrigued, because Laura had pointedly told him nothing about her mother, and raised huge questions with her evasive silences. Laura was at work, and Andrew pumped Ms. D'Amato for tidbits about his girlfriend's childhood, only to find it took a master interviewer with a whip and a chair to shut her up.

The picture Ms. D'Amato painted was of a rocky but rewarding odyssey, adrift on the edge of America, where her kids had discovered themselves as individuals before their time, but had grown strong and wise. In between lectures about how to toilet-train cats or keep turkey moist with a coat of mayonnaise, she rambled through lovingly airbrushed memories until Andrew began to doubt that any of the children knew their mother at all. He was still listening to Ms. D'Amato chatter when Laura walked in, and he tried to pass the phone to her. Her reaction would have been calmer if he had pointed a loaded gun at her head.

After that, he covered for her, apologizing for her when Ms. D'Amato vented her suspicions. Ms. D'Amato told Andrew that she liked him, and that if anyone could help Laura work out her issues, he could. It wasn't until they started couple's therapy, that Andrew got Laura's side of the story.

And now, here he lay, alone in the monster's bed.

Andrew rolled over with exquisite care, slightly amazing himself that he could do so. He was sore from neck to tailbone, and his head throbbed mildly, but nothing worse than a hangover, and his toes wiggled when he told them to. If he'd seriously injured himself, Dean would have taken him down to the hospital, he hoped. He sat up, feeling a bit dizzy and like someone took a shit in his mouth, which wasn't beneath his brothers at all.

His brothers. They treated him as a stranger, offering only grudging respect after he married into the family, but they'd carried him up from the lake and laid him out. Like family.

Weird fragments of his dreams, mismatched jigsaw pieces, bubbled up in his mind. Waiting—sinking—falling . . . the naked lady in the lake—

That part wasn't a dream, was it?

He got off the bed and pushed around the gauntlet of boxes, marveling at the thoroughness with which everything had been packed. Three plastic Roughneck trashcans lined the hallway, all filled with bagged and tagged trash.

A growling hum from the living room drowned out the TV, became a choked sound Andrew recognized from his brief stint in corporate America: a document shredder choking on too big a bite. He came out into the living room, found it halfway converted into brown cardboard, even the stuffed pet shrine reduced to a pyramid of labeled cartons. Dean sat at attention on the couch, sorting through a shoebox of old photos as he watched Fox News.

No Dom. No Mom.

"Thanks, man," Andrew said. "For taking care of me."

Dean gave a little shrug that might've been dismissal. "Sure, whatever."

"How can you stand those douchebags?" Andrew asked.

Dean tossed a fistful of photos into the box and clapped the lid down. "Who are you talking about?"

"That dick," Andrew pressed, pointing at the bejowled, bloviating pundit on the screen, eager to talk about something outside the house.

"He's a truth-teller," Dean said. "He's mopping up the floor with that pussy from your side." Some shaggy-haired punching bag with a pocket protector wore the liberal straw man suit on Dean's show, and the wingnut panel was pushing him around like high school bullies behind the auto shop.

"They're saying we should get deeper into a war that everybody knows is a disaster, and they want to shovel more young men like you into the meat grinder."

Tits, meet wringer. "I don't see you volunteering to defend this country. The men who fight don't need candy-ass titty-clutcher liberals crying for them. They know—*we know*—about the costs of war. You could never understand that, Andy."

Warming to the topic, Andrew came over and sat on the back of the couch. "But the war's a farce. I don't begrudge you your fetish for killing the heathen brown Islamists with your smart missiles, but wouldn't you rather do it for a good reason, instead of keeping gas prices down?"

Dean pinched his temples and squinted at the screen. "I don't have the energy for this right now, Andy . . . But if you don't like the way we do things in America, maybe you'd be happier somewhere else."

"Or maybe you would be. I mean, I get the feeling you think everything would work better if it were run like the Navy . . ."

"No argument there . . ."

"Or like a business. So it must suck for you to have to put your life on the line to defend a bunch of hippie ideas like freedom of speech and government making people's lives better. You'd be happier defending a fascist dictatorship, is what I hear you saying. What do you love about America?"

Dean rubbed his temples harder, trying in vain to keep his brain from popping out like a jack-in-the-box. "It's the greatest nation in the history of the world. It's God's country. It's—"

"No really, what do you fight for? Not what everybody says they fight for. America's great because we're free? When the assholes who started this war are shredding the Constitution, just like that . . . " Andrew flicked a finger at the document shredder.

"If you're not an enemy of the state, why would you have anything to hide from the government? Freedom isn't free, Andy. It doesn't mean freedom from responsibility. Everybody's free to shoot their mouth off until somebody holds them to account for it."

Wow, this was a milestone, or close enough. The first time, Dean had ever threatened him. He finally was a part of the family. "We're free to worship and speak and associate as we choose, until we end up on a no-fly list or Camp X-Ray, but we can go duck hunting with assault rifles, without getting locked up. Your brand of patriotism is the blind, bloody-minded jingoism that the cavemen felt, the day they invented flags. You'd be just as happy under Stalin or Hitler—probably happier, because you'd get to hunt down everybody who disagreed with you."

"Maybe, maybe not, but God put me here, and you should get down on your knees and thank Him for sending people like me to protect you, like it or not, from the animals who want to run you down in the dark . . . "

"It must really piss you off that you fight to defend the rights of people like me. You must know just how Jesus felt every day, when you're launching those missiles at those grid plots on that map."

"I should have known better than to expect a civil

political discussion from you, Andy. I'll let you walk away because you're my sister's husband, and you probably got brain damage when you fell off that kiddie swing, today."

"I'll stop if you'll do me a favor. Stop waving the flag in my face. I love my country, and I would die to defend it. But I don't have to agree with you to be an American, and I shouldn't have to join the military to be taken seriously as an adult. As you pointed out, I am your sister's husband."

"Well go do something adult, and I'll try to treat you like one with a straight face. Go pack up the kitchen, and make us some fucking dinner."

"OK . . . listen, man . . . I'm sorry . . . " Andrew rubbed his back, trying to put out the rhetorical grease fire he'd set. "But what the fuck is going on here, man? Where is everybody?"

"She's not here, *man*," Dean replied, making the monosyllable sizzle with scorn. "Wouldn't be the first time she up and bugged out."

"Where's Dom?"

"With some girl."

"Bullshit."

Dean smirked at the TV. "Some guys catch all the luck, and all the diseases. Weight Watchers in the freezer. Dom ate your Pop Tarts."

Andrew started across the room to the kitchen, when he noticed the wastebasket beside the shredder. It was filled almost to the rim with confetti: white papers and yellowed old documents, but mostly piebald strips of Kodak photos. "Why're you shredding up all her old pictures, Dean?"

Dean looked at him for the first time. His eyes were so glassy and far away, Andrew could swear he was drunk as a poet on payday, but every other part of him was so tightly locked down, it hummed—like the shredder, when it got too choked with childhood memories to tear them all up. "They were mine. I can do whatever I want with them."

Weird. Dean sounded twelve years old. This strapping, clean-cut Reaganaut who ordered sailors around for a living, was drowning a kid deep down inside himself. Oh, well. Behind every great man of destiny lurked an untreated psychosis.

Andrew went into the kitchen, wishing Dom was here. *He* could rip into Dean about crying.

The kitchen was a lazy mover's jackpot—a mismatched set of pots and pans, some tumblers, mugs and plates, a toaster, a microwave and a popcorn popper. The cupboards were almost bare, with only a few cans, ramen packets and boxes of generic macaroni which had been chewed open by mice. In the pantry, he found more random stale foodstuffs, half a palette of 9 Lives canned cat food and two forty-pound bags of dog and cat kibble.

And not a single dog or cat in sight.

Leaving out a couple place settings and mugs for coffee, he boxed up the rest of it more or less to naval specs and labeled them in silver Sharpie. He went to the freezer and found a few frostbitten Weight Watchers dinners— single-serve lasagna, beef stroganoff and eggplant parmesan—and a couple ice-cube trays. He wrung a tray out and dropped a couple cubes in a tumbler, filled it with water from the sink. It tasted of silt, but it was cold.

He saw something black and many-legged in his glass, dumped it out in the sink.

Bees. In the ice cubes.

Four or five of them, wings clasped against their furled abdomens, antennae drooping over unseeing compound eyes.

Was this Mom's idea of a joke, or a diet? He looked around the room. Out in the country, a bee swarm could take refuge almost anywhere, even inside, but they would have noticed by now. Maybe the fucking things just flew in when Mom was making ice cubes, and she didn't notice before she left.

He realized he'd left the freezer open, and bumped it shut with his shoulder. Coupons and clipped *Far Side* cartoons fluttered in the breeze like pinned butterfly specimens, so he glimpsed a flyer stuck in the bottom strata of fridge crap. He blinked, then brushed all the other shit away and picked it out. A flyer with an emblem at the top, a grubby Xeroxed woodcut of a bee on a flower that looked like a mechanical gear. In blurred type, it read:

FROM YOUR NEW NEIGHBORS

The New Coverdale Valley Colony at Leviathan House has taken up residence in your area to perfect a self-contained utopian commune and develop strategies for a sustainable human future. We chose this site because of the ideal and isolated locale, and the tradition of experimental living throughout its history. We pledge to act as good neighbors, to respect your peace and privacy, and hope you will return the favor and support our endeavor with your good will and prayers.

At this delicate time in our development, we humbly request that the clearly marked boundaries of our property be treated with neighborly respect. We look forward to reaching out to you at such time as our communal bonds are strong enough to admit contact with the outside world, and to becoming a good neighbor to the community at large.

Thank You,
The New Leviathan Colony

Andrew dropped the flyer on the table.

"I don't hear packing!" Dean shouted.

"Sir, yes, sir," Andrew barked back, and started unfolding a fresh U-Haul carton from the flat stack on the breakfast bar. In the living room, Dean dug clods of photo-fetti out of the teeth of the shredder and resumed feeding it pictures.

Outside, on the patio, something heavy fell over. Andrew went to the sliding glass door and flipped on the light switch.

A rusty aluminum lawnchair lay on its side beneath the living room picture window, motes of upset dust floating in the harsh floodlight.

Andrew opened the door and called, "Dom!"

Only the symphonic trill of the nocturnal insect kingdom answered. The moon and stars poured brilliant silver showers down on the overgrown lawn, but not a ray of it penetrated the cloistered black ramparts of the pines crowding the edge of the yard.

Something swooped down out of the dark, silent and sleek, and was gone before Andrew could flinch. It dropped into the shaggy thicket of the lawn and flapped up into the sky, stirring air against Andrew's cheek. The only sound was the squeal of the field mouse it snatched up in its claws. Andrew whistled in awe at the owl's performance.

Where the hell was he? If anyone could hook up in this godforsaken wilderness, Dom would. Andrew thought of the waitress at the diner; low-hanging fruit even Andrew could have picked, in another life. Uninvited, the naked lady in the lake haunted him so hard he almost saw her there in the kitchen. It wasn't a dream, he knew, but he didn't say anything to Dean as he wandered back to bed.

CHAPTER 8

DEAN HAD A lot on his mind.

The plan was halfway to completion, and if Mom never showed up, so much the better.

Too wired to sleep, he'd moved away from the TV to sit at the dining room table and perform his nightly ritual; tomorrow's punch-list, a randomly selected passage from the Bible, and his conviction list.

He'd burned through the first two items, but he was choking on the third. So far, he had written and underlined . . .

WHAT I BELIEVE
#1: *I believe that Mom . . .*

He had written and crossed out, . . . *ruined my life when I was little. She messed me up so bad, that I have blacked it out.*

That was weak. No one could mess up his life, but him.

He went back to shredding photos until his vision started to blur.

He caught himself grinding his teeth. He should put in his retainer. Dean took excellent care of his teeth. A winning smile was important, if you wanted a future after the Navy. Since he'd started talking to Dom about coming up here, he'd been having the dreams about his teeth, again. In the dream, he clenched his jaw so hard that his teeth shattered like candy, or simply popped out of their sockets when he tried to scream at his mother, choking off whatever he meant to say. The shipboard chaplain told him it was a normal symptom of anxiety, and to face his fears with God's guidance. But Dean could not tell the chaplain, or anyone, about the *other* dreams that were coming back—

He surprised everyone when he agreed to come up with Andy and Dom because Dean was his own man, with his own plan. The men under him on the ship knew it, his neighborhood knew it, his wife and kids sure as heaven knew it. And if his family didn't see it, they could all go to hell.

Dean could never come up here alone, never face her without losing it, and everything that might come after. No, as he sat here, feeding the evidence of his childhood into a shredder, and his mother into boxes and dumpsters, he almost wanted to weep with relief at the new vistas looming ahead on his horizon. Visions of destiny, unclouded by shadows of the past.

It was like sneaking into a bear's den to steal treasure, or diving to the bottom of a septic tank, to drain the damned thing and be done with it, so he could stand for what he was, and never fear the mud and slime of his past. He could look his muckraking enemies in the eye with a winning smile and deny he had any idea what they were talking about. They must all be lies, or he would remember.

But here and there, evidence peeked out, of years of shame and poverty, converging on a vanishing point that was a hole in his life.

He'd found more than a few innocent snapshots, unmarred by Mom or her boyfriends, or the bruises they left. These would do nicely to build up the story of Dean Kowalski: West Point Navy officer, devoted husband, churchgoing Catholic, and your Republican candidate for state legislature.

Dean kept his eyes down on the shoebox filled with

photos and loose pages from a journal. He'd taken down all the mirrors and framed pictures along with all the other crap hanging on the walls, even the damned taxidermy pets, but he sat facing a big picture window that looked out on empty blackness, and was thus a mirror.

Dom sat facing him on the other side of that black glass like the partition in a prison's visitation room. When he looked for too long, he could see tattoos seeping out from under his reflected skin.

Though he could not remember all that burned him up inside, he knew they were both full of the same poison. He had only managed to contain it, to squeeze it out like venom from a snake, a tiny bit at a time. But it was still in him. No matter how hard he prayed, it still seized his hand when he lost patience with his wife or his youngest son, who was a devil for breaking his daddy's things. No matter how he sacrificed himself to duty, it still drove him to lose his temper when his authority seemed in question, and when that happened, he burned to lose control and become a beast. No matter how he loved his wife, it still kept him awake nights with tortured fever dreams of other lives, other women, pleasures untasted, forbidden things worth torching everything he'd built.

But he would rise above it. Already had. Here, tonight, he could put it all behind him.

A picture of a line of children in tall wheat grass, swaddled in dirty blue robes. They wore bags slung on their hips like millet gleaners, and bent to pick at the ground. Dean recognized himself and his sister, looking up at the camera with that special glassy reproach they reserved for Mom, who must have snapped this during a lull in whatever repulsive hippie orgies kept the grownups occupied at the ashram or commune or squat in question.

Dean guessed that he was about ten in the photo, his sister nine. Dom was nowhere to be seen, so it was a snapshot from the heart of the lost year. He looked into the blank but wizened face of his boyhood—grubby, blistered and grave like a Dust Bowl Okie, but vulnerable in a way he had never allowed himself to be since.

He squinted, mouth a lipless wrinkle, but his eyes yawned in a silent scream for help. His mother had not answered. Soon after this was taken, his father swooped in and took Dean and Laura back home, and later, got Dom out of the reform school. But whatever had happened could not be erased, only buried. It was happening right there in the picture, in the boy's mind, broiling with terror over the memory and the unborn ghost of what would happen to him that night.

The child silently begged his mother for rescue, but now he begged Lt. Cmdr. Dean Kowalski for release. And Dean, who could be merciful, granted it by feeding him into the shredder.

He sat back and looked at his reflection in the picture window, eager for an audience to share this moment of unadulterated triumph. He'd been having the nightmare again, the one where all your teeth crack and shatter like rotten eggshells and your face collapses in on itself like a rotten jack o'lantern, so it felt like a dream coming true when two of his molars cracked and splintered under the lockjaw strain of his grin.

He choked on his broken teeth. His feet kicked like a hanging man's, driving the chair back from the table and against the wall. His reflection mocked his sudden fit of terror, exaggerating his crybaby grimace and emasculating his manful yelp of surprise when a black shadow behind his reflection moved.

Something outside.

He knew instinctively who was out there. He almost heard Dom's guffaws before he realized they were only in his head.

Dom lived to kick him in the jewels, to trip him up and drag him down to Dom's level, to the playground, the strip club, the jungle. He couldn't stand to see Dean proud of his hard-won life, hated anyone who held values, or character, or self-discipline. To make up some story about a girl and go off into the woods, only to spy on Dean, would both perpetuate Dom's dubious legend as a man-whore and allow him to play summer-camp pranks.

Dean got up and went to his duffel bag. He checked the action on his automatic, chambered a round and flipped the safety off. Dom's problem was, he had a child's sense of humor. He thought Dean couldn't take a joke, but if he wanted games, he would see how grown-ups played.

They had been so much alike, once. From the same egg, they'd been a split soul in two bodies for most of their childhood. When Mom and Dad broke up, they clung even closer together, sharing a bond that shut out even their little sister. When they fought, they only externalized the turmoil that goes on in every human soul. Together, they could have withstood anything.

So Mom took them apart.

Her boyfriend Roy was the worst of them. Running from the law in three states, he never held a job, and his anger was a seething, molten thing like magma just under his skin.

Dean didn't even remember what they'd been arguing over when they woke Roy up. All he remembered was that huge, hairy, drunken bastard taking him by the arm and yanking him into the air, jerking him and cracking his arm like a whip, or like a rattlesnake when a real frontiersman breaks its neck.

Until then, Dean hadn't even noticed that he was her favorite. Dad had always dressed them in matching outfits, and when Mom took them away, they dressed from a common pool of thrift store castoffs. He never thought of himself as separate from Dom in any way, and the little extra treats she bestowed on him on the sly, he always shared with his brother. Food did not taste, music did not sound, nothing was funny, unless Dom was there to reflect the pleasure of it back at him.

But she chose, that night; she picked Roy over Dominic, sold him down the river to a reform school in the state they happened to be at the time, and kept Dean, with a purple plaster cast on his arm, the whole summer. Her whispered voice, husky from Pall Malls and vodka, "You're Mama's real boy. Mama loves you the most, Dean. Mama's going to fix it . . . "

The cast outlasted Roy, who abandoned them at a rest stop in Wyoming a month later. If Mom didn't stand up for them when Roy was mad, she strove to make his hangovers into a family court with endless interstate harangues about just how much he'd fucked up. He went out to take a piss, leaving them sleeping fitfully in his rusted-out Chevy Vega, and hopped a ride on a semi, or wandered off into the badlands to be eaten by wolves, if there was any justice.

They camped at every rest stop on the way back to California, feeding on trash from the dumpsters, when she ran into her next boyfriend, who ran what he called an "ideal living commune."

At the start, after months of living in a car and separated from Dom, it'd seemed like paradise. Mom's new boyfriend had room for all of them, and food, if they worked to help grow it, and love, lots of love. He had dozens of other girlfriends and stepchildren and children, love for all God's creatures. Even now, it made Dean sick to his stomach to try to remember what happened on that farm.

It was best not to dwell. The past was not his fault, and now he had started to lay it to rest, to burn it and bury its ashes deep.

He would not let himself do anything tonight that couldn't be taken back, but he would take Dom further than he was willing to go, so far it would have to end.

Dean went down the hall and flipped on the bathroom

light and turned on the shower, then doubled back and crept through the living room to the sliding glass door.

The redwood deck wrapped around two sides of the house. Half the planks were loose or warped out of true, but he moved with a ninja's stealth to the steps leading down to the weedy backyard. His guts went cold and clenched up, a fist filled with shit and Weight Watchers. It was the old game, the pure simple thrill that the Navy, at its most challenging, had only just scratched. Hunting his nemesis as he was himself hunted, circling and striking, merging like snakes gobbling up each other's tail.

Ear cocked for the slightest arrhythmic sound, he zoned out to the layered threnodies of night insects all around him, blanked his mind with each silent step in the endless journey around the house. His dark-adapted eye took in feasts of moonlit detail. Beards of rust trailing from the seams in the vinyl siding, the prefab shack was rotting from the inside out.

The owl on the low branch at the edge of the property; the fathomless darkness between the trees where the hills grew steep and framed the valley where no roads led. Everything tried to tell him how easy it would be, and how good, to win, once and for all.

And a new wrinkle in his brain-terrain presented itself: tonight, it was real.

They weren't pointing their fingers and saying bang (well, one of them wasn't), and they weren't using the painted plastic toy Roy used to rob gas stations under the specious impression that the law was softer on fake armed robbery.

The game that probably began in the womb, when they vied for nutrients and *lebensraum*, the game that never ever ended . . . but it could end for good, tonight. Mom was gone off to God-only-cares where.

No, lord God Jesus, what are you thinking?

This was the kind of hotheaded stupidity that only

Dom could push him to. And in the end, it would be Dom's victory, for he had no other purpose than to mess with his brother's life. It was Dean who had something to lose, Dean who had a plan and a destiny.

Dean took a deep breath, held it and slid the clip out of the pistol, pocketed it and let the breath out slowly, picturing all the ugly impulses spinning off into the night air like dying germs.

Thank you, Jesus.

He would still scare the shit out of him. Dom would creep in the front door, hoping to catch him jacking off in the shower. He caught him once when they were eleven, and never let him forget it. That Dom himself had no shame, beating it on long car trips, in public restrooms, and in front of God and everybody in the showers in high school, only added to his humiliation.

He would probably try to snap a shot of Dean with his new camera phone.

Dean slipped around the corner of the façade and ducked behind a desiccated acacia bush. The darkness was profound, with oak and pine trees towering over the house blocking out most of the starlight, but there was enough to make out a silhouette on the porch, leaning over the railing to block out the buttery yellow glow through the goldenrod curtains.

Mindful of the crushed gravel of the driveway, Dean knelt and crawled closer to the porch. If he stayed low until he got up close, then sprang out of the bushes alongside the railing, the motion-sensor lamp over the garage light would go off, and hilarity would ensue.

It stood as still as a statue, but Dean could see that if it was Dom, something was seriously off-kilter.

The railing blocked his view until he got within arm's reach of the railing. He took a deep breath, held it, and jumped from cover.

"GET ON THE GROUND, TURD-BURGLAR!"

The blinding spotlight struck like lightning and a rush of white and yellow eyes and red-flecked teeth and claws whirled and snarled at him.

"Toshiro!" Dean jumped back and raised the gun. God, it was just Dom's damned dog.

He thought seriously about putting the clip back in.

When Dom got thrown out of his apartment, he'd crashed on Dean's couch with Toshiro in tow. The puppy ate his Clancy hardcovers, pissed in his bed and left non-minty chocolates on his pillows, and what he did to his wife's stuff was too foul to describe. When Dom joined the Army, she demoted Dean to the couch until he got rid of the dog. He sent it to the one place he knew it would not be refused, to the one person who truly deserved such a beast. It was worth the two-hour tirade he'd suffered on the phone to get Toshiro shipped upstate to live with Mom.

Toshiro barked at him once, lazily. Clearly, he remembered Dean as an old enemy with a new weapon, and wisely leapt from the railing and sprinted across the yard.

Dean looked down and noticed he was standing in a long two-legged shadow. "I see you, fudge-packer—"

He spun and pointed the gun. Dry, rustling tangles of ivy snared his feet when he tried to take a step back. Something chopped at his chest and hurled him back across the yard so hard he hit the wall of the house and the vinyl siding shattered under his shoulder. A little eep of pure terror escaped just as his windpipe closed like a cheap soda straw. The gun bucked in his hand.

The blast from the one round left in the chamber bathed his face in white-hot light, but he squeezed his eyes closed. In the moment of noon-bright light, he'd seen Dominic's face.

Dean collapsed, wheezing, "Medic!" He had been trained to replace a damaged trachea with a plastic tube; you could even use the cartridge of a ballpoint pen, in a pinch . . .

A burning breath trickled into his lungs. He was bruised, but not broken. His shoulder hurt more where he'd hit the house.

Even the insects had gone dead silent in the wake of— whatever it was. It was real, though . . . wasn't it?

The yard was empty. A straggly piñon pine huddled against the house by the porch, scrawny branches thrust out to invite him to walk into them again. That must have been what it was.

Oh shit, it was like freshman year at the Academy all over again. He was losing it . . . losing it big time.

"Dom?" he croaked. A sip of cool night air, sweet as communion wine, slid down his recovering throat. "Dominic, you okay?" He got up and looked around.

There was nobody. No body.

The thought gave him no comfort. If he let his guard down, they could try to get in again. And if they weren't real, it was worse, because then, they were already *inside*. They had as much claim to his mind as he did.

He'd slipped up. He walked into a branch in the dark and accidentally discharged his weapon. No harm, no foul.

Dean went back into the house and locked the doors. He checked on Andy, who snored in Mom's bed with the covers tangled up around his legs and a pillow over his head. If he had a concussion, it was probably a bad idea to let him sleep.

The crybaby would be fine, Dean knew. He hadn't hit his head on the shore at all, anyway, just knocked the wind out of himself. All the way back up to the cabin, between gulping and sobbing, he babbled about some naked chick he saw on the shore until Dean gave him some sleeping pills from Mom's cache.

He pictured, for a distasteful moment, Andy the gump making it with his sister, who was, he freely admitted to himself, no great catch. Lord, what losers their kids would be.

He laughed, feeling a warm, buttery balm coat his soul at the comparison of himself to Andy. He meant no harm, and that was the trouble. People like him slipped into your family, your crew, your country, and they seemed so reasonable and meek that you didn't think to push them out until it was too late, when their reasonable talk-things-out approach started to tap-dance on your nerves and drag every decision out into a passion play. Everything had to be explained and debated, and before you knew it, they'd undermine and sabotage your authority at every turn with their godless, liberal moonbat bullshit.

Dean went back to the table and brought in the shredder and another box of photos. He'd keep busy until morning, then go for a run, maybe try to catch a nap after he got the flakes up and working on their share of the punch list.

But first, he wanted to finish the conviction list. Each day, he wrote his beliefs, big and small, specific and general. Tonight, he skipped the God, family and country entries. Tonight, he wanted answers from himself. He took up the pen and finished the sentence.

#1: *I believe that Mom . . . is dead.*

It didn't lift any weight off his chest, to see it there in print. Maybe he could get one of those fake newspapers from the county fair. That would be a funny white elephant gift, Dad would get a kick out of it, for sure, ha ha.

Ding dong, the bitch is dead.

It didn't feel good, because it didn't feel true. He took up the pen and changed the period to a comma, added, *and she's still trying to drive me insane and ruin my life.*

Wrong. Wrong, all wrong. Unworthy beliefs, unworthy thoughts that would yield unworthy actions. Mistakes, weakness, catastrophe. Failure to plan is planning to fail. He tore the sheet off the pad and balled it up tight, crushing his fingernails into it until it was a tiny bolus of bleached pulp, ink and shame, and popped it in his mouth. Without benefit of water, without even letting it soften in his saliva, he dry-swallowed it, relishing the hurtful track it carved down his bruised throat.

When he felt he had atoned and prayed himself clear of the offense, he took up the pen and began again.

WHAT I BELIEVE
He underlined this title until he tore the paper and set the pen down, waiting for inspiration to strike.

CHAPTER 9

ANDREW WOKE UP CHOKING.

Shrouded in a tangle of hairy, dog-oily blankets, he rolled off the bed and hobbled to the bathroom. Morning sunlight, brutally bright, poured in through the parted curtains. A straggly bush pressed at the window, casting bobbing shadows of fruit the size of human baby heads. Pomegranates, ripe and ready, but the birds had already pecked the blood-red hulls open and gutted the clusters of seeds, so each fruit gaped a shrieking jack-o-lantern grin as it knocked at the glass.

It smelled like someone was baking cookies, but he knew better. Mom seemed to have a thing for candles that smelled like sweets, from vanilla to pumpkin pie and chocolate chip cookies, and every room in the house smelled like a different cause of type 2 diabetes.

Wracked with nausea, he gagged over the sink, sneezing convulsively until bile scoured the walls of his sinuses. Fucking dog hair. He wasn't even allergic, but the miasma of dust, dander, oil and hair made him feel like he'd been smoking camel-shit in a hookah through layers of burlap.

His back and arms throbbed from his fall yesterday, and when he examined himself in the mirror, he saw they were studded with itchy welts. He lost count after ten or twenty. Out in the country, it could be mosquitoes, fleas, ticks, chiggers, spiders or a million other goddamned things. One of them on his shoulder still had a tiny stinger jutting out of it, with fuzzy venom-sacs attached.

He wasn't allergic to bees either, but he loathed them. Insects could bite to draw blood or defend themselves, but a bee was just a bullet—totally expendable. When it drove its stinger into flesh, the barbed weapon anchored itself and ripped out its innards, so the spent drone sacrificed itself to deliver a wound that didn't even wake him up. And the stinger itself, once torn from the body, still convulsed, pumping its venom into the enemy of the hive.

She hadn't come back. He rinsed his face but skipped the soap, a fissured and stained brown bar studded with bristles that looked like cactus needles. Perfect for self-flagellation. Out here alone, a person could go quietly and quickly nuts. And Mom hadn't started out with a full deck.

A weird thought struck him, just then. Had Dean opened every closet? They'd walked around the property, but maybe they weren't finding her because they were looking for an upright body.

An awful idea, and he disgusted himself with the thought, but what if she turned up dangling from a pine tree, or facedown in a ditch up in the hills? Another inert, obsolete thing to be packed in a box. Maybe then, Laura could relax . . .

He took out his cell phone and checked the signal: one bar. He didn't want to seem needy, but no matter how he rationalized it, he *needed* her. He needed to talk to her about yesterday, vent about her brothers and uncork a bit of spleen over her sending him up here alone; but mostly, he just needed to hear her voice, to know she was waiting for him to come home.

Harden the fuck up, Andy.

He jotted off a quick text message—*Good morning, honey—miss you*—and pocketed the phone.

Andrew took a piss and washed his hands again, changed into fresh jeans and his favorite Radiohead T-shirt. Out in the living room, everything but the TV and the shredder had been packed up. The TV ran Fox News with the sound muted.

Golden spears of sun through the dining room window made the lazy parade of dust and hair dance. Dean sat at the table, making out a list. He gave no sign that he saw Andrew come in. He didn't look like he'd slept. Splashes of sweat plastered his Naval Academy T-shirt to his chest. On the *Barney Miller* Eyebag Scale, he'd drooped from Chano to Yemana.

He smelled coffee, but found none brewing.

"Dean, you want some coffee?" he asked.

Dean shrugged.

"You go for a jog this morning?"

Dean scowled, but didn't look up. "I went for a *run*."

"Was anyone chasing you?"

"No . . . "

"Then you were *jogging*."

Not rising to the bait, Dean resumed trying to make the memo pad spontaneously combust with his gaze.

Andrew tried to remember where he'd seen the coffee the night before. He poked around at the cans in the pantry—okra, pumpkin pie filling, cranberry sauce, garbanzo beans and a bunch of mystery cans with the labels peeled off.

"Fucking bees stung me in my sleep last night," Andrew said.

"A little poison won't kill you."

"Venom," Andrew corrected. "Plants and animals contain poison so they won't get eaten. Animals use venom to kill other animals."

"Whatever."

Andrew found a big Folgers can between the Glad sandwich bags and a generic fabric softener, and cracked the rubber lid. This shit must be a decade old.

At home, Andrew never sipped anything less than

Starbucks, and even that tasted like pencils, next to his birthday stash of Jamaican Blue Mountain beans. He scooped some of the petrified crap into the basket filter on the Mr. Coffee machine when he saw something white peeking out of the grounds. He reached in and took a closer look. He slapped the lid down. "There's no coffee."

His hip tingled and he took out his phone, but it must've been a phantom nerve response, because his inbox was empty.

Dean gave no sign that he heard or cared. His jaw muscles popped and worked like he was chewing rawhide, or biting back a gout of crypto-fascist bile in response to one of Andrew's liberal barbs at the Xmas dinner table.

Andrew sidled past him and dropped the coffee can in the trash, peeking at the list. He'd get no other hint of their marching orders for the day. The header at the top of the list, underlined until the ballpoint pen had gouged rips in the Century 21 memo pad, said WHAT I BELIEVE.

Dean's hand covered the list. "Nobody likes a spy, Andy."

Andrew mumbled, "Sorry," left the kitchen in a hurry, crossing the living room and turning into the green shadows of the hall, and walked face-first into a muscular wall.

Andrew stumbled back, yelled, "Jesus! Dom, you scared the shit out of me!"

Dom stood in the hall with his sunglasses on and his windbreaker zipped up. "Hey," he said as he shouldered past Andrew.

"What happened to you last night, man? We were worried—"

Dom's face looked bloated and flushed, like he'd slept on a bed of pummeling fists. He turned and went into the bathroom.

"Hey, I was here first—"

"So were the Indians," Dom said, and kicked the door shut.

Just before the door slammed, Andrew caught a glimpse of Dom that pinned him to the moment for a long while after it passed. Dom noticed the mirror, flinched and threw up his fists as if he'd blundered into a stranger, and reflexively challenged him to fight. Animals and birds did that, not people. Wasn't it an elementary test of sentience, to recognize one's own reflection?

Dom must be massively hung over. Probably a good story there. Dom was usually eager to share the details of his improbable adventures, and he was always hung over in the morning, if not still wasted.

Andrew pounded on the door. "Hey, man, fine if you don't want to talk, but there's still work to do. We left you the garage boxes to pack, okay?"

Dom said something that Andrew barely made out through the door. He thought it was, "Okay," or it might have been just a wordless animal grumble, but as Andrew retreated down the hall with the Folgers can, he thought that Dom might have said, "No . . . staying . . . "

Dean was still sitting at the kitchen table. The pad in front of him was blank, except for telegraphic slashes where his underscoring had stabbed through the previous page. His musclebound jaws strained and twanged under his skin, to hold something back or force it down. Had Dean eaten the list?

"What're today's marching orders, Lieutenant Dean, sir?"

For a long minute, it looked like he wasn't going to answer at all. He set the pen down on the table with a too-deliberate click and laid his hands out in front of him like weapons he'd been cleaning and oiling all night long. "We'll go into town," he finally said. His voice was so low and strangled, it might've come from his ass. "See if the Sheriff knows anything. Maybe she fell off the wagon, again."

Andrew just stared at Dean. Any other time, if he'd heard it second or third hand, he'd laugh until he shit himself. But right now, he could only stare and wish himself away, because so much about Dean suddenly made sense, from his anal, authority-worshipping attitude, to his frantic shredding party last night. It was all in the coffee can.

Dom shouldered past him, making him jump a little, but for a change, he didn't get two for flinching. He might've been a beaded curtain for all the notice Dom took of him. "Go into town. Good idea . . . need supplies."

Dean drove, but he didn't try to pop in his Sean Hannity audiobook, and Dom didn't reach for a Slayer CD. Nobody talked.

To fill the silence, Andrew fiddled with the radio: Great sizzling plains of static, interrupted only by squalls of redneck warbling and creepy Christian pop. He settled on the clearest signal. A monotonous baritone voice bathed in crackling distinct from the reception problems, like the fireside ambience of an old LP, or a shortwave signal rebounding off the ionosphere, sixty years out of date.

"It was on the seventh day of the lockout. The strikebreakers brought axehandles and brass knuckles and baseball bats, and the company sent over Pinkertons, who threatened us with guns.

"They knocked me down and hooded me, and worked my ribs with their bats. None of them said a word, and I didn't give them the satisfaction. Then one of them got down close by my ear . . . and he said, 'Renny, don't make us drag your family into this . . . '

"I told him where to go, and how I could take all they could dish out, and how he could kill me and mine, but there'd always be more of us. He laughed then, and he told me, 'You want to take good care of your family, Renny, 'cos you ain't ever gonna make another.'

"Then he had his goons take hold of my legs, and just so I'd know it was sharp, he sliced my cheek down to the bone with his straight-razor. Then he told them to take my trousers down—"

"Enough of that shit," Dean snapped. He reached to change the station, but Dom leaned across Andrew and caught his wrist.

Andrew pressed himself back against the seat to stay clear of the straining arms locked before him. Still stunned at Dean's language and temper, saying, "Hey, assholes," over and over without expecting a sensible reply, he only noticed the tattoos on Dom's arm just as the fight in the truck got serious.

Andrew looked at the throbbing forearm and saw something new on the bewildering tangle of shark and octopus that sheathed it. So realistic he flinched at first glance, before he saw it was a part of the design he'd never noticed before. A bee, fat and furious as life, seemed to waggle and dance as Dom twisted his twin's arm backwards and the wheel spun and the road went out from under the truck.

"Hey!" Andrew screamed. "Goddamit, watch the fucking road!"

The right wheels jounced and bit into the soft soil on the road's shoulder. The whipping procession of trees swerved closer, like the teeth of a saw, clipped off the passenger-side rearview mirror with a nasty clap of flying metal and atomized glass. Andrew screamed again as he chopped at the locked arms in front of him.

Neither brother gave any sign that they noticed. Andrew caught the wheel, jerked it out of Dean's loose grip and spun the truck to the left. They lurched against each other and the centerline swung under them, wheels squealing and the huge yellow Hummer in the oncoming lane blaring its horn.

Dean snapped out of his trance and put both hands on

the wheel, fought them out of the path of the Hummer, which flashed by with a final honk and a bunch of rigid digits pressed against tinted windows.

"Maybe I can find a wingnut show, with some kid crying about how his gay college professor forced *Das Kapital* and a blowjob on him, Dean, would that make you happy?"

"Just turn it off," Dean grunted.

They drove on in silence. The cool morning breeze gushed in the windows, rippling Dom's tangled black hair and the filthy Motorhead shirt stretched across his musclebound chest. Andrew found he couldn't quite look at Dean after what he saw in the coffee can. He risked a sidewise glance at Dom, noticing in a totally casual, not-gay way that he looked bigger today.

His biceps was thicker than Andrew's thigh, and looked denser than lead. His neck bulged out wider than his ears and throbbed with inner tension, as if Dom held every muscle in his body contracted to its uttermost, coiled to explode.

On the flesh just under his left ear, where flaming dice rolled and mermaids dragged drowning sailors to submarine catacombs beneath the veil of his shaggy hair, Andrew saw two more bees, capering busily under the skin. The ink that rendered them was slightly more vivid, the skin around them flushed and scabbed with dried blood. Fresh work.

"See something red?" Dom growled.

Andrew averted his eyes.

The road leapt over a narrow gorge with a waterfall and kids in bib overalls with fishing poles sitting on mossy rocks. The guardrails were piebald with smears of paint and hastily patched up where more than one car had misjudged the angle of the turn.

Beyond the last span, the shoulders drew up on either side of the road and became rusty granite walls; then, around a hairpin bend, they closed over it to form a tunnel. Andrew saw corrugated steel walls and stained pine support beams, then the tunnel spat them out, and they were driving down Main Street. A green sign said *UTOPIA, Pop. 552, Elev. 2,800 Ft.*

Dean pumped the brakes and stopped just short of the bumper of an old Chevy Blazer with SHERIFF'S DEPUTY stenciled in peeling green paint across the tailgate. He felt Dom tense up beside him, and stifled the suggestion that they stop and ask for help.

Main Street twisted and swooned down a mountainside so steep that the sidewalks were staircases. The town clung to the steep wall of the valley and spilled out before and below them in as unlikely a locale for human habitation as ever Andrew had seen.

The houses and shops were a curious mix of Depression-era public works and alpine half-timber design, and unlike every other small town in California, no attempt was made to cater to tourists. He saw no motels, no souvenir or T-shirt shops, no fast food chains. They passed a soda fountain, a grocer, a leather goods store, and a realtor with hundreds of For Sale listings covering the front windows, but Andrew took note of many shops that belonged on Telegraph Avenue in Berkeley. A world music store featured African metal percussion instruments in its windows; a pale white man with graying dreadlocks swept the front steps, suspiciously eyeing the non-indigenous passersby. Another store seemed to sell only huge chunks of crystals, geodes and other New Age minerals. An enormous graphic of Andre The Giant as Che Guevara peered out the window of the next shop, a converted neo-Victorian with carts and hand-trucks of books on the porch under a sign that said FREE—PLEASE TAKE.

"So," Andrew asked, "what's the plan?"

"We'll go talk to the realtor about Mom's cabin. Then I want to get some decent chow for the ride back to Sacramento."

"What about your mom?"

"What about her?"

"You're cleaning out her house, and taking her shit to a new town. That's going to look suspicious."

Dean flashed a snarl at the traffic, a slow pickup towing a speedboat. "If she's really gone, this is the best thing to do. We'll call the sheriff's after we get to Sacramento. If we walk it in now, they're liable to try to hold us until she turns up."

This was fucking ridiculous. Andrew knew he should count to ten and choose his words carefully. "Why would they hold *us*? What did *we* do?"

The twins sat like silent bookends.

"Fuck it." Andrew leaned over Dom and opened the passenger-side door. "I'll call you."

Dom made no move to get out of his way.

"Andy, stay in the truck," Dean snapped.

Dom lifted Andrew out and dumped him on the street. Dean gunned the truck down the hill so the passenger door slammed shut, swung onto a narrow side street with a shriek of burning rubber.

Andrew jumped up on the curb and looked around. He could've sworn he'd seen people on the street only a moment ago, but now the steep sidewalks, broken up by crooked stairs that wound up between the moss-furred brick and granite buildings, were empty of pedestrians, the road, gaping potholes revealing crumbling river rock cobblestones, desolate.

He took out his phone. Three bars, and it was late enough. If he took a few deep breaths, he could sound casual. He thumbed her number, waited, got her message center. He hung up without leaving a message.

The bookstore beckoned, and Andrew gave in.

If he never bought another book, he would need two lifetimes to read the books he already had; but when he found himself in a strange town, shopping in bookstores, especially used ones, provided the muted mix of the familiar and the foreign, and the DNA of the collective unconscious of the area, that he felt he learned something valuable with every book bought, whether he read them or not.

The books on the freebie carts were dogeared Marxist tracts, hobo memoirs, little red Mao books, and histories of the Wobblies, HUAC trials and union wars. Andrew poked through them, but half the books disintegrated when he picked them up, and the rest had black mold-speckles on them. He opened the door.

A cacophony of tinkling bells pealed. The same radio show that had assaulted them in the truck played on a crappy speaker somewhere in the back, and a crackly Stan Getz record raved at itself from an antique phonograph under the stairs on the left side of the store.

The floor-to-ceiling shelves started just inside the door, and a counter, half-buried in receipts and flyers, peered out from ramparts of stacked books like a pillbox.

A bent old man with a silver beard that tickled his belt buckle straddled a stool behind the counter, chewing a meerschaum pipe and contemplating a ledger. His eyebrows stood out like moth's antennae from behind wire-rimmed spectacles perched on a nose like a cuttlefish bone. His vest was crowded with buttons and pins with Che and Einstein and messages like CENSORSHIP CAUSES BLINDNESS—READ! When he smiled, the ghastly yellow teeth threatened to tear the skin off something. "Can I help you find anything, comrade?"

"No thanks . . . " Andrew started, but the stacks were unlabeled, and the sections seemed to bleed together, if there was any rhyme to the layout at all. "Uh . . . d'you have a science fiction section?"

"You mean like the Warren Report, or Ronald Reagan's biography?" The clerk chuckled. "Not as such, no. Fiction is a decadent distraction, and we deplore it."

"Okay, well, I'll just look around . . . " A useful idea occurred to him. "Do you have anything about local communes?"

"Oh, there were never any successful communes around here, son. That's how the town got its name. It was settled by folks who gave all they had to this or that boneheaded utopian scheme, and they tried to run the town as a collective, too. Lasted about three weeks."

"You don't believe in them, then. I thought—"

"No self-respecting Marxist would have any truck with utopianism. So you've got a toy communist state on your farm. It doesn't bring you any closer to revolution."

"Right," Andrew tried to break in, "but what about—"

"You know, a lot of folks think the communes were a hippie fad, but they had utopian communal societies in Nathaniel Hawthorne's time. Now, the Kahweah settlement had a lot going for it, but the timber companies screwed them. And Llano Del Rio, down south, lasted quite a while, but their leader, he—"

"That's cool, but I was wondering if you had anything about the Leviathan Colony in Coverdale Valley, the one that was here in the Twenties? If you don't, maybe there's a library around here?"

The clerk seemed to wrack his brains, or maybe he was just trying to decide how badly he wanted to make a sale. His tongue squirted out from under his tea-stained mustache, and his eyes darted around behind his spectacles like lightning bugs in twin killing jars. "Seems to me, there never was a real history of that experiment. It limped along for a few years, but never went anywhere, really. Nobody took it seriously from the start; newspapers who took note at all had a field day about them settling in that old madhouse."

"Old what?"

"Oh sure, the Grass Valley retreat was one of the first private criminal asylums in California. Much more progressive than those snake-pits at Mendocino or Stockton, if by progressive, you mean sterilizing the retarded and scalding catatonic patients with live steam ... But they ran afoul of the political spoils system, and they boarded it up right before 1900. But if you're interested in socialist mental hygiene ..."

Andrew smiled and shrugged as the clerk upended his bottomless windbag of tangents and trivia, while he digested the idea of the commune inhabiting an abandoned insane asylum. Maybe it was built on an Indian burial ground, too. "So," he finally interjected, while the clerk searched for a monograph of Swedish mental institutions, "what happened to the commune?"

"Oh, what always happens to pie-in-the-sky utopian socialism? It foundered on ego and poor planning, like so many before and after. Some people thought it was a Bolshevik plot, like an advance invasion force, but like I said, it never amounted to much."

"Do you know anything about the new commune, the people who are there, now?"

Again with the tongue and the eyes, until Andrew suspected that he was signaling that someone was listening. His fingers fiddled around in the air, like the right book was floating between them, invisible. Then he darted out from behind the counter and into an alcove screened by several layers of beaded curtains.

Upstairs, the jazz record was arrested in mid-crescendo with a rude squall as someone yanked the tonearm off the vintage vinyl. Thudding footsteps on the treads drove Andrew back among the stacks. He flattened himself like a Wanted poster against Natural History.

A scratchy acoustic guitar took up a trudging rhythm, over which a tired black voice sang, "Which side are you on, my people? Which side are you on?"

Elephantine leg-shadows spilled down the stairs. Andrew took in a deep breath of the musty, book-rot stink, usually as comforting as church, but now it was like wads of wet pulp paper stuffed down his windpipe. Tiny, furtive scratching sounds right behind his head made him whirl around and startle a moribund beanbag of a rat gnawing the mildewed binding of a biography of LaMarck.

LaMarck professed that animals evolved by striving—that reaching for the higher leaves on gum trees stretched a giraffe's neck, and they passed the strain and striving on to their young. Darwin left him on the dungheap of junk science, but the idea always appealed to Andrew, that by trying and failing, he might still pass on that unkindled spark to his children, who might just make it.

The shadows stretched, then receded back up the steps with a bit more grace than they'd come down. *Which side are you on, my people?*

The beaded curtains parted and the old clerk puttered up the aisle to him, holding out a cup of steaming tea. "It's maté, very good for the nerves and digestion."

"Sorry, I'm not a big fan of tea. I like coffee . . . "

"It's good for all humanity . . . " The clerk rattled on about tea as Andrew looked him up and down, noticing the Band-Aid on his neck, uneasily clinging to the wiry white hairs at the border of his waterfall of beard. A little trickle of pus dribbled out from under the gauze, and one end of the bandage hung loose, like he'd been scratching it. Andrew thought of the bees in his bed, and the bees in the freezer, and the bees on Dom's arms.

"My brothers are looking for me, I gotta go . . . "

The clerk dropped the teacup on the floor between them. Andrew started to kneel to help clean up, but the clerk handed Andrew a book and pushed him, not ungently, towards the door. It was a slim, faded red journal with the binding gnawed away.

"They're making a horrible mistake up there," the old clerk whispered. "The workers—cutting off their own heads, you tell them that. Not so they can hear or think for themselves, but you tell them. Tell Sprague. Without the head, the body dies."

Which side are you on?

Andrew caught the book, reached for his wallet, but the old clerk stopped him by grabbing his arm in a shaky vise. "You'll find a way to pay," the clerk whispered.

"But I have money—"

The clerk hissed through his tea-stained teeth, shifty eyes like a student terrified he'll be caught helping the world's biggest idiot cheat on a test. "Your money's no good here."

Andrew backed up to the door, again setting off the tangle of bells. The jazz record came back on, and the old clerk bent and blotted the spilled tea with the sleeve of his gray flannel shirt.

Out on the street, Andrew caught the town red-handed. An old hippie in tie-dyed spandex riding gear buzzed by on a mountain bike, and a pair of husky Slavic women with scarves over their hair stomped down the street with a leash of children on a harness, like sled dogs. The deputy's Blazer screeched off with lights flashing down up Main Street, headed out of town. Within seconds, they'd all disappeared, as if there was a gunfight scheduled. Andrew strolled down the sidewalk, drinking in the glow of the sun and the purity of the air.

He covered two blocks, his eyes mostly on the book in his hands. The cover was blank. The title page had a photograph of a huge, ugly stone house like a Victorian debtor's prison, with a regimented group of about one hundred arranged in front of it like a West Point graduating class, except they were coed, wore plain gray smocks and held shovels and other tools instead of swords.

Beneath it, CONSTITUTION & MANIFESTO OF THE LEVIATHAN COLONY, by Dr. H. Xavier Sturtevant. And beneath that, a block print engraving of a honeybee.

He took out his phone and tried Laura again. This time, he'd leave a message, maybe even vent a little.

A shadow fell across the book. He heard footsteps pacing alongside him, even as he smelled clove cigarettes and French fries.

Laura's bored outgoing message kicked in. He killed the call and pocketed his phone. The sun, too-bright white tearing through the too-thin alpine sky, dazzled him when he tried to look up.

"Whatcha reading?"

This was his least favorite question in the whole, wide world. Sometimes, he wished he had a t-shirt that said something witty and misanthropic like I LOVE PEOPLE— I LOVE TO READ ABOUT THEM IN BOOKS, or TALKING IS FOR PEOPLE WHO CAN'T READ. Nothing flippant and nasty came to mind, just now, and he looked up with nothing to say, even as he realized that this might be the shadowy party on the stairs, and he might not be allowed to have this book. The business with the tea had been rather covert, the clerk's paranoia and cryptic message all the more reason to be afraid, because everyone in this town could be, for all he knew, as insane as the clerk.

"A book," he said pithily, feeling like an ass, for he saw a book in her hand, too. A Penguin Classics edition of L'Autreamont's *Chants Of Maldoror*, no less: the most obscure and intense of the French Decadents. He'd tried to read it in college, but couldn't get high enough to grasp anything more than rootless nightmare images and an overwhelming cloud of cloying, surrealist morbidity.

"So . . . who was that on the phone?" she asked, a sly lilt in her voice that made him reply, "Nobody."

Why did he say that? Why didn't he say, *My wife?* He usually loved to say *My wife*. It sounded grown-up, and yet it freed him from grown-up bullshit. *I'd love to come to your Super Bowl party, but my wife . . . Wish I could go out with you guys, but you know how the wife is . . . No, I*

*won't buy you a drink, sweetheart, but maybe my wife
will . . .*

"Do I know you?"

"May," she said. "I waited on you?"

From the restaurant, he realized. "I didn't recognize
you, with your hair down—"

"Thanks," she said, and blushed, hot rouge thawing
white, heart-shaped cheeks almost blue in the shade. Her
ebony bangs flapped in a veil across her eyes in the crisp
breeze, prickled at base of skull and nape of neck, where it
was clipped short enough to show goosebumps.

It didn't take much out in the sticks, he supposed. Any
strategy more elaborate than clubbing and dragging them
back to your lair must play like Casanova. "Those uniforms
suck, and the tips are for shit, but you can't make any real
money out here, without breaking the law."

What the hell did she mean by that? At sea, he tried to
keep her talking. Girls liked to answer questions, to talk about
themselves. He figured she wasn't originally Californian, since
she lacked that lilt in her voice that most girls from the
coast used to make every statement sound like a question,
unsure of anything from their names on down. But why
would someone come from out east, and settle here? "You
grow up around here?"

"No, I've been all over, but you know how it is . . . "

Did he? "Yeah, tell me about it . . . "

"You tear yourself in half, trying to figure out who you
are, trying to fit in. Into a town, into a family . . . "

He nodded dumbly and asked, "You need a ride
somewhere?" Where the hell did that come from?

She fished a pack of Camel Filters out of an unseen
pocket in her dress, tapped out a cig and lit it with a
tarnished silver Zippo. "You have a car?"

"I—my brothers and I, we came in a truck, but there's
room . . . " He did not want to be a trim coordinator for
Dominic. He'd nail her before dinnertime, and reward

Andrew with a lewd account of the conquest over breakfast.

He'd never cheated on his wife. If he didn't keep up his appearance as well as he had when he was single, it only helped mark him as spoken-for, and removed all temptation. Marriage made him secure; he could be an asshole at work, and not worry about getting laid at the Christmas party. Girls seldom smiled at him, except when they bagged his groceries or sold him a Whopper. Even if he never touched her, he realized he intended to hoard this girl's extraordinary smile for himself. "Do, do you live around here? I mean, I'm just asking . . . "

"No, I have a place up by the restaurant . . . I just come down here for the glamour." Her smile, when she didn't cover it with her nervous hands, was just the kind of fractured prettiness that Andrew defined as true beauty. One chipped tooth dimpled her lush lower lip, and her eyebrows, one split by a thin little scar, arched as if she saw into his mind and all his half-formed schemes. There was a shy wildness, an unspoiled, feral wisdom behind it. If you said the right thing, this girl might do something crazy with you, or to you.

Just knowing that the world had such creatures in it, and that they could see him and smile at him, made him both exultant and vaguely sad. He felt like a bald, fat old man flirting with a coed at a wedding.

"My brothers *are* assholes, though . . . "

She laughed a little. "If it'd be weird, I understand," she said.

It was like puberty all over again; each reply that occurred to him more idiotic than the last.

"Well, listen," she said, but then nothing for a long moment, looking down at her coy feet in big steel-toed purple boots drawing little shapes in the crust of pine pollen on the sidewalk. He looked her up and down and she seemed to brighten, skin, hair and faded paisley-print dress, for drinking in his gaze. "Maybe you'll come around, later."

A phlegmatic six-cylinder growl and a sharp squeal of rubber jolted him out of his mooning. Dom's truck emerged from an alley and nosed the curb beside him. "Yeah . . . um, that'd be cool. See you, um, May . . . "

He opened the door of the truck, but Dom didn't slide over or get out, just sat cigar store Indian-style, forcing Andrew to climb over him and sit in the middle. The bed was full of boxes.

When he turned to look at May, the street had taken her. Dean flipped an uncharacteristically reckless U-turn and headed out of town as fast as Main Street allowed.

"Who was that?" Dom asked. His flat, uninflected tone was barren of accusation, even of curiosity.

"A girl. From around here."

"What'd she want?" Dom sounded half-asleep.

"My dick."

"Um."

Dean brought the truck around with a squeal of scorched rubber and floored it up Main Street and into the tunnel. Nobody spoke.

CHAPTER 10

THE SOUND OF the engine and the wheels eating up the root-buckled tarmac were the only accompaniment on the trip back. Dean sat behind the wheel like a sleepwalker, but the tension wound up inside him set the truck to vibrating out of sync with the engine, as if he was running in the red and close to flying apart. Andrew wanted to shrink away from him, but there was nowhere to go.

On his right, Dom spread out like all his bones were disconnecting and reintegrating in new forms inside the overdeveloped house of muscle. In his lap, his big, gnarly hands twitched and grasped a dream of something, pulled it apart. The bees inked into his skin danced their secret codes.

Trapped between opposing poles, wracked by magnetic forces that pulled them toward certain mutual destruction, he could only sit, tongue-tied and vaguely ashamed. Caught red-handed talking to a girl from town. A book in his lap he suddenly felt he needed to hide. Andrew tasted ions in the air, sensed the electricity swirling around the three of them, seeking only a tiny, shiny glint of something to ground it and draw down the lightning.

When the truck finally came around the bend and turned up the rutted drive to Mom's cabin, Andrew almost tried to break the uneasy silence. Something stupid, even if it made them find common cause in mocking him, if only it would undo what seemed to be deciding for itself, what would happen next.

Dean stopped at the edge of the yellow, weedy lawn and killed the engine. The moment stretched out like the clouds of dust raised by the truck, the ticking of the engine and the droning, screaming dream of the cicadas, but nobody moved to get out.

"I gotta piss," Andrew said. His voice sounded like he was eight.

Silence. Stillness. Bookended by the twins, Andrew waited. If anything happened, it would not be because someone decided it, but only because someone lost control. Very well, then.

"You know, you guys need to figure out what the fuck we're doing out here, and get it done."

Dom didn't move. Dean bit down, let out a sigh that, if a bird flew through it, would kill it stone dead. "You really don't want to stick your nose in this," he said.

"Into what? Family business? I'm here, aren't I? I'm your sister's husband, and if that doesn't make me family, I sure wish somebody would've told me before I came up here, because this is bullshit."

They both looked at him, laser-guided resentment burning into him in stereo so he could only stare straight ahead at the cabin.

"We're packing up," Dean said, "and we're leaving."

"We're staying," Dom rumbled. "I know where Mom is."

Dean glared and shot back, "I don't fucking care."

"Let me out," Andrew snapped.

Both of them popped open the doors and sprang out so fast he thought he'd made an impression on them, when he saw them crossing the lawn at a fast clip to the front door, which was hanging open, and a silhouette filling the murk of the doorway.

"You in there!" Dean shouted. "Come out and show yourself!"

Bees circled Dean's head. He swatted at them with a

prissiness that reminded Andrew of old women walking through spiderwebs. "It's because you're so goddamned sweet," Dom sneered.

"You boys settle down now," the man in the house called out. With his hands up, he stepped out into the sun. It was a sheriff's deputy, maybe even the one they'd passed in town. Lurching over a potbelly and favoring one crooked leg, the gray-haired deputy did a yeoman's job looking unafraid of Dom and Dean.

They flanked the deputy as he came down the porch and onto the lawn. Seeing neither of them was armed, he put his hands down. "I stopped by because folks down at the Pond said you were asking after Ms. D'Amato."

"She's our mom," Dom said.

"And your door was open. We're out in the country, but we've got more than our share of crime." The deputy looked from Dean to Dom, and then, searchingly, to Andrew. The brass nametag above his badge said SCOVILL, L.

"Yeah, there's all kinds of criminals," Dom said. "Somebody steal your truck?"

Scovill hitched his thumbs in his Sam Browne belt and rocked back on his bootheels. "I parked up the road a piece, in front of your neighbors' place. There're some kids next door, who need the fear. You boys look like you've already got it in spades. What's the trouble?"

He looked at Dean as he asked this, turned his back on Dom and Andrew thought, *oh shit, no.* Dom took a step and one arm cocked fit to throw around the deputy, arms big enough and trained to kill silently . . .

"No trouble," Dean said. A bee drowsily probed his ear, and he slapped it hard. His voice was low and begrudging, each word dragged out by sheer will, like Dom with a hangover. Andrew thought of *One Step Beyond* urban legends about twins sharing emotions, memories. Maybe that's why Dean hated him.

"Our mom told us to come up and help her move, so we're here."

"She's gone missing?"

Dom shook his head. "She's around. We're just waiting for her . . . "

Dean took up his brother's stalled thought with eerie aplomb. "Then we'll be taking her down to Sacramento."

Deputy Scovill's smile was as shiny and worn-out as the seat of an old pair of jeans. Now he was getting annoyed. "Folks say you were afraid she'd come to some harm. There's a girl, named Jenny Treadwell, lives with her folks in the next valley, about halfway to town. Her folks said she went out last night to meet a boy, and never came back or called."

Dom looked away and settled his fists on his hips. Andrew had seen him do just that about half a dozen times, in bars or on the street, just before he knocked someone's teeth out. "What's that to us?"

"She's just turned seventeen."

"Again . . . what's that to us?"

A whole litany of items rolled behind Deputy Scovill's gray-green eyes, but he hawked and spat on the lawn. "No reason, just talking. If you boys are your mother's sons, you want to know she was being looked out for. This ain't the middle of nowhere, but it's on the way there. When I came down and saw the door hanging open and the place cleaned out—"

"The moving truck's right there, sir," said Dean. "She's moving. There's no trouble."

Scovill sized the twins up once more, subtly shifting gears as he decided something. He shrugged, touched the brim of his hat, started to walk away. "Well then, boys, I'll leave you to it. If you don't hear from your mom by tomorrow, you might call the office in town. We've had some mountain lions and bears coming down into population, so don't get to feeling too safe." He stopped and turned on the twins, ignoring Andrew completely. "And one more thing."

"What?"

"If that damned devil-dog's still here when you've gone, there'll be hell to pay, and that's a promise." He turned and shuffled down the drive.

Dean and Dom raced for the door. Looking over his shoulder, Andrew followed the deputy down to the road. "Sir?"

Scovill turned, but said nothing. His flushed face and fitfully blinking eyes buttoned up when they regarded Andrew, but it was plain to see he was spooked. Maybe Dom was right, and they had caught him doing something underhanded in the cabin. Maybe he'd seen something inside that they hadn't, yet. Or, most likely, he was just scared of the twins.

"I'm, ah, Ms. D'Amato's son-in-law."

Deputy Scovill took off his hat and swatted at a bee that circled his face. "Those boys listen to you?"

"Not really, sir . . . I came up to help their mom move, but we haven't seen her . . . "

"What's really going on here, son?"

"I don't know, and nobody's talking to me. But I heard there's this cult, or something, up the road?"

"Not a cult, just a commune." The deputy sounded vaguely offended. "And they're gone. Whole works folded a couple months ago."

"You know that old man, who lives next door . . . ?"

"I know he's nuttier than a squirrel turd. Sprague's best left alone. "

"Right, but he says they're still up there. And I've seen some things—"

"That's why you should get the hell out," Scovill barked. "Soon as your in-law shows up, get in the truck and skedaddle on down to Sacto."

"Why?"

"Tourist season's over, son," the deputy said, and turned away to hike down the driveway, waving dismissively at Andrew, or just warding off more bees.

Andrew wanted to say something else, wanted help, but for whatever reason, he couldn't shout out that Dom took the jailbait girl into the woods last night, then came back alone like a broken robot. Maybe the deputy was under the same trance as everyone else in this godforsaken burg. Maybe he was a crook. Maybe he was just a sensible fucking guy.

In the front yard, on his way to the truck to fetch the book, he heard them in the house. Shouting, cursing.

Andrew felt like a thief as he reached in the open window and picked the slim red book off the seat. This wasn't his family. He hadn't been born into it, but he'd married it, tied himself to it. God, how he wished Laura was here, or they were together somewhere else.

Coming back across the lawn and passing the open door, no way was he going in there, when Dom appeared, charging for the doorway. Dean in hot pursuit slammed him into the wall and kicked the door shut. The whole façade shook. A brown potted fern tumbled off the porch railing and shattered. The force of their bodies thrashing around inside threatened to smash down the front door and roll out into the yard.

I am a part of this family, Andrew told himself. *I am Laura's husband. I am my brothers' keeper.* All that bullshit.

Resolved, he crossed to the porch before he thought better of it, and grabbed the doorknob.

It was locked. On the other side, he heard the crunch of drywall, thundering, stamping feet and grunted curses.

"Open the goddamned door!" Andrew thought he sounded pretty damned good. His voice didn't even crack.

"Fuck off, Andy!" Dean shouted. "Family business!" Dom roared, before they went back to killing each other.

God damn it, he was tired of this shit. If they were going to fight, they could kill each other, for all he cared. But he had to try harder, for Laura. He stepped down off the porch and went around the cabin to the back door. Through the window, he could see them grappling, a shadowy, four-legged blob with its hands at its own throat.

He reached for the back door when his phone rang.

Son of a bitch, he hadn't been able to get a signal out here, all day. Muffled by his pocket, Laura's ringtone was a brain-needling beep version of "Some Enchanted Evening" from her favorite movie, *South Pacific*. A gesture to show how well he knew her, it felt like he earned her a little more every time he suffered through it.

He dug the phone out and answered it. "Hey, baby."

"Andrew, what's going on, up there?"

"Oh, not much . . . can't find your mom . . . your brothers are fighting . . . Sheriff wants to nail Dom for statutory rape . . . Dean's gone all Yul-Brynner-in-Westworld, and Dom's acting like a zombie . . . the usual . . . Um . . . I'd ask if I could call you back, but I don't know if I could get through, again." He stood rooted, afraid to move his head, for fear of losing the connection. "I've been thinking a lot, about what we talked about before I left . . . "

Silence.

"Hello?" he asked.

"I'm still here," she said, but nothing else for a while. "I've been thinking, too, hon. I wish I didn't make you go up there with them. It wasn't right—"

"No, baby, no. I wanted to . . . I mean, I want to help you and the family, and if I can do anything, then—"

"I wanted you to go, so I could have time to think, Andrew. I needed time, and some space."

The sharp, measured tone set him back on his heels. She'd prepared this speech. "What do you mean, you need space? You're my wife. You wanted to be my wife."

"I know that. We dated for two years and we've been

married a little over a year. It took longer than college, but I finally got what I wanted."

"What's the deal, Laura? Why are you doing this to me now?"

"This isn't the first time, is it, Andrew? It's the same argument we always have. Every step forward you take in the adult world, I've had to push you. Every milestone in our relationship, I've had to force out of you. You surrendered, but you never let me forget it. And I'm tired, Andrew. I'm looking at how far I'll have to push you to get us through this life together, and I'm saying, right now, I'm sorry, but I can't do it anymore."

He was speechless, but only because he was floored by how many things he could say, if he really wanted to join battle and burn the whole thing down. *I gave you everything you wanted; sure, I need you, what the fuck is wrong with needing you, why would two people promise to be together forever if they didn't need each other to get through life; life with you is no fucking picnic, either . . .*

"Don't do this to me right now, baby," he murmured into the phone. "Don't do this to us, please? You're just . . . in a bad mood, or . . . "

"Or on the rag, right? I've been on the rag like this for almost two years, now. But that's not how you're supposed to feel all the time, is it?" She sniffed back tears. "I thought I could help you grow up, Andrew . . . I still love you, honey, and I probably always will. But I can't be married . . . "

"What're you saying, honey? You wanted me to leave town with your brothers so you could hit me up for a divorce long-distance? Are they in on it? Are they supposed to keep me up here while you file the paperwork?"

"I wish . . . I wish you were strong enough to have this conversation like a grownup, Andrew. I wish you could handle the truth . . . " She trailed off, biting back a big wet sob. There was something else.

"What can't I handle, Laura? What's going on, that you

think you're doing me a favor, by keeping a secret?" It felt like shit, accusing her, but it felt better than being helpless, clueless. He almost wanted her to be having an affair. It would make everything automatic.

"I'm sorry, Andrew . . . I can't talk to you right now, if you're going to—"

He waited for her to drop the other shoe, but he lost her next words in a wash of static distortion.

Call Dropped, said the phone.

He almost threw it into the woods. He stifled a scream, but the momentum of it drove him across the backyard, away from the crazy old monster-woman's cabin with the twins still fighting inside, away from all this bullshit that was suddenly, totally somebody else's problem.

Fuck it.

Almost floating, he went for a walk.

CHAPTER 11

DEAN SAW BLACK SPOTS. His fist had all the strength of a kitten's tail when he tried to punch his twin in the kidneys. Dom wrenched him around by his neck, bent him to his knees on the baby blue shag living room rug. "You're going up there," Dom grunted in his ear, "one way or the other."

Playing by the rules, it always ended like this. Dean could hold his own in a boxing match, but Dom fought like a barroom thug. Fine, if that's how he wanted it . . .

Dean snaked his sweat-slick hand between Dom's straining legs and gave his package a long, hard honk, hung onto it like an emergency brake on a train as his brother went ragdoll on top of him.

Dean expected his twin to be incapacitated long enough for him to disengage, but Dom lashed out with his fist and pasted Dean in the mouth. His lip split and two teeth rattled in their shredded gums. Gagging on blood, he could only spit at Dom as the fist came down again, bursting his nose.

Dean's hands went up and he tried to roll away, tap out, throw in the towel, but Dom was past caring, this time, and all Dean could think was, *why was* he *always the one who held back?*

"Get out!" Dean screamed, locking up Dom's punching fist with one arm and throwing wild jabs with the other, kicking out with both legs. How many connected, he couldn't see through his snotty tears, but he knew he had

Dom's attention. "Bad twin!" His voice ratcheted up to a crackling preadolescent shriek. "Get the fuck out! Nobody wants you here!"

Dom ripped himself free and scuttled back against the far wall, beneath the gaping hole they'd made when they spilled through into the living room from the entry hall. His sides heaved, and he bent over to vomit up his lunch. Strands of bile hung from his swollen lips when he rasped, "Fuck you, weak twin." He lay back against the exposed 2X4's and smiled that crooked smile that always got him out of trouble. Dean would give his soul to make a lampshade out of that smile.

"You want to hear a funny story, Deano? When you got married . . . remember how you made fun of my hair? I was just back from basic, and you rode me about my whitewalls, about copying you, remember that? When I came to wedding rehearsal, I was looking for you and I walked into that room where the bride gets ready.

"She's a pig now, but before she pumped out that litter of pups, Janice had a smokin' hot ass, didn't she? I fucked her eight ways from Sunday, right there in the church. She called me by your name, but I think she knew. She never asked about why I was wearing an Army uniform. Anyway . . . just thought you should know why I always get your oldest such nice birthday presents."

A plosive growl spraying bloody foam from his lips, Dean grabbed two handfuls of shag carpet and pulled himself upright. Before he could decide what to do with Dom, his twin rushed the door, flipped him the bird and slammed it going out.

Dean said a prayer for strength. When he'd said it twenty times, he still felt like shit, but at least he stopped shaking.

Outside, he heard Dom start up his truck and spray gravel, roaring down the driveway, then a squeal on the pavement and mocking silence.

"We'll see who's weak," he said to the empty house.

Using the walls as a crutch, Dean dragged himself to the bathroom and flipped on the light. A ghastly red mask greeted him, a shiny muzzle of gore drizzling from his mangled nose and shattered mouth. Horrified, he examined his teeth one by one. An upper canine and a bicuspid were loose, and the corner of an incisor was chipped, but none of them had fallen out, thank God.

A hot strap of leaden tension girded his head, a piercing ache settling in as the endorphins from the fight wore off. Bruises and welts marred every patch of exposed skin, and his arms were too sore to remove his torn T-shirt.

He cleaned himself up as best he could with water and toilet paper, since the contents of the medicine cabinet were boxed up somewhere in the living room. His nose was broken, but not critically so. Unless he got it set by a doctor, the straight aquiline blade would heal as a crooked hook, like Dom's. God damn his brother. Every blow removed another point of distinction. Dom's ferocity this time was unprecedented, but Dean was pretty sure he'd given as good as he'd got.

The hell of it was, Dean loved his brother. He loved being a twin when they were kids. Their presence was remarkable, and the way they could bamboozle anyone who thought they knew which was which, never got old. But it was always Dom who broke the illusion, who tried to set himself apart.

When they were little, they used to watch *Star Trek* reruns every afternoon. Dom's favorite episodes were the ones where the crew encountered their evil alternate universe doppelgangers, or where Kirk got split into two Kirks by the transporter. Back when they looked exactly alike, Dom would draw a moustache on his face with a Magic Marker and say he was the Evil Twin. Dean would play along, calling himself the Good Twin, but Dom always ruined it. The opposite of the Evil Twin was the Weak Twin.

They came from the same egg. They were one man in two bodies. Each half-man looked at the other and despised him for all the qualities the other had, that he lacked, hated how those envied qualities ran amuck in the other and made a parody of balance. Only when they stood together against a common enemy, were they anything like a whole man.

He wanted to lie down. He needed to start loading the truck. Mom or no Mom, he was leaving in the morning. Just as soon as he found what he was looking for.

He'd taken the house apart, examined and packed everything with little or no help from Dom or Andy, and still he hadn't found it. And this, more than the tension with his twin, more than the strain of remaining in this house, had taken its toll on his nerves, for he knew not what he was seeking, knew only that it must exist, that he must destroy it, though he could not imagine what it was, and had built his life upon a lie.

If he could find it, he could lay to rest all doubt about his past; but first, he must face it, and he knew that, whatever it was, he had once suppressed, buried and forgotten it as a defense against insanity.

But was this not insanity?

What could it be, that he blocked out? He'd faced all manner of threats without breaking a sweat. He'd seen men die; he'd overseen a weapons crew that fired artillery that incurred terrible casualties in Operation Desert Fox, and never missed a wink of sleep. Surely there was nothing on earth he was afraid of, so what could this thing he searched for be, if not a phantom? There was nothing here. He'd faced his fear and found nothing but unpleasant memories, easily shredded.

So why was he still afraid?

The house was empty. Only the dining room set and a few kitchen accessories remained. He would tie up those loose ends and load as much of the truck as he could by himself. If Andy showed up to help, so much the better, but if he didn't reappear before the work was done, he could hitchhike home, for all Dean cared.

Steadier now, he went back into the kitchen, when he figured it out.

Mom's comfort mechanism, after the booze and cigarettes and drugs were denied her, was food. She snacked constantly. He'd found potato chip bags and Weight Watchers candy wrappers under every stick of furniture, treats hidden in the linen closet and in the backs of cupboards, as if she was hiding them from herself for sleepwalk-snacking. Stress drove her to eat; eating was safety; if she had something to hide, she would hide it with food.

He pulled the string for the light in the pantry. The stocks were sparse; she hadn't been to the store lately. A few Campbell's soups and marginally edible canned vegetables. Andy was supposed to have packed this shit up. *What a fuckoff . . .*

Andy had gone to make coffee this morning, but said there was none, then threw the can away, then took out the trash.

Andy never did anything on his own without being asked more than once. Dean went outside to the trash cans, dug out the kitchen trash bag and tore it open, spilling the contents on the ground between his feet.

He realized he'd been standing there looking at the can for a long while. He was building this into something it probably wasn't, giving it power over him, and he didn't even know what it was. Soon, it would be nothing.

He picked up the can and pried off the plastic lid. Inside, he found a clump of rancid coffee and a sheaf of faded photographs.

Dean squeezed his eyes shut and took a deep breath, held it. He reached into the can and took out a picture. He pinched it in his fingers for a while with his eyes closed. He could shred it without looking at it. He didn't ever have to know.

That would be weak. Dom could never have weathered what he went through. It was hard to be the favorite. Dean was strong.

He looked.

It was from the same period as the snapshot he found last night, maybe from the same roll of film. Dean and Laura in their blue robes, sitting on a big bed with Mom and a witlessly grinning man with long hair and a full, bushy beard. The man had his arms around Laura in a possessive, familiar way, and Mom was doing the same to little Dean. Everybody looked stoned. Dean's smile was an undertaker's trick, achieved with cotton wads and cardboard jammed into the cheeks.

He looked at the next one.

The same scene.

Minus the blue robes.

Dean's stomach rumbled and shot up runners of acid to the back of his palate. His jaw clenched, teeth gritting, glutted with blood from the raw sockets in his gums.

He looked at a third.

Mom and Dean on the bed. Laura, in the background, crying.

A low, breathless moaning, "No" came out of Dean's battered mouth.

He didn't look at a fourth. He didn't need to. He could remember, now. He could feel this time, and all the other times, without going further. He remembered Mom's whispered entreaties, the commands of the bearded man, night after night, Mom so big, so rough with him, so fierce when he failed, so proud when he did what they made him do—children of sin—children without sin—

The can fell from his hands with a dull clang. The pictures curled up in his fists. He fell back against the cabin, biting back vomit, fighting back tears.

So many pictures.

He went inside and fired up the shredder.

Nobody would remember, now, nobody could prove anything. It never happened. Never happened.

What never happened?

Exactly.

Loud as the sound was, at first he thought it came from inside his own head. Something smashed the front door off its hinges. A wrecking ball crash, and the door flew across the entry hall and into the family room in halves.

Dom was back. Dean dropped the pictures and spun around to go for the gun. It was in his duffel bag in the living room. "No more games!" he called out. The bright, tight echo of his voice bounced back at him off the bare walls. It was a sound he loved, and everywhere he'd lived, he furnished and decorated as sparsely as he could to still keep that echo alive. His wife was a good God-fearing wife and helpmeet, but she sure could clutter up a room with all her shit. Just like his mother—

Something with boulders for feet walked through the front of the house into the kitchen. Dean caught a glimpse of a shadow as it passed the hole in the wall.

Dean checked the clip, thumbed off the safety. Who else could it be, but Dom? Dean's mind was quick, but it ran on deep tracks. Even derailed as it was, he could not imagine anyone or anything but Dom in the house. If it wasn't his brother, back for a final rematch, it must be some trick of the mind, now completely off the track and hurtling blind through the dark woods of nightmare.

The kitchen. The pictures, scattered on the floor. Dean raced back through the dining room and into the kitchen with the gun level in front of him.

The refrigerator door hung wide open, and someone rummaged inside it. Wire racks clanged and grated. A Clausen's pickle jar with only green juice and a few bits of onion in it, tumbled and shattered on the linoleum, and he heard the faint sound of a flat, rasping tongue lapping at the condensation on the fridge's interior, like a dog on a hot day.

Dean crouched and approached the fridge from behind, then lifted his leg and kicked the door shut as hard as he could. "Surprise, asshole!"

The door slammed into the looter and swung back, shelves and smashed plastic compartments scattering everywhere. Dean gripped the pistol with both hands.

Burglar or grizzly bear, he would face it down, kill it dead and paint his face with its blood. He was a warrior, the Strong Twin, the Good Twin, and nobody would ever hurt him ever again.

A hand grabbed the top of the door. Looking at it, Dean did not waver with the pistol, but he wet himself, just a little.

It was the size of a snow shovel. Gray, wrinkled skin like a rhino's hide, calluses on calluses. Chipped, cyanotic nails like chisels dimpled and tore the dingy white sheet-metal facing on the refrigerator door.

With a screech of violated metal, the enormous hand ripped the door off its hinges and swung it at Dean like it was a pillow.

Dean was already shooting. Two bullets punched through the door, two more into the big gray thing that stood up out of the empty fridge, and a fifth into the ceiling as he reeled away from each wicked swipe of the door.

In the brief but furious internal debate over whether to continue shooting or evade the attacker, who apparently could give two shits about the flying lead, Dean tried manfully to keep the impossibility of this situation in a box, to be unwrapped and pondered at his leisure.

He elected to flee when the refrigerator door launched at him and slammed into his back. With blind momentum and paralyzing force on his side, he left the kitchen at high speed, crashing into the dining room table and sliding across it with the refrigerator door heavy across his shoulders.

Over the far end of the table, he slid and pancaked on the shag rug of the living room. One of his arms refused to help him get up, but he rolled out from under the refrigerator door, pointed the gun back into the dining room and scooted back towards the sliding glass door, prehensile ass-cheeks carrying him away with all due dispatch from the thing that lumbered after him.

It had to turn sideways to fit through the doorway. It came at him on stumpy elephant legs with its arms outstretched, huge, gray, naked, headless, wrong, wrong, wrong—He shot it twice more and threw the gun, just like in those stupid monster movies Dom always watched, but it kept coming.

Dean turned and threw the sliding glass door open with his functioning arm. The other was dislocated, and screamed blue murder as it ground around out of its socket. His feet didn't care what the rest of him was bitching about, didn't care if this was a nightmare; they got under him and threw him out of the house and across the ruined sundeck, running away into the night, but he only got three steps from the door before he ran into another one. This one was bigger. He tried to feint left and duck right under its impossibly long, thick arms, but it was faster, too.

CHAPTER 12

THERE ARE CLUES, signs and portents, by which you can tell if you're cursed.

Dogs always bark at you. Cats let you pet them, but then, as if at some prearranged interval decreed by their master, Satan, they turn on you and maul your hand. Concerts and films sell out just when you reach the head of the queue; beer kegs drain, rollercoasters break down. Streetlights fizzle and burn out as you pass under them. Girlfriends dump you with a spooked tone in their voices as they try to explain that it wasn't you, it was—and hang up.

You might dismiss these signs as random chance or bad karma, but when all that is good in life withers at your touch, sooner or later, you have to accept the pattern before your eyes and realize that someone, somewhere, is fucking with you.

Andrew had learned as a child how to put up with almost anything, and think it was normal. His father blasted his music in the car. Andrew sat in the back on his monthly Dad weekends, straining to pick out the words and music from the roar of wind through the open windows. Dad didn't believe in air conditioning. Oh, he acknowledged that such an invention existed, but he'd be damned if he'd waste gas on something so trivial as comfort, when he could simply open the windows wide and drive faster. (Later, Andrew discovered that Dad had it exactly backwards—AC didn't consume that much gas, while the open windows added drag and wasted energy.)

Whenever Andrew tried to talk to Dad in the car, he turned up the stereo. Andrew came to believe that his father represented himself to his son in the music he played in lieu of conversation, and took what lessons he could from it. Bob Marley and The Clash shaped his political manifesto; *Slow Train Coming* was a sermon in faith—respectfully rejected, because Dylan sucked ass; and Fleetwood Mac schooled him in affairs of the heart and convinced him to avoid cocaine. Yes, music was how Dad communicated all his hard-won wisdom for dealing with life's milestones. *Dark Side Of The Moon* was on repeat on his CD player when his girlfriend Pam found him on his back on his futon with a bottle of Seconals in his belly and vomit in his lungs.

But the funny part was, he believed Dad when he said that his sound system—a Pioneer AM/FM cassette pullout with five-band EQ, four hundred-watt Kenwood speakers—was the best money could buy. The bass was so crisp and hot and alive, even through the deafening wind, that a deaf-mute could rock out to it.

It was not until junior high, while riding home with his friend Scott's brother who was a senior, and he was bitching about how he'd blown out a door speaker rocking *Straight Outta Compton*, that he heard its like again. Dad had been driving around for years with four blown speakers, and told his son it was supposed to sound like that. Andrew's whole musical nostalgia was filtered through an irritating sonic raspberry, and he'd come to think it was how music should sound.

Andrew did not realize until just now, this afternoon, how he had done the same rationalizing alchemy on every other aspect of his life.

The trail led him up and away from the cabin in steep switchbacks, but when he turned to look back, winded but gratefully free of cigarette-craving, the property was hidden completely by the dense screen of firs. The book, he discovered, was still in his hand, the faded scarlet boards of the cover drinking in the oil and sweat from his palm, leaving a damning print across it.

He looked around for a place to sit, but the incline was too steep, the skirts of needles on the trees swept all the way to the dusty earth, so there was nowhere to sit out of the sun. The afternoon was fading fast, the sun retreating like an old dog at the home stretch of a long walk behind the jumble of mountains to the west. Where had the day gone?

He kept walking. Marooned in northern California on a botched intervention, stranded between two brothers at war with each other, abandoned by his wife; if he didn't keep walking, it would catch up to him. He had no idea what it would do, but he had never been so afraid of anything, as he was of finding out.

Why me? he kept asking himself, a wheezing knee-jerk whine that kept the real questions at bay.

An undigested chunk of Psych 101 bubbled up out of memory, one of those simple Big Ideas that fleetingly made college seem like a key to enlightenment: Fundamental Attribution Error. We fuck up because of circumstances, karma, luck, addictions—outside forces, mysterious and mundane, that always make us late, drunk and dumb at the worst possible moment. For others, these things happen because of who and what they are. You were late to work and hung over because your roommate kept you up and the traffic was awful; your roommate was late to work because he's a drunk.

He had, long ago, come to terms with his flaws; it was liberating to acknowledge that he was a flake, a coward, and a sorry excuse for a man who would, in any tribal society with manhood initiation rites, eke out his days doing chores with the womenfolk. Nobody ever taught him to assert himself or go after what he wanted. He was a master of hindsight, of figuring out the right thing to do and say the day after it mattered. Damaged goods, and proud of it.

When Laura came along, they seemed to fit together. Their cracks matched—her need for control and understanding fit with his passivity and need for validation. He needed someone to get behind him and push, sometimes. Wasn't that why some men prospered, while others failed? Raised mostly by his spacey, disengaged mother, Andrew thought he, at least, understood women; but apparently, his experience only served to make him act like one in his marriage.

He loved Laura like a drowning man loves air. He could feel how much he loved her like the waves closing in, like drowning in that old, cold ocean.

His ring finger was swollen around the plain white gold wedding band on his right hand. Flushed from the hike, his hands looked like bloody, inflated surgical gloves, but his ring finger was purple.

Andrew despised jewelry of any kind. The idea of wearing metal to represent marital status was straight-up ridiculous. He'd never understood it, and the ring never became more than a weird intruder, never a part of his hand. He rotated it on his finger and tried to slide it off, but the blood-engorged flesh of his knuckle wouldn't budge. A surge of panic hit. He twisted and tugged the ring fit to tear the flesh off like a sock. "Shit, shit, fuck, get off!" he screamed against clenched teeth. He forced himself to stop. *Count to ten, dumbshit.*

Andrew sat down against a tree and held his hand up above his head for a few minutes, flexing his hand and making a fist to work the fluid out of his fingers. Then he slicked up his finger with sweat and oil by running it through his hair. It still hurt a little, but the ring slowly unscrewed like a wingnut and finally sat in his palm like a coin, its diabolical enslaving powers dispelled, for now. He resisted making a melodramatic gesture like throwing it into the woods, and dropped it in his pocket.

The night he met her, at a Halloween house party, he'd worn an elaborate costume with a too-convincing rubber zombie mask. He shambled through the crowd, grooving on the anonymity, enjoying the drunk girls who crushed sloppy kisses against him for camera-phone snapshots, sipping a vodka & Red Bull through a straw jammed up the mask's nostril-slit. Peering out the other nostril, he saw her, and immediately ditched the mask.

She wore a low-cut red velvet gown, slit to mid-thigh. Her striking heart-shaped face was painted like a Dio De Los Muertos skull. Ornate black curlicues like skeletal ivy filigreed the false rictus on her pouting mouth, made drowning pools out of her gold-flecked deep brown eyes. A cruelly cinched scarlet vinyl corset heaved her cleavage at him, framing the tattoo of a blazing sacred heart on her breastbone. She caught him looking at it, probably felt him drooling on it. She'd smiled at the thrift-shop shambles of his costume, chatting him up with a pointed lilt that winked at his marginally charming awkwardness.

She utterly tamed him in five minutes, keeping him at bay so he couldn't talk about himself, but offering no details about herself. She set him on fire with intrigue and then she left, begging off despite his slightly slurred pleas for her to stay. "I'm sorry," she said, "I'm not a people person . . . but I like you."

"Well," he'd asked, struggling mightily to fix on her eyes and not on her oppressive rack, and still come up with something not stupid to say, "what kind of person are you?"

She didn't tell him, but she gave him her number. It didn't occur to him until the next day that she hadn't even seen his face.

He had to work harder than he ever had to be present

for Laura. When he first looked in her medicine cabinet and saw the ranks of prescription medications, he'd balked at asking her. He'd wait for her to bring it up, and when she never told him what she was dealing with, he figured she had a handle on it. Little things, like the way she trembled, one body part at a time, as she drifted off to sleep, made him hold her closer, love her more, but he knew that he never reached her. Even after they'd lived together, even after she asked him to ask her to marry him, he felt like he was hardly halfway to the place where she really lived.

It was a real feat of psycho-judo for her to insist this was all her fault; she'd wondered, herself, so many times, who she'd be and what kind of life she'd live, if her childhood had not so badly fucked her up. He never had an answer because in his heart, he believed that if she had not been so fucked up, she probably never would have given him her number at all.

The trail dragged him up the mountainside and over a ridge, and now, he did sit down. His rubbery legs shook under his elbows. Sweat beaded on his face and streamed down his neck like columns of ants.

The shadows of the evergreen trees around him were blue-black and deep enough to swim in. Before him, the sun cut through the forest in discrete golden spears. Andrew breathed in through his nose and held it for a five-count, expelled it slowly through chapped lips. Concentrating on his breathing like this, he felt his pulse ebb and his mind stop chasing its tail.

Below, the canyon widened out into a meadow, clear of trees and brush but overtaken by weeds. The trail shadowed the ridge up the mountainside, which got serious towards the peak. If he got that high, he'd probably decide to jump off.

Andrew left the trail and ran down the slope to the meadow. As he came out of the trees, the sun dazzled him so that he had to shade his eyes.

The soil was corrugated with the furrows of tilled farmland, but the harvest must have come early. Broken stalks and a few corncobs lay trampled in a net of footprints, as if buffalo stampeded the crops.

Andrew was startled to see a looming gray figure hunkered in a stand of sedge at the center of the farm, a headless man with absurdly broad shoulders and one stump of an arm raised to warn Andrew away. Just a statue, he realized, forcing a chuckle at his nerves, but it did remind him of what he thought he saw at the lake.

The statue looked new, but was smashed up and scattered like a ruined bust from ancient Rome, after the barbarians rolled through. The pedestal on which it stood was smeared with dried feces and the ankles were chipped away as if something had been gnawing on them. Staring at it as he walked, he tripped over the severed hand, grasping a hammer.

Across the small field, huddled in the shade of the mountain, Andrew saw the façade of the big house from the picture in the book.

Someone came out here to build a dream of a perfect human society in a shuttered madhouse eighty years ago, and someone else had come out here only recently to try again. Though not a Communist, and a natural raised-by-hippies cynic, Andrew could get behind the idea. He knew they seldom worked, especially when artists were at the helm, but it was a nice idea. How could anyone come out here with that idea in their hearts, see this place, and not just walk away? What kind of maniac would try to create a utopia here?

The picture had shown a dreary, Dickensian workhouse, so devoid of ornament that it might've been erected by giant ants; great rust-scabbed granite blocks piled into a long, cumbersome eyesore slitted with narrow horizontal windows like snipers' boltholes, but the grim determination of the colonists assembled before it gave it an air of ominous grandeur. Misguided they might be, but lazy or unserious, never. What must the New Leviathan colonists have thought, when they arrived here, in their Prius hybrids? Did it still seem like a bold adventure, a lusty pastoral romp, or did they begin to suspect they'd been had?

In the flesh, it was positively ghastly, the charmless ruin of a Soviet orphanage, or a debtor's prison. Rubble, rotten timbers and other debris littered the parade ground in front of the house, and the bluff masonry walls leaned out from the sinking foundation, as if the building was holding its breath. A lone, peaked observation tower jutted up from the center of the awesome pile. Shading his eyes and staring at it, Andrew thought he saw light reflected off metal or glass in the iron-barred shadows beneath the conical roof. Dancing motes of gold orbited the tower in the dying honey-colored sunlight.

Humming "The Lunatics Have Taken Over The Asylum," he crossed the field. He noticed that much of the acreage underfoot had been taken over by wildflowers. Some of the heartier species had come back from the trampling they'd suffered, but Andrew wondered why the people had cultivated them in the first place. It wasn't quite large enough for a commercial crop, which needed tents and irrigation systems up here. Maybe they did it for the symbolism, or maybe they were just really shitty farmers. Or maybe, he thought as he dodged a zealous honeybee that buzzed his face, they weren't farming flowers, but bees.

He opened the book and flipped through it. No interior illustrations, and the prose was in cyclopean bricks of archaic, Latinate prose, with long chains of clauses the author must've known were hard on the eyes, but his solution was to abuse caps lock.

THE HEAD OF STATE

As the QUEEN BEE is to the hive, and the MIND to the BODY, so is the OVERSEER, in the early stages of the utopian COMMUNE, seemingly a TYRANT. The will of the individual, so enshrined in western thought, is divine in solitude, but the aggregation of willful individuals is like a festering colony of maggots, fit only to shift for himself.

Just as MAN cannot learn to become a HONEYBEE, no man can truly surrender his will to the collective, until it is taken away. Thus, the OVERSEER is the lowliest SLAVE of the PROLETARIAT, for he must tirelessly SERVE and safeguard each CITIZEN, and direct them to the best service of the COLONY. Where the ultimate goal of all human government is only the preservation of stability for the ruling elites and the continuance of power, our goal is a higher one.

The OVERSEER rules without check at the outset so that the COLONY is tamed and attuned to its unification into ONE DIVINE BODY of the UTOPIAN STATE. When the MANY wills become ONE, the OVERSEER renders himself obsolete as a TYRANT, and joins the body as a central, but sublimated cell among many, the seat of reason for the body of the state, and yet its most abject slave.

Dean ought to read this, Andrew thought.

Actually, the author made Lenin and Marx sound like Falstaff and Hunter S. Thompson. How could grim, dogmatic shit like this appeal to anyone with half a brain, let alone haughty leftist intellectuals? Communism might be the hook, but this thing was a cult. To pampered, jaded, guilt-wracked liberal elites, this might seem like some sort of atonement. The heavier the yoke, the more they'd bend to it . . . for a while.

The old man, Sprague, had tried to tell him about the commune. It made no sense then, and Andrew had to strain to recall it.

So close to utopia. The first Leviathan colony, we never had a chance . . . but the new one, I thought they were different. They became the state. They went further than even Marx could have imagined. But something always goes wrong, doesn't it?

Deputy Scovill said they were gone, the commune dissolved, and to stay away from Sprague. The crackpot in the bookstore had tried to warn him—to send a warning to the other side . . .

There's two factions now, and no neutral parties. Zero against One, body against mind, labor against capital. It's simply not in human nature to take the final step, to let go of power. But that shouldn't have been a factor, this time.

The book Sprague was writing was a new manifesto, a sequel to the one Andrew held in his sweaty hand. All Andrew wanted to know, then, was where Mom went. Sprague had tried to tell him.

One side or the other took her in. Scabs make a settlement less likely, but anything to break the siege.

In the truck, Dom said he knew where Mom was. Weird since he went in the woods, and the new tattoos, the bees—

The huge double doors were much newer than the surrounding structure, but they were scarred and battered. Brown stains and shards of splintered rocks littered the porch at the top of a wide staircase. The stone stank like the vestibule of the landmark theater he and Laura went to, where bums and wandering dogs relieved themselves.

The plain stone lintel over the doors was inscribed with an epigram that caught Andrew by surprise. He'd expected some solemn Marxist slogan, or a totalitarian haiku from Mao's red book. Instead, it only said, *E pluribus unum*, same as any dollar bill. *Out of many, one.*

He pushed on the doors. They didn't budge an inch. Peering into the crack between the doors, he saw only graded planes of shadow and the silhouette of an enormous fencepost barring the doors.

If the place was abandoned, wouldn't there be a padlock on the outside? Looking around, he saw no windows within reach of the ground, and dense stands of flowers around the foundation buzzed with the drowsy menace of bees.

Circling the building, he found two doors on the rear, but both were ten feet above the ground, and no stairs or ladder to reach them. Behind the house, a cliff piled with huge boulders offered the promise of a better view of the roof, but no trail presented itself, and the climb looked dangerous. He sat down in the shade of a fir tree and laid the book on his knee. He was too stirred up to read, but he didn't want to think, right now.

He felt, rather than heard or saw, the presence coming up behind him, out of the woods. The hairs at the back of his neck bristled and stood out, and his skin prickled in gooseflesh as a chill breeze carried a half-familiar scent to his nose.

"You don't want to go in there," she said.

He looked down, composing himself. "Why not?"

"Before the new commune moved in, kids would go up there to party, and somebody almost always got hurt. People say it's haunted. The new one didn't have any carpenters or stonemasons, so it's still not very safe."

He wanted to ask her what she thought she knew about him. In his current state of mind, he was ready for anything, and the stupider the better. But the exquisite gravity of her presence, the uncanny timing, stifled his inner turmoil in the best possible way.

"You're not ready to go there yet." She reached down to take his hand and lift him up. "Besides," she added, right beside him now, "I bet you'd rather come with me."

CHAPTER 13

GIVEN DOM'S CURRENT MOOD, it was probably a bad idea to blast Motorhead.

The road went round and round the mountain, twisting back on itself and shunting him from one two-lane blacktop to another whenever he took a drink.

He drained the silver flask from under his seat—cherry schnapps, left behind by a chunky blonde chick from Riverside he met at a SDSU party—and tossed it out the window. He couldn't find the landmarks that he'd noted on his way in. His mind was a sulfurous fog of murky but malevolent intent. Sweat like battery acid ran into his eyes.

One minute, all he wanted was to get the fuck out of these woods, and the next, he was consumed with thoughts of Mom and the house and all the vague promise locked up inside it. Dimly aware that he was going in circles, he drove faster, turned the stereo louder, and pounded his frustration out on the steering wheel.

It was at the peak one of these jags that he saw the dirt turnout at the elbow of a hairpin turn, and impulsively yanked the wheel to send the truck down it. Loose gravel squirted out from under his wheels. Seven veils of fine brown dust obscured the rear view, and the road was too narrow to turn around. This was not the way out. But it might be the way *in*—to what, he could not or would not say, least of all to himself.

Lost, getting loster.

"Fuck!"

Dom pounded the wheel again, dealt it a sharp blow like he always did to let off steam when driving away from a big mistake. But this time, the wheel snapped clean off the steering column with shocking vigor and clipped his jaw as it zinged off the roof.

His reflexes kicked out, but when he floored the brake, the truck slewed down the steep dirt road into a rightside skid with no way to control it. The wheels locked up on the loose gravel, the truck a runaway sled. The road didn't stay straight, either, but curled to the left. Dom saw stout fir trunks flying past, the shoulder vanishing into his blind spot. He pumped the brake. Ahead, looking out the passenger window, he saw the looming bulk of a white Blazer parked on the shoulder for half a second before he crashed into the back of it.

Maybe it was the *perfect* time to be blasting Motorhead. But it was a rotten time to have no seatbelt on.

The front right bumper of Dom's truck hit the Blazer's tailgate like a hammer through a paper plate. The engine block popped off its cheap refitted mountings, rebounded off the Blazer and battered down the firewall and came to rest in the soft berth of the driver's seat, where Dom had been sitting only a split-second before.

On impact, Dom flew across the bench seat and smashed into the passenger-side door like a pinball out of the chute. The unlocked door gave way with only token resistance, ejecting Dom's body into the forest at a good portion of the forty miles per hour the truck had racked up before impact. Limbs flapping in the breeze, he shot through the phalanx of trees and crashed into a stand of waxy-leafed brush.

It took less than two seconds for all of this to happen. It took another thirty for Dom's brain to catch up, whereupon he curled like a burning leaf into a fetal position on the crushed branches that broke his fall, and rested for a while.

Anyone else would have put on their seatbelt before tearing ass all over unfamiliar mountain roads. Anyone else right now would probably be dead.

Lucky. Just enough luck to keep him running.

The trucks lay intertwined on the edge of the road. His pickup absurdly resembled a he-dog mounting a bitch, but in his ardor, he'd broken her hind legs and smashed her snout into an unyielding pine trunk. Steam, coolant and other vital fluids gushed out of both wrecks.

The Blazer's red and blue roof lights strobed and spat shadows.

Shit, there was his luck. A cop car.

In the half hour or so he drove through the woods, he hadn't seen another car.

He tested his limbs. Everything hurt, but everything worked. From his shoulder down, his whole right side throbbed from its dispute with the door, and he was scratched and bleeding in a dozen places from his flight, but otherwise, in far better shape than he deserved to be.

All things considered, he felt pretty fucking good. Accelerated. Adrenaline pumped through him like a good cocaine surge, and when he waved his hand in front of his face, it seemed to move faster than he could see.

It was difficult to breathe through his nose, though. Boogers grew spiky and scabby like the day after a good coke binge, like the Magic Rocks Dean got for his eighth birthday. Dom—jealous because he only got Silly Putty—dumped them down the toilet, but Dean was able to keep them from getting flushed for almost a week, and they grew into a tiny crystalline city that endured until the next chili night.

He tried blowing his nose and rooting around with his finger, which almost wouldn't fit. It was almost as if his nostrils were closing up . . .

Dom got up, wary eyes looking for witnesses, and crept up behind a tree where he could see inside the Blazer. If anyone was inside, they were gone, now. The weird silence pricked at his nerves. In the city, sirens would stir the air before the hot metal stopped ticking. Someone would have called 911.

He could claim that someone stole his truck and wrecked it. He'd gotten away with it once before.

But out here, who would believe it?

Where was the fucking deputy?

One way or the other, staying here was stupid.

He retreated into the woods, found a safe spot to sit and think that offered a view of the road. He squatted and scratched at himself. His muscles jittered with restless energy he couldn't suppress. Like a good coke binge indeed, the initial rush crumbled and left him starting to feel fatigued.

Shock. He had to fight it, chase that buzz. He'd been going to the house, looking for it, when he crashed. He'd tried to bring Dean, and even Andy, with him. They were needed. The family needed them and anyone else he could bring, especially girls.

Dom got up and hiked uphill, alongside the dirt road.

A light through the trees made him freeze and take cover. It was stationary, and illuminated a wedge-shaped slice of the wall of a cabin, a sliding glass door, and a sundeck.

Dom moved closer in a crouch, planting his feet silently. A strange but irresistible sense of childlike glee took him over. A curtain blocked the view through the sliding glass door, but he heard loud music and saw light shining inside. Presently, a slim, appealing silhouette crossed in front of the door, holding a beer.

Dom's luck was once again running in the black, at the expense of everyone else. He recalled what the asshole deputy said about leaving his truck in front of Mom's neighbor's place. *There're some kids next door, who need the fear*. He wondered if the cop was inside, and what kind of party must be going on in there, that they hadn't heard his entrance.

Closer still, to the edge of the treeline, he dropped to his haunches when he triggered a motion-sensor light that bleached the deck and the faded coat of Astroturf that served for a yard.

The cabin was a two-story Bucky Fuller fuckpad deluxe, hexagonal in shape and deeply mid-70's in design. The front door was on the second floor, and reached by a maze of stairs and decks like scaffolding that made the cabin look unfinished. A familiar yellow Hummer was parked in a carport around the back.

Something about it made him want to stalk around humming the *Mission: Impossible* theme. It looked as if it should have uniformed lackeys patrolling it, guarding some powerful douchebag who was hiding from Chuck Norris. It was a bolthole for rich folks (pigs) to do things that even their neighbors in elite retreats like Aspen or Palm Springs would never tolerate. There was no skiing anywhere around here, no lake big enough to float a yacht, and the summer season was over, and never really began, after the last big forest fire. He could bet that whatever was going on inside would not be a group singalong by marshmallow-toasting Girl Scouts.

Dom screened out the rising insect symphony around him and homed in on the music. He could hear the Percolator going hot and heavy inside. The more he listened, the louder and clearer it got, more present than that acid trip where it first revealed itself. It had been right *here* all the time, some cosmic message just for Dominic Kowalski. He climbed the stairs to the front door, trusting that he would know what to do when it opened.

A scorched-oak placard beside the door told him he was about to experience THE SEXAGON. What kind of asshat named their cabin and put up a sign?

He knocked. Nobody answered. Well, the music was

pretty loud. The little piggies were partying most heartily. He hadn't brought any beer or drugs or chicks. Why should they let him in?

A fugitive thought swam up out of his blood: *From each according to his means, to each according to his needs.* And Lord, but he did have needs—

Lightning ran around in his body. His muscles flexed and tore and grew. The adrenaline pumped him so high, he thought *he* was the Percolator. The prowling, powerful flashback phenomenon was like an action hero's theme song, coiled and muted, yet drowning all other sounds to cover his approach. His cock and balls shriveled up so small and numb he had to grab them to be sure they were still there, but they would be ready for duty, if called to serve.

He knocked again. He felt rather than heard the floorboards creak. He could almost smell someone on the other side of the door, but they didn't open it. In the city, they'd have a peephole to scope him out. In the city, they could call for help.

Behind every door, there stood someone who thought they were in control of the situation. A locked door was where the social compact got as serious as most homeowners were willing to take it. They figured nobody who might harm them or take their treasures would actually go to the trouble to force their way in. They didn't know how easy it was, if you simply gave no fucks.

Little pigs, little pigs, let me in!

With one hand, he knocked . . . then knocked the door down.

Inside, a skinny, longhaired kid stood in the doorway with a green plastic bong like a tenor sax in his hands, frizzy red locks still flapping in the breeze of the door coming down. His jaw rested on the collar of his faded Phish T-shirt, while his free hand still dug in the pocket of an Army surplus jacket that might once have been Dom's.

Behind him, another college-aged guy, less Berkeley and more Abercrombie & Fitch, with a meshback trucker hat that said TOWN DRUNK on it. Determined to live up to his title, he wore a bedsheet toga, and looked to have already puked on himself.

Bummer, Dom thought. *A sausage fest.*

"Dude!" screamed the longhaired kid, "What the fuck?"

Dom grinned and looked around. The second floor was a gallery with tiled floors and a respectable wet bar, with doorways opening on bedrooms and a bathroom with a Jacuzzi, but most of it was a balcony overlooking the ground floor, which was a massive game room.

"Holy shit," Dom grunted. "You spoiled little punks got air hockey?"

The longhaired kid whipped around to run, crazy legs piling up the throw rug behind him like Shaggy running from a cartoon monster. Dom lunged and caught that flapping orange flag of hair, twisting it into a leash, brought his arm down and around in a deadly windup over his head like cracking a whip. That it had a hundred-and-fifty pound college dropout at the end of it did nothing to slow the motion. The kid followed his fistful of hair like a marionette, yanked clean off his feet and sailing through the air and out over the railing when Dom released him, bong and all, screaming down into the game room.

The kid crashed facefirst into the white expanse of the air hockey table head cocked at a jauntily fatal angle on his compound fractured neck. A black girl and a blonde jumped away from the table, dropped their paddles and clamped their hands over shrieking mouths.

Holy shit, Dom thought. *They've got chicks! And air hockey!*

The girls ran for the doors, the blonde headed for the sliding glass door in such a panic she'd go right through it, the black girl making for the bathroom. Dom vaulted over the balcony railing and landed both booted feet on the tabletop *Ms. Pac Man* machine.

A volcanic burst of sparks and vacuum-sealed smoked glass erupted, but he was already in midair again, arms thrown out like an all-star tackle bringing down the game-winning receiver in the red zone.

The blonde was yanking on the handle for the sliding glass door and, not seeing the lock, faltered one fateful step to look back. Dom tackled her and they went through the glass together.

Dom rolled with the impact, took the concrete on his back with the girl wrapped up in his arms. When they hit, her forehead cracked into his hard enough to knock her cold. He rolled over and took in his path of destruction. It made him laugh. He'd done all that, and he didn't even ache. He felt great!

Effortlessly, he scooped the unconscious blonde and carried her back into the cabin.

The kid on the air hockey table didn't move, but the corona of blood from his face danced like carbonation bubbles on the whirring cushion of air. The puck floated lazily around him, before getting mired in the grisly business spewing out of his ear.

He turned to go after the other girl when the Town Drunk came stumbling down the stairs, woozily aiming a Glock 9mm and shouting at him to stand still and put his sister down.

"Fuck that," Dom cackled, and came closer.

The gun went off in the drunk kid's hands, surprising the shit out of him. The recoil whipped the gun back and the hammer split his lip. The bullet shattered the stained-glass lamp above the billiard table.

"Shit, chief," Dom said, "put that thing down. You're liable to hurt somebody." He dropped the blonde on the green felt, balls clicking and strolling away from her lithe, limp form in pink sorority pajama top and panties. "OK, try it now."

A big neon Budweiser sign exploded behind Dom and fell off the wall with his next shot.

Dom grabbed the trashed *Ms. Pac Man* console, hefted it and found it seemed to weigh less than a medicine ball. "I see your problem, bud. You're closing your eyes when you pull the trigger, and you're jerking it. Keep your eyes on the target. I'm right here . . . "

The kid got off one last wild shot, holing the oak paneling above Dom's head, before the airborne tabletop video game slammed him into the wall. He sank to the floor with the two-hundred pound console in his lap.

Looking around, Dom was stunned at the luxury these pigs wallowed in. Pictures on the wall of Town Drunk and the blonde with Mom and Dad—twinkle-eyed, clean-cut Christian soldiers of prosperity, one and all. Dad with Governor Terminator; with the President, at some thousand-bucks-a-plate fundraising jerkoff; lifting his arms amid a crowd at a victory rally. Daddy was some sort of politician in Sacramento, he concluded; he sent his spoiled little piggies up here to get their naughty jollies out of the public eye.

He went to the stereo and killed the CD, an irritating techno trance mix. Not the Percolator at all, but a cheap facsimile. But it had led him here, to play.

He went over to the bathroom and knocked the door down. Inside, the little window beside the shower stood open. The bitch got away. Oh, well. He knew he was not alone in the woods tonight. The only thing she would not find, out there, was help.

Onward and upward. Dom climbed the stairs and checked the bedrooms. The first was unoccupied; a safe in the wall above the round bed hung open. The kid must have gotten the gun out of there. He itched to check the safe for cash he could use to get out of here, even as he dismissed it. He had no need of money, anymore, and he knew damned well he wasn't going anywhere.

The next bedroom was occupied. A Jacuzzi frothed and swirled in the corner, making a swampy morass out of the room. Pictures sweated and warped in their frames; condensation dripped from the rafters, and a boy lay in the tub with his head propped against the edge, mouth slack and eyes half-lidded. The whirring pumps and the sloshing water were almost loud enough to drown out his snoring.

An even bigger bed dominated this bedroom, and a naked girl lay spread across it on her back, legs akimbo, one hand clutching a condom . . . no, a balloon.

Dom went over to the guy in the tub and gently nudged him under the water. It didn't wake him up. He sank for a while, then floated back up, facedown.

Dom found a fifty-pound pressurized steel tank on the floor beside the Jacuzzi. He picked it up and looked it over. Too good to be true. Nitrous oxide, his favorite party favor.

Holding the tank up to his lips, he opened the valve wide and took a mighty hit, expelling all oxygen from his lungs to fill them like a bellows with magic laughing gas.

Bubbles tingled up in his vision, obscuring the world and taking him away to another world of pure light and energy and the Percolator, throbbing and bubbling away at the center of the universe. Scooped up out of his body and into the chaotic maelstrom of Outside, he saw it all from a cosmic height, and relaxed. For all his acting up, all his desperate ploys to stand out, all he'd ever really wanted, was to belong. And now, finally, he did.

Holding his breath, he padded over to the bed and climbed on, straddled the girl and leaned in close. Her hair was dark brown, damp, arranged around her head in a careless spray. Her full breasts spread in luxurious puddles on her slim torso. He leaned in and clamped his mouth over hers, and exhaled.

With the first burst of nitrous, her eyes fluttered and regarded him blankly, and her arms and legs struggled against him. As he pinned her and passed the gas to her,

her resistance became shocky and unconscious, spasms of an unmanned vessel. He sent her far away, but her body responded just fine to his gentle stroking. His paws—bigger, clumsier than he remembered, but stronger, too—tugged her nipples and kneaded her flanks. She clamped her legs around his hips and undulated against his groin. She didn't know or care who he was, or where she was, but she wanted what he wanted.

He tore off his jeans and ground his pelvis against her bare slit. She giggled and threw up on the pillow, then tried to kiss him.

His conscience was speaking Greek. The angel on his shoulder jerked off in his ear. He was so ready for this, but downstairs, somebody hadn't gotten the message—

Dom tugged at his cock. This had never happened to him before. The girl squirmed under him, wanting it, so why couldn't he make it work?

He rubbed it and tugged it, getting kind of pissed. This was his cock, and if his hands could smash doors and steering wheels, surely his cock had evolved in direct proportion.

It came off in his hand.

There was no pain, no more sensation than taking out a baby tooth, or peeling off an almost-healed scab. He held it in his hand and looked at it for a long while. Was this shriveled Vienna sausage really his *cock*? When would a new, improved one grow back?

The reality of it dawned on him when his fingers traced his groin. Around the vacated socket, the muscles of his thighs and belly were thickened, the skin becoming a hide that barely registered the pressure, let alone the touch, of his fingers. He was changing.

Dom looked down at the girl with new eyes. She was not for him, but through her, he could get himself back. She was for the family. He and the others, the ones who still lived.

He tossed the withered organ away. He saw and thought more clearly without it, anyway. There would be other pleasures . . .

There was still the question of how to get them back to the house. As if his thought was a radio wave, a swarm of bees came in the open door and settled on the bodies, glossy golden robes, dutifully stinging them and rolling off to die in their hundreds. Dom picked up the girl and carried her over his shoulder out of the cabin. The Percolator guided him again through the forest to the house.

He could learn to live with this.

CHAPTER 14

WALKING THROUGH THE WOODS, the trail was steeper and shrouded in purple shadows. Andrew's slick-soled Vans couldn't get traction, but she took his hand and steadied him. Her slim, alabaster fingers felt like stolen money in his sweaty grip. Whenever the trail crossed another or abandoned them in stands of brush, she always chose the right path. Dimly aware that this wasn't the way back to Mom's house, he didn't question her.

He didn't know what to say, let alone what to do. Thoughts bubbled up half-formed and popped, leaving him more flushed and confused the more he tried to decide what he wanted this situation to become.

She only smiled at the trail and the sky when he tried to make eye contact, that sly, shy smile that said she didn't know what was happening either, but also that she knew everything, and savored his helplessness.

When he did try to get her to talk, he was almost out of breath. Going down the folded, jumbled slopes took more out of him than going up, and he'd been under a full head of angry steam, before. "So . . . May . . . what happened . . . to the people up there?"

She grinned that secret grin, made doubly entrancing when her teeth trapped the tip of her tongue. "The commune broke up. You know how it is, when people can't make things work out . . . "

What *did* she know about it?

His mouth started to work its ugly magic, to spew the bile he'd been stockpiling since the phone call, since before he came up here, since he'd first begun to see the cracks in Laura's façade. But he bit it back. This was not the kind of thing that happened to him. It was a chance to drop all of it and become someone else, if only for a while. WWDD? He asked himself. He wouldn't go on a whiny bitch-rant about his estranged wife . . .

He saw her flash that peculiar quirk of a smile whenever she caught him looking at her, heard her stifle a giggle when he stumbled over a root for gawking at her. Did she know more about him than she let on? Or was he just milking his doubt when he should just do what Dom would, and accept it?

"You tired?" she asked in a wry tone.

"Shit no . . . you got a cigarette?"

She slapped his arm, her expression stormy. "Don't be stupid. This whole forest is dry as the Sahara. You could burn it down in a day with one match, so don't ever let me see you smoking in these woods."

"Okay . . . " The vehemence of her reply made it hard to look at her. Everything before had been so sly and understated. Sure, she made her home here, but the sudden harsh edge reminded him of her weird crack about Dom and Dean being first against the wall when the revolution came. It didn't sound like her, so much as a prerecorded message left by a real dick.

What are you doing, man?

Laura said there was something she couldn't tell him. He knew what that meant. As a serial monogamist from age fourteen, he only broke up when he had a new one on deck. He did so as painlessly and with as little cheating as possible, but it was how relationships had always worked for him, and he thought he smelled something of his own need for validation in Laura. She had someone in the wings, or something had happened that opened her eyes, and she didn't credit him with the guts to hear about it. He'd show her who was a grown-up, or he'd show himself.

One of Andrew's earliest intact memories was of drinking a bottle of weed killer when he was four. He vividly recalled opening the shed in his grandmother's backyard and taking down the heavy brown bottle, but he had no idea of what was going through his mind. The bottle might have reminded him of the beer his dad sometimes let him sip to amuse his friends, before Mom kicked him out. But he remembered the skull and crossbones on the stained label, and the alien word that jarred his nerves with its ugly complexity: FORMALDEHYDE. He remembered the eye-watering vapor that wafted from the bottle's wide, open mouth, the stringent taste of the stuff as he swigged it down, the sleepy tingle spreading out from his mouth as, cell by cell, he began to die. But he did not know why he couldn't stop drinking.

Most of all, he recalled the sensation of queasy invincibility, almost of divinity, as he staggered from the shed to the house like a poet on payday, and begged a glass of milk. He felt as if he had only just awakened to find himself in this body, this life, and delighted in every detail of it, cherished the notion that he was here only by choice, a dreamer in a hammock in Heaven, and could take his pleasures as he chose and move on when it suited him.

That heavenly euphoria was ripped away when he drank the milk, which curdled violently in his gut and made him vomit. In the emergency room, with the doctors and nurses and social workers screaming at his mother while they pumped his stomach, he had reached out for it and found it gone, amputated, and felt a desolation such as only the old can feel, in the face of death and hell. No mere drugs or alcohol could ever come close to getting him that high, or making him that free, as that draught of poison. Until today . . .

May led him on a secret trail through the woods after

the sun set behind the mountains, and the limpid pools of shadow swelled and drowned the trail. Night fell like the dimming of the house lights in a theater. He stopped once, thinking he'd heard a crash and a wailing siren, somewhere down the valley, but it was hard to say what it was, let alone how close. Another time, she'd stopped and he'd almost walked into her. Almost lost in the chirping of the insects, he thought he might have heard a muffled pop like gunfire. He looked at the nape of her neck, stole a grazing touch on her shoulder, dabbing his fingers in the clammy sweat that he could smell over the tang of pine pollen and sun-roasted soil.

They'd walked further than he would have alone, when she said, "Here it is," and threaded a path into a stand of blackberry bushes.

"Aren't you, um, worried about bears?" he asked, making her chuckle. It had been a long time since he'd intentionally made someone laugh.

"Used to be a thing, but they killed the last one a few years ago. Now it's always tweaker season."

Behind her on the narrow path through the thorny brush, blistered with overripe berry-clusters and fizzing with bees, he didn't see her trailer until she climbed onto the doorstep. Broken glass and less wholesome trash crunched underfoot. He blinked and saw the blackened outline of the silver Airstream, and recalled seeing it from the road.

"They tried to burn me out last Christmas," she said, the same way most people would ask you to excuse their untidy living room.

Inside, the charred smell vied with cigarettes and cloying incense, but the damage was almost imperceptible, aside from scorch marks around the plastic-wrapped windows.

May bustled down the narrow aisle between the kitchenette and the breakfast nook, passed through a clattering wall of beaded curtains into the bedroom. "Wait right there," she said.

An odd, uncomfortable silence followed. He wobbled, afraid at an animal-infant level of leaving fingerprints, of getting the stain of anything here on him. What the hell was she doing?

What the hell was *he* doing, here? He always asked himself that, no matter where he went, and seldom had an answer worth repeating aloud occurred to him. The emotional fallout from Laura's nuclear phone strike had only just settled in his mind, and had not evaporated or drained away. The toxic stew seeped deep down into his psyche, poisoning his reasoning and everything that grew on the thin topsoil of his heart. But you had to cleanse the soil, to grow anything new. Time to change his actions, and change himself.

What would Dominic do? he asked again.

From the dank depths of the trailer, music beckoned. Sleepy, liquid tones, rendered nasal and bright by puny speakers and the crackerbox acoustics of the trailer, but he recognized it as the Cocteau Twins' *Victorialand*. Vintage rainy-day makeout music for opium-toking Goths.

He skulked back to the curtains and stood watching her, sure she knew and expected nothing less.

She raised her arms and her flimsy print dress seemed to slither up and off her lithe body. Underneath, she wore only a sheer black bra and black stirrup stockings that made smoked glass of her long legs and framed the trimmed black tuft of hair between them. Her skin was whiter than milk.

"Nice moontan you got there," he observed. She wrapped the dress around herself as if she'd only just realized he was there. Her face stiffened. "I don't tan, I just burn," she said defensively.

Jesus, he was bad at this. He wondered if he'd ever been smooth at talking to girls. Laura had suffered, rather than enjoyed his sense of humor, and every instant conquest had involved some quantity of alcohol in one or both bodies.

"I wasn't teasing," he offered. "I like it."

She unclenched a bit, but reached for a robe. Whatever had been about to happen might not happen at all, now.

He thought of Laura—of how her long black hair trapped the moisture from her morning shower, so it was always cool, deep down at the roots, on hot days, as if the night retreated at dawn to hide inside her head. He pushed those memories back and emptied his mind until it lay as blank as a sand garden after the rain.

Unbidden, his hand parted the beaded curtains and the rest of him slithered in after it. He invaded the closet-sized space with her, leaving her only a step to retreat before she backed into a vanity with a boombox, incense burners, candles and a hodgepodge of cosmetics and hair product jumbled onto it. She just stood there, close enough that her breath—Altoids, Camels, deep-fryer grease and sweet, mysterious girl-chemistry—filled his nostrils.

The moment stretched out; her face magnified. Tongue wet chapped burgundy lips, eyes dilated. He smelled the subtle tang in the sweat that beaded on her flushed skin. Her excitement almost made his eyes water as it evaporated into the stifling air.

"May," he started to say, when she kissed him.

He thought he'd been kissed before. He'd had tonsillectomies from drunken sophomores, and hickies in his freshman high school year that made him the envy of the media club. He thought he knew what they were talking about when they spoke of the spark that set a true kiss apart from the meat-on-meat friction and chemical warfare of all other human contact.

With that one kiss, May took him to school.

She ate his mouth. Her lips caught his unawares and melted his rigid defensive rictus, nipped his lower lip so a tear of blood stood out, then lapped it off and roved to his ear. Her tongue grew bolder, teeth nibbling his earlobe, goosing his pulse and making him sag at the knees. It hurt, but not enough to stop. If he spotted a tube of herpes ointment by the sink or found a straight razor under her pillow, he could not stop now.

He let his hands roam over her body. Her skin was softer than his wife's, softer than smoke, downy ivory velvet sheened with sweat, the foreign spice of which set his brain buzzing. It excited him even more to hear her breathing quicken in his ear, feel her runaway arousal kindle a feedback loop with his. She was so much more responsive than his wife, more than anyone he'd ever had.

He kneaded her arms back and wriggled between them to caress and squeeze the delectable meat of her breasts. It startled him to find a ring dangling from her erect nipple, like the pin on a hand grenade. He pinched the nipple as hard as he dared and gave the ring a twist.

She shuddered. She gasped once, then let out a low moan and crushed his mouth in a kiss like a guard gives a convict in the showers of a women's prison. He smelled a bloody ozone scent and felt waves like a breaking fever coming off her, and knew that she had already come.

Her tongue traced the arterial throb at his throat, rasping his skin raw like a cat's. He flinched at her touch, heard her dusky laugh under his jaw. He reached out and took her by her spiky black hair and tugged her head back.

Her eyes rolled in her head, almost shutting down, shocked at getting so quickly what she didn't dare ask for. His turn to laugh; he kissed her hard, crazed with the alien angles and behaviors, the unholy novelty of the body in his thrall, the perverse thrill of watching his clumsy, unassuming self dominate her.

May's hunger, her wildness and the unfamiliarity of her angular, underfed form, drugged him beyond recall to reason. His fingers ran down the serpentine arch of her spine to squeeze her ass, baffled and trembling over the frail contours of her ghostly flesh, worlds apart from the sleek solidity of his wife. Through his sticky T-shirt, he felt the jutting rivets of her transfixed nipples grazing his chest, the muted thunder of her heartbeat.

Her mouth had drained some vital spark from him. He fed on her and took it back. Her hands pawed his back and clutched at his ass. Her hips gyrated against him. She thrust one leg between his and ground into his overeager cock. Then she pivoted and tossed him off one hip like a judo master. He fell onto the narrow Murphy bed at the back of the trailer. He slid backwards across burgundy cotton sheets, cool with sweat-residue and steeped in her perfume.

She pounced on him and went to kiss him, but bit his lip again and slid down him and tore his pants off like Christmas. In another moment, he was in her mouth, praying not to come right then and there.

His hands tangled in her hair, but she batted them away. Through the glossy veil of her bangs, her eyes lanced him with a vacant intensity, as if some wilder spirit had possessed her, and rode her as she rode him. Throttling his cock with one white-knuckled hand, she searched his eyes for a reflection of her possession, a kindred elemental.

You could never tell how a woman felt about giving you head. Some would never touch it, paralyzed by a nightmare vision of the man's tackle as a slimy snake to which one must make awful sacrifices, to conjure a child. Some dutifully took it in, but let it wither on the palate like a disgusting vegetable waiting for the right moment to be washed down quickly or spat discreetly into a napkin. There were those who seemed genuinely mad for it, but Andrew had only read about them in letters of dubious veracity in *Penthouse*.

May's eyes never closed, never flicked away from his as she bathed the unbearably sensitive root of his shaft with her pale pink tongue. Here and there, she introduced her teeth to keep him on edge, but she worked with the selfless assurance of a maid building a fire, milking a cow, though her urgency showed some feral longing that was more powerful by far than any naïve notions of tenderness or love.

Andrew lay back on the rumpled bedclothes and closed his eyes. She worked on him in rounds, building his desire, coaxing more blood and fire into his organ until he gasped and almost came, then swirling his balls one at a time in her cool, red mouth and biting his thighs to edge him off.

He wanted to fuck her, wanted even more to turn her around and return the favor, but she pressed him back down on the bed with one black-nailed hand splayed flat on his soft belly.

He tried to settle into the alien moment, let his eyes roll around the compartment. Tapestries and bolts of faded burgundy velvet quilted the ceiling like the dilapidated lining of a coffin. The cellophane windows snapped and rippled as a shrill gust of wind shook the trailer.

The formica walls were shaggy with clipped magazine ads and album art, marble-eyed sirens and androgynous eidolons gazing at him from darksome crypts, icy catwalks and stygian hate-holes. In the corner beside his head, the clippings almost covered an older stratum of family snapshots.

In one, a reedy, bright-eyed girl of about five grinned a bit too hard into the camera. In the background, a blurred constellation of colored lights and horse heads, the mad rush of a carousel. The girl's little arms were trapped by a meaty woman's hand, in the midst of being dragged away from a merry-go-round ride.

Other shots of May as a child, in rest stops and diner booths, opening meager Christmas gifts in seedy motel rooms, always holding a plump woman's hand, always resolutely out of frame. He'd never seen any of the places before, but something about them spread a rancid shadow of familiarity in his brain.

Not the subject, but the scene; not the girl, but the photographer. The cheap thrift store clothing, the framing, the quality of the camera, seemed all too familiar.

Up in the corner, beside the window, another picture: an arrangement of robed figures gathered round a bed. A tapestry with some sort of Tibetan mandala hung on the wall behind them, giving the bed the elevated nature of an altar or a shrine. Most of the figures had their faces blacked out by cigarette burns, but the woman in the center and the boy lying beside her were left intact. A baby lay in the crook of her arm, mouth clamped over the nipple of her left breast. The boy cupped the other breast, pendulous, mottled and manhandled, as large as his head, eyes empty and glazed over by pleasures far beyond his years. Beside the bed, a girl with dark brown hair stood with her hands knotted in the front of her robe as if to hold in a scream.

Her face was scoured out of the yellowed, faded image, but Andrew knew, in a single, scrotum-clenching instant, that it was Laura. He didn't need to guess, because he'd seen the rest of the pictures from this roll, in the coffee can at his mother-in-law's. The boy was Dean, the woman was his mother, and the baby was both his daughter and his sister.

May.

An arctic blizzard swirled through his bowels, a cold so fierce he sat up and closed his legs on May's head. He pushed her off him, too hard. She tumbled across the floor and hit her head on the vanity. A drawer slid open and lipstick clattered and fell into the sink.

"Jesus," she hissed, sloe-eyed, slurring. "It's okay, if you want to come in my mouth."

"Not okay," he said. "It's *so* not okay. I can't . . . " He chose his next words very carefully, rejecting several drafts of a diplomatic way of expressing that the girl with his dick in her mouth was both his sister-in-law and his niece. "I mean, who are you, anyway? Why me . . . ? Why did you—"

"Me?" She rose up on her knees and cocked her hip so her ring-pierced tits swung and the cleft between her legs winked at him. "I'm May D'Amato. Who the fuck are you?"

Ugly, unworthy thoughts blew around in his head like cash in those tents radio promotional contests use, where a rube jumps and flails like an idiot, as a fan whips it around in a cyclone. All of them were trash and small currency. Was this instant karma? Did he ask for this?

"I don't see a ring," she coyly said. Her hand brushed his, touched the raw, white band of skin at the root of his right ring finger. He jerked away, feeling at his front pocket, but the ring wasn't there. "You came here. You knew what this was."

"You knew those guys at the diner, didn't you?"

"Your brothers? I never saw them before, but I just moved up here a few years ago."

"To be with your mother."

Finally, her smile soured. "She's a bitter old bitch. But you'd know. You know what Laura is like."

"You know what you are . . . and you could . . . still do this?"

"What *I* am? Just what am *I*, Andrew?" She smiled at him again, but the smile had no guile in it, no seduction. She was turpentine boiling on an untended stove when she licked her lips and said, "I won't tell if you won't."

He stepped over her, nearly tripping as he zipped up his jeans. She reached for him, but he retreated down the narrow passage. He didn't touch her, but she rebounded off his passive deflection and threw herself on the bed, letting out a shuddering sob that nailed him to the creaky plywood floor. "I didn't mean to cause trouble," she moaned, "but that's what I do . . . "

"You," he started to say, but he was so far out of his depth, he couldn't catch his breath. "I'm sorry. About all of this. You and I shouldn't . . . we just shouldn't . . . "

"I didn't even want to," she cried. "I was supposed to keep you away from the house, because you're not indoctrinated yet, but I was supposed to make you want to . . . and you were really sweet . . . but he doesn't know what to do with you . . . "

"You're not making any sense," he said. "Are you feeling okay?"

May rolled over and reached for a pack of Camels and a Bic lighter on a shelf beneath the window. "The revolution," she said, in a hard, dry voice, "needs many strong backs and strong arms, and one strong mind. If it fails . . . " Her voice trailed off as she looked at something through the layers of plastic.

"I still don't understand. I don't believe in Communism. Nobody does, anymore, not even the communists."

"But in Russia, Communism believes in you." With a lilting giggle, she lit her cigarette. The stink of it made him want to vomit. Some fresh air, that's what he needed—

The window stretched and tore. A massive gray hand snarled in May's tousled black hair. She screamed like a fire alarm. Beat at it with her fist, the cigarette, but it dragged her halfway out of the trailer before Andrew could shout, "Hey!" and grab for her legs.

May slid out the window on her back buck-naked. She clawed at the enormous paw and broke off her nails in its hide without tearing it, her legs kicking under Andrew, but all his strength and weight didn't slow her down. He rode her into the dark, into the arms of something that filled the night outside the tiny trailer.

Without thinking, without any rational calculation of risk or reward, right or wrong, he let go of her legs. Her body was jerked out from under him so hard, he had friction burns where he touched her. Hanging halfway out the window himself, he kicked out his legs and hooked the sill with one hand while the other reached stupidly out for May.

She was gone. Only the flapping tatters of the plastic bag around the window frame and her screams receding like she was in a speeding car, and thunderous trampling like horses or faraway bombs, to say it wasn't all a nightmare from which he was about to awake.

Andrew backed away from the window. He crashed into the vanity, fumbling behind him for the boombox and yanking its cord out of the wall. The music choked off and he heard something sharp scrape against the formica and fiberglass wall at his back.

Another window right beside him, not wide enough for him to be pulled out, but big enough for something to reach in and grab him. He dropped to the floor and scuttled under the bed, pressing himself in among piles of spiky heels and soiled socks and panties and wigs and dust bunnies. He cocked his ears for the slightest sound, but only the wind stirred outside, moaning through the trees and flapping the ruptured cellophane window like it was sniffing for him.

For all he knew, they were lying in wait outside, or maybe they had no use for him, and he could just walk away.

There's two factions now, and no neutral parties.

The woman at the shore, clothed in bees, and the thing that crushed her skull. Not nightmares conjured up by his concussion. Andrew curled up tighter on the floor and closed his eyes, simply frozen up, praying, *Please God, I learned my lesson, now let me wake up . . .*

CHAPTER 15

DEAN AWOKE TO PAIN.

He couldn't focus on anything beyond his body. His injured arm dangled and flopped, galvanic twitches ripping through heedless meat. It must have just popped back into its socket, and the shock of it awakened him. Scalding bile flushed his throat and sinuses, spilled out his mouth and into the dark.

Had he blacked out? A furious mental inventory ensued. Had he been drinking? Had he let go, like that one time in college, or that disastrous shore leave in Okinawa? He remembered fighting with Dom and losing, and then finding the pictures . . . Jesus, what had he done?

No answer came. His brain lolled on the floor of his skull like a beached jellyfish—on the roof, rather, for he hung upside down, carried like a dead rabbit through the woods.

It was too dark to see much. He hung over someone's shoulder. A few stray rays of dying sunlight through the trees, but the shadows gathered between them in a violet flood. He could only see that he was a long way from the ground, and that his bearer dwarfed him the way he dwarfed his oldest son.

Dean brought up his knees hard into his captor's chest. He tried to roll off the shoulder, but an arm as thick as his waist encircled and squeezed him until he saw spots and shit his Dockers.

Paul was a good boy. Excellent grades in kindergarten, never made a mess, teacher's favorite at Sunday school, and, truth to tell, Dean's favorite. The other three were, quite frankly, a study in diminishing returns.

But Paul had a temper. He threw tantrums when he didn't get his way, and he and Janice were forever at loggerheads as to what to do with him. At every birthday party he'd ever attended, sooner or later, Dean had to scoop him up and take him to the minivan for a spanking and time-out of duration and intensity to suit the offense.

He was only four, but you had to give the little man credit. He hit and kicked and bit for all he was worth over a handful of piñata candy. He hurt Dean pretty bad more than a few times. If Dean wasn't so proud of him, he might lose his own temper and really hurt the boy, but he always knew that one day, Paul would channel that angry energy into success, and would laugh with him about these times. He wondered if Paul would laugh right now, if he could see his daddy, a freshly spanked brat in the arms of a monster, borne off for a time-out.

Slowly, like a frail old woman lowering herself into a hot bath, Dean examined the insane nightmare bullshit that now confronted him and conceded that maybe it was not such bullshit, after all. Someone came into the house. They kicked his ass and clotheslined him. Now they were carrying him off, to—where?

Bigfoot. Deformed cannibal hillbillies. That Commie cult. All of the above. This last, at least, made sense. He'd still been reeling from the beating Dom gave him, when that motherfucker came at him with the fridge door. His memory wasn't even good enough for government work, but it made a sick kind of sense. Commies. Knowing Mom like he did, it made sense she'd run off and join another cult.

They were taking him to her.

He was helpless—

No. Never helpless. He was an Eagle Scout, third in his class at Annapolis—he was an American, goddamit—and if these Commie faggots didn't put him down posthaste, he would stomp the pink shit out of them.

The long, loping stride of his captor tightened up and accelerated. The lungs beneath him heaved like bilge pumps. They were ascending a steep slope. The legs were like an elephant's, gnarly with muscle and baggy with tough gray hide.

First chance he got, he'd tear its fucking head off.

Dean took a deep breath and held it, then sprang into action. Kicking and flailing at the monster's back, he jerked and dropped free. With a grunt of surprise, the thing let him fall, but he hung in the air for a pregnant split-second, long enough to feel shock at his altitude, to see he'd torn his palm wide open hitting the thing, to look up at the thing and try to see its face and think, *someone beat me to it.*

He hit the ground squarely on his tailbone. The shit in the seat of his pants squelched up his backside, the stink and the shame of it forgotten in his pain and panic as he saw it through tear-glutted eyes. The impact jolted the wind out of him and cracked his spine like a bullwhip. He lay on his side and looked up, useless legs flopping in front of him like dying eels.

He saw those mighty shoulders, knife-blade bones sprouting out of the joints like antlers, flex and reach out huge arms and wrecking ball hands to catch him. Between those shoulders, however, he saw only a stump with a hole in it. Knurled wrinkles and folds around the mouth might have harbored eyes and nostrils, but they were an afterthought. Its head was less than a lamprey's—no eyes to see, no brain to think—only a mouth working silently round jagged teeth, wheezing breath like moldy compost in his face as it stooped and picked him up. Too weak even to scream, Dean sobbed and let himself be carried away.

Dean flew through the woods on its back until the

shadows won and plunged the world into night. They crossed a plain of high grass and brambles in the relative glare of starlight. Out in the open, his captors galloped in long, mechanical strides, wheezing with effort and as much fear as things that ran around without heads were capable of expressing. Repulsed, he could smell it coming off them like cat piss.

Dean covered his face and swatted at razor teeth slicing his exposed skin. Grasses absorbed mica from the soil and made defensive weapons out of their foliage. Knowing this did nothing to soften it, or soothe the crazy-making burn of his sweat in the cuts. If only his closet-case brother-in-law were here, Dean could shame himself to stop crying.

He could see the length of the plain through the lashing grass, a long meadow nestled between sentinel peaks and bordered on all sides by a secretive phalanx of forest. At the far end of the plain, a huge gray house stood against an almost sheer wall of boulders. Monolithic in the gloom, inert but for a lone light in a tower looming high over the featureless ruin, confirming in Dean's fevered mind that it was an old prison.

Exhausted, his captors shambled gratefully into the shadows of a clump of live oaks, and in its shelter, the thing set him down.

The bed of leaves and rotten acorns beneath him rustled with disturbed insects. In the stillness, he heard a rushing deeper than the evening breeze, muffled by terrain, but not much distance. Running water.

Thinking they meant to rest, he went limp and feigned unconsciousness. At the right moment, he would escape. He had to try, if he was a man.

They didn't give him a chance. Three long deep breaths, and he was scooped up on another monster's shoulder, while his abductor turned and ran back out into the night.

Through slitted eyes—still playing possum, he told

himself, not because he was afraid to look—he saw it. The new one was not so tall, though still half-again Dean's height; muscles more compact, limbs less rangy and without the serrated bone spurs that mutilated Dean's hand. With a flat, wheezing grunt of effort, it carried him back under the live oaks and up a short slope.

They passed through a barn door and into a huge ruin like a rude timber cathedral. Jumbles of chiseled stones and termite-riddled pine and oak beams showed in the fugitive rays of moonlight through the collapsed roof. A necropolis of shadowy wreckage rose up around them. A circular saw blade the size of a palace gong loomed over the rubble, a rusty, shark-toothed moon.

Deeper into the ruined sawmill, the thing carried him, into the dark and down with the subsiding floor, underneath a gallery that buckled and groaned overhead like the hull of an ancient slave galley in a storm. It set him down, not ungently, on a bed of petrified sawdust, turned and stomped off to some new task.

In the guttering dark, he could see only shadows. But all around him, he heard breathing. Phlegm-choked bellows worked at the moldy, dust-choked air. Great tree-trunk feet padded timidly among mounds of debris, converging on him.

His tears dried up, but Dean could not control his shivering. His skin all prickled gooseflesh, blood and bruises, he couldn't tell if he was warm or cold. Slipping into shock, he fretted, but he'd be damned if he'd let these Commie freaks have their way with him. Swallowing his terror and creeping nausea, he forced himself to stare them down, but they seemed not to have an eye between them.

Each stood about seven feet tall, and half as broad at the shoulders, which were padded and buttressed with callus and cartilage like a linebacker's armor. Like the ten-foot behemoth that kidnapped him, they had no heads to speak of, but only faceless stubs with hippo tusks gritting in gaping mouths like garbage disposals. But some sense guided them closer around him.

Their huge, freakish hands splayed out before them, callus-padded digits extended like blind men warming themselves at a fire. Wounded, grievously burned, porcupined with splinters and tenpenny nails, but trembling with raw, childlike eagerness.

Dozens of them, crouching and shuffling in the dark. Dean shuddered with loathing as the details of their bodies pressed in on him, making him wish for darkness.

That these things were from the commune actually relieved him, because it explained it down from the unacceptable to the merely impossible, which Dean had learned to entertain over years of digesting conservative commentary. It made a kind of sense, at least. They were communists, and thus capable of anything.

"You fucking Red losers got ears?" he shouted. As one, they flinched. Dean drew confidence from this. Rolling up onto his knees, he stood and raised his fists in a tae kwon do attack stance. "Fuck Marx! Fuck Lenin! Stalin liked it in the ass! Mao raped babies! Come on and get me, you pinko pussies!"

The sound of his voice seemed to hurt them, so he shouted himself hoarse, turning to give each of them a dose. There was scarcely space to take a step in any direction, but they shook, helpless. They flinched when he jabbed at them, though whether they could see or hear him, or just felt the air move, he didn't know.

He feinted right and ducked, fully intent on darting through their massed ranks of clumsy, clubfooted legs. Quicker than he could see, his fists were wrapped up in one massive paw and whipped behind his back.

Dean squawked just like his son, when Daddy snapped him up in mid-tantrum. His arms got levered up over his head, bending him at the waist. He mule-kicked behind him, jarred his leg as if he'd kicked concrete. They bowed him lower. Dean screamed as his shoulder wrenched and almost popped back out of its socket. "God damn you, fight fair! I'll kill every one of you with my bare hands, one at a time! I . . . "

Before his eyes, a giant's paw rose up, holding a pith helmet with opaque black netting draping down—a beekeeper's hood. Dean jerked away, but only succeeded in popping his arm back out. Sagging, biting back shrieking fits, he could do nothing as they slipped the hood over his head. What the hell kind of game was this?

Then he saw that the hood was not opaque, but filled with bees.

Dean would tell you—if he could talk—that to get as far as he had in the Navy, indeed, in life, you had to learn to love pain. During Hell Week at Annapolis, he suffered tortures that nearly undid his sanity and his manhood. He persevered and discovered, in the end, the value and necessity of hazing tactics. They weeded out the weak and taught the strong the most important lesson in life.

There is nothing to fear in pain. When one has walked through fire for a cause, even if that cause is only to prove himself, the strong man finds a kind of pleasure in pain, a corporeal blessing, as potent as the afterglow of good sex. Pain awakens, Dean would say, the essential man, empowers him to crush down all obstacles. With a mighty warrior roar, Dean steeled himself for pain.

Bees flew into his mouth.

Dean whipped his head around until something tore in his neck, but he only agitated the trapped swarm. Battalions of stingers pricked his face, his ears, his neck, his scalp, his eyeballs. His skin welted, blistered and burst, tears, plasma and venom spurting, drowning wriggling, eviscerated bees.

His arms and legs never arrived on the scene. He couldn't feel, let alone control, anything outside the hood, and his body might be doing the Funky fucking Chicken right now, for all he knew.

Pain did nothing to restore the essential Dean, either. The unbearable agony awakened something less than an animal, a craven abortion slinking back to the womb of shock. But eventually, it did help him escape. Pain drove him right out of the driver's seat and into a catatonic fugue. He was far from sleep, but there were dreams.

When he came to, Dean floated on the euphoric bubble he recalled from boxing at the Academy, or the most knockdown dragout fights with Dom. He could feel only a golden halo of numbness where his head should be, and everywhere else a blinding wash of universal goodwill, as if his body had atomized and become an abstraction, a bleeding-heart ghost of Scrooge on Christmas morning. He couldn't see much of anything beyond the radiance of his own ecstatic, near-death bliss. He felt drunk—but unlike every other time he got seriously wet, he didn't feel angry.

All those wasted years, he'd prayed for the holy spirit to come into him and drown his doubt, for the false idol of patriotism to sear away the scourge of his fear, until only his will to believe supported him. He'd built a bridge out into a void. He'd wrapped himself in a coat of thorns to ward off the world, but he wore it inside out. He'd built a graven image out of his unfulfilled longing for a father and called it God, never realizing that God lived in his fellow man.

Where were those dickless commie bastards? He wanted to show them how wrong he'd been, how selfish, how stupid. He wanted to thank them. He wanted to tell them about his dream.

Surging up through the trivial physical pain, he felt something from outside himself that, at long last, enfolded his heart. He felt recognized and validated; it needed him, and it promised struggle and reward.

He shared their pain, their wordless pride in their work, and he endured with them the confusion and rage of the strike. Their home, their hope, their head, was lost.

They had given everything to the commune, shed all but their power to work, and in return, they were turned out to starve in the wilderness. Never meant to interact with the outside world, the commune had split open and exposed itself to infection, as both sides reached out for comrades in the struggle.

His heart rent itself open and bled for them. He wanted to help. Now that he understood, he wanted to make things right.

His eyes were swollen shut, gummed with pus-crust and venom. He tried to knuckle them open, but his hands were gnarled blister-mittens. He wept, and presently, he could see.

Dean lay on his side in a small, bare room of rough-hewn granite, and littered with bodies. Eight men and women lay sprawled out or in fetal wads all around him, flannel and denim and hick and tourist togs caked with dirt and shit and golden slime, faces and hands scabbed and turgid with beestings, disfigured like drowned floaters dragged from a river bottom. Dean's heart leapt. Comrades!

Several of them were dead. Stiff and blue, necks crooked, limbs bent all wrong; broken during their abductions, he supposed—*contents may settle during shipping*. The survivors slept, dreaming new dreams, drooling honey.

He wobbled and collapsed the first time he tried to rise. He landed atop the body of a girl. She was naked but for the rags of black stockings. Her creamy skin was livid with cuts, bruises and stingers, countless quills, more than the others, because her acrid sweat told him she was already indoctrinated by a rival hive's venom.

He read somewhere, or heard on talk radio, that in the ancient world, highborn women like Cleopatra would sting their lips with bottled bees to make them more full and luscious. Dean's wife, Janice, had lips like a goldfish, flat and fishy and always gulping something down. He'd done his duty by her and God and yielded a family, but it wasn't hard to resist fornication for pleasure with those thin, uninspiring lips to kiss at night. You could feel her teeth through them, for Christ's sake. She'd read in one of her dumb magazines that it turned a man on, if you shoved your tongue in his mouth, and he'd had a devil of a time disabusing her of the disgusting notion.

But looking at these lips, on this girl, in this place, despite or because of all he'd been through, he felt a stirring in himself that no Bible verse could tame. His cock, one of the few parts of him not beaten bloody tonight, pressed through the shreds of his Dockers. He looked around, saw only glassy eyes and honey-dripping mouths. He felt like a new man in a new world. This girl, everything told him, was for him.

He reached out and stroked her breasts—smaller and more inviting than his wife's slack, lopsided dugs—brushing away stingers and tugging the silver doorknocker ring transfixing her nipple. Even this revolting pagan self-mutilation only stoked the roiling heaviness in his groin, and he reveled in wringing a groan from her when he twisted it.

The harlot moaned and moved against him in a way that said she was less than half-asleep. Her slim hips thrust invitingly at him. Her dyed-black hair still veiled her face, smeared with gobbets of comb-fresh honey, but Dean had no interest in her as an individual.

She was faceless. He was making love to the body politic, to the whole of womankind. His pleasure in the act was nothing more or less than the joy of labor. He was a tool, just like the lumpen proletarians who jumped him, doing his duty. His current job—and hers—was to make more workers. Maybe a soldier, like himself, or even a leader, which the colony desperately needed, right now—

She arched up and kissed him hard, biting his lip.

Mechanically at first, he kissed her back, then with clumsy ardor as his frigid fear of his own sexuality thawed, exploring and exulting in her like a drunken beast.

When her tongue darted into his mouth, he did not reject it, but delighted in its soft invasion, even when she regurgitated into him. It was a sweet and sour nectar of honey and stomach acid. He swallowed it with vigor, sucked more from her.

They bucked and writhed as one across the body-strewn cell, until he pinned her against the bars. He probed her slit and found it hot as a melted gun barrel, but dry like his wife's turkey. He dipped his hand in the pool of honey in the gaping mouth of a dead old trucker and slicked her up, lubricating her labia and clit and the tightest pussy he'd ever known. She mewled like a cat, scratched him and licked his open wounds. He got another gout of dead man's honey to slather up his cock, hurtfully engorged and by God half again its normal size.

All of this was permitted. It was vital labor. As he mounted the girl and began driving her against the bars, she chanted, "Get it, comrade, get it," in ever more breathless gasps. A horde of workers shuffled up to the bars and pressed against them, as if to bask in the warmth of the fire that had been doused in their sexless bodies.

When he came, he died almost a greater death than he had endured in the hood of bees. White light engulfed him and showed him the glory of the world he would help to build, repopulate and defend. He hugged the girl to him and cried out for joy. Still erect, he continued to thrust into her as she screamed and screamed for more.

Dean knew duty was a whore. But he served it, as always, like his life depended on it.

CHAPTER 16

IN THE DARK, Andrew thought he would feel safer.

But with the dying of the last rays of sunlight, the dark outside pressed up around the trailer and came alive with night noises.

In the city, he realized, it never really got dark. There was always light, or light pollution, from somewhere. Out here, with no artificial lights, and no starlight, no moonglow, breaking through the forest, the dark had a solidity, a presence that could eat you alive, all by itself . . .

Little gusts of wind found his hiding place and sniffed him like a dog, deciding whether or not to bite.

Whatever was out there might still be waiting, or it could have left with May. He didn't even want to let himself dwell on how he felt about that. Maybe it took her away to its lair, or maybe it just tore her apart and ate her out there, and was waiting for seconds. Maybe it had carried her off and was now strolling back, and he'd wasted the chance that she'd bought him.

He was still manfully struggling with his dilemma when he was forced to act on instinct. He felt the itch of tiny legs on his neck, but, tarred with sweat and feathered with puffs of dust, he barely noticed. He was still shaky with unspent adrenaline and prickled gooseflesh, and wet all over from pissing his pants.

When the stinger plunged into his skin, it felt like a white-hot thumbtack. He screamed, "Fuck me!" and slapped at his neck, thrashing around in his hidey-hole. He smashed the bee, but its stinger lodged in his skin, venom sacs torn out of its abdomen, pumping toxin into his bloodstream.

The bees here were not normal bees. They got into shit, like they were *looking* to sting people. They were the symbol of the commune.

He stuck his head out from under the bed.

A dim candle threw a red pool of lesser murk at the far end of the trailer. The air danced with buzzing black motes.

Stirred by some damnable insect certainty of his presence, a seething swarm circled over the bed, like in the cartoons, where the swarm formed an arrow or an exclamation point in the air. Then it dove for his exposed face.

Andrew sucked wind to scream, and inhaled gobbets of dust. He clawed at the sheet hanging off the edge of the mattress and ripped it down, corkscrewing himself up in a shroud while bees alit on him and tried to sting him to death, or something worse.

Coughing snot and bee carcasses into the sheet, he wriggled out into the open, humping across the floor like a caterpillar. The sheet bound his arms at his sides, but he hunched against a wall and got up on his knees.

Sightless, hyperventilating, he heard and felt bees spasming in bottled fury in the folds of the sheet, but he forced himself not to melt down and toss his only protection away.

The air crackled with them. He felt their tiny bodies bouncing off his swaddled face as he staggered blindly down the single-wide trailer in search of the door.

A shapeless orange glow led him into the living room. He knocked over something that popped and shot out sparks when it hit the floor, and then he found the door, but he couldn't get a hand free to turn the knob. He felt stingers jabbing through the burgundy sheet stretched over his face, wings beating the sodden fabric taut across his mouth.

Their rage, and his terror, ripped from Andrew any pretense of self-control. He ran screaming until he hit something and turned to run in a new direction, sweeping pictures from walls and popping open cupboards and cabinets that dumped shit on him, driving him even crazier. Stingers pricked his arms and scalp when he mashed them into the walls. The location of the door, the concept of a door, was long forgotten when he threw himself headfirst into, and ripped through, a barrier of yielding plastic. The sheet metal windowsill barked his shins, folding and dumping him out into the black woods.

Tumbling end over ass-end, he rolled shrieking over rocks and rotten pine needles until he came to rest in a blackberry bush. Thorns shredded the sheet and unwound him, but scored his hands and forearms with hot, shallow welts. A few tardy bees settled on him and stung, but he was too exhausted to react. Their venom actually seemed to soothe him, slow his breathing and suppress his panic. He was one of many. He was not alone, just out of sync.

Over his head, the swarm roared in a cyclonic funnel, but the humming motes bunched in flying knots that fell to the ground and died. The bees were stinging each other to death. Two swarms engaged in an all-out dogfight around and inside the trailer. He couldn't tell them apart, but they had no trouble scenting their enemies. At least they, like the others, had forgotten him.

Out of breath and retching dust and bits of bees, he lurched out of the blackberry patch and followed the land downhill, hoping to find the road.

The treacherous slope was broken up with boulders and brush, and he barely caught himself before he blundered into a rusty snarl of barbed wire strung between the trees. Beyond it, the hills rose up to a crest with no sign of a road, but he saw a light way off through the trees, dim and tiny as Venus. He was too out of breath to say anything more than, "Thanks, God," but he meant it.

He took his gratitude back when he got closer. The guiding light was a flood mounted under the sagging eaves of the roof on the rear of Sprague's cabin. If the old man had lied about having no phone, he would force him to call the sheriff. If not, Andrew would take his truck into town. The old man kept a shotgun by the door. He'd rush inside and take it. Then he'd be in control of the situation. Hopefully, with control would come the idea of what the fuck to do.

In a big black stand of brush just before him, something stealthily moved, leaves and needles crunching underfoot. Andrew crouched, turning to run, when the bushes parted and someone tackled him.

Andrew's legs got tangled and swept out from under him as his attacker wrapped him up and hurled him back down the slope, then fell on top of him.

"FREEZE, GODDAMIT!"

Milkweed seeds and dust swirled around him to obscure his attacker. He didn't see the first blow, just felt it on his cheek and upper lip. Knuckles wrapped around metal. He screamed and shut his eyes, seeing a whirling, churning purple limbo. The beating could go on forever without disturbing his sleep, if he just kept his eyes closed.

"Look at me, you son of a bitch!"

Andrew opened his eyes, but all he saw was a fist with a big chrome-plated revolver aimed at the bridge of his nose. He went crosseyed staring up the barrel. Trying to put the brakes on his runaway panic, he earnestly addressed the gun. "Sir, please—"

"What's your fucking game, pissant? You come up here to hurt some local girls, maybe start a few fires, and fuck with the yokels? Well, who's fucked now?"

Andrew's assailant knelt on his arms, cutting off their bloodflow, so his fingers began to tingle and go numb.

CODY GOODFELLOW

Andrew kept blinking and shaking his head until he could
see past the gun. In the dim glow from the distant light, he
could make out only wild, tousled gray hair and a drooping
mustache, and the faint gleam of sweat on a ruddy, furious
face, the glint of a starburst of metal on his chest. It was
the deputy . . . Scovill, L. *Thank God,* Andrew thought.
Who says you can never find a cop when you need one?

"Something funny, boy?" Scovill rapped Andrew on the
forehead. The sight on the end of the barrel split his brow.
Blood ran into his eye. "You must be fucked up out of your
mind, to do what you did to my cruiser. Not a patch on
what you did to those kids . . . "

Andrew was so terrified, he somehow wet his pants
again, but he couldn't control his mouth. "I didn't do
anything to your car! I was looking for help . . . I was out
here with a girl, and someone took her, and the bees—"

The deputy shook him until his teeth rattled. "Bullshit!
You left your black '94 Nissan pickup at the scene!"

"I don't even have a goddamned truck!" Andrew did
not just lose, but threw down the frayed reins of his
temper. What was the cop going to do, arrest him? "My
brother-in-law has a pickup, but he took off about an hour
ago! I don't know where anybody is, and I just want to get
the fuck out of here! If you're gonna arrest me, do it and
take me to town, but if you're not, then please, sir, get your
gun out of my face before I try something really stupid."

By the end of this inspired tirade, Andrew's voice had
modulated from a shrill shout to a level but deadly earnest
indoor speaking voice. Deputy Scovill seemed to ride it
down from his own heights of hysteria, hitching breath and
head-swiveling tic slowly running down to fatigue and
disbelief. He stared down the barrel at Andrew's twitchy
but unblinking gaze for a long while, but finally thumbed
the safety on his revolver. "Tried to tell you idiots to get out
of here," he said. "Now we're all fucked."

Andrew felt the ground going soft under him, panic

sucking him under. He generally got along great with cops. He called them sir and they saw that he was harmless, and let him go. He trusted them to take control of the situation, and they had never let him down. "What is going on out here, sir?"

Scovill patted his hair, looking surprised to find his hat gone. He looked around and holstered his gun. "I . . . I wish to God I knew. Every vacation cabin in the valley has been looted, and every local I checked in on is missing. There's somebody out there, maybe a lot of them, and they're up to some shit, is all I know. Now, where're your brothers?"

Andrew bristled with nervous anger. "How should I know? Who cares, let's just call for help and get out of here!"

Scovill pursed his lips disapprovingly. Andrew saw a lecture in his eyes about how family should stick by each other. Andrew began to protest that they weren't his family anymore, but the deputy batted the stillborn rant away like a flying pest. "I can't go anywhere, damn it. I told you, my cruiser is totaled, and cell reception is for shit out here. And the goddamned phone lines are down from here to the Wyatt place, a mile over the ridge. I was heading for that pinko shitbird's place when I saw you."

Andrew could still see the beacon of the spotlight through the trees. He could even make out a slice of timbered wall and a patch of earth beneath it, but just then, something passed between him and the light, blocking it totally, though it hung ten feet above the ground. "There's got to be somewhere else. He's . . . not cool with company."

Scovill mopped flop sweat off his face. "There's nowhere this side of the diner at the pond, and they're locked up for the night. I was working that missing girl, but nobody's up here, save for your family, and those damned congressman's kids. Some of the summer places were busted up. I figured it for vandals or burglars up from the city, but most of them weren't closed up for the season. We're good and fucking cut off."

"What about those kids—"

"They were the first place I checked, after I left your mother's cabin, but somebody was already there . . . " Ashen at the memory, the deputy shook out a soft pack of Camel Filters. Andrew asked for one, but Scovill disappeared them and lit the one in his mouth. "When they look at that, they're gonna say a rabid black bear or a grizzly did it. They're gonna leave everything that makes a lie of that story out of the report, because no man could've done it."

"They're not men. I saw them take a girl—the waitress who lives in the trailer—and they are not regular fucking people."

"I could give a shit *what* they are," Deputy Scovill growled. "Men or not, I'll sure as shit kill them, if I can."

"Great, man. Awesome plan. But it's dark, and there's a lot of them. Can we just go?"

"You sure are eager to walk away and leave your kinfolk out here," Scovill said. He stopped looking around and fixed Andrew with a pinched stare that seemed to glow with its own light. "If your family ain't mixed up in this, why're you so hot to ditch them?"

Everybody thinks they want to know. "They're my wife's brothers, and she—I don't know if they are mixed up in this or not. I think Dominic went up there, to that old communal house. He said he knew where his mother was. Something happened to him, anyway. He wasn't right, after he came back . . . "

Deputy Scovill got to his feet but crouched as he moved up the slope towards Sprague's cabin. "Come on. Sprague's place is the only one out here that still has lights on."

Suddenly, the light went out again, blocked by a wall of blackest night that towered over the stout deputy.

Scovill hissed, "Jesus," and raised his gun, but never got to fire. Something stepped out of the shadows and swatted him aside like a scarecrow. He lifted up off his feet with a hideous bleat like air leaking from a balloon, then flapped and flailed about over Andrew's head. Hot arterial blood spattered him like a sultry summer shower.

The thing that struck the deputy vigorously shook its massive arm, but daggers of bone growing out of its massive forearm pierced Scovill's throat and transfixed his skull. Try as it might, the lumbering giant could not shake the still-spasming deputy off itself.

Andrew felt the spell of fascination break as the creature's other arm cocked to do the same to him.

Ducking under the flopping boots of Deputy Scovill, Andrew threw himself off the trail and into a thorny stand of brush. The arm dropped and clove the air down Andrew's back with a bullroarer whoosh.

Brittle branches skewered him and tore away what remained of his shirt, but he scrambled blindly through it to hit a pine trunk, creeping around to put it between himself and the monster.

The monster barked like a sea lion and thrashed the bush, uprooting it and laying into the tree. Scovill's boot kicked Andrew in the head, but he hugged the tree and bit his tongue to keep from screaming. With ass-puckering intimacy, he heard the thing scrape the impaled deputy's body off on the other side of the tree. The sounds of chattering teeth and flesh tearing on bone and bark made his stomach rebel.

He had to shake off the absurd and infantile notion that if he couldn't see it, it couldn't see him. It had no head, for God's sake, so maybe it had already forgotten him; but it had ambushed them. Collecting himself and unclosing his eyes, he pushed off the tree and ran up the slope, looking desperately for Sprague's floodlight.

From the first step, Andrew's legs buckled, lungs burned, steeped in fatigue poisons and spent adrenaline. Since his last day of high school gym, Andrew never had to run for anything more urgent than a bus, a midterm or a job interview. He ran for his life now, comically uncoordinated. Much fitter than his body, his mind raced ahead of him, but only in circles.

He was weak, stupid, worthless. He didn't deserve to survive. Run, hide or fight, he was going to die like Scovill or be dragged off to a worse fate, like May, whom he couldn't save. The emasculating stench of his failure as a man had driven his wife away, and now, out here, it was going to kill him and anyone who threw in with him. Hurled into an impossible nightmare, running scared through the woods in the dark, he saw his weakness balanced against the feather of his courage, and found wanting. And for all his wit, for all his formidable powers of bullshit-spinning, he couldn't even figure out what the fuck was going on.

Tree trunks, thorny brush and slippery, sharp rocks battered him, but he was running ever faster and more recklessly, when he heard something coming after him.

The indistinct tree-shadows became stark silhouettes before him. He stumbled into a clearing painted brilliant yellow-white by the light mounted on the roof of Sprague's fortified cabin.

Andrew jumped over the row of steel feed tubs. In midair, he noticed the naked woman standing in the yard.

Andrew skidded to a stop just out of her reach. Even with her face turned away, he knew she was the lady from the lake.

Fiery red hair hung down over the left side of her face, but when she turned to open her arms to him, the black mass obscuring the rest of her head hummed and danced in the floodlight.

"Comrade," she buzzed, "do you serve the blessed hive of the state, or anarchy?"

Only yesterday, he saw one of those headless Bigfeet smash her skull in with a rock. The gaping cavity of her skull bulged with honeycombs, alive with dancing bees.

With a hive as a surrogate for her pulped, waterlogged brain, she had not so much recovered, as the bees had recovered her. In a livid, curling cloud, they spewed out of her right eye socket like a genie from a lamp.

"Do you serve the head or the hand?"

Which side are you on, my people?

Andrew looked away from her face, then away from her body, which still could stop traffic, even after the fish and the crawdads had gotten their fill of it.

Retreating back into the trees, he saw shadows moving to intercept him, just outside the light. He turned to run around the cabin, but a stitch in his side folded him over before he crossed the yard. "Mr. Sprague!" he breathlessly whimpered. "Help me!"

The naked woman crept up behind him, hissing, "Anarchist!" The bees formed a sword above her busy, hollow head.

Andrew staggered backwards, trying to get the cabin wall at his back, but he dropped to the dirt when a shotgun blast went off.

He rolled like he was on fire, ears ringing, thinking, *I'm shot, I'm dead, how do you like that shit?* He rolled over and over to flatten himself against the cabin.

The naked woman took another step, flapping jaws wheezing propaganda, but nothing above her nose remained. Orphan bees whirled in crippled orbits around her stumbling corpse until it finally toppled.

The windows were all boarded over. Andrew saw the shotgun aimed at him through a bolthole and froze with his arms grabbing sky. "Please don't shoot, it's me—"

"Get to the damned door, now!"

Andrew pulled the shreds of his shirt over his head and ran on all fours around the cabin. Bees alighted on him in flocks. He was stung on his back and belly and arms, but the orphan swarm was under attack by other bees. Just like at the trailer, just like these freaks, they were at war.

Batting away insect dogfights, crunching drifts of dead bees, Andrew circled the cabin and alighted on the porch, coughing his lungs halfway out his mouth.

The door swung open before he could knock. When he lurched inside, Sprague slammed and bolted it, cocked the shotgun and pointed it at him. His greasy, colorless hair was corkscrewed up like he'd been sleeping, and the bags under his eyes looked like mail sacks. "Which side got to you first, boy?"

What did he mean? The commune? The townies? May? The Bigfeet? The bees? "I don't know! I hate everybody right now! This whole fucking thing is fucking bullshit!"

Sprague didn't lower the gun, but let out an asthmatic cackle. "Good! You've been stung by both sides. Now you're ready to fight."

CHAPTER 17

AT FIRST, Dom had quantifiable reservations about his new family.

It was not so much that he had left one dysfunctional clan only to find himself in another, as he felt as if he'd rejoined the Army.

All his life, Dom had let a smile be his umbrella, *fake it 'til you feel it* his primary credo. If you were smiling, Mom's boyfriend didn't smack you to stop your crying; bullies and teachers figured you knew the score, and didn't single you out; girls figured you had all the answers, and gave it up.

Boot Camp Sarge didn't buy the smile, but eventually gave up trying to break him. Among the other recruits, wobbly saplings tied to the stout sticks of their rifles, Dom was the mighty oak who never broke. He made it look effortless, yet drove his CO insane with his inability to even pretend to give a shit. *Five miles, Sarge? Sure, if we can't do ten,* he'd say, knowing Sarge had his ass afire with hemorrhoids. It was all bullshit, the smile said. Nothing signifies. Everybody liked Pvt. Kowalski, the lovable fuckup.

Nobody at the big house was buying the smile. He felt like an idiot when he came in carrying the girl. The zombie tweaker let them in the front door. His head was bashed in, and shards of glass and wood stuck out of festering wounds all down his back. Bees buzzed in and out of his ears, and a gnarly antler of honeycomb protruded out of a hole in the base of his skull. Dom wondered if anything human still lived behind that toothless grin, and if the bees were just hitchhikers, or if they were filling in for the damaged brain. If they thought he'd sit still for that shit, they had another think coming.

Only a dozen comrades remained, and most of them were damaged. In less desperate times, they would all have become nursemaids or workers. The Tower had tried very hard to make them all soldiers. In large doses, the honey could totally reshape them in hours, but the first, rushed, indoctrinations didn't even produce a single viable worker, and the Tower was reluctant to try again. But it had other methods of throwing its weight around.

Dom caught hell in a way he couldn't shrug off, when he brought the girl up to the cells. Pain like a cloud of bees descended and stung him. He was getting used to the way the venom steered you when it got into your bloodstream, and bees could only sting you three, four hundred times, before you didn't feel it, anymore. But this was different. When he looked down, there were no bees. It was all in his mind, which only made it worse.

It was a chemical reprimand, a deluxe chewing-out and PT worse than pushups. Hot white agony throttled him as soon as he set the blonde down on a pallet. He sank to his knees and flopped like a landed catfish while it sank in.

He was not to kill, except to defend the Colony. He must learn discipline. He relived the murders inside out, soaking up the pain he dealt out in his first ecstatic burst of power. Dead and damaged converts were of limited use to the Colony. Was he so stupid, so selfish, that he would let the Colony die?

He hated himself. He wished himself dead. He was unfit as a soldier, a disease defiling the Colony when its survival was already uncertain, when the body itself had betrayed it and plunged the perfect state into internecine war.

"I'm sorry," he said, through jaws shivering as if he'd been doused in ice water. He wept for the fate of the Colony, and for those he'd killed. He was out of control. Someone should shoot him before he went rabid again.

Paralyzed, he looked up through tears at the tower. He felt the crushing weight of his interrogator relax just enough to let him speak.

"I want to do good, but I'm weak. I can't always figure out the right thing to do right away, and what the fuck do you expect? Look what's happening to me!"

He tried to raise his arm, but could barely make it twitch, though his forearm was thicker than his thigh with new muscle hard and knotty as heartwood from an oak. Stretched and strange on his overtaxed skin, his tattoos were fading under scabby gray layers of callus and warts.

His voice sounded weird, a basso rumble like massive stones grinding together that seemed to come from somewhere far south of his lungs. "Help me! Tell me what to do!"

The pain stopped. His whole body unclenched, tension bled away, pins and needles of blocked circulation pricking him inside and out. Dom sobbed with relief and started to get up, but the Tower wasn't done with him.

It wasn't a voice that spoke, or even words in his head. He felt the purposeful, authoritative weight on his mind, and in the blink of an eye, he simply knew what must be done.

They were outnumbered, outclassed and boxed in, but the enemy had limitations. They were dumber than a box of Polocks, and every day without leadership, they got dumber, going feral. Only one old man kept them alive. He fed them, protected them from the outside world. He had assassinated their queen, stolen a hive and turned it against the Colony. The traitors abducted and converted the hillbilly bitch who led him out here, snatched her away right under his nose, and had taken or damaged several of their most successful recruiters. No doubt the old pretender schemed to become the head of the Colony, himself.

With his eyes closed, Dom could see the old man and his shack, a panoramic mosaic compiled by thousands of diligent compound eyes. He saw the striking workers lurking in the shadows, waiting for feeding time like refugees from a ruined zoo.

And he gave a wordless, preverbal growl when he saw strikers carrying bodies through the woods. One of them, draped like a rag over the shoulder of a hulking, stub-headed marauder, was his brother Dean.

The old man abetted the traitors to prolong the strike, which he had almost certainly orchestrated from the start. With the old man liquidated, the strike would end, the body would be healed, and the Colony would be whole. Pain and pleasure in syncopated jolts nailed Dom to this wish.

And if the old man should prove too fragile to bring back whole and alive, so much the better.

A final shock galvanized Dom and sent him racing from the cell, where two hooded workers had begun to inspect the girl and feed her honey.

A handful of new recruits waited at the foot of the stairs. They looked at him with the same vacant expectation an old dog gets when it's time for a walk. Pathetic, scarcely begun to change, glaze-eyed vacationers and local rubes, but they carried guns, or else the guns carried them. Talk about your chickenshit outfits.

A few of them, he had to admit, had some sweet ordnance. The big bleach-job waitress from the Pond diner cradled a sawed-off 12-gauge; a tubby dittohead in overalls had a lever-action deer rifle, road flares and a rusty red gasoline can; a pimply teen who looked like he could pick a mean banjo with his toes had his granddad's vintage Garand M1 and a police revolver; the tweaker trio had a

Mossberg pump shotgun and a smart pair of Glock pistols that probably came from the Sexagon; but the one that knocked his dick in the dirt was an Ak-47 with a brace of extra banana clips on the shoulder sling, resting in the unworthy arms of a crosseyed kid in swim trunks and a life jacket.

"Too much gun for you, Alfalfa," Dom said as he took it from the kid's unresisting hands. Creepy, the way the kid's eyes just studied the upturned end of his nose, the vacant, lip-biting smile, like he was playing a videogame. Maybe in his head, he was. This was a lot of new shit to soak in, and Dom was all for whatever it took to make him a good soldier—*fake it 'til you feel it, little dude.*

A bee alit on Dom's cheek and did its waggle-dance for a moment before deciding on just the right spot to plant its stinger. The pain was less than a pinprick, and the message in the venom was worlds apart from the word of the tower.

Make your mother proud, Dominic. You were always my favorite.

They followed him out the door into the night, as silent and driven as the swarm of bees that led them through the woods to Sprague's cabin.

CHAPTER 18

FOR A LONG TIME, even after Andrew stopped hyperventilating, the old man only stared at him. He didn't demand an explanation, or scoff at the scatterbrained story of Deputy Scovill and the monster, when Andrew tried to stutter it out. He waited for Andrew to rattle to an exhausted stop, and only kept staring.

Finally, Andrew snapped, "What? Are you going to do something, or what?"

Sprague painfully stood and crabbed into the kitchen with the shotgun in the crook of his drumstick arm. He returned with a cup of steaming black tea. He resumed sitting and watching, waiting for Andrew to sprout horns or fart bees, or something.

The tea was strong and sweet, and though he preferred coffee, it seemed to unclench the laced fingers of tension around his heart. His pulse settled down so he couldn't hear it in his ears. Was he calming down, or going into shock? "I don't . . . don't care about what's happening, or why . . . I mean . . . you can do what you want, it's your lives. I just—I want to know . . . what this has to do with us . . . "

Sprague snorted. "You're here and human, that's all." He creaked out of his chair and switched off the lights. Andrew heard him shuffle over to the nearest window, which was, like all the others, boarded up. "You think the world's a playground, and you'll never have to fight for keeps. You've been living in a bubble, youngster."

Andrew wrapped both hands around the cup and stole the warmth from it. He felt very, very cold, except for his countless beestings, welts and scratches, which throbbed with a nuclear heat. The old man had plastered his injuries with some kind of waxy, herbal resin, which he called propolis. It itched like new skin growing, but he found the epileptic jangles of his thoughts spooling out in coherent sequences again. He felt entirely too calm; he couldn't even muster up the craving to smoke a cigarette.

He'd been lucky. Deputy Scovill, May and his brothers probably had not. He should feel guilty. He should feel glad. Worried about Dom and Dean, and his erstwhile mother-in-law. Something . . .

Sprague peered out a slot in the boarded window. The harsh floodlight glare from outside painted his craggy features in chiaroscuro relief. "The only perfect human society," he said, "is one alone, living in seclusion."

The sartorial, puffy tone of Sprague's voice snapped Andrew back to his college days. "Thoreau?"

"If he said it too, he was on the money." Sprague closed the drapes. "They were trying to do a great thing. Do you understand that? They were proud, idealistic people. They believed in the cause . . . and in mankind. They thought that if they could just do it right, the world would have to see, and it would change . . ."

Andrew's eyes had adjusted to the lambent darkness, fed by the low red glow of the potbellied stove in the corner, so that he dimly saw Sprague hobble back to his chair and sit with his shotgun across his knees. "The commune—the first one—had its problems, but I believe that for a time, there were no happier people on earth. We used to wish that the world would go away . . . not for them to die, but, if only we had a world of our own, if it had to start all over again with us, we could make it perfect . . ."

"You were there, then? That'd make you about, what, a hundred?"

Sprague leaned forward to warm his hands at the fire. "I was born there, you little shit. There were fourteen of us. I was the first. I grew up in that house, until the Colony broke down. Every man there was my father, every woman my mother, and all of them my teachers. I could read and quote Marx by my third birthday. Could you do that, young man?"

Andrew shrugged, feeling oddly smug and pleased with himself. He wondered what kind of herbs were in this propolis shit. "That's really impressive. How'd that work out for you, in the real world?"

"I was five before I saw anyone from the outside, and seven when I first saw a city . . . when the Colony dissolved."

Sprague looked as if he might begin to cry, so Andrew tried to cheer him up. "The house looks like a jail. What's the deal with that?"

"It was a sanatorium in the old days, but we didn't need to lock ourselves in. It was to keep the bastards out. You don't understand the times—"

"I think I know what a jail looks like, and I went to school. Not a fancy private communist school, but—"

"You've read a few books, but books are all lies, history most of all." Sprague's eyes glinted and he thrust out his chin. "Line up all the bad facts and dates and bury them alive, and they take the story that flatters them so they can feel good about the blood they stepped over to get power. They never let you see how uncertain it was to live in those days, those dates. What could have happened, and all the little things that did happen, that nobody wants to recall . . . ."

The old man leaned further, cocking the shotgun to command Andrew's attention. "Don't roll your eyes at me, junior. Nothing you can do out there now, and you won't help anyone if you don't know what you've walked into.

"In those days, the fat cats were terrified of the working man, and with good reason. They saw what happened to the Tsar. They knew that Socialism had roots in America. The men who built the unions banged their heads against the ignorance and fatalism of the worker, and faced the Pinkerton armies. They took beatings and shootings and bombings, and many died or got deported, or rotted in jail. They didn't do it to join the fat cats, or replace one tyrant with another. They saw it as the first step to creating a new world. There was a time when it looked like they just might succeed. People believed in it at first, but in a war, you stop fighting for anything, sooner or later, and fight just to fight.

"In the end, it didn't amount to much. The Wobblies started throwing bombs, and the FBI was created in '24 to hunt Anarchists and Reds, and they never missed a trick pissing on us in the press. The labor unions had to throw us overboard to get clout, and the New Deal was a soft revolution that stole our thunder for good and all. And there was no relief in the 'Worker's Paradise,' either, let me tell you. Even before Stalin, the writing on the wall was in the same peasant blood, as before. We were orphans in a land that hated us for trying to set them free."

Sprague sat silent for a long minute, adrift in bitter memories. Andrew thought of prompting him with another question, but held off. The old man talked about history before even he was born as if he'd lived it and bore its bitterness in his bones, absorbing it from a commune of outcasts from birth. Andrew still shivered with displaced adrenaline at the landslide of fucked up events that had thrown him here, but exhaustion and the stillness of the moment left him powerless. He sipped the sweet tea and stared into the fire.

"The movement needed a symbol, a guiding light to remind them what they were fighting for. Some still foamed at the mouth for revolution, and some threw their votes away for Debs or Sinclair, but a few hardheaded fools still believed that if they could just break away and start fresh, the world could see what a perfect state looked like, and maybe then, they might wake up.

"One hundred men and women sold what little they had, and pledged the money to buy the land. We lived in tents while we fixed up the old sanatorium, tilled the soil and put up a sawmill. Our only neighbors were the timber companies. They fought tooth and nail to kick us off, and they weren't above burning us out, even if it destroyed the forest they wanted to chop down. We had to build strong and defend ourselves, and we had to learn to live together.

"It looks like hell now, but in its time, it was full of laughter and songs . . . artists painting and sculpting, carpenters making furniture, everyone taking turns making food and clothes and all the things we shared . . .

"I was born during the work, in a tent in that clearing. It took over a year to finish it. By then, there were already rifts, and changes in the plan. I remember fights over the future, over large and little things.

"The leader, Sturtevant, never got his hands dirty with anything but ink, but he was a bully lecturer. Came out from Berkeley after he lost tenure over some flap at the science department. Everything according to scientific principles, but always, 'As above, so below.' If it was good enough for bees and ants, he said, it was good enough for us.

"He had the final say, but the group got fed up and put their loudest shouter at the head of them. Bart Dunlap was a union leader in Frisco. All they did was fight. Sturtevant had become another Lenin, a tyrant who relished his power too much, whom they blamed for all our misfortunes.

"In the end, he hardly ever came down from that tower. We put it up to watch for men from the timber company, trouble from outside, but there were . . . incidents, at night. Sturtevant decided we needed watching. He ripped off the roof, replaced it with bars and glass. He just sat up there, watching us through the night. He saw everything we did. I had nightmares about him, and thought he could see those, too.

"He said that until we all learned to give ourselves up

to the collective and stop fighting, he would not step down, and we would never become a true socialist state. If we were not born and raised in a capitalist system, we could take to it like ducks to water. We were all complacent, selfish babies without him, and would never progress without a hard hand.

"Each side blamed the other until they couldn't live together, and everyone walked away. Legally, Sturtevant owned the property, and he beat back every attempt to liquidate the collective. We walked away with our clothes and what we could carry. He hanged himself in the tower . . . "

"Listen, I'm sorry—"

Sprague banged the shotgun sharply on the arms of his chair. "You don't know enough to be sorry! Sorry is something you see on TV, that makes you feel guilty in your big plastic house with all your toys, and your rock concerts! Makes me sick to hear you young people whine like a bunch of baby birds, always screaming for more . . . " Now the old man's dander flared up, he sputtered angry Donald Duck noises in spasmodic misfires of anger. *Confound you young whippersnappers! Get off my lawn!*

"Sir," Andrew replied, "with all due respect to your shotgun, I didn't pick when and where I was born, and you have no idea how hard it is, today—"

"Hard! You have no idea what hard is! When I was a boy, they told me the revolution was already won, God damn it! All men were brothers, all women sisters, and all shared the toil and wealth, as a family should. Then he kicked us out, and I found out it was all a lie.

"We lived in camps, rode the rails, followed the crops up and down the state. We got beat and robbed, thrown in jails, but we did not scab! We went to work where we could, and we struck with the workers, and that's how I got these scars, boy. And I'm not a fucking bit of sorry. It's still and always will be a rich man's goddamned world, but I did my part to fight the inevitable."

Peace of a sort stole over Sprague's crumpled scowl. "And when I got too old to work and too tired to fight, I came back here. It's peaceful. No more strikes and speeches, no more running and hiding . . . just the wind in the trees, and the birds and the beasts, and only my ears to hear them. At the end, it felt like the answer, at last. One man, in seclusion. Utopia, at last.

"And then, about a year ago, they came."

"Those things out there?"

Sprague angrily snapped open the shotgun and fished in his shirt pocket. "Damn it, they're not things!"

"Whatever they are, they're not human . . . not even close." In his head, Andrew felt like he was tumbling down rapids, trying to hold onto anything that felt solid. "Those . . . people of yours killed a cop and dragged a girl into the woods. They probably did the same to my mother-in-law, and every one of your neighbors. They don't look like people, and they sure as hell don't act like people . . . and you're feeding them! Who the hell are they?"

"They're the Proletariat. The New Leviathan commune. They were young, idealistic people who believed, just like we did. But they took it too far. They changed. They became perfect workers, but they were still too human to escape the troubles. Their leader is still too human, by far."

"And that . . . lady . . . outside." *The one with the beehive hairdo* . . . "She looked a lot more human than the others, and you wasted her."

"She's a scab and a spy," Sprague said irritably, as if Andrew had missed the obvious. Wincing with pain, he pinched the spent shells out of the breach and replaced them with fresh ones. "When the workers went on strike, the Tower tried to recruit scabs. She brings their loyalist bees to propagandize and probe our defenses. I've worked up an immunity, but they're still a damned nuisance. And she's just a scout. They'll come back before dawn."

Andrew jumped out of his chair and started for the door. "Then let's get out of here now!"

Sprague pointed the shotgun at Andrew and cocked the hammer. "Sit down, son. There's nowhere you can get to, that's safer than where you are."

Andrew pondered how serious the old man was about shooting him. At this distance, he could cut Andrew in half with his eyes closed. And it wasn't as if he knew where to run. He patted down his pockets. His phone was gone. He sat down.

"When I heard that someone was coming to form another commune, I didn't believe it, but I tried. I wanted for someone to get it right, and on that spot, where there was so much hope, at first, maybe they could succeed.

"I didn't like Grodenko from the start. He was a big political philosopher over in Russia, and some big pinko money brought him here and set up the new commune on the QT. He was an asshole, but he got people to believe he shat roses. Immigrants, mostly; Russians, Ukrainians, some Poles . . . and a lot of scientists. There was a kind of cult around him, just like there was around Sturtevant. I saw the same cracks right at the outset . . .

"But they had worked the problem and came to the same answer I had, because they tried, in seclusion, to become one man. They didn't get there, but they went way too far, to turn back."

"Those things . . . "

"The Proletariat. Commune workers, fractured along the same lines as before. He took all their power, their minds, but he wouldn't join them. He sits up there in his tower, haunting the house and gathering scabs to rule over, but he'll wither and fade. The head and the hand are at war. The hand can grow a new head quicker than the head can grow a whole new body.

"Maybe it was the ghost of the old failure that spoiled it, or maybe it's just the nature of mankind. But they are so much less than men, now. They need a new leader, or they'll die, and he will win."

"What made them change? The beestings? What're they, magic bees?"

Sprague's scowl returned. His knurled hands wrung a groan from the stock of the shotgun. "And I thought you were a smart boy."

"It's impossible. Radiation doesn't do that . . . and genetics—"

"I don't know or care much for gene therapy and retroviruses, but that's how they said they did it. Bullshit, says I. They changed because they wanted to. Haven't you ever wanted something so much, it changed you?"

Andrew thought of Lamarck, and then of Laura, and suddenly couldn't meet the old man's eyes.

"You're a smart boy, alright. And you want to change, even if you don't know into what. I hope that'll be enough."

Andrew looked into his empty teacup. A dollop of half-dissolved honey dripped from the bottom. The feverish heat of his wounds consumed him down to the core. His stomach turned itself inside out, but somehow, he couldn't gag, couldn't expel the poison.

"That's the worst thing about war, young man. The terrible symmetry. The other side does some dastardly, evil thing, you have to do it, too."

A crack and pop outside sent Sprague back to the viewing slot. "What happened?" Andrew demanded. "What's going on out there?"

"Bastards shot out the light." Sprague peered out into the dark and raised the shotgun, fired twice at nothing, and hunkered down to reload.

Something slammed into the back wall. A shelf fell and sprayed books across the floor.

Scrabbling and pounding went up the wall and across the roof, stopping directly above where Andrew sat.

"Old man! Come out, or we'll burn you out!" It was a booming voice, flat and bright as if through a bullhorn, and utterly sure of itself. Dom's voice.

Andrew stuck his finger down his throat. Maybe he could make himself throw up. But he'd had some honey in his coffee here, only yesterday.

Dom's stomping tread crossed the roof in two mighty, shack-shaking bounds. A metallic squeal that must be Dom ripping open the chimney. A gout of fluid splashed on the bed of embers in the stove. Puffs of sulfurous smoke gushed out into the room. He'd pissed down the chimney, but something in his urine made the fire rear up with toxic gusto, blazing green and spilling out onto the floorboards.

Dom's stomping war dance shook loose a splintered roofbeam that missed Andrew's head by inches. Coughing and retching, Sprague hobbled to the stove, aimed and fired at the ceiling.

Andrew rolled out of his chair and ran from the room, ripping down the Soviet flag and heading for the nearest open door. He shouldered the door shut behind him and dropped onto a toilet seat.

Looking down at his shoes, muddy and bristly with burrs and thorns, he tried to will himself to be calm. Next to the toilet was a stack of old *Mother Jones* and *International Worker* magazines, which Sprague apparently used in lieu of toilet paper.

What would Dean Do? Dean would not freak out. Dean was an asshole, but he would keep his powder dry and not go off half-cocked, and all those clichés, and then he would sit down and make a punch-list. Yes, Andrew would do that. He stared intently at his shoes, now, and tried to figure out the Next Thing on his punch-list.

The scabs were outside. Dom was one of them. None of it made a lick of sense, but every time he thought he could deny it and wish it away, the situation got worse and tried to kill him.

Okay, think. What's the Next Thing? What are you going to do?

He felt a weird, warm euphoria in his belly, a languid

voice that told him, *relax*. All was as it should be, and good things would happen if he just stayed put, or maybe went to sleep until it was all over. Maybe this was shock, or maybe it was something worse.

Two walls of the bathroom were draped with black muslin curtains. He hadn't seen any windows that weren't boarded up when he came running in, but he would get out, if he had to pull nails with his teeth.

He turned to lock the door, but of course there was no lock, why would a hermit need to lock himself in his own bathroom?

He heard Sprague fumble with a latch and snap a padlock on the bathroom door. "Stay in there, and don't make trouble. You'll be safe." The doorknob turned, but the door didn't budge.

Trouble? Don't make trouble? Oh, he'd make trouble, alright.

Andrew ripped down the curtain. Almost in the same dramatic motion, he screamed, wrapped himself in the curtain and tripped over the toilet trying to back away.

There were no windows. The two curtained walls were floor-to-ceiling plexiglass, set in about two inches from the timber and crumbling plaster wall.

It was an observation hive, the biggest he'd ever seen. Tens of thousands of bees toiled over an expanse of honeycomb that filled the gap and spread across the wall like a mathematical fungus. Armadas of drones waggled and danced at the fringe near the ceiling, darting in and out of a gap at the top, which must lead outside.

To cut through the log walls, he'd need a chainsaw. To get through the bees, he'd need a flamethrower. He sat and clenched himself tight and tried to think of a less impossible Next Thing to do.

The teeming, festering industry behind the glass, pure and unstoppable as the hunger of sharks or fire, made him snap inside and drove him to the door. Pounding on the solid oak only bruised his fists, but he beat them until they bled, screaming, "Open this fucking door, Sprague! Let me out of here, you crazy motherfucker!"

But Sprague couldn't hear him for all the shooting.

CHAPTER 19

At LONG LAST, Dean knew peace.

He felt love. He swam in it, flew through it, ate it and shed it like radiation back to the collective.

For a time beyond measure, he ate and slept and made love to all of the women—and, in his enhanced, unhinged state, more than one of the men—in his cell. When he was spent, they fed him honey, nothing but honey, and then more honey. He choked on it, but forced it down and opened his mouth like a baby bird for more. Stuffed to bursting, he burned it all up fucking and sleeping, blackout catnaps that left him sore like he'd worked out with weights, and ravenous for more of everything. But it was not a senseless orgy. With each meal, with every coupling, came deeper understanding.

This was not his destiny, but only a transition; not a cell, but a cocoon. Until today, he thought he was the shit: an outstanding badass Navy officer, a warrior for Christ, devoted husband and father. Until tonight, he was a maggot. A larva. Nothing and nobody, lost in his own sham of self-importance, chasing a ghost of security. Now, he was *becoming*.

The collective was divided, dying. The Colony was under attack. He would become what it needed most. A defender.

He could tell by the inferior grade of honey given to the other men that they were to be workers. Gradually, the stink of them became repulsive, and a measure of his ecstatic universal love was shed like the booster of a rocket. If only the Colony could have found more able-bodied, tough-minded men . . . but given time, they could make them.

While the Colony was equality incarnate, because of the emergency, all of the fertile women had become breeders—Hero Mothers, in the Colony's darkest hour. Dean couldn't get enough of them, nor they of him. Their silken bellies were swollen with equal parts honey and semen. He could feel the ingredients reacting inside them, and in himself, strange vibrations and stranger silences, as of the body holding its breath at a cellular level, before leaping into a drastic structural change.

When the changes finally came, they sighed and fainted, but twitched and squirmed in their changing skins, dreaming, becoming. Some parts visibly withered, while others ripened and burst forth in brash new forms. The Colony was finding the best use for each of them, and making them its own.

Dean awoke from a feverish sleep when he heard squealing and smelled a fear-fog of worker-urine throughout the sawmill.

A runt of a soldier stalked by the open door, booming sea lion barks echoing after its thunderous footfalls. Dean's body wanted to go back to sleep, but he pummeled it into alertness, strained to get a sense of what was happening.

The miasma of messages was confused, conflicted. It warned of abandonment, chaos, famine and bloodshed, but the cause was a knot of mangled rumor.

He heard the soldiers' guttural croaks join in a chorus, whipping themselves into a fury. The whole mill trembled with their bestial roars of defiance.

The Colony was under attack! His heart sang to join them. His voice was an asthmatic hyena howl, but he found the strength to reach a crooked brick wall and climb it to stand upright, push through the unguarded door and out to the starlit gallery where the soldiers huddled.

There were six. The smallest stood seven feet tall, the largest almost twice Dean's height. In the silver-blue glow dripping down through the shattered roof, their bone spurs and knotted piston limbs took away any sense that they were men, or even animals. Machines forged by a bloody-minded war god, they embodied absolute violence, even in repose.

They did not deign to notice him as he wobbled out into the open. He had only just begun to become one of them. They gave one final blistering collective shout and streaked out of the sawmill in a tight pack.

Dean ran after them. A worker stepped in his way, but when Dean barked wordless outrage at it, the lowly creature bowed and backpedaled with submissive paws upraised.

Out in the night, with the warm wind on his bare skin, he felt as if his transformation was complete. If Dom could see him now, he would shit himself and run crying for Mom.

Shameful, that such childish junk still cluttered his brain. Like he never could before, he simply wiped it away. His mind became a crystal prism, and the world rushed through it, almost blinding him with the rich new spectrums of detail he must always have missed for thinking about it, yet somehow absorbing and responding and carrying him as fast as his new legs could on the trail of the soldiers.

The scent of them led him along the forested border of the meadow where the big house loomed and plotted, and the fields lay ravaged and untilled. Over rolling ridges and down reckless slopes, he ran like he carried the game-winning pigskin. Only briefly did it strike him strange that they were running from their home to defend it. The scent of imminent peril was undeniable. They were scared, so he was scared, but he could not afford to let it overwhelm him. He would crush his fear, and then he would crush the enemy, wherever and whatever it was.

He heard shooting, and screams. Soldiers called off with clipped, almost subsonic growls from the undergrowth as they circled the little four-room log cabin on the bluff.

Dean raced up to the weedy backyard clearing with his heart thumping in his throat, leaned against a tree and tried to catch his breath. A bullet whizzed past him and chipped off a branch just below his ear. He ducked and covered his head. He felt hot blood flush his face, making his head swim. Nobody said anything about guns . . .

Unfuck yourself, sailor! Screamed his reactive brain. *Wars are fought with a varied arsenal of weapons, but mostly guns. What kind of fight did you think this was going to be? This isn't Wild Kingdom.* But his fellow soldiers had no guns, and seemed not to know what they were.

From cover, he scented the trails of the workers all around him. He saw a row of tin tubs like feeding troughs for grazing livestock, and three bodies out in the open yard. Two were unenhanced scabs, infested with angry bees, but the third was a true worker. It flipped itself over and tried to drag its leaking bulk back home, but a wild volley of automatic rifle fire strafed it. The worker wheezed in resignation, but kept crawling. Dean ached to do something, but fear choked him. He was still becoming. What was he doing out here?

A soldier ran across the lawn, its balls-out loping stride like that of an Olympic long-jumper. It was like a bucking bronco, or a successful missile launch, a thing of terrible beauty unleashed as a brief but absolute demonstration of pure, precise force.

It should've gone right up the wall of the cabin and taken out the shooter on the roof, but the muzzle-flashes lit up the soldier before it could even reach the dying worker. The bullets didn't stop it, but blowing fist-sized chunks of flesh out of its torso threw off its gait, so when it finally crossed the yard and sprang for the roof, it was so much unmanned flying meat. Still, the soldier fought for every inch of roof, forcing the shooter to empty the clip point-blank into it, before it sagged and dropped to the ground.

Dean trembled with rage. Cowardly bastard!

The forest shook with the barks and hoots of enraged soldiers on the move. Dean collected himself and prepared to join them.

"Traitor!" screamed someone behind him. Dean pushed off the tree and felt the steel heat of a buckshot blast parting his hair. Prone on the ground, he tensed and cast about him for the enemy.

A big blonde woman in a filthy waitress uniform sighted him down the stubby barrel of her shotgun. Bees swirled around her like berserk electrons, but she stood queerly still, like she awaited further orders from headquarters. Her lumpen bulk and the way she leered and lorded over him reminded him of someone he'd always wanted to kill.

Please, Lord, he prayed. *Make me hard.*

He was all over her before she could pull the trigger again. His forearm slammed into her collarbone and drove up under her chins. Despite her impressive girth and wide linebacker's stance, his charge threw her off her crepe-soled loafers and laid her out on the rocky soil.

Dean threw all his weight behind his forearm and crushed her larynx. His toes dug into the ground and his knees pinned her to the ground.

The shotgun clanged off his skull time and again, but he hardly noticed. Hiccupping blood in his face, she bucked him halfway off and tried to turn over, but he pushed harder, harder, until he heard something in her wattled neck decouple and snap free, like a big Thanksgiving drumstick coming off the bird.

It wasn't enough. This scab bitch tried to kill him, his brothers and sisters. He found a rock that he had to lift with both hands, and raised it high. If he knew in his heart that this was not Mom, it did not diminish his 4th Of July glee one iota when he brought the rock crashing down on the enemy's fat, repulsive face. Or the next time, or the third . . .

More shooting, more screams, recalled him to the moment. A loyal soldier, its vocal pitch soaring with the agony of failure, tumbled from the roof, but another clipped the shooter's legs out from under him with a sweeping arm. The gun went off again, punching the soldier back and illuminating the pained but still smiling face of the coward killing Dean's true family.

"DOMINIC!" Dean pried the shotgun out of the dead waitress's surprisingly sturdy grip. He could not wipe away the inborn fury, now, and did not try. His anger was a gift. He lovingly unwrapped it.

A husky good old boy in deer hunting camo broke from cover and hustled across the open to the back wall of the cabin. A shotgun poked out of a slot in a boarded window and opened up. The hunter's left arm came away at the elbow, but he dove and dropped against the wall under the shotgun and knelt over a big red gas can.

Dean came across the lawn in three strides at an angle so the inside shotgun couldn't hit him. Bullets criss-crossed the space around him so slowly he could almost see what caliber they were. He put the shotgun up the unsuspecting arsonist's nose and pulled the trigger. The headless scab flopped on his back and let out a hellacious fart by way of an epitaph.

Dean collected himself and tried to compile a mental punch list. Storm the roof; disarm and/or neutralize the enemy; fuck the enemy's eyesockets until the break of dawn.

"Hey, weak twin, what're you waiting for?" Dom sprayed a salvo into the roof. Dean heard someone inside yell for help. The voice sounded familiar.

Dean flattened against the wall. "I'm waiting on you to fight like a man, you fucking yellow pussy!"

"You are what you eat," Dom replied.

Dean took a deep breath, centered himself, and lobbed the gas can into the air.

"Gotcha!" Dom crowed, and fired.

Dean was looking right up at it when it exploded. A ragged high-noon sun popped overhead and lit up the yard way back into the trees. Dean saw the soldiers and scabs frozen in animal wonder at the sudden, blinding lightshow, until a flying wedge of shrapnel sliced his scalp to the bone.

He heard Dom cry out, "Ow, fuck me!" Dean reflexively covered his head, but forced himself to leap and grab the eaves of the roof before the fiery rain had fallen from the sky.

Dean's head popped up and surveyed the roof. He saw only a litter of blood and shells on the slanted plain, but when he turned and looked up at the sky, he saw Dom's lopsided grin as his twin swooped down out of the air and planted a Size 13 steel-toed workboot in Dean's mouth.

Whipped off the roof like a swatted fly, Dean flew head over heels and crashed to earth in a puddle of burning gasoline. He bounced with the rippling shockwave of his brother jumping off the roof.

Rolling, rolling, spreading the hungry, licking flames, Dean tried to get closer to Dom where he landed, to get under his rifle and grapple it away from him.

Dom tossed the rifle away, another toy that bored him. "Okay," he sneered, "let's fight like men." He yawned and popped his knuckles, swatted away angry bees. "Waste of bullets, anyway."

Dean smothered the last tongues of fire, but now, he was ablaze with doubt.

Dom had changed, too.

He looked taller than when they last fought. About thirty pounds heavier, too, and none of it fat, as if he had undergone a second puberty in the last few hours. Blisters, singed hair and shreds of embedded metal marred his face and chest, but none of it seemed to faze him.

Had all the changes Dean underwent been only in his mind? Dom always could make Dean feel small when he wanted, but Dean was literally dwarfed, a stunted beanpole next to his twin.

Dom took a hesitant, staggering step away from Dean, as if he'd already forgotten the whole thing, but then rounded and bent down to look him in the eye. "Oh, almost forgot," he said. "Mom said to say hi."

Then he hit him.

Once, when he was a high school junior, Dean got hit by a car. He was out running after dark, in the hills around home. An early drunk driver whipped around a corner on the wrong side of the road with his lights out, and knocked him sprawling across the hood of a parked car.

The driver got out and mumbled some slurred Spanish, looked around for witnesses, and then sped away, leaving Dean rolling and cursing through tears that, in America, some worthless welfare puke could do such harm, and then just amble away scot-free.

The outrage and the shame were about the same, now. The pain and the damage were much worse.

Dom's fist tunneled into his gut like a mortar shell. Spiny knuckles shredded skin and muscle. A tidal surge of blood and fluid evacuated his devastated bowels, splashed out mouth and asshole as he tumbled onto his back and rolled end over end across the grass. Dean stifled a monsoon of sobbing. He was still a man, and men did not cry.

"Crybaby, crybaby, whatcha gonna do?" Dom sneered, "when your big, bad brother comes beatin' on you?" He stalked around Dean's crumpled form like a sumo wrestler, cracking himself up.

What the hell is happening? Dean demanded of himself. He had been reborn, rebuilt and sent out naked and invincible as a Spartan helot, but Dom had sided with the enemy, and instantly put him in his place. "Fuck you, you evil fuck," was all he could say.

"Don't hate me 'cos you ain't me," Dom replied, and kicked him in the face.

Though he threw up his arm lightning-fast to block or even trap Dom's foot, the blow whipsawed him off the ground. The air rushing all around him shivered with Dom's whooping laughter and cry, "AND THE KICK IS GOOD!"

Dean hit a tree square between his shoulder blades, slithered down to curl around it like a wet rag. Dean tried to pray for strength, but he lacked the strength. Dom came closer, eyes wide with mock-concern. "Did wittle brother fall down? What's Mommy gonna say?"

The tree wrapped itself around him and lifted him up. He lolled on the branches, helpless, trembling. His splintered ribs jabbed every breath. His mouth was a junkyard of loose and shattered teeth, bloody gums and tattered tongue. He couldn't breathe through his nose, or see through his right eye. Somehow, the words got out of his mouth, and even if they sounded like a bloody mush of nonsense, his twin still understood. "I'm worth ten of you, Dominic. You never had to work for anything. I earned what I got."

"Yeah, you paid for yours," Dom admitted, flexing his monstrous arms, "but I got mine for free."

The tree pushed Dean upright and shoved him at Dom. It was a soldier. His brothers—his real brothers—had his back. Dean rushed his twin and threw punch after punch at his face and abdomen, screaming as he pounded away, "You stole everything! You were a freak! You never should've happened! You joined up with them just to fight me, because you've never had anything in your life but fucking with me, and you never will! You're not even a man! You're just my shadow!"

The volume, if not the force, of the attack set Dom back on his heels. He made no attempt to defend or cover himself, but just soaked it up like he had to be reminded why he ought to get off his lazy ass and finish this fight. In the end, it was Dean who stopped, when something under his arm dislocated and tore, and he felt all the desperate strength leak out of him.

He sagged against Dom in a boxers' clinch for a moment, then danced away before those enormous fists could catch him, but they didn't come. Dean wobbled and barely stood upright, mopping blood and sweat out of his good eye.

Dom took a step towards him, the throat-slash smile going sour on his face, finally at a loss for a snappy comeback. Bees settled on his head and shoulders in a buzzing, stinging hood, stopping him in his tracks. His eyes defocused like he was taking a phone call. A soldier clotheslined him, kicking with its serrated spurs at him as he fell and opening a rip that filleted his thigh to his knee.

The cabin was burning, but it still stood. Workers swarmed out of the trees to stamp the flaming grass and smother the burning timbers with their massive paws. The battle was over. The enemy was routed. The realization was like puppet strings holding Dean upright, skinning his split lips back in a feral grin. They had won.

Dom rolled to his feet and looked around, saw no one standing with him, and three soldiers closing him in. "Oh, I see how you are, now," he said. Retreating to the trees, herded by the soldiers, who seemed to be holding back out of deference to Dean, Dom pointed and jeered until he was out of sight. "All that God-bothering America-hoorah talk you lorded over me for all my life, but you join up with these pinko dead-enders. Are they giving out free pussy? I might just sign up, if they're desperate enough to take you."

Dean laughed. "You have to believe, bad twin. You have to want to change. And I know you can't."

From the shadows, Dom laughed even harder. Always the last word. "Oh well . . . I got it pretty good now, anyway. Next time, maybe you'll be bigger, but so will I. I'll always be able to whomp you, but I won't kill you until Mom says I can."

The hateful name yanked on Dean's frayed strings. "Where is she?"

"In the big house, little brother. She got born again, too. You should see her. She's everybody's mom, now. Everybody's but yours."

"God damn you!" Dean howled. "God damn you to Hell!"

A soldier swiped at the trees and chased after Dom, but he was gone, limping at breakneck speed into the darkened woods.

Dean tried to walk, but his legs failed him. Another tree caught him and carried him away. This time he did not fight, but gratefully went limp, and succumbed to dreams.

CHAPTER 20

From *A Manifesto & Chronicle of the New Leviathan Colony*, by Dr. Leon Sturtevant, PhD.

The idea was so simple, that Nature discovered it soon after life itself began on earth. Or rather, it was the first step, but it hardly came quickly; for millions of empty years, single-celled anarchy rampaged across the earth. The pressure to adapt and conquer the newborn world drove a renaissance of innovation, but Nature wasted her fledgling powers on destruction, and left only fossils visible under a microscope.

That first crucial step towards complexity came when single cells learned to cooperate. United, the toiling masses of cells specialized and diversified into organs, even as their descendants diversified into discrete species, all parts subordinated to the common good of the body, and they thrived.

With specialization came the strategic importance of centralized vital organs, without which the organism would die. These elite cadres of cells cultivated their elevated status to consolidate their power and gorge themselves on oxygen and nutrients while the body toiled and sacrificed.

Once sown, the seeds of inequality spread and made predatory tyrants of the "higher" animal kingdoms, while the oldest, the simplest, pursued the most enlightened cooperative societies.

As above, so below—as with the internecine class warfare in every complex living creature, and the parasitic inequality of the stratified food chain, so with the self-proclaimed crown of creation, humankind.

With the advent of true self-awareness, a cardinal paradox arose, for man was never so blind to the evolutionary imperative of true communism, as when he began to think. Endlessly proclaiming, *I am*, he wallowed in the empty luxuries of the self, and vacillated between hibernation in pointless contemplation of the cosmic indifference of God, and rabid spasms of wanton violence which put the divine cruelty of his most bloodthirsty pagan deities to shame.

Human society obtusely mimicked the strata and rhythms of the animal kingdom it conquered. Big fish ate little ones, scavengers feasted on the wreckage, and everywhere, gentle messiahs were hunted and devoured for the crime of defying the sanguinary gospel of predator and prey. Divided by nations, religions and cultures, they celebrated difference by hating it, never seeing that they were not only one race, but one body, one living being rending itself asunder.

Because they could not be made to see the threat—not only to their own survival, but to the balance of life on earth—in their fearful and selfish greed, they had contained or killed off all species that might succeed them, and degraded the earth into a charnel house. If they could only be made to live as One—

Some scattered cells of the body politic have tried to awaken the human animal to throw off the chains of its flawed nature, but their techniques for unifying the people were crude and, in the end, always fell back on violence. The inequality in the system ran deeper than the noblest schemes for perfecting the human herd. Tyranny lives in every cell. The current bourgeois social models have only incubated new and more ruthless species of it.

PERFECT UNION

Tragically, even revolutionary communism as practiced in Russia has not proved immune to the decay of human evolution. Those who set themselves as the Head of the new proletarian state never set down their whips, never truly shared in the pains and labors of the Body they tried to rule. The People gave their hearts and their minds, and became the arms and legs of the Body; but the Head could not surrender its selfish *I am* fantasies.

The Body, deprived of the sense that the Head took for granted, could not accept that the Head did not take its turn as the hands and feet, could not grasp that the Head toiled also, or that the sweat of the brow was as hard-won as that of the back or the arms. Time and again, the grand experiments failed. Headless Bodies stumbled and starved; severed Heads faded or fled to wither in history's shadow. For it has forgotten the truth of the maxim that has ever fed the fires of revolution: WOE UNTO THE SHEPHERDS WHO FEED NOT THEIR FLOCKS.

Never has debased humanity come closer to reproducing the ideal division of labor as it has in this place, at this time. Never has its hope and faith in pure communism been more clear-eyed or devout. Nowhere have united cells of men given more deeply of themselves to the good of the lumpen Body, in order to awaken it to the real possibility of a human Utopia.

For true Communism is impossible, in any human society. The salvation of Man and Nature is not to be found in the doctrines of Marx or Lenin and the Soviet Comintern, but in the radical overthrow of the human ego in every head and heart, and an absolute revolution based upon the perfect Utopia whose unheeded lessons buzz at my window as I write this.

I speak, of course, of the life of the Hive.

CHAPTER 21

"**C**OME OUT, BOY. It's safe, but we have to hurry."

Andrew was wound up so tight that he threw himself at the door the moment it opened. Sprague blocked him, but the old man had his arthritic hands full with the shotgun and padlock. Andrew easily shouldered him aside.

His eyes burned. The living room was a boundless cavern of inky dark, obscured by stagnant smoke that parted reluctantly as he waved his arms. Was the cabin on fire?

Boiling panic sent him six directions at once, but he couldn't find the door. The fire had gone out, and the only illumination came from bulletholes in the roof. Sprague boarded up the last windows when he was in the bathroom.

He'd heard shooting and hammering from within, and shooting and shouting from without, but the shouting scared him the most, because the voices were familiar. Dom and Dean were out there, and they had changed, but they had not changed at all: they were just intensified. All things considered, he was probably safer here in the burning cabin.

Three miles to town. It was only three miles to Utopia; even he could walk that far. Three miles through mountainous pine forest in the dark, with those hulking, murderous things out there, lunatics with guns, and his brothers . . .

"Where can we go? Where are we safe?" His brain

ached like it was swelling up with a fever and pressing on the walls of his skull, an egg ready to hatch. When did it get so fucking cold? "Nowhere, nowhere is safe . . . "

"They're gone," Sprague said. He shuffled out of the hall with the shotgun crooked in his arm. "They came here to kill you, and they'll be back."

"Why me? What the fuck did *I* do to them?"

Sprague took a baling hook from the wall and bent painfully at the knees, tiny gunshot pops, and hooked a ring in a floorboard. "Not what you did, nor what you are." He hauled a square trapdoor up out of the floor and leaned the shotgun against it. The square of opaque darkness at his feet greedily inhaled the smoke. "What you will be."

"You poisoned me! Son of a bitch, you drugged me? With that honey?" He grasped, way too late, the meaning of the bees inked on Dom's skin, the roaring beasts with his brothers' voices outside. All of them had been touched and were starting to change, claimed by one side or the other in this insane siege. "Why did you have to drag us into it? What do you need us for?"

Sprague turned to look at him, and though no light could cut through the smoke, a lambent yellow glow seeped from the old man's eyes. "It's gone too far to stop, now. Grodenko wants them back, or dead, and he'll just start over. He thinks the body of the state is his body, but he's not a god, yet. He can be stopped."

"I don't care about stopping anybody. I don't care about these . . . things, or people, whatever . . . I just want to go home to my . . . my wife . . . " Even as he said it, the untruth of it slipped through his hands like eels. He had nowhere else to go, did he? Nobody cared; nobody needed or wanted him around. Dizzy and half-sunk into shock, he knew that safety lay in being needed, and someone needed him very badly. Alone, he was nothing . . .

"They'll protect you," Sprague said, "until you can protect them." He took out a flashlight and, with much lip-biting and hissing, strapped it to the shotgun barrel with a roll of duct tape. "When you become what they need you to be. You're their last and only hope."

"Then they're even more fucked than we are."

The old man shrugged, as if he knew that quite well, but then he turned on the flashlight and aimed it at Andrew's eyes. "Now get in the hole."

The tunnel was not much bigger than an animal's burrow. The floor was fouled with loose rocks and puddles of scummy water. The walls scraped Andrew's shoulders and the uneven, root-festooned roof bumped his head, but he hurried, holding the last burning breath he'd taken in the cabin as long as he could.

Andrew was not claustrophobic, but his fear spiraled out of control every time the damp earth crumbled under his questing hands and tumbled in showers down his back. The dripping water—from the septic tank?—the feathery touch of dangling roots on his face, like cobwebbed fingers, made him want to scream.

The creeping certainty that any moment, a sudden sound or motion would bring the tunnel down prodded him fumblingly on, even as it became a certainty that they would never reach the end. At least it preoccupied and protected him from a hidden, half-hearted idea he didn't dare frame in his mind—that when he broke out of the tunnel, he must try to escape.

Sprague wheezed and faltered with every step, but kept close behind Andrew. The flashlight beam slashed the ground just before his feet, disorienting rather than guiding him, making the dark before him like a wall of coal. The first glimpse of a faint gray light at the end of the tunnel, Andrew let his breath out and inhaled the sour air of the tunnel. He smelled the spiky tang of pine pollen, and felt a chill current of fresh air stirring against his face.

Sprague turned off the flashlight. Andrew rubbed his eyes, but they would not adjust, and only filled the dark with elaborate phantoms. He seemed to wallow in a bog of mottled purple phosphene worms. Vertigo overtook him, sending him stumbling over roots and rocks. At last, he saw moonlight through the trees.

The tunnel let them out into a tiny hollow screened by granite boulders and mesquite brush. They couldn't be more than a couple hundred yards from the cabin, but Andrew had no idea where to run, even if he could. Nowhere was safe.

The old man crept by Andrew and maneuvered out of the hollow by creeping sideways among the jumbled, lichen-furred rocks.

Andrew was afraid to move before his eyes adjusted. If everything would just slow down, he could get a grip on his fear, but he recognized the treacherous wheedling voice that had pinned him under the bed in May's trailer when he could have run, before it was too late. It was much too late now, he knew, but he had to keep moving.

Sprague leaned against a fallen log, halfway up a slippery ridge with no trail. Andrew almost busted a lung catching up to him, painfully aware of how much more fit the old man was. *Boy, I'm gonna be sore, tomorrow.*

A fresh squirt of hot, unadulterated pain, like a lifetime of New Year's hangovers, wracked his brain. The murky earth went shaky under him, the moon and stars turned cartwheels. He stumbled into Sprague, who caught him with a grunt and shoved him upright.

"Fuck, fuck, fucking fuck!" Andrew whispered. Each curse seemed to release a little of the pressure roiling in his skull. His ears popped like he'd just come down from cruising altitude in a jet. Something was wrong with him. Though his vision bulged and the colors bled, he blinked and rubbed his eyes until they could focus, and he saw that the log was not a log at all.

Sprague dripped tears on the freakishly huge corpse. His knurled hands stroked the blunt turret of its head like a blind man searching to close a corpse's eyes. He turned his flashlight on and off, on and off like a nervous tic, or like he was signaling someone. "I think this one was named Marcus," he said, "when they had names. He came from Gdansk. Short-tempered, liked to drink, but he was a good worker. He fought hard and gave his life for the cause."

The dead worker's skin was dull gray and wrinkled like an elephant's, padded with thick plates of horny callus like a rhino's, where it was not ruptured by bulletholes and splashed with blood, shiny and black in the moonlight.

It looked unreal, because it had no eyes, ears, or nostrils, only the gaping mouth at the apex of its neck-stump. Andrew noticed rows of open cysts around the mouth, like a garland of tiny, blood-red desert flowers poking up out of the spiny skin of a cactus. The wounds did not appear fresh, nor did they look like wounds at all, come to that. The inflamed, petal-rimmed cysts resembled experimental sensory or sex organs. But his first impression had been closest. They looked like little cactus flowers, and the bees still alit on them.

Clever design—they could transmit their venom-messages without ripping out their stingers. It reminded Andrew of all those pointless arguments with Dean about evolution over Sunday barbecue. Eyes showed intelligent design, Dean repeated over and over; nobody ever got anywhere with ten percent of an eye. Andrew wasn't sure if that quote about the one-eyed man in the kingdom of the blind was in the Bible, but it should be. Andrew wished Dean could see this incredible adaptation, of flesh into flower, to serve a new network for connecting human hardware—

The corpse's stout, overdeveloped limbs reminded Andrew of pictures of elephantiasis victims in old medical books. Despite, or because of, its humanoid structure, it looked at least as weird as anything Andrew had ever seen wash up on the seashore.

But Sprague insisted it was a man. He mourned it, when he had coolly blown away the arguably more human people who came out of the woods. "If this thing," Andrew stammered, "if it's a man, he had people, right? Family, friends? Won't they come looking for him?"

Sprague pushed himself out of his squat, hawked a lunger into the dark. "The Colony was his family, his friends. People with tight-knit families aren't drawn to try to make new ones, boy. Grodenko was careful to pick candidates with no lasting ties to the outside world, and they cut off all contact months ago. Nobody expected to hear from them for a year."

Andrew's eyes roamed over the ugly, rough-hewn contours of the worker once more. "This happened in less than a year?"

"No," Sprague said as he lurched off down the open slope. "The changes didn't really get going on their bodies until a few months ago . . . It took weeks, but if the need of the Colony is great enough, it only takes days."

Sprague half-walked, half-slid down a slope carpeted in dry pine needles and leaves, using the shotgun as a walking stick. Andrew started after him, but let out a high, wordless cry and sprawled on his ass trying to crab back up the slope.

A tree stepped out of the dark in Sprague's path. Sprague hissed, "Shut up," and the silent giant picked him up. Andrew tried crawling to the top of the slope on all fours. Another worker was waiting for him at the top. Without so much as a sigh of effort, it threw its arms around him and swept him off the ground.

In a grove of live oaks near the top of the valley, the workers set them down. Sprague patted the faceless thing on its shoulder and went through a gaping door in a broken wall of granite and cut timbers so old they looked like fossilized bones in the yellow-red light of a bonfire within.

Andrew hesitated only a moment before he followed

the old man into the ruin. It wasn't the worker clomping up behind him, or the fear of what else was out in the woods tonight. It certainly wasn't that he trusted Sprague, who only seemed more insane, now that the things he raved about had been proven true. Andrew clung to the hope that he had reached bottom, and could not be shocked any more than he already was.

He stopped trying to count them after twenty. There were dozens—most of them workers, but a small clique of soldiers took pride of place around the fire. It would look like a scene of a Stone Age tribe, if any of them had heads. Sprague further upset the patina of sanity by shuffling to the fire to warm his hands, imposing a monstrous deformation of scale. The shortest of them stood almost seven feet tall at the shoulder. None of them moved or reacted in any visible way to the old communist as he set his shotgun down and splayed his crooked hands to the flames.

Andrew stood frozen. Had they not noticed him? Was he a captive or—even weirder—a guest, since he came with Sprague?

Their bodies were like organic machines, tools without any of the God-given earmarks of natural birth. Naked, they had no nipples or breasts, no genitalia. They looked unfinished, fashioned of clay like the golems of Hebrew legend; but they were the most refined tools ever made of human flesh, half-human automatons, raised only to work, but they clearly had no work to do here.

But they did, he saw at last, have eyes, of a sort: tiny, expressionless spots, barely darker than the surrounding hide, around the flowers on the muzzle of each worker and soldier, so that they saw, however crudely, in all directions at once. Somehow, the vestigial eyes were harder to look at than the ear-flowers; barely functional and less expressive than a potato's, they distilled the surrender of the Proletariat. Each of them had all but given up his right to see as an individual, in return for the connectivity of the hive.

All other improvements, if one could call them that, only made them fitter for work. Their arms and knees had ball and socket joints, so as to bend backwards as well as forwards, so that the difference between front and back on their bodies was more or less moot.

But in what way were they an improvement on human bodies, on workers with heads and minds of their own? Were uniformity and silencing dissent so important? The workers looked like some Soviet tractor-engineer's dream of an ideal worker. Perhaps the ruthless efficiency of the bees had inspired it, but like everything human beings did by committee, it went south, and hard.

Andrew shivered from cold and shock, but he dared not approach the fire. He moved deeper into the sawmill, clinging to the shadows of an overhead gallery. He heard sounds behind the silent tableau around the roaring fire; hushed animal grunting and short, sharp cries that, even in this place, could only mean one thing. Someone was getting some.

Picking his way around jagged piles of debris, Andrew saw remnants of the things they built here, when it worked. They must have made a lot of really big chairs.

He heard a female voice cry out. It came from one of a row of cells with broken oak doors hanging off their hinges.

In the last of them, bodies lay entangled in sticky shadows, stiff like castoff mannequins, yet some strained and pumped at each other as if in the throes of wet dreams. Not so much fucking, as pollinating each other.

Alongside a fugitive voyeuristic twinge, Andrew felt a numb, driving curiosity that took hold when his rampaging panic simply ran out of steam. He thought he recognized the voice of the girl, and someone else . . .

Fishing in his pockets, Andrew found a lighter and flicked the wheel. It didn't catch, but in the spark, he glimpsed a red-faced ruin of a man, naked and plowing into a slender, white slip of a girl who looked up at him with glazed, bottomless eyes. In the dark, he heard a mushy croak, punctuated by porcine grunts. "We're going . . . *uh* . . . as fast as we can . . . *uh* . . . comrade . . . "

Andrew flicked the lighter again. Starved on the dregs of butane in the disposable plastic reservoir, the feeble blue glow barely reached the back of the shallow cell, and only added mystery to the horny pile of human kindling. The mangled fornicator was his brother-in-law. Incredibly, it was not Dom, but Dean. Or rather, a cunningly sculpted replica of Dean, executed in tenderized flank steak.

The girl was May.

Against all odds, this found an untrampled nerve in Andrew and bit into it. "Jesus, Dean, what are you doing, man? Get off that girl. She's . . . she's not your wife . . . "

Dean thrust once more and gave a dislocated groan as he came inside her. May twisted around on his cock like he was killing her, and she could already see heaven.

"Andy," Dean said, and all the contempt he could stuff into the name oozed out. "Don't talk to me. Don't look at me. This is what men do, Andy. This is a man's job, a warrior's job. If you were ever going to be a man, it would have happened . . . before now."

Fine. *If that's how you want it, dickhead . . .* "Dean, that girl you're fucking . . . " *It's a real small world, bro, and maybe God does have a plan, just like you're always preaching, every goddamned chance you get.* The lighter burned his thumb, and little polyps of melted plastic began to leap out of the flame, so he let it go out. He'd seen plenty. "Dean, meet May. She's your daughter, and I guess since you fucked your mom when you were ten, she's your sister, too."

Dean lolled back on his bed of flesh, bodies smeared with honey and swollen like those ants that hang from the roof of the nest with their abdomens hideously bloated with nectar, from which all the hordes of ants line up to drink. By staring very hard, Andrew could just make out his darker, blood-daubed form against the pale flesh of the others.

Dean seemed to go to sleep, his congested breathing deepening. But then he said, "You couldn't understand, Andy. You're so frightened of responsibility, you trained your wife to do it all for you. She knows you're not a man."

Andrew fired up the lighter again, popping the blister on his thumb. "What the fuck do you know about me and my wife? She never talks to you. She thinks you're the biggest asshole in the world, next to your father."

"She never told you . . ." Dean chuckled and coughed. "Oh, you got her trained. Laura's a crazy bitch with no future, but she's no idiot. She was dumb enough to give it up to you, for whatever reason . . . but when push came to shove, she knew you weren't father material."

"Are you fucking insane?" He tried to hold back from just screaming at Dean, because he seemed to think he knew something. Andrew and Laura had talked about having kids. In bed at night when they were just living together, they'd joke about names and how they'd raise them, and where they'd go to school. It was a cute conversational game, but Laura would always round it out with something like, "I wish I could know I'd be a good mother." When he tried to comfort her with some off-the-rack wisdom about how instinct took over when a woman became a mother, she bristled at his sexism, then rolled over and doggedly pretended to sleep.

It hurt him that she smeared his reasoning, but he really believed it. Laura was so generous and patient when someone truly needed her help. When something needed doing, she usually did it before he even noticed a problem. He knew, when a few months had gone by without the job fight, that she had left it to him to find a stable career that could support a household. If he wanted children, he would have to earn them.

It was very hard, indeed, not to just curse at Dean, when he brought this shit up. Now, here in the middle of all this . . . Dean, with his litter of towheaded pups packed into the family Christmas card every year in matching sweater vests and bow ties; Mr. Red-State America, career Navy dittohead Dean, fresh from fucking closing the wreath on his family tree, presumed to lecture him about the responsibilities of a parent. Oh fuck, if he only had the patience, Andrew could write him a song about it.

"Fuck you, Dean. You know better than anyone what Laura went through. When she's ready, we're going to start a family, and it won't be a fucking baby factory like you and Janice . . . "

"No, Andy . . . " Dean laughed himself into a *petit mal* seizure. "No, you won't."

"What do you know?"

"I know she got pregnant six months back."

"Bullshit!"

"Relax, it was yours . . . She called Dad and she cried, and he told her it was a sin, but to follow her heart. He doesn't think you're worth a lick of shit, either, by the way . . . "

The headache flared up again. A vein in his temple turned into a viper biting his brain. Andrew dropped the lighter. What he needed now was a weapon.

"She scraped it. Went in while you were out of town for one of your concerts . . . She blamed herself, but it was written all over her, that she did it because she knew it would be a mistake, with you."

Andrew backed away from the door. He looked around for a hefty beam, or a hammer. Maybe he could take Sprague's shotgun, and the workers would let him kill Dean, the champion they had apparently chosen to repopulate the colony . . .

"But don't take it so personal, Andy. She went back to the doctor when we left San Diego. She got her tubes tied. Didn't want to wind up like Mom, tied down to a bunch of fucked-up brats like us. She won't be making babies with anybody, and good riddance, says I. If I knew Dad was going to pay for it, I would've kicked in something extra for plastic surgery, or whatever. After all she's been through. She deserves better than you."

Andrew ran for the fire and Sprague. "I can't stay here. Fuck this place."

"You can't leave, Andrew . . . "

"Watch me! I've had it up to here with your shit, and these fucking things—"

Two soldiers stepped in front of the door. Andrew saw more than he wanted, of how they turned the ugly dream of the ideal worker into a nightmare of potential carnage. If the workers were tools, the soldiers were weapons. They were pointed at him.

"You can't leave. They can't let you. You are too important to them, now."

"Fuck them, and fuck you, too! This experiment is a failure! It failed! Look at them! Let it go!"

"You can't let it go," Sprague said, crestfallen. He lost all passion to persuade, but he came to Andrew and put his hand on his shoulder. "It's already too far along."

He showed Andrew a mirror.

CHAPTER 22

BEFORE THE FIRST rays of the rising sun crept through the bars of his cell, Dom leapt up and embraced the day with a smile and a song in his heart.

He had not really slept, and had run himself ragged with other duties all night long, but he felt rejuvenated, now. New. His wounds had scabbed over and were half-healed. He doubted that Dean could say the same.

A new day, a new Dom, hotter and harder than ever. Sourly, he noted that his cock showed no signs of growing back, but no biggie. He needed no one and nothing. But they needed him.

There was a lot of extra food at breakfast. Only two survivors had returned from the raiding party. They made a motley crew at the oversized trestle-tables of the dining hall. The girls from the Sexagon wadded honey and moldy Wonder Bread into their mouths and stared fixedly at his sly smile. Deaf to his Winnie the Pooh jokes, they topped off their gurgling gullets and buzzed away to their duties.

As he watched his own hands mechanically feeding his mouth, Dom noted that he seemed to have lost his sense of taste, but not his appetite. Even the Town Drunk turned out, dragging his crushed pelvis and shattered legs behind him, to get his ration of honey. He bore Dom no hard feelings, but he didn't liven up the conversation, either.

The pain of his failure still ached in Dom's bones. He'd cut down a soldier and two workers and clobbered his brother. His night was pure magic. Deep down, he still thought, *fuck the old man*. But his brain tied itself in knots with forced remorse, the waves of mute accusation from the Tower, hours dragging like years of crushing interrogation, crying and gorging himself on honey. He had not slept a wink. But in the night, he had grown. He would not fail, this time.

Somewhere out there, Dean was recovering and growing. Dom had to be bigger.

Dean. A traitor to state and family, he got sucked into the first club that would take him. Dom thought it more than passing funny that this time, jackboot-licking Dean was out there with the savages, and Dom was on the inside, with the brains, the power—and Mom.

And today, he had a mission.

The Colony needed new citizens. The drive to indoctrinate the neighbors had run its course, but had done nothing to break the stalemate. Dom had a picture of the rental truck fixed in his mind. He was to get it and bring it back to the big house.

Walking through the woods, Dom felt the sun penetrate his skin and nourish it, though it made him itch where the gray, leathery callus was spreading, covering the Detroit Redwings logo and the devil chicks on his chest and the lone swordsman on his back in dense, fibrous exodermis.

The woods were quiet, but he could feel eyes on him; bees bumbled around, just out of reach, tangling in deadly dogfights and sometimes trying to sting him.

Deep down, he had an itchy feeling that didn't sit well with his devil-may-care nature. Surely, the outside world would take notice of what was happening here. He might be strong, but he was not invincible, and if the real Army turned up, they would be wiped out.

While he was out at the old man's cabin, the Tower sent someone to clean up his mess with the Deputy's truck.

With a loop of chain around the bumper, they towed it on foot down to the road where it overlooked the big pond and pushed it in, with the headless Deputy Scovill in the driver's seat. Then they pushed Dom's truck up to the Sexagon and left it in the garage.

But the law would come around, he knew. They would come looking for the deputy. Fucking mafia in blue, always trying to kill his buzz.

Dom saw the necessity of acting fast, and all his uncertainty fell away. They would come, sooner or later, and the only way the Colony would survive was if they had more people and a new home. The confusion over the wreck only had to last for a day or so; if it worked, they would not need to hide much longer.

He saw and heard nothing alive as he walked down the slope overlooking Mom's cabin. Had the bees stung all the birds and the beasts? What side were they on? The idea of harnessing a flock—or pack, or whatever—of deer, and turning it on the workers tickled him to laugh aloud, but it wasn't his job to have ideas. The Head of State sat up there scheming all day long in the Tower, and Dom's job was to bring the schemes to life.

The moving truck was still parked in front of Mom's cabin. He remembered when he'd left, not twelve hours ago, still seeing red from his tangle with Dean, still screwed up in his head from the first throes of his transformation.

It was like coming back to an old elementary school. Everything looked cheap and small. The damage from the fight made him laugh. Had all that bullshit really been so important? From his new, enlightened perspective, the irrational rage that had driven him, the ties of the family, were like toy handcuffs, easily broken and tossed away by the new man he had become.

A flash of filthy white squirted out from under the truck as he stepped out of the trees. Dom felt an odd pang of relief and confusion, of something returned that he'd forgotten he lost. His hands spread out, but he had to search his mind for the dog's name.

"Toshiro!"

The dog pranced around him, nervous paws dancing on the pea gravel, ears cocked. A weird bark and whine came from his red-stained muzzle, a low growl from deep in his throat.

"Come here, boy," Dom said, trying to make his voice low and harmless, even as his hands flexed in front of him. "You know me, buddy."

The dog was his, but it was dangerous. Toshiro called no man master, but he had accepted Dom as a kindred spirit, and given him something worth much more than submission. If the dog would come with him, maybe the Colony could use it, but Toshiro was his own dog, a lone swordsman, a dog after his own heart . . .

Dom took another step closer, wondering what his hands would do when he caught the dog, when Toshiro made up his mind. He barked louder, the same way he barked at strangers. His head ducked down low and he leapt at Dom's throat.

Dom jumped back in shock. His left arm came up to block the flying hound's snapping jaws. Teeth like jigsaw blades gouged his hand and wrist, stabbing through his tough, piebald hide where, only yesterday, the ink under his skin had rewritten itself into bees.

Dom spun like a drunken discus-thrower and slung the dog away, but Toshiro clung to him like a killer crocodile, clamping down on the bone for all he was worth. A bear trap with ninety-five pounds of flying muscle behind it, Toshiro tore twenty-six holes in his flesh wide open.

Dom whipped Toshiro over his head and turned to smash him against a tree trunk, but the wily devil dog let go and flew through the air, landed sliding across the gravel and vanished into the undergrowth.

"Fuck!" Dom screamed, and pounded the high-impact

plastic wall of the U-Haul trailer. His bloody fists went through it like toilet paper. It took him almost a minute to let the rage boil over and flow out of him.

Fuck the dog. He had a mission.

The keys were tucked in the sun visor, but the U-Haul truck didn't have a CD player. He had to count to ten to keep from breaking off the steering wheel, when he adjusted it.

He was taller and heavier than yesterday. The fresh clothes from the cabin he'd changed into, a baggy black track suit, clung and rode up and felt like he would burst out of it, Hulk-style, if he exerted himself. The bandages from the truck's first aid kit were still wet with his blood, but he could feel the bite wounds closing. It almost hurt worse than the bite itself, but he was in no state to argue with the results. It was a miracle, how the Tower turned honey into muscle.

Agitated, he twiddled the knob past country and Christian pop until he came to the local public station. Over a solo acoustic guitar dirge, a grim, reedy voice sang of a factory strike like it was a lost book of the Old Testament. Men on horseback trampled workers and smashed men's heads in with truncheons. The workers locked arms and sang, *So look for the union label*, or something, until the union-busters busted them, one and all. It wasn't Motorhead, but it did the job of washing away his confusion. The dog rejected him because he belonged to something.

Of course, it made things a bit thorny, that the heroic workers were shut out of the big house, and he was, himself, a union-busting scab.

This was why communism had never worked, before. Too many chiefs, and not enough braves. Dom knew who the boss was. He had felt the raw authority of the Tower as it showed him his place in the new order. He had endured its touch as it forced his growth as fast as his body could stand it. He had felt its wrath, and knew that it could effortlessly pop his skull.

Boy, Dean-o, you sure picked the wrong side. Again . . .

Dom backed the truck out and smashed into Mom's Cadillac. The cumbersome sedan rocked and settled on its flat tires. Bumpers locked. Dom ripped the rusty grill off the Cadillac. It clanged and dragged in the dust behind the truck as he slowly brought the truck's blunt snout around and aimed it down the steep driveway. It felt so good on so many levels, that he let fly a hearty belly-laugh that shook the whole truck.

As the U-Haul truck lumbered onto the paved road, stripped gears and barefoot brakes screaming, Dom kept a weather eye out for cops, but he saw only a lone cyclist in fruity tie-dyed spandex tights, humping his mountain bike up the grade past Mom's driveway.

Weighing the pros and cons of mowing the hippie down, Dom decided he'd probably wreck the truck trying. The cyclist passed without incident, iPod earbuds tucked into his helmet, serenely oblivious to the other vehicle in plain sight, the totaled white Bronco's rear end peeking out of the shallows of the pond, just a few hundred yards up the road.

Even to Dom's art-hating sensibility, the sight was deliciously surreal. In plain daylight, the wrecked pigmobile cried out to be investigated, towed to Sacramento and combed over by diligent, serious-minded pigs, maybe even feds. One of their own was fish food, and nobody seemed to have noticed.

A cold thrill, an ass-puckering promise, tickled his bowels. The Percolator slunk into his hearing as a tense, suspenseful lurking cue. There were no bystanders in the valley, now. Anyone who came in would have to choose a side.

In the new world, nothing would stand in the way of the Colony. Their opposition was nothing but buzzing alien insects, and would be crushed. That Dom would lead those doing the crushing was a foregone conclusion. *To be strong is no crime*, he told himself. He served a greater good that could absolve any excess in the pursuit of glory.

The Pond Diner was deserted, the boat landing chained off. Halfway to the little island in the lake's center, two men sat in a little fishing boat. From the frantic waving of their arms and their faint caterwauling screams, Dom guessed they had discovered the bees.

He saw no one else as he drove past the Sexagon— noted with only a demure handpainted sign bearing the stately pleasure dome's sobriquet—and onto the narrow, rootbound dirt track beyond it, that led to the big house.

He had to slow to a crawl to negotiate the pines crowding the road and scraping at the trailer. He took his time making a three-point turn into the unmarked driveway of the big house. The cumbersome ten-foot trailer broke branches off desiccated pines, which piled up on the hood. The wheels locked up and skidded down stretches of soft gravel. Panic gave him the slight mental leverage to wonder if the plan was as perfect as the Tower believed. When had the Head of State last gotten out of the house?

As he forced the truck through the stubborn woods, he felt a host of eyes upon him. It taxed him not to jump out of the truck and go after them, but there was no stopping the bees from spying, and this plan was vital. He couldn't fuck up again, just could not. Let them try to figure out the genius of the State. Let them try to stop it.

At last, the truck broke out of the forest and into the open meadow. Dom was hard-pressed not to gun it and execute some jumbo-sized donuts on the tilled plain. But he refrained even from honking the horn as he rolled up to the front porch and killed the engine.

The wind chased itself around in the long, yellow grass. Bees buzzed, but none brought a message for him. What was wrong? Had he fucked up again?

The doors flew open, and four hooded scab workers rushed down the steps to the back of the trailer. Dom got out and ambled over to meet them. Scanning the treeline, he saw nothing, but he felt them. He gave the forest the finger and pissed in the dirt, hoping Dean was watching.

The workers unloaded the truck like ants dismantling a picnic, shuttling Mom's furniture and boxes into the house as quickly and quietly as their shaky, half-remade legs could carry them.

Dom picked up the La-Z-Boy recliner and followed them, figuring that the sooner the truck was cleared out, the sooner he could continue his mission.

The caravan shuffled through the great hall and down the kitchen stairs to the cellar, a gloomy gallery lined with barred holding cells. A striking worker slouched in one of the cells, too big to lie down, and starving. Bones jutting out of rumpled, elephantine hide, shaking with palsies from repeated interrogation, yet the defiant worker had somehow resisted all gracious attempts at forgiveness and reindoctrination.

The dumb fuck had a peanut for a brain and a bunch of sockets for receiving commands from the State, but all those sockets were blocked with anarchist propaganda, and the Tower's attempts at a reunion had only caused allergic reaction and toxic shock.

Dom had a sinking feeling that he was not meant to know this, that the striking workers were dead to reconciliation, that the enemy's poison propaganda was stronger than the Tower's all-embracing love. He wondered if he would be punished for knowing this, the next time he was called before the Tower. Whether he told anyone or not probably would not matter. What with the bees stinging him to do this and feel that, and the Tower constantly picking through his brain, he didn't know how he was communicating to anyone, but he knew that the last thing he should be doing, was making plans or asking questions.

The mute scabs led him through a narrow passage with a heavy iron gate propped open across it, and into an open space almost as vast as the great hall. All around him, he saw dozens of cribs of plain and uniform design, lovingly crafted out of local pine. All of them were empty.

The movers set down their burdens and hurried off at a dead run for the next load. Dom dropped the recliner and looked around. Crates and steel drums were pushed back against the wall, and a boiler rumbled and hissed in the dimmest corner of the cellar.

A droopy, toothless crone in a pink housecoat set about arranging the furniture with a will that far outpaced her tired old body. He squinted and wracked his brain before deciding this was not his mother.

The heat down here was wet and musky. Condensation dripped in Dom's eyes. He looked up and saw a colossal spaghetti-tangle of tubes of slick gray organs, dangling and bobbing with huge nodes here and there, like overstuffed garbage bags turgid with busily fermenting new life, and disappearing into holes drilled in the cellar's roof, the granite foundation of the house.

And suspended in the midst of it, connected, trapped, enslaved by it, yet so inherently regal that he found himself bowing, hung the queen bee.

"Hi, Mom," Dom said. "You look . . . good."

CHAPTER 23

ANDREW WAS AWAKE long before dawn.

What little sleep he got, he'd endured in an empty cell in the back of the sawmill, wrapped in an itchy woolen army blanket. Every time he dozed off, he was jolted awake by the creeping sensations like insects crawling over him. His eyes were crusted over, his limbs half-deflated balloons, floating on phantom winds.

Even allowing for the bites, stingers, wounds and filth of the last two days, he could not deny the rings of inflammation around his neck, and clustering at the base of his skull. The sweat pouring from his neck was oily and pungent, and smelled of honeysuckle. Ecstatic bees clustered and bathed in it. He tried to resist scratching or tearing them out, for the tiny flowers blooming out of his skin were tender and as delicate as rice paper.

The weirdest part was that he wasn't freaking out, when he had every reason to. He woke up to find Sprague kneeling over him. He itched all over. He was encrusted with dead and dying workers and redundant drones. They fell from his face like sand and took to the air.

Andrew shrieked and batted at his hair, which was crawling with lively workers. Their sleepy buzzing didn't quaver as they flew away. Their wings, he knew without knowing, beat two hundred times per second, producing a steady monotone an octave below middle C.

In that moment, he belatedly realized whom the old

man looked like. If George Orwell had taken up bareknuckle boxing, then retired to become an alpine hermit, Andrew would swear, the results would be the cadaverous fossil leering over him. The wrinkles etching his face showed the scars of a prizefighter's lifetime of losing fixed fights.

"Don't mind them," Sprague said. "They're just getting to know you."

"I don't *want* to know them," Andrew whined, hating the self-hate cracking his speech. "I never asked to be a part of *any* of this." Never quite sure they were all gone, Andrew kept combing his fingers through his hair, but the more he touched himself, the deeper his insecurity became. His hands came away with feathery tufts of loose hair. He stopped while there were still a few patches of hair left, but wherever he'd scratched, he was bald as an egg.

In a reedy, declamatory tone, Sprague quoted,

"Clear from the head the masses of impressive rubbish;

"Rally the lost and trembling forces of the will,

"Gather them up and let them loose upon the earth,

"Till they construct at last a human justice."

"Meh," Andrew said. "You write it? It sucks."

"Auden," Sprague said, a bit hurt. "I thought you knew books."

"Hate poetry."

Sprague watched him for a long while. "It's hard, I know."

"What do you know?"

"I know enough to envy you, youngster. If I was twenty years younger, it would be me, but this old body couldn't take the strain." Sprague rummaged in his knapsack and handed Andrew a fistful of big, granular vitamin pills and a canteen.

Radiation poisoning? Had they dosed him? Radiation didn't give people superpowers in real life. It made hair and teeth fall out, organs bleed, and twisted healthy cells into festering cancers. His arms and legs were pale and atrophied, like when he spent his eleventh summer in a body cast. He felt weak enough to blow away on the next stiff breeze, but he wasn't dying. He was changing.

Andrew refused the vitamins, but gulped the lukewarm, silt-laden water from the canteen. If Sprague was poisoning him, it was too late.

"I'm hungry," he said.

Sprague held out a mason jar packed with brown ooze. "There's honey."

"Fuck you. That shit's poison."

The sour wrinkles in Sprague's face deepened, as if looking at him sucked the moisture out of it. "You kids have more knowledge at your fingertips than the foremost thinkers in my day, but you never want to know the truth. So long as you're warm and fat and safe, and somebody else is doing your fighting and dying far out of earshot, you don't care what the world's turning into—"

"Fuck you, old man! You can judge us young whippersnappers from all the way out here, in your Unabomber shack? You have no fucking idea what it's like to be young, today. We want to make the world a better place. But every generation before us has fucked things up a little worse, and passed it on. Now *we're* supposed to fix it? *I'm* supposed to fix it? I just got here! Look at them! It's all broken, Sprague, and nobody can fix it!"

Sprague's knees popped when he pulled his forlorn carcass upright. How long had he been sitting there, watching Andrew sleep with a bee-beard? "Maybe you're right. But if what you do when you have a chance counts for anything, then you'd better decide if you really have it in you to make a difference. Because *you* have a chance."

Andrew's brain throbbed. "How could this happen? It's insane . . . bodies don't just change like this. People don't . . . turn into . . . things . . . "

"It happened because they wanted it to happen. When people of like minds come together, if their will is pure and focused, nothing is impossible. At the old commune, all the women had their curse at the same time, and all of us fell asleep within minutes of the last bell. That's why your government hated communism more than fascism, because of the power of people working together. When Mao told China to kill sparrows, they wiped out billions in days."

"Yeah, Mao was the greatest. When they limited everybody to one child, the people obeyed by murdering or abandoning their daughters. Glorious cultural revolution, my ass."

"The problem wasn't that they changed," the old man said. "They didn't change *enough*. In Russia, the problem was corruption. The people never saw true communism, because the bowl was made of holes. If all the people were truly unified, if their commitment to the common good was more than mouth-music, they would not be human anymore. They would become something better."

Sprague watched the Colony workers sleeping in piles around the dying embers of the fire. Their breathing was wet and raspy, like a nursery filled with colicky babies, but synchronized and soothing, like the ocean.

One of them tended the fire, dropping logs onto it with no regard for kindling the embers. With a puff, the fire went out. "This wasn't how it was supposed to be. Somewhere down the line, the communal idea got perverted . . . maybe Grodenko took too much from them into himself . . . Maybe it's just that goddamned madhouse."

Andrew watched them until it sank in that he was irrevocably one of them. He touched his head. Would it wither and rot off, or would a new one just pop out of his neck like a permanent tooth? He didn't want to look in the mirror again, but he had to.

His fingers told him that it hadn't been a nightmare.

His hair was falling out, and his eyes bulged like they were about to pop. His skull felt like a prize pumpkin in his shaky hands. *Bees in my bonnet.* He was becoming something else, filling a gap in the collective left by the strike. Nature hates a vacuum.

"It doesn't just happen," Andrew snapped. "How did they do it? What's in the honey?"

"In the Soviet Union, they saw the end coming, but they didn't just lie down for it. History's already lying about that, too, making it look like communism just went away and everybody cheered and went shopping.

"But they fought it, some because they believed in the idea, but mostly, they were afraid of change, or losing their own power. They tried things . . . near the end. They chased all kinds of crazy ideas to keep the dream alive. One program got past the drawing board, but they must've had a moment of clarity, because they put it on the shelf and forgot about it.

"Some damned fool of a genius over there put together that the brain created moods and memories with chemicals a long time before they figured it out over here. They knew about serotonin and oxytocin, all those juices that get pumping when we're in love, or just happy. They thought that if they could induce and regulate that state in every citizen's brain, everyone would feel good about Communism again."

"Yeah, that makes a lot more sense than just getting rid of corruption. Brainwashing people with beestings."

"Not in practice, no, but the drug was made from the bee venom. These people were used to having absolute power and zero accountability, and their backs were against the wall. If it sounds crazy as a bag of assholes, it was the least ambitious part of the project.

"They wanted to revive the old collective farms, and remake the ideal Soviet worker. The venom would give them their minds, but they needed to make them totally dependent, totally reliable. To them, it was the unwritten final step in the evolution to true socialism. To make the workers truly workers, and nothing else. To industrialize the messy business of producing the failed state's greatest resource, its people.

"They set after it like they did Sputnik, for a while, before someone pulled the plug. They erased the project when the Soviet experiment failed and broke down. But somebody remembered, and Grodenko came here to test it."

"He just *came* over here? To California?" Andrew scoffed. "Bullshit. They had to know who and what he was, when they let him and his magic bees in. He had to have backers. This never would've happened, if someone in charge over here didn't want it to happen."

Andrew awkwardly stood and crept out of the cell. The sky had lightened to fresh denim blue with the imminent sunrise. The Colony workers had all risen and stood around the smothered fire. Bees crawled around their eyespots and tiny flower-ears. As Andrew approached the ring, the workers bustled off.

"Where are they going? What's going to happen?"

"I hardly know," Sprague said. "What did you tell them to do?"

Andrew turned. "What did *I tell them* . . . ? I didn't tell anyone anything . . . "

Sprague hobbled over to the fire ring, using the shotgun as a cane. "The bees carry messages. They came to you for orders. They chose you. To tell you the truth, I'd just about given up hope—"

"But why me? If you want a leader, you picked the wrong guy. I'm not that smart. I couldn't crack a thousand on the SAT, and I flunked my driving test four times. I—"

The old man bent over the fire, poking the smothered embers with a stick. "*I* didn't pick you. When I saw what the commune was turning into, I took a few hives and started trying to agitate them, break the lines of command, force them to reorganize and choose a new leader."

Flinching as if someone took a swing at him, Sprague raised his voice as he tried to convince himself. "It was for their own good. I caused the strike, but it never would have gone this far, if the collective didn't need a new head. The communal will can be failed by its leaders, but it is never wrong. Nobody gets to choose family, young man. Your new family needs you."

Out of the shadows, Dean lumbered, pushing through the knot of workers gathered around Andrew and Sprague. His body was still mottled with eggplant-hued bruises and crusted with blood, but his wounds had scabbed over. To heal so fast, he must have gorged himself on the lion's share of the Colony's dwindling honey supply. His face still looked like a hamburger deathmask, but he stood a head taller than Andrew when he stared him down. Dean had always used his four inches of height advantage like a judge's bench to look down on Andrew, but he now seemed lordly, not at all shaken by the insane chain of circumstance that had led them here.

"Need you, Andy," Dean said. "Come on."

Though it made him seasick, Andrew forced himself to meet Dean's gaze. "Go to hell, Tweedle Dean. I'm not going anywhere with you."

Dean's superior scowl cracked like a bullwhip, but before he could bark, Sprague interceded. "The head of state should be protected. He's vulnerable—"

"I want what's best for the collective," Dean said. His lips clamped tight over his teeth like they pained him, or were trying to escape. "Big house trying to break the strike. We need someone who can drive." Harder than ever to read, Dean never took his hooded eyes off Andrew, but his spasmodically flexing fists promised to tear Andrew's head off at the earliest opportunity.

"I can drive a car, soldier," Sprague said. "And I'm expendable . . . "

"Sure you are . . . but I'm not carrying your ass, and you're not one of us."

One of us, yes . . . he's still human. Andrew was about to tell Dean off again, when the bees came back. All at once, they swept in and roosted on him like a cloak, enfolding him and dancing on his hypersensitive skin.

Andrew saw the forest with thousands of compound eyes.

Everything those roving eyes saw on their patrols knitted into a panoramic model fluttering through his brain, overwhelming him with a kaleidoscope of perspectives until he dug in his mental heels and found he could navigate the hallucination like a map.

He saw the sawmill from every angle at once, and the meadow, and the big house, and instantly, he knew why Dean had come to get him.

He saw the U-Haul truck parked in front of the big house in the dawn's first golden light. A bucket brigade of battered, half-transformed workers filled the trailer with white wooden crates. Beehives.

Dean skinned his swollen lips back in a humorless smile. Andrew stared, put off not so much by the bilious insincerity of his expression, as by his teeth, themselves. They looked bloated and soft and translucent, like boiled peas or pearl onions, budding out of the burgundy pulp of his gums.

"He'll be safe with me," Dean growled.

There was no time for debate. Dean led Andrew into the woods, away from the meadow. They crossed the overgrown dirt road to the colony house at a run, aware of armies of eyes on them, less than half of them friendly.

Andrew felt shaky, top-heavy, drunk on transmitted swarm-visions. The way he walked, thrown off-balance by his throbbing head, reminded him of a baby's first steps. The splashes of sun falling between the trees dazzled his eyes and made his sluggish blood dance, but the shadows chilled him like a mountain stream, and plunged him into the head of the hive. If he focused on it and let Dean lead him, he found the memory of the bees' vision crystal clear in his mind, could see himself bumbling through it. They had circled the big house and were traveling parallel to the paved road. But still, he had to ask Dean what they were going to do.

"We have to stop the truck in the woods. They've got guns at the big house. Soldiers are watching, but I thought you'd know all this, Andy. You're the big brain, aren't you?" The sneer in his voice could strip paint.

"I don't know what you're so pissed about," Andrew replied. "You're getting an awful lot of pussy, for a married man. If we're supposed to be on the same side in this shit, maybe you could try to stop being such a dick . . . ?"

They paused at the top of a slippery slope overlooking a gully choked with granite boulders. Dean took Andrew's hand to steady him, but then he did something strange.

Crushing Andrew's hand in his thorny paw, Dean yanked him off-balance and slung him down the slope, planting a swift kick in Andrew's skinny ass for good measure.

Andrew tumbled down the slope in a ball. The hard, rocky soil took nips and rasping licks off his back and arms, but Andrew kept his hands up and around his tender head. His legs didn't curl up like they should because the howling pain in his tailbone seemed to be gumming up the lines of communication. Desperately, he caught a sapling halfway down the ridge, clung to it and screamed, "Why?"

"Don't worry," Dean murmured as he effortlessly jogged down the slope to kick Andrew's hands until he let go, "I won't hurt that big, precious brain of yours."

Andrew slapped at Dean's feet, but Dean kicked him in the ribs, just under his right arm. He wheezed and rolled, continued his sliding descent down the slope. Screaming for help, Andrew barely managed to land feet-first against a car-sized boulder. He wanted to hug it. "What is your fucking problem? I thought we were on the same side."

Dean trampled the sapling, somehow casting a deeper shadow over Andrew, even in the forested shade. "You're going to be the brains of the new order, I guess. Whatever . . . But you're sure as hell never going to be the leader."

Andrew rolled off the boulder and put up his fists. If he wasn't so short of breath, his chest already burning with an overdose of adrenaline, he would have laughed at himself. He had not thrown a punch in anger since middle school. He enjoyed football and boxing and Jet Li movies as much as the next guy, but he had no instinct for violence, and worse, the very idea of punching another person in the face, of driving his fist into the soft tissue, bursting lips and eyes with his bare hands, nauseated him.

In his last real fight, Andrew instinctively backed up until cornered, then lashed out in a spastic slam-dance of short-circuited reflexes that left him feeling poisoned, and his opponent certain that he was crazy. Win or lose, after every fight he had ever been in, Andrew puked his guts out. Andrew was enough of a red-blooded American to hate this about himself, if not to seek to overcome his fear of violence.

Dean cocked a smile of blissful unconcern. He stood there with one hand around the trunk of the sapling like he was holding it up. Then he kicked off the slope and fell on Andrew.

His feet never touched the ground as he traveled the thirty feet of empty air like an actor on wires in a Hong Kong action film. His upraised arms, his engorged lats fanned out like batwings, seemed to scoop the wind, so he did not fall, but fly.

Andrew saw him coming, but had only started turning to run when Dean tackled him and crushed him into the boulder.

Dean screamed louder than Andrew, on impact.

Andrew felt his brother-in-law's jaw smash into his shoulder, heard the mandible snap shut, teeth gnashing, but not clicking like hard enamel-coated bone should. There was an explosive, squirting sound, and a slash of hot wetness jetted down Andrew's neck.

Andrew must have lost consciousness for a while. Dean was talking, low and soft. "And that's why the old order broke down. But we're not going to make the same mistake again." Dean sucked in a breath with a shuddering grimace, biting back an eye-watering jolt of pain. "The *leaders* are going to lead, this time. The people who take the risks. You've got a big brain for storing lots of trivia bullshit, but you couldn't lead water downhill, could you, Andy?"

Andrew's temple already knotted into a bump where he hit the rock. All that came out of his mouth was, "Fuh," along with a spray of blood.

"So you're going to be the head of state, and you're going to do the remembering and calculating, and you're going to give the orders, but they're going to be *my* orders." Dean hissed and spat blood. All his front teeth were gone, but they had not fallen out. They had burst.

Tatters of soft-boiled enamel and streamers of gristle and naked nerves dangled from Dean's gums. Every breath, every movement of his tongue, made his face contort in spasms of agony, animal rage and robotic apathy. With every breath, Dean seemed to be learning to like it. "Do you understand, Andy?"

Slowly, afraid his head might fall off, Andrew nodded.

Dean tugged him upright. Andrew struggled to get his legs under him, but Dean dragged him over the boulder-strewn gully like a doll. "Now, this little lesson is the gentlest I'm ever going to be with you, if you forget your place again. And if you try to run off or betray the collective, we'll just see how vital you really are."

Andrew was too shocked to resist, too sick from his

body's crippling reaction to conflict. Dean dropped him against a pine tree, then hiked up the opposing slope and down a game trail that led to the fancy hexagonal cabin up the road from the big house. Nothing Andrew could say, no argument he could offer, seemed worth the effort. Dean was a soldier. He lived for this shit.

"We'll get along fine, just one big happy family," Dean said, "but you just remember who's the fucking daddy."

CHAPTER 24

WHEN DOM CAME back out of the house, he smelled Dean on the hot, dusty wind. He didn't need the bees to tell him that his twin was running around out there. "Good morning, little brother," he laughed.

The U-Haul truck bounced in the ruts going back out to the road. The new cargo was much lighter than Mom's shit. Feeling jaunty, Dom flipped on the radio, dialed in a fuzzy country station and sang along with Willie Nelson.

When the truck broke out of the forest and lurched onto the cracked tar, Dom spun the wheel hard left, but still almost ran off the right shoulder. The front bumper took a divot out of a Douglas fir that crowded the road. It took heaps of self-control not to just floor it and bobsled down the long, loopy slope to the pond.

His orders were to drive the truck into Utopia without attracting attention and meet the agents who would take care of the rest. He knew there would be more orders, more fun, once he had delivered the propaganda. Utopia's last census lied by a mile, but the town still had at least a hundred inhabitants. The Tower had been most emphatic about its hope for a bloodless revolution, but these things were only ever neat on paper.

Case in point: the little convoy of pigmobiles parked on the shoulder overlooking the pond where Deputy Scovill met his untimely second end. Two Broncos, a towtruck and a green sedan that must belong to some county official were lined up along the shoulder. The sheriff, a bull-necked, sunburned bald bastard with a walrus mustache, wallowed in the pond with the towtruck driver, trying to get a chain around some part of the Bronco's pulverized rear end to drag it out.

A deputy leaned against the bumper of the lead Bronco, crushing his hat in one hand and smoking a cigarette. He looked all of nineteen, and still green from losing his breakfast. As Dom rumbled down the hill towards them, the deputy perked up and stepped into the road with his arms out wide, clearly a little nervous that Dom might run him down.

At first, Dom considered doing just that, and ramming the pig caravan for good measure. But his orders were specific about not attracting attention.

Dom braked and coasted to a stop calculated to make the deputy take just a single step back, and to dent his smug pig pose a little. Besides, it might serve the collective good best, if he *did* attract just a little attention, right now . . .

And just like that, he was alone.

Andrew sagged into a crouch against the boulder when the sound of Dean crashing through the woods had faded under the rustling of the wind in the trees. The loamy soil under him was damp, and seeped up through the rags of his jeans.

Dean said, *Don't move*, and took off in the direction of the neighbors' cabin. After a long while, when the burning in his chest became unbearable, he indulged in a deep, cautious breath. He was mildly surprised and relieved when Dean did not appear and hit him again.

All the attitude had been shocked right out of him when Dean threw him down the slope. Everyone seemed to have found a new niche, except him. Dean was as big a hard-on as ever when he wasn't turning into Bigfoot, and

Dom had gone native, as well. And whatever was happening to Andrew, the angst and humiliation games of his old family had followed him into the new.

He never asked for any of this. All he'd done was fall in love with a girl and try to build a life with her . . . and now, for a colossal clusterfuck of reasons, that was over. Yet here he still was, saddled with everyone else's problems, everyone else's insane fantasies of what made a family, putting their relentless, digestive roots into him, remaking him into what they wanted . . .

Andrew started to cry.

Nobody gets to choose family, young man.

His busy brain buzzed and waggle-danced strategies and tactics and plots within plots, but he couldn't will himself to get off the ground. His arms and legs trembled, both avid to go and in abject terror of making any move until Dean came back, even if something worse came . . .

He wished he had someone he could talk to, someone he could trust. If he had any guts, if he was a man, he would run parallel to the road down to the Pond Restaurant, steal the car parked outside, haul ass to the next town south and call the fucking cops. They would come in with the FBI and the National Guard, and sort shit out for good. Once they saw what was really going on out here, there would be no TV cameras, no show trials, no survivors.

Assuming, of course, they took him at his word. When Sprague had shown him the mirror, he had reacted almost as Dom did, the morning after he went out in the woods. He touched his reflection to see if it wasn't some kind of prank, or a funhouse mirror. It was happening even faster, now. If he could get away from Dean and out of the woods, would they take a look at him and lock him up in a secret government lab, or just shoot him down?

The realization that stopped his tears was not a relief, but only a deepening acceptance that the terror riding him now would probably do so forever.

He was one of them.

Your family needs you.

Andrew got up, still feeling a bit dizzy, and walked towards the road. He kept his arms out to catch himself against trees, but he felt stronger with each step, as if the choice had put him in touch with the ones who depended on him, as if his good faith made a direct conduit for their strength.

He heard the low, gurgling growl of a big truck granny-clutching down the hill. He was unarmed and worse off physically than yesterday, but he kept walking. His mind was alive with scenarios, but somehow, the omens of chaos and doom did not make his pulse run amok. His legs stopped shivering.

There was much he could do.

If Dom reached Utopia in the truck, he could simply dump the hives in the town square and hope for the best, but the results would be chaos and bloodshed. The big house was taking a huge risk by reaching out to indoctrinate the town. They would have to quietly get most, if not all, of the residents to control the town and stifle any calls for help. Andrew remembered the cranky old freak in the bookstore. The big house had advance agents in the town. If they crashed some kind of mass event in Utopia, hundreds of scabs would flood the forest and besiege the sawmill. The strike would be broken, and the Proletariat doomed.

No. Not doomed, he told himself. They didn't need the big house. The Proletariat had already won, hadn't it? It didn't need the old head, anymore. It had him . . .

His web of thought tore apart as he realized the truck had already passed him. He tried to run, but stumbled, catching himself on a tree when his momentum proved too much for his wobbly legs.

He didn't have to stop Dom. Just slow him down. Dean would catch up to him, and that would be the end of it. His fear of Dean was now greater than of his own death, but he knew with equal certainty that Dean would put a stop to it. That was his job, the one he had been born again for.

Andrew ran, throwing his wobbly body downhill, racing recklessly to keep up with his heavy, throbbing head. The ground got steeper, slotted with erosion ruts and exposed roots. He screamed, "DOM! Wait!" just before he spilled out on the road.

The sudden transition to a level and hard surface upended Andrew and sent him tumbling. The broken pavement was little more than a gummy coat of tar over loose gravel. Andrew hissed at his skinned knees, but levered himself up and staggered down the road after the U-Haul truck.

It was about a city block ahead of him. The echoing squeal of the truck's brakes brought him up short. He could only see the top of the orange and silver box trailer around the bend, but as he came closer, he saw a line of cop Broncos on the side of the road, and he almost wept for joy.

Andrew started running again, but it was a mug's game. A stitch in his side lanced every breath he took, and every step seemed to take geometry proofs and signed forms in triplicate from his brain.

The sheriff and the other deputy were parked on the shoulder, sandwiching a green sedan. A towtruck idled on the ridge overlooking the pond. The operator ran the winch, which stretched out to a third Bronco half-sunk in the muddy brown shallows.

A young, pimply deputy stood beside the cab of the U-Haul truck with one hand on his sidearm, and a thickset man in shirtsleeves and rubber hip waders stood at the back, intent on the padlock securing the loading door.

Andrew tried to shout, "Stop! Get away from the truck!" but the cracking croak that came out of him didn't carry.

The deputy noticed him and shouted something, approached and unsnapped the strap over his pistol.

The driver's side door of the truck opened, and Dom emerged. Andrew couldn't believe it. If you shaved Bigfoot and dressed him like a Motorhead roadie, you'd still have to beef him up with steroids and feed him live pit bulls to measure up to what Dom had become.

The deputy never had a chance.

Deputy Craig Wilmott stood by the cab, eyeballing the U-Haul's suspicious driver while the sheriff ran his license. His apple pie complexion was flushed, his sweat flowing in rivers, Adam's apple bobbing, but he didn't give an inch.

"C'mon, chief," Dom muttered, "let me get out and stretch my legs."

"Nossir," the deputy piped, clearing his throat twice to sound like a cop, "you stay right there, and keep your hands where I can see them."

"You boys are pretty upset about something," Dom said.

"One of ours," Wilmott started to say, then caught himself, and went back to the silent stinkeye treatment.

"I thought I'd be in town by now, Deputy sir. I had a lot of coffee with breakfast, and I sure could use a pit stop. Gotta drop the kids off at the pool, y'know what I mean?"

The deputy tried not to crack a smile. Sheriff Bialecki appeared at the passenger side window, pondwater sloshing in his hip waders, and looked Dom up and down. His eyes bugged out at the patchwork of scabs and scrapes and all but obliterated tattoos covering his bulging, hulked-out body. "The hell happened to you, son?"

Dom smirked and shrugged. "You should see the other guy, sir."

"You came up here in a black Toyota pickup, is that right, Mr. Kowalski?"

"Yes I did, sir," Dom nodded, taking it all very

seriously. "My brother took our mom down to Sacramento in it yesterday afternoon."

"Is that right?" The sheriff turned Dom's driver's license over and over in his hand. Though he was short and stout and bald, Bialecki carried himself like a full bird colonel. His bushy gray eyebrows knitted in concentration, looking pained at each new fact. Dom almost missed this game from the Army. "Your name isn't on the rental contract, and he took your truck . . . When did they leave? Have you heard from them since?"

"Yessir, they're at Mom's new apartment, sir. I guess you know it's not the safest place for a woman alone, out here . . . "

"Well, I sure would like to talk to them and find out how they got down there in that truck."

"It's old, but I work on it myself. Almost one-fifty on a rebuilt engine. Say, Sheriff, you're Polish, right?"

Bialecki arched his mustache at him, like an open hand cocked back to slap.

"No, sir, I just meant to say, I'm Polish, too. My dad's really into genealogy and shit, and he tracked down our cousins in Krakow . . . "

"Well, I'm pretty sure they didn't get far." Bialecki flipped the license onto Dom's lap and scratched his stubbly, sun-blistered scalp. Dom respected old guys who realized the tide was going out, and just shaved it, rather than trying to comb it over or grow a mullet. "We found all kinds of fragments and a whole headlight from the vehicle that struck my deputy's truck last night. We're pretty sure it didn't happen here, but we're all but certain that a Toyota pickup truck was involved."

"You should be real sure, sir, if you're going to go saying stuff like that."

"Well, we haven't had any of those CSI nabobs come out to take paint scrapings, and we can't seem to be able to get a goddamned ambulance out early on a Sunday morning, but we're pretty good at simple detective work, when we have to be."

The sheriff held up what was in his other hand. Bent in half and still dripping mud, it was the front license plate from Dom's truck.

Dom wished he was wearing his shades. He felt his eyes pingpong around from the sheriff and back to the trailer a moment too long.

"My deputy and very good friend Lonnie Scovill is dead, Mr. Kowalski. I aim to get to the bottom of it with both feet."

"Sir, I hope you do, honest-engine, and I'm real sorry for your loss, but I just don't know anything about it. Let me come down to your office in town and we can talk this over, but if I have to leave the truck somewhere, I have stuff in the back that I need to account for—"

"Better you just stay put, Mr. Kowalski. We're going to have a look in the back."

"It's locked," Dom said. "My brother has the key, but it's just my mom's furniture and personal stuff . . . "

"Your brother . . . the one you say was driving your truck yesterday."

"Dean. He's . . . well, I love him, he's my brother, you know? But every family has one, I guess. He gets into trouble . . . "

Looking over Dom's gnarly, tattooed hands on the steering wheel, at his haggard, hungover face, Sheriff Bialecki said, "*He's* the wild one?"

"I'm *pretty* sure there's nothing back there but my mom's furniture and junk, but you're welcome to look . . . "

Sheriff Bialecki glared at him, trying to winnow out some sense of the truth, but he didn't see Dom's smile when he ambled back around the truck.

"What's so funny?" Deputy Wilmott demanded.

"Nothing much," Dom said. "I guess it's just a funny day."

"God damn it, Craig," the Sheriff snarled, "try to get a signal and get that damned ambulance out here, pronto!"

Wilmott looked away up the road and shaded his eyes. "What the hell is that? Sheriff!"

In the rearview mirror, Dom saw a funny little guy like a fugitive from the *Alien Autopsy* video, running down the road waving his spindly arms and squawking like he either wanted a lozenge or to grudge-fuck a crow. His big, balding head had a halo of bees humming around it like electrons. His ungainly dome threw him off-balance as he jogged, and he almost fell down every few limping strides. It took Dom more than a few seconds to recognize the pathetic, pumpkinheaded effigy.

Deputy Wilmott turned away and didn't take notice when Dom got out of the truck and walked up behind him. "Look at that, Sheriff! It's a goddamned saucer-man!"

About thirty yards away, Andrew stumbled and fell prone on the tarmac, but the geek took a big deep breath and sobbed out, "Don't open it!"

Sheriff Bialecki looked up from the lock, which he'd been trying to pick with no success. "Craig! Escort Mr. Kowalski back to the vehicle!" The sheriff squished a couple steps toward Andrew, but thought better of getting closer. Andrew looked like he carried the plague. "Now, just calm down and be still, because I can't understand you. What's wrong?"

As Wilmott spun to cover Dom, he drew his pistol, but Dom palmed his hand and crushed it. The automatic went off twice, once into the air, and once into Wilmott's thigh. The deputy squealed and dropped. Dom let him go and pointed the pistol at the Sheriff, who had drawn his a half-second late. Admirable, because he looked to be having a heart attack.

"How'd you expect to catch crooks," Dom barked, "if you don't even know how to pick a lock?" He took hold of the padlock and wrenched it free so hard, the bolt spun off into the woods.

Andrew came crawling up to the sheriff's boots. "Stop him . . . Don't . . . open . . . it . . . you'll die . . . "

Covering the sheriff with Wilmott's gun, Dom undid the latch and yanked the loading door open.

"Shoot him . . . you've got . . . to stop him . . . "

The sheriff clutched his chest with one hand and waved his revolver with the other. "Don't you move, big boy . . . "

Like an old-fashioned window blind, the door rolled up into the roof of the trailer. A solid shockwave of agitated bees gathered over their heads.

"Sheriff," Dom shouted, "I'm sure this'll explain everything."

Not again, was all Andrew could think.

The roaring swarm engulfed the sheriff and the deputy and rolled over their buried forms to get at Andrew.

Too weak to stand, let alone run away, he could only throw his arms over his head and cry. Tiny bodies drummed on his back, but nothing stung him. It was like wave after wave of rice flung at him, but not a grain landed. All around him, in a corona around where he lay, the ground was powdered with dead bees. Hundreds more flew at him, but within a few inches of his cowering body, they simply dropped dead.

Holy shit, I did that. If anything, he felt even weaker than before, but the swarm changed course and avoided him.

The sheriff finally tried to shoot Dom, but it was anyone's guess where his wild shots went. The deputy ran in circles across the road and past the towtruck, hurled himself into the water.

The towtruck driver jumped in his truck and rolled up his windows, but thrashed around in a conniption behind the wheel. The man in the green sedan was behind his wheel as well, doing something to himself . . . Andrew focused, saw him inject himself in the neck with a syringe.

Untouched at the heart of the bee-storm, Dom crossed his arms and nodded. "I love it when a plan comes together," he said. "How about you, Andrew? How's your new family treating you? Looks like they're feeding you the royal jelly."

Andrew made himself stand. Bees in ankle-deep drifts crunched underfoot. "Dom . . . we're all trapped in this situation . . . but it doesn't have to be our fight . . . We can end it . . . "

Dom dragged the loading door down slowly, leaving it propped open a few inches so the retreating swarm could pour back inside like a genie returning to the lamp. "Yes, we can. Oh, indeed, we can do that very thing right now." Dom cracked his knuckles. Each joint snapped like a starter's pistol. "See, I'm working here, Andy. Do I come to your place of business and slap the dicks out of your mouth? Do I?"

Andrew felt his grip on consciousness slipping, but he bit his lip until he tasted blood to stay focused on Dom. He tried to will whatever he'd done to the bees on his brother. It was nothing personal; a lot of crazy shit that was nobody's fault had happened, but Andrew was tired of eating all of it. *Have an embolism, a stroke, a grand mal seizure, you bullying son of a bitch!*

Dom tried to come closer, but he seemed to walk into a high wind. His fists swiped at the air, but he couldn't get any closer to Andrew. The strain on his face alone showed the force of the wind, which didn't stir a single pine needle, but Dom's muffled grunts told Andrew that the wave he resisted was one of pure pain.

"Fuck it," Dom finally said. He tilted his head, listening to the wind. "Catch you later."

A moment later, Andrew could hear it, too.

Dom sprinted back to the truck and jumped in, popping the brake and letting it roll before he got the engine started. When it caught, the truck jarringly laid down a patch that set the hives in the trailer tumbling like dice in a cup.

The civilian in the green car gunned his engine and tried to ram his way out of the bracketing Broncos. Backing into one and then thrusting into first gear to slam into the other, the green car careened onto the road with its bumper dragging and peeled out, heading for town.

Andrew stood alone in the road, alone with the mounds of bees covering the bodies of the sheriff and the deputy. He turned and raised his arms at the growing rumble of the canary yellow Hummer from the neighbors' cabin. When it came around the bend, Andrew's stomach dropped into the seat of his pants.

Dean was doing fifty at least, and when he saw Andrew, the Hummer accelerated, bore down on him and only swerved to miss him when Andrew did not leap out of the way. The Hummer's customized horn sounded a deafening blast of jingoistic challenge as it passed.

I am quite unashamed, he thought, *of pissing my pants, right now.*

For Dean, the whole world seemed to slow and grind to a halt. The road was a frozen arena, in which only he and his brother moved. As if from the air, he could sense Dom up ahead, as everything between them faded to transparency. From their first game of tag, every touch football game that ended in bloody fisticuffs, to the lessons of the beating he took last night, had honed his mind for this.

The Hummer was a disgrace. Every design feature that made the military-issue HMMV a durable, maneuverable transportation asset had been sacrificed to lull the civilian idiot driver into delusions that he was invincible, and protect him from the carnage the top-heavy piece of shit would inflict when he lost control of it. The back wheels fishtailed badly on the Sexagon's gravel driveway, clipping the mailbox at the bottom. On the tarmac at last, the Hummer dug in and launched him down the hill, but it took real elbow grease to steer the flying shitbox over the meandering contours of the valley.

Through the trees, the raw golden sunlight glinted off chrome and orange painted steel on the move at an oblivious elephant walk. Dean floored it.

Now we'll see, Dean thought, *who's weak*.

The high-crowned road slipped off to the left and dropped over a little hummock, the Hummer floating over the peak, wheels barely touching the road, kissing the uneven tarmac of the steep downward slope with a screech. Dean swore and yanked the wheel hard left.

Andy stood in the middle of the road, ankle-deep in piles of dead bees, with two bodies in brown uniforms splayed out before him. His girlish arms flailed, his mouth made a big, empty O that lined up perfectly with the targeting sight of the Hummer's hood ornament.

One iota less effort, and all the complications Andy embodied would be rendered moot. Like Stalin said: *No man, no problem*.

Dean had found it hard to think clearly about what to do with Andy from the beginning. When he came along and the collective adopted him as the new Head, Dean was wounded to the quick. He was everything a leader should be if the collective wanted to survive, while Andy was a bedwetting pissant. It hurt his pride until he realized that nothing had changed. The Head of State was still a sunken-chested wimp, and if Dean couldn't keep him under his thumb, then they deserved to die out. But Andy obviously had a hard time following even the simplest orders.

Dean swerved across the double yellow line and goosed

the horn as he blasted by Andy, who flinched and fell down. A gaggle of sheriff's vehicles and a towtruck flashed by on his right, and then the road leveled out as it circled around the pond. Up ahead, Dean saw the boxy outline of the U-Haul truck limping around the next bend, and sped up.

Dom cursed the U-Haul rental company, the National Transportation Safety Board and the limiter that held the truck's speed down to sixty-five. Only three miles to town, but he knew Dean was gaining on him.

Then he saw the green sedan in the rearview, growing huge and swerving to pass him on his left.

If that motherfucker was a civilian, Dom was the Pope. He swung the truck across the centerline and judiciously applied the brake. The sedan tried to feint back to the right, but smashed into the rental truck's built-up rear bumper.

Chrome and a gusher of radiator fluid dumped out of the shattered grill as the driver fought to keep his car under control. Watching him in the left rearview, Dom chuckled and pumped his fist in the air, then went to look for something good on the radio. He barely noticed the flash of garish yellow coming up fast behind the fading sedan. When he did a double take and looked behind him, he couldn't see it anymore, but he could hear it.

The speedometer needle kissed the safety limiter. "Fuck!" Dom braced for impact.

The green sedan hovered in the Hummer's path like a holed ship, brake lights screaming, floundering across both lanes trying to regain control of itself and get around the U-Haul truck. Dean barely got by without hitting it, which almost certainly would have sent him flying into the tender mercies of the old-growth pines crowding the road.

His heart raced like he had jet fuel in his blood. His mind zeroed in on the truck like it was packed to the rafters with everything that ever let him down, but he cracked a carefree smile as he scissored by the green sedan doing seventy. The driver flailed at the inflated airbag mushrooming out of his steering wheel, quite unable to control his still-racing car. Dean didn't believe in evolution, but he was a staunch supporter of the Darwin Awards.

Nothing in the way, now, between him and Dominic.

With the cool surrender of a kamikaze pilot, Dean dropped in behind the hulking trailer and floored the gas.

The rental truck drifted left across the centerline. The Hummer ate up the distance and smashed into the scuffed black truck bumper.

The bumper folded under the trailer, but Dom kept the truck on the road. The loading door slid up. White wooden crates tumbled out and shattered on the Hummer's hood, exploded in clouds of livid insect fire. Whole hives of bees coated Dean's windshield. The wipers swept them away, but smeared the glass with a paste of guts, wings and chitinous debris. The long silver tongue of the loading ramp slid out of the U-Haul's crushed bumper assembly and dragged behind the truck, spraying rooster tails of sparks off the tarmac.

Dean dropped back to fight the chaotic forces trying to throw the Hummer into a spin, then sped up again on the next straightaway to come abreast of the truck. The road climbed a long, bumpy incline and vanished over the crest, where a green sign pointed to the junction for the state road to Sacramento. Dom waved his huge gray arm, inviting him to pass with a big shit-eating grin on his face in his rearview mirror.

Dean swung hard left across the centerline and floored it. The rental truck was maxed out at sixty-five. They were almost axle-to-axle when they went over the crest of the hill.

A rickety old Ford camper conversion filled the oncoming lane, less than four car lengths from smashing head-on into the Hummer. Dom flashed a big thumbs-up and closed the gap with the camper.

Dean sucked in a breath to scream. The hot, arid summer air turned to liquid nitrogen as it flowed over the exposed nerves from his broken teeth. The world went white. Blind, torqued out of his mind by unbelievable pain, Dean stomped the brake.

The Hummer stood up on its front wheels. Dean felt every ounce of the huge SUV pile up on his back. Letting off the brake, he tried to wrench the wheel hard right and drift into the wake of the rental truck, but the Hummer was not designed for such precise, high-velocity navigation. The front wheels locked up and shrieked as the road shredded the tires. The hulking SUV was suddenly a bobsled, shooting down the double yellow line sideways.

The camper squeaked past the rental truck with inches to spare, but clipped the wildly swinging ass-end of the Hummer, winding it up like a top. Dean saw the road and the woods and the passing truck become a dazzling blur, the Hummer a centrifuge. He lost count of how many times he spun, but the trees stopped him with authority.

"All right!" Dom crowed, and reached for the radio dial. This was a moment made for Motorhead, but the best he could find was Rush. It wasn't particularly celebratory, but he did sort of think of himself as today's Tom Sawyer, so he grooved on it.

He slowed down and cruised with the flow of traffic. A punkass little hybrid that looked as if it was made of recycled Big Mac containers put-putted in front of him, and an irregular flow of oncoming traffic decided him against trying to pass. Nobody followed him, which was just as well, because his loading ramp still dragged along behind him.

A few passing cars honked at him and pointed at this or that. Dom waved back and smiled. One mile to Utopia. He could hear the Percolator in the engine, and knew that he drove with destiny. "Them don't know who they fuckin' wit'," he shouted.

The road ahead slalomed down the face of a canyon and crossed the falls on a narrow concrete bridge, then the tunnel, then the town. The hybrid seemed to want to stop to check a map at each turn, and Dom rode the brakes, shouted, "Come on, pussies!" when he glanced in his rearview and sucked in a breath cold as a toothache.

He'd always said it until he believed it, that Dean was the weak twin, the uppity afterbirth, the shortchanged accident, while Dom was the real deal. But he should have known Dean would never let it be this easy.

Dean shredded the Hummer's airbags in a frenzy with his bare hands. Coughing white powder and bright blood, he kicked the door off its hinges and dropped to the forest floor. The Hummer hung suspended sideways on the trio of Ponderosa pines it had uprooted on impact.

Every breath was torture. The last of his teeth had split open like rotten fruit in his jaw when he hit the dashboard. The nerves sparked like downed power lines in his mouth, but now he welcomed it. He did not need his teeth. He needed the pain to clear his head.

The road was quiet when he climbed up onto it. The camper sat sideways on the shoulder, fifty yards away. The driver stumbled out of the cab and jogged after Dean. A tubby guy in khaki and flannel fishing gear and a bright splash of blood covering the right side of his face, he looked like he'd just shit himself, and was choking on the maelstrom of mixed emotions he felt when he saw Dean come lumbering out of the wreckage, beaten, but far from broken.

"Oh my God, are you okay? That was . . . what the hell were you doing, trying to pass like that, you dumb son of a bitch? You're lucky I'm not a younger man, or I'd—"

Dean started running.

He was big and heavy. His feet on the tarmac sounded like the clopping of Clydesdale hooves. Every step sent a jarring lance of pain up his legs, every breath sent thirty-two bolts of lightning into his brain.

He had to go faster.

He threw himself into it like he did in track that first year in high school, before they bussed in all those black kids from bad homes with bad grades and long legs, who made a mockery of his every heroic, tendon-tearing sacrifice. All those times he almost won, he pictured Dom just ahead of him, duck-stepping, endzone dirty-bird dancing and smiling like it was nothing, why couldn't he keep up?

He ran harder. A lather of scalding sweat and blood flew from his arms and legs, stung his eyes. Steam poured off his back. He ran faster, his heart and lungs a furnace that fed on fat and muscle, blood and bone. He got lighter and ran faster.

Racing through the junction, he passed and cut off a Toyota pickup towing a ski boat, and passed two more trucks going up the next grade. He was made of fire. He was the collective's last chance.

He passed people mowing the lawns of fancy summer cabins set back from the road, tourists in their Volvos and Jeeps turning to gawk as they passed, a blissfully unaware young Asian lady with an iPod, jogging with an Irish setter that reared up on its hind legs and snarled at him.

He passed them all in a blur, leaving none of them quite sure of what they saw. Even before he crested the ridge overlooking the falls, he could see the radioactive beacon of Dom right through the intervening mountain. He was a smart missile, locked on the same target for twenty-seven years.

He came over the ridge and saw the U-Haul just crossing the bridge behind a bug-shaped hybrid sedan. He redoubled his pace and it was like the truck was standing still, though he saw its wheels spinning, grit spraying out from them as Dom tried to overtake the hybrid.

Dean threw his legs out in giant moonwalk strides and hurled himself at the trailer. It was just like stealing second base. He jumped on the trailing loading ramp, which instantly broke free, then used the inertial boost to fly headlong into the back of the trailer.

The half-open door soaked up his weight, but he dropped back onto the road, barely caught the shattered bumper and ran to keep up. He tore a strip of metal from the bumper and stabbed the left rear tire.

The jagged steel gutted the whirling rubber all the way around in a split-second. He risked a glance up and saw Dom's face in the rearview mirror. Stunned, punctured. That look was sweeter than a lifetime of valentines.

The truck slewed left to pass the hybrid, its back end fishtailing even worse once Dean slashed the other back tire. Settling down on its rear rims, the truck dragged itself across the bridge like a racehorse with two broken legs. Dean let go and tumbled across the span to crash into the abutment, and watch what he had wrought.

Dom struggled valiantly to negotiate the tunnel, but Dean pricked up his ears and realized, with a squirt of bitter noise that passed for laughter, that he needn't have worried. Whoever fought for their side in Utopia wasn't much smarter than Andy, but they sure earned the worm, this time.

As Dom fought the moving truck's palsied steering wheel and floored the accelerator, he was quite impressed with himself, for the truck remained more or less in its own lane.

The ambulance coming at him with lights and sirens going full-tilt, however, did not.

Through the dazzling kaleidoscope of red and strobing white light, he could see her face flattened out like an empty rubber mask in his headlights. The girl he'd won and lost on the way to the big house, the one who'd been sent to bring him to the Tower, but got snatched away by the egg-sucking anarchists. The one with the bees in her business—

Shit, Dom thought, and reached for his seatbelt.

The ambulance and rental truck collided head-on with a combined speed of almost a hundred miles per hour. Both heavy, high-profile vehicles, the outrageous energy of their abrupt and brutal fusion ripped through both vehicles like storm waves in a tiny pond, and vented its fury on the respective vehicles' occupants and contents.

The back end of the ambulance rose up and struck the roof of the corrugated steel-lined tunnel, ringing it like a bell.

Dom tensed every muscle and rode out the impact with his feet braced against the firewall. Tendons and twisted cords of torque-wracked muscle strained and snapped in his thighs and lower back like firecrackers going off under his skin. The blizzard blast of safety glass and the ballistic kiss of the safety bags blinded him to her arrival, but he felt and heard her—whose name he still couldn't remember—rocket out of her own seat and into the cab of his truck like so much catapulted meat.

For a second, there was something like silence, if you tuned out the Percolator, the ticking and dripping and sizzle of hot metal and the tortured roar of the bees in the trailer. *Ha ha, Dean's never gonna get his deposit back . . .*

Dom pushed open the door and spilled out onto the road. The tarmac was slippery. Streams of ghastly green fluid forked around his feet. The maple syrup smell of scorched coolant smothered the coppery smell of blood, but his eyes burned with the gasoline vapors coming from the ambulance. Plastic gas cans spilled out the gashed windshield. She'd rigged it up like a bomb.

What to do, what to do? The end of the tunnel was only a hundred feet ahead. He started to limp back to the trailer to open it, when he saw someone with a rifle come shambling up out of the window of daylight at the Utopian end of the tunnel. Dom popped his knuckles, eager to tune up on someone to shake the dust bunnies out of his brain.

"I . . . we . . . tried . . . to stop . . . her, Comrade," the man shouted, hacking coughs chopping the words into wet, garbled parcels, "but . . . she . . . she killed . . . my . . . my . . . "

The old geek was bent over at the waist with a gnarly spinal curvature, like he'd never heard of milk. His long, silver beard was flecked with yellow spittle and a pipe was clenched in his teeth. He wore a blood-spattered gray sweater and jeans, and a vest with lots of smartass buttons on it. The shotgun in his arms seemed to be dragging him forward, as much as he carried it. He staggered after it up to Dom and managed a shaky salute. "Long live the glorious revolution, comrade. We've been waiting . . . for you . . . "

Something stirred in the cab of the U-Haul truck. The old bookseller hoisted the shotgun and emptied both barrels into the girl on the seat. "Traitor . . . cancer . . . "

"Let's move the hives," Dom croaked. He hawked and spat two yellow, cracked teeth and a gob of blood. He turned and looked back down the tunnel, but saw no sign of Dean. Strange—

The old comrade was fumbling with the latch on the

trailer when Dom heard the crisp chrome rasp of a Zippo lighter. Dom threw up the loading door and jumped back as the remaining hives emptied out into the tunnel. Quite undeterred by the sleet of bees clumping on his face, the old man threw himself into the trailer to grab for the nearest overturned hive.

Rounding the corner of the trailer, Dom saw the rich golden flame and glint of silver in the girl's red, ruined paw, dangling out over the road where the gasoline flowed in rivulets from the smashed ambulance.

Maybe he could have dived after the tumbling lighter right then, and perhaps he might even have caught it, if there was nothing left of Dominic Kowalski in the perfect soldier he was becoming. As it was, his distracting thoughts were not fretful musings on the fate of his own skin, but a deep, solemn regret that he never got to fuck this chick.

He did not flinch or take cover to save himself. He started to leap for the lighter just a split-second too late, and still might have caught it, if the roiling fumes of the gasoline did not lick up at the falling flame and embrace it in a brilliant consummation that washed over Dom like morning on Mercury.

"What the hell kind of crazy stunt was that?" somebody demanded. Rolling over, Dean saw a reedy, pot-bellied college kid in Birkenstocks, a faded String Cheese Incident T-shirt and flannel pajama pants. He must have come from the hybrid, which was parked on the shoulder, just beyond the bridge. Dean couldn't find the words to tell him where to go.

Bees roared out of the tunnel, a superswarm of at least a dozen hives, but going the wrong way. The hybrid driver ran for his car, but the bees brought him down just short, and buried him. They descended on Dean, but he swatted them away. Something in his sweat seemed to turn them off. The dozens hanging from his skin by their trapped stingers caused him no pain whatsoever.

In the tunnel, the rental truck exploded.

The force and fire came out the mouth of the tunnel like birdshot from a blunderbuss. Hair blazing like a mad villager's torch, Dom staggered out into daylight and looked around like it came as one hell of a surprise that he wasn't waking up in some strange girl's bedroom. "Well, fuck . . . " he observed. "How the hell d'you like that? Hit an ambulance . . . "

A secondary explosion, much bigger and chunkier, hurled shrapnel at them. Dom caught a lot of it and was flung into the air right over Dean's head. Wreathed in burning bees and kicking at empty air, he sailed over the bridge railing and plunged out of sight with the falls.

Dean leapt to his feet, collapsed against the guardrail. The fiery daylight danced with static energy that entered him and undid all his pain. It was, he knew, the love and will of the Proletariat. He roared at the sky, sharing with them the joy of his victory.

He was still congratulating himself when the speeding green sedan ran him down and dragged him into the fiery tunnel.

For once, common sense prevailed.

The first thing Andrew did was get out of the road. No one else tried to run him down, and nothing stirred. The sheriff and deputy still lay spread-eagle on the road, dusted with dead bees.

Something else Andrew had learned about bees: their stingers were meant to be used again and again on other insects. The complex epidermis of higher animals trapped the stinger and tore it out. It came as quite a shock to the bee, to the extent that anything could, to find itself disemboweled by its own weapon.

His own flying eyes descended on him now, but they could show him little. In violet, black and white, the truck and the Hummer battled until they went out of range.

There was nothing between him and freedom.

He still felt weak and starved. The last thing he needed right now was a cigarette, but the craving for honey was worse than what he imagined heroin withdrawal must feel like. His brain burned. He needed more of the stuff, or something bad was going to happen. He didn't dare hope that the bad thing would be reverting to normal.

When the bees found him, it was like his second wind just got beamed to him out of thin air. He was stronger, and he felt them at his back, far away and yet under his skin with him. They did not think, but they feared for him.

He shopped for a new car. The towtruck was still tethered to the dead deputy's truck in the pond, and the sheriff's keys were gone, but the deputy had left his in the ignition. Andrew took a minute to pull his withered legs and ass up into the high seat. Once he got in, he managed to turn the Bronco around and coast down the hill, only once accidentally turning on the siren.

The morning was still and quiet; more so, surely, than any other day, when the Pond Restaurant would be open, and tourists frolicking in the sunshine. It wouldn't last. He needed to talk to someone, anyone, he trusted. There was no one but Laura.

He stopped at May's trailer and skulked around the thorny berry patch until he found the trail that led into her nest. The sense of dislocation froze him in his tracks. He was here only yesterday. He would have recognized himself in a mirror only twelve hours ago, but he had already changed into a stranger. *I'm sorry, baby*, he thought. *I'll fix it; I'll make it right . . .*

The door was still shut, the windows through which

May had been dragged and Andrew fell still flapping in the breeze. He listened for signs of life before he touched the door. If anything bigger than a rat was inside, he didn't think he could take it.

He opened the door and let it swing wide to clang against the blackened silver skin of the trailer. Nothing stirred, or at least nothing that felt threatened enough by Andrew to present itself. Gingerly, he crept up the folding metal steps. He felt the strength of the collective failing him. Was something wrong, or were they withdrawing their support, because he was scheming to betray them?

They did not think. But they wanted—they needed—him.

He needed her. To know she was safe and far away from all this, holding out some hope of a sane refuge when he got free, and he would do whatever it took to save that place, anything. He would change, he'd show her, she'd see how much he'd changed, already . . .

The cell phone was right where he'd left it, under May's bed. He picked it up and hit the button. Battery Low, it said. *So what, fuck you, can I pretty-please get a fucking signal?*

One bar. *One Voice Message*. From Laura.

He thumbed the button to play it, but he had to hang up and redial twice because his hand shook so badly. When he finally got it, the message crackled and cut out, so he didn't trust her words. But he melted at every syllable she spoke.

"Andrew . . . honey, where are you? I've been trying to call . . . but I still don't trust myself to say the right thing . . . You know how I am . . . " She sniffed, wiped her nose, and sighed. "I need to talk to you, we really need to talk . . . I'm sorry about how I was before, I was mad at myself, mostly . . . I made a big, big mistake . . . but I was mad at you for just letting me . . . Why couldn't you . . . just once . . . ?"

She started crying.

"Shit, I don't want to argue with your fucking machine . . . OK, long rant short . . . I was wrong to send you off like this . . . and I know I need to face my mother, if I'm ever going to get better . . . You can't fix this. You could put everything on the scale against it and . . . It's not your fault, is what I'm trying to say.

"Whatever happens, um . . . I need you to call and let me know everything's all right up there, or else I'm coming up . . . I'm leaving tonight, after work . . . "

"Oh Jesus . . . oh shit . . . oh please, God . . . " He hit the Message Details button. Had she sent it today? Was she on her way up? Had she sent it last night? Was she already here . . . somewhere?

Replace Your Battery, said the phone, and died in his trembling hand.

"Andrew, baby, come here . . . "

Andrew jerked at the sound of her fifty-thousand volt whisper.

In the shadowy alcove of May's bed, Laura knelt on the tangled sheets. She moaned and writhed as if in the throes of a fever, or one of her elusive, earth-shattering orgasms. "Missed you . . . so bad . . . "

It was too much. Andrew hugged himself. Every fiber of his being ached to run to her and throw her down and ravish her, begging her to understand, thanking her for this second chance . . . but he quivered with unbearable terror. "Laura," he choked, "what are you doing here?" *Who got to you first?* He had to know. *Which side are you on?*

Rocking her hips as if he were already inside her, she tossed her long black hair and caressed herself, from her heavy, full breasts to the generous, gyrating curves of her hips. When her insatiable hands doubled back, she hiked up her skirt, exposing crotchless fishnet stockings that framed the shaven treasure he knew so well and missed so much.

But he saw nothing familiar between her legs.

Laura's pale olive skin was pitted with hexagonal pores; the tessellated pattern spread across her belly and thighs like a rampant tropical skin disease. Lost in ecstasy, Laura stroked her inner thighs and parted her honeycombed sex with both hands. Her eyes rolled back in her head and her breathing quickened as if a ghost were eating her out. Bees poured out of her vagina and came for his face.

"Stop it, Laura!" Andrew threw an arm up across his eyes and dove at her. His nerves threatened to overrule him. She was contaminated; a scab, sent to destroy him. The bees in his bonnet told him so: *She doesn't love you.*

"Be with me," Laura growled.

He crashed on the bed and rolled over to find himself quite alone.

His mind was changing . . . growing. His imagination was growing with it. Only his sanity was shrinking.

When the workers came to the door of the trailer and carried him back this time, they bore him as tenderly as a swaddled infant.

CHAPTER 25

THE REMAINDER OF the day passed quietly.

Andrew sat beside the fire ring, watching the sunset shadows steep and ferment like wine in the corners of the sawmill, staring at the cell phone, willing it to light up. Sprague hovered around him, offering him honey from a mason jar.

"I have to recharge my phone. I need to talk to my wife." What would he say to her, if he could? *Hey baby, I haven't had a smoke in twenty-four hours!* When he tried to quit at home, he'd pick up a smoke and just as reflexively reject it, flush with false willpower, only to pick it up again and light it a few minutes or half an hour later. Laura would say this grossed her out worse than the smoking. *It's like you're tripping on two drugs,* she said.

"You mustn't go out," Sprague scolded. "You almost got yourself killed, you selfish fool. The collective—"

"If I really want to leave, you think you can stop me?" The bravado of this statement would have made a room filled with sane people laugh.

"They'll stop you. You're too important, now."

"Then why don't you do it? Tell one of them to go!"

Sprague's shriveled, shrunken-apple head shuddered with tired mirth, as if Andrew's density had finally tipped the balance between vexing and ludicrous. "There's nobody outside who can help us, Andrew. There's no point trying to drag anyone from your old life into this."

"That's the goddamned point! My wife is coming up here!"

That stopped his wheezing, muted laughter. "You aim to stop her?"

"Yes . . . I mean, I want to see her . . . but not like this!"

"There won't be a better time later, son. This isn't summer camp. If she really loves you, then she will come and join you. If not, then it doesn't matter. This is your family, now."

Andrew furied at Sprague a while longer, but it got harder to keep his argument straight as his fingers, swatting and brushing away hovering bees, sank into the soft folds of his skull. Like an overripe pumpkin, the bone was pliable and spongy, the sutured petals of the petrified rosebud cranium unfolding, the busy, buzzing honeycomb hideout of his brain rising like yeast, sweating an oily, spicy fragrance that lured the bees in ecstatic, implacable waves, and sent them bumbling away freighted with the encoded pollen of his will.

Whatever her emotional state when she arrived, Laura was not going to understand this. Who could?

When he was in doubt about Laura's emotional state at home, Andrew would check the medicine cabinet. When a manic phase took over, she swept through the house in a cleaning frenzy. To touch her in the midst of such a phase was like waking a sleepwalker. She might tremble with bottled anxiety, or she might hit him like a grabby stranger on the street, before she remembered herself. Asking her never got under the rhino-hide of What's Wrong, but he learned to read the signs and portents in the fruit of her frantic labors, like an ancient Roman *haruspex*, divining the will of the gods by spilling the organs of sacrificial beasts.

His paltry handful of deodorants, shampoos and shaving supplies might be lined up opposite hers on the shelves in a trench war of toiletries, or hemmed in like outnumbered explorers about to be devoured by savage cosmetics or segregated completely by a brutal apartheid, and relegated to the ghetto under the sink. Once or twice, he'd found them paired, his unscented Sure Solid beside her Powder Fresh Secret roll-on, his toothbrush spooned beside hers on the little cradles, instead of behind the faucet, encrusted with its own filth. Such subtle attempts to reconcile their lives had given him hope that she was at least trying to reach him. Maybe what he should have done was help her make a clean break from all the toxic waste of her childhood. Maybe a radical change, a new life, was exactly what they needed . . .

A soldier shambled into the sawmill, shoving aside workers even as they tried to clear a path. Blackened from head to toe by blood, burns and road rash, the looming, wounded effigy twisted its toothless mouth in a grimace that alone identified it as Dean. Animated solely by anger, he approached the fire ring and held out something. It took a second to grasp that it really was what it appeared to be.

"Who the hell is this?" Dean barked, waving a man's severed head by the hair over the crackling fire. His voice was distorted, mushy, as it coughed out of that old man's mouth. Toothless, but the jaw muscles only seemed larger, taut cables, the gums fraying away from exposed jawbones honed to keen edges, like the beak of a parrot.

Andrew gulped, choking out, "I don't know . . . " even as he remembered seeing the bland, sandy-haired man in the green sedan injecting himself with something during the bee attack, just before he drove away. "He was down at the pond with the sheriff . . . "

"I wasn't talking to you, Andy. I'm talking to your senile old boyfriend, here." Stepping over Andrew like he was a puddle, Dean cornered Sprague, who tried not to cower. "Do you know this asshole, yes or no?"

Sprague spat in the flames and glared defiantly back at

Dean. "Who can know a man better than one who ends his life? No, I've never seen him."

"Liar!" Dean backhanded Sprague with the severed head. The pithy, gridiron clonk of knocking skulls resounded through the sawmill and startled bats out of the rafters. The old hermit whipped back and lay supine against a pile of splintered stones. His cloudy eyes unscrewed from his brain. He made no move to block the next blow.

Andrew rushed Dean and leapt onto his arm when it cocked above his head. Dean lifted him off the ground and slung him loose. He flew, and would have landed in the fire ring, but a worker moved to catch him. Two soldiers converged on Dean, a head taller than him despite their lack of heads.

"You're freaking them out, Dean," Andrew said. "Don't lay a hand on him again, or I don't know what they'll do to you."

"Are you *threatening* me, Andy?" Dean dropped the head in Sprague's lap. The old man didn't react. Andrew couldn't tell if he was breathing. "Are you so smart now, that you already forgot our little talk?"

"You know the way things are," Andrew said, feeling an alien confidence lifting him up, driving a ramrod up his flimsy spine. He felt the worker's skin against his—warm, almost hot, and transmitting an electricity that gave him the strength to face Dean. "We're all a part of this, now, and we have to cooperate. You're bigger and stronger than me, and I'm weak and a liberal candy-ass titty-baby, but I guess somebody thought I was smarter than you."

"I love the collective," Dean grumbled, straining for calm, without a trace of irony. "I have laid down my life and killed for it. What have you done, besides piss your pants and get in the way? You're just a tourist, Andy, like you always were."

Andrew felt the air around Dean charged with bees

vibrating in A major, a martial throb signaling their readiness to ball Dean at a twitch from his brain. "Wow. Day before yesterday, you loved America. You called me a faggot for defending the idea of communism. They changed your mind as much as they changed your body, just like they did mine. It's not a game any more, is it?"

"You don't know what's really going on," Dean gritted.

"Well, why don't you tell me what's going on? Or do I have to wait for another bee to sting me to find out?"

"We're under surveillance. That sneaky bastard I deep-sixed was a government agent."

Andrew didn't expect this. But he should have. They talked about it this morning. "What kind of agent?"

"What difference does it make? They're spying on us! They're just waiting to see what happens. He said their inside man told them the experiment was *near critical mass*, his words."

Andrew ached to throw Dean's pompous words from the other night back in his face—*Only enemies of the state should worry about government surveillance . . . what do you have to hide?*—but that Dean was dead and gone, and this one wouldn't recognize itself in a mirror. "You killed him."

"Of course I killed him! He was a spy!"

"He was a spy, and you killed him, so now they will have to conclude, when they find his headless corpse, that he didn't cut himself shaving, and they're going to come in here with helicopters and tanks! It'll make Waco look like a Girl Scout cookie drive!"

"So ask yourself," Sprague hissed, cradling his head, "what path should the Proletariat take?"

"We've got to get out of here, now." The how and where of it began, even then, to assemble itself. Plans shaped, scuttled and rehatched in his mind, almost beneath his notice. When the hive breeds a new queen, the drones separate. The old queen leaves with half the hive to swarm in search of a new home. There are no disputes, no *coups d'etat*; the real ruler of the hive is a ghost called *instinct*. Its enforcers, the pheromones, preside over the bloodless succession. How lucky for bees, that they have no ego.

"Fuck that," Dean snapped. "We're going to war."

"Fuck you!" Andrew stretched up on his tiptoes to get in Dean's face. "If I decide what the collective does, we're gone! You cast your vote when you ripped that guy's head off."

"The colony is still not whole," Sprague said. He propped himself up against the rocks. A lump like half an egg was already forming on his forehead. "He still holds their minds. He won't let you go until you give him a war."

"But I don't understand why! The Proletariat needed a new head. And . . . for better or for worse, they got one. We don't need the big house, we don't need the scabs, and if we stay here, we're all going to die!"

"You have no idea what he stole from them . . . how much untapped power the human brain has, and so many together, aligned . . . He thought the state should be one body, but that it should be *his* body. He took their *minds*, Andrew."

Incredible. How long had this situation grown into itself, slowly collapsing, the insane gravity of this perverse dream warping the minds of all involved, to make them take hostages and make them leaders, and think to inspire them with pity? If there was a pill for Stockholm Syndrome, now would be a good time to pass them out. "And what the hell do you expect me to do about that?"

"The Proletariat chose you. They trust you. You're going to go in there and get them back."

"That's insane! Unless Grodenko is some kind of Big Bad Wolf, and we can cut him open, and Grandma spills out whole and hearty—"

"A Big Bad Wolf," Sprague interrupted, "is as good a way to describe Grodenko, as any. Before there can be any talk of leaving, he must be put down."

"That's just what I'd expect a *spy* to say. Agent provocateur, is that what you put on your income taxes?"

"Andrew, you can't believe that hogwash. That's what they used to do. They'd start rumors and plant phony evidence to turn us against each other. This idiot has doomed us. If you had taken him in hand properly—"

Dean came up behind Andrew, whipped him around too fast. Andrew threw up a defensive arm. The soldiers around him would have gored Dean with their forearm spines, if he intended harm. But he shoved a valise into Andrew's chest. "Here, read this shit. It was in his car."

Andrew took the bag. It was slippery with tacky blood. Pegs of safety glass spilled out of its brown leatherette folds like fake diamonds. "Didn't you read it?"

Dean frowned, a cramped, schoolyard bully face. He was searching the bulkheads and footlockers of his shipshape brain for an answer, but nothing satisfied. "You're the brains, you read it."

Andrew dumped it out. Maps, receipts and transcripts, with phone numbers and coded notes scribbled throughout. And pictures—forest scenes with fuzzy humanoid silhouettes in the background, *In Search Of Bigfoot* outtakes. Grainy blowups of the big house, with a pair of scabs idling on the porch; one with a rifle on his hip, and no pants, both faces blurred by black, meteoric haloes. A couple clearer shots of workers gathering food from steel troughs. Taken from inside the cabin.

Andrew looked sideways at Sprague. "Fucking spy."

"How dare you, boy! I tried to tell you they were watching! When you first came snooping, I thought *you* were a spy! Stumbled into this days ago, and you think you know it all!"

"The more I know, the worse I feel." He turned and walked away from all of them.

His head throbbed like an egg about to hatch. Athena was born fully grown out of the brainpan of her father,

Zeus. During her gestation, the goddess of wisdom and ingenuity forged her helmet and breastplate, driving the god of thunder mad with divine migraines.

"Fine," Andrew wheeled on Dean. "You want a war?"

"You don't know how to defend yourself, let alone fight to win. Leave it to me."

Shame and rage over the beating Dean dealt him had simmered in Andrew's guts all day. Dean's flat contempt now was the tickle that goaded him to vomit it out. "Teach me to be a winner, Dean, since you know it all. Teach me how to be a man. Show me how to beat down everyone smaller and weaker than me. Show me how to bend others to my will, make them tools and then throw them away.

"That's exactly what all these people revolted to get away from. And even with most of their brains scooped out, they reject that bullshit. Teach me, so I can explain it to them, and maybe they'll let us use them the way they wouldn't let the big house use them."

Scalding heat poured out of Andrew. It seemed to burn Dean, to hurt him worse than his grievous wounds. As he spoke, Andrew seemed to grow, to loom over Dean, who sank to his knees like someone cut his tendons. His ruined skin flushed, on fire inside, and sweat broke out. His mouth hung open and his eyes teared up, but never once blinked.

"Leading isn't about beating everyone else into following you. It's about getting them to want to cooperate. Wolves run in packs, but what did they ever make, that mattered? Everything good the human race ever did—and everything bad, for that matter—they did because they could work together, the strong and the weak."

Dean nodded like it cost him money.

Andrew could almost see himself through Dean's eyes, as if through clear chips of ice in his head, slowly melting. "You understand, don't you?"

Dean just nodded again.

"Dean, what's my name?"

"You . . . " Dean's mouth worked like the words were the first he'd tried to speak after a stroke. "You . . . are the . . . the Head of the Proletariat."

"Jesus, man . . . what's wrong with you? My name's Andy. What's your name?"

This took Dean even longer to assimilate. He wasn't trying to remember. He was waiting for Andrew to tell him the answer. "I . . . am," he finally said, paying a bill in foreign currency, "a fist."

Andrew turned and grabbed Sprague by the shirt. "What's happening to him?"

"He joined the Proletariat," Sprague said. "He's a part of the Body. He won't try to hurt you, anymore. He knows his place."

"What the hell are you talking about? I didn't do anything. What happened to him?"

"You absorbed him. You both offered your talents, your hearts and minds to the Proletariat, and they are being redistributed. From each according to his means—"

"Yeah, fuck Marx, okay? Dean is an asshole, but he's a human being. What's the point in reasoning with people, if you can just rewire their brains? I'm supposed to lead, but if everybody else is a yes-man robot, what fucking chance do I have to make a right decision?"

"All arguments are resolved in you, now." That old utopian gleam shone like klieg bulbs behind Sprague's owlish eyes. "You're becoming a leader."

"This is fucked. Even if we win, there's going to be a bloodbath, tomorrow. The cops will come, and the feds. We can't hide a bunch of fucking Bigfoot freaks . . . "

"We will. There are invisible nations within this one, son. The Proletariat will survive, and one day soon, when the oil runs dry, and the cities go dark, the colony will grow. Your people won't be torn by strife or despair; they won't pine for the old machines. You will be all you need in that new world, and your people will take over all that is. The revolution," Sprague concluded, bloodshot eyes welling with tears, "will finally come to pass."

"But I need him . . . He knows all about this shit . . . " But now, so did he. Andrew discovered, all at once, that he actually knew quite a lot about warfare, especially sieges. At West Point, Dean wrote a huge research paper on siege warfare from Troy, Masada and Jerusalem to Stalingrad and Khe San.

The big house was well-fortified but poorly manned, and had no artillery but what the Tower could move by itself. If they improvised some rams and covered ladders, and pursued simultaneous focused assaults on the entrances above—and belowground, they could break through and take the objective in a matter of minutes.

The Tower would make another attempt to indoctrinate the town, if it hadn't already. Every day would add to its numbers, while the Proletariat declined. They would have to do it tonight. Now.

"Dean," he tried again, very slowly, "what do you think we should do?"

Dean stood with the other soldiers; not waiting or pacing, but simply parked. "We should fight," he said. It was no more nor less than Andrew expected, and he could not say for sure that he didn't just stick the words into a dummy, and pull them back out. *What did I do to him?*

The soldiers echoed his grunted reply with harsh, clipped barks, which spread in a chorus of guttural croaking from the workers.

Bees settled on Andrew's skull and danced with a new urgency around the pouting sores on his neck. They had been doing that, he noticed, for quite some time. The things they told him, he simply knew; the plans that fluttered in the back of his mind, they lifted from him as pheromones or radio waves, or whatever. They began, now, to relay his commands to the whole hive.

A weird silence stretched out around Andrew, as the entire Proletariat, forty-four bodies and one mind, coiled itself like a spring. Andrew felt the energy that buoyed him in his fight with Dean roll out like a shockwave over the group. A message he barely understood flowed like nerve impulses down an invisible spine to the feet and fists of a gigantic, ghostly body.

As one, they heard him. As one, they went to work.

CHAPTER 26

THERE WOULD BE no joy, today, in the big house.

Dom rolled with the mountain stream, gargling screams as the rocks pounded ingots of shrapnel into his back. His right arm hurt so bad it must be broken. Everything else felt worse.

When the stream dumped him out in the pond, he had only two thoughts. One, that this pain would be a Tijuana blowjob compared to what he would go through when he got back to the big house. And two, Dom would greet the next sunrise wearing Dean's face for a loincloth.

Crawling out of the pond to sprawl on the muddy shore, he was at a loss for a landmark; the towtruck and Deputy Scovill's Bronco were nowhere in sight. Weird, how the bubble around them just kept swelling, but never burst.

He almost wished the pigs would descend en masse and force them to circle the wagons. Faced down by a common enemy, the Tower calculated that the strikers would fold, and with Andy and the meddlesome old hermit running things, they were better off headless.

Andy.

In all the hullabaloo and mishagoss of the last couple days, he'd plumb forgotten about his brother-in-law, until he stumbled out into the road. Dom had scented right away what he was becoming.

Anybody else, he would have snapped their neck and never looked back. But he had just begun to get used to the idea of the little dork joining the family. He found it easier to accept Andy than Dean did, and had come to accept, if not respect, his sister's husband. For the sake of Laura, whom he truly loved, Dom had let Andy slide.

At first scent of Andy today, a newly upgraded instinct told him what to do, but he was of two minds about the act. When Andy resisted with such uncharacteristic gumption, a circuit breaker got thrown in Dom's brain, and he defaulted to his original orders. Dom had blithely carried a freight of ambiguity all his life, and was sick of it. It unnerved him, now, to be of two minds about anything. The assurance of being in line with the Tower was like cocaine, except it worked.

So much had changed, inside and out, and yet nothing had. They were still a family, still divided, and at war. Joining the Colony only heated the conflict. But one way or the other, everything was going to sort itself out, today.

He dozed for a while on the warm mud, basking in the sun like a bull alligator, supremely content in his ancestral domain. Time didn't quite stand still, but kicked off its shoes for a lazy soak; in the pristine alpine silence, the Percolator slowed to a glacial gurgle.

A mule deer doe crept down to the water, not more than ten feet from where he lay. She looked him over and saw no threat. Nimble as she was, Dom saw how one hind leg dragged through the cattails, a rusty wreath of barbed wire snarled around the tawny, sleek muscle.

He held his breath. The doe came no closer, but didn't flee after drinking her fill. He needed to do something simple, something pure, to shake off the chaos of the morning: Dean thwarting him, the wreck of the truck, the disappointing outcome of his mission, and the wrath that awaited him at the big house.

Slowly, cell by cell, he planted his weight on his hands. Fiber by fiber, he tensed and lifted himself up off his sucking bed of mud.

The doe flicked a sidelong glance at him, but betrayed no glimmer of suspicion that she had strayed into an episode of *Wild Kingdom*.

Favoring her wounded leg, the doe lowered her head again to drink.

"Go time," Dom said.

And it was, but not for him.

His blitzkrieg attack came unglued the moment he put serious weight on his right arm, which was worse than broken. His forearm bones popped out of their sheaths and jabbed through his skin, gritted on nerve like teeth biting down on an electrical cord. The pain was nauseating, appalling and glorious in its world-warping enormity. Muscles seized up and went limp under him. He kissed mud.

The doe whipped her head at him, big beautiful Bambi eyes on fire with surprise. She bunched up to spring back to the shore, but her own bum leg betrayed her. She only faltered a single step, and would have recovered in an eyeblink, but a flash of white overwhelmed her and slammed her into the water.

Dom saw it all through a curtain of violet spots. His left hand was little better than the right, because of that fucking dog.

The doe broke water and lunged, but Toshiro rode on her back like Satan's own lawn jockey. With that vicious muzzle stuffed full of Dom-chewing teeth, he had already shorn off one velvety ear and bit deeply into her tawny throat. Most of the spume and foam that splashed off the doe was red as she tried one last evasive maneuver, bogged down and collapsed on her side.

Toshiro descended on the still-kicking carcass, dragging it onto the shore and into a stand of cattails. His white coat dripped rainbows when he went to work ripping out the deer's throat.

"That's my dog," Dom said, in awe as much as ironic

pride. Whatever tissue-thin pretense of being a mere "dog" he might've claimed, Toshiro had long since renounced it, along with his master. He was a wolf.

Dom had seen Shiro run down squirrels, gophers, crows, possums, cats, rats and Mormon missionaries, but never had he seen so pure and perfect a predator in his dog, or any living thing, up close. The Colony soldiers came close, but they were machines, bearing the tool marks of somebody's improvement on the human body. They hadn't been tested in the woods much, and the other night had pointed out numerous design flaws. But his damned dog was a killer to lick them all; he would still be out here roving when they were all dead and gone, because he needed nobody.

Toshiro turned to look at him. A lazy growl escaped his bloody muzzle, but he paid Dom no more mind than he would any other scavenger. That sly red doggy smile told him there was no point waiting for leftovers. Returning to his lunch, Toshiro lifted a hind leg. Hot piss splashed Dom's cheek.

Dom gingerly eased himself upright and limped away from the pond. That damned dog would get his, one of these days, but not today.

His shitlist was already full up, and it wasn't even lunchtime. Now would be a perfect opportunity to cut out and get some, except that was all behind him now, since his dick fell off. Funny how he kept forgetting that.

All was quiet as he crossed the road. The breeze died in the whispering pines, and everything seemed to go to sleep as the heat of the day piled up.

Shit, he sure could go for a cold beer. He itched all over, the way the Army trained you to feel out in the open in a free fire zone. What if the other side got guns? He giggled at the image of those brain-dead, ham-fisted golems trying to plink him with a sniper rifle. Did they still have thumbs? Dom hadn't thought to bring a gun when he left the big house. But Dean was on the other side. If Dom got a new toy, Dean always whined until he got one, too. It wasn't funny, anymore.

Bees bumbled around his head in a pissed-off question mark, but no help came to bodily usher him to face His Master's Wrath. Maybe if he'd broken his leg, they could spare some wheels to pick him up. He'd played the army of one for this bullshit outfit long enough, without any tangible reward.

Was it his fault the bitch in the ambulance totaled the U-Haul truck in the goddamned tunnel? Sure, in theory, but if he hadn't stopped her, she might have kamikazed the big house. What the fuck did the Tower expect? He was only following orders. If everything that went wrong was his fault, what good was following orders, anyway?

Through the trees, over hills and mountains, he felt the eyes of the Tower fall upon him and peel him open.

Those eyes razored his unworthy meat, rolled it back and stuffed the cavities between skin and muscle with angry drones. Every step he took made their weight heavier upon him, multiplied his agony. He kept walking, unable to stop.

Bees burrowed into his nostrils and ears. When he had to breathe, they flew in squadrons down his throat.

They danced and dueled behind his eyes. They crawled and caroused on the folds of his brain. His broken, bitten arms would not twitch to wipe them away. And still, he kept walking. The stingers in his pincushion brain pricked deeper, pumping their venom until the burning fever made a drunken scarecrow strut of his walk, and he couldn't even scream. There were no relentless lectures in his brother's voice, no word-pictures, no rebus condemnations, just raw, pure punishment.

Dom wept. For the Colony, for his selfishness, for his failure. He had only ever wanted to be useful, to belong, but he always fucked it up. Whenever he listened to the devil on his shoulder, the colony suffered. They would almost be better off without him. Surely anyone else could have driven the truck into town—the sluts from the Sexagon, even the Town Drunk, if someone else worked the pedals. Any of them could have got it there without arousing the self-righteous engine of doom that was Dean Kowalski.

Dean.

Hundreds of new converts lost because of Dom's arrogance. Their last hopes dashed by the lowest of them all, the greatest disappointment . . . If they could do so without being poisoned, they should eat him. He could serve the Colony in no other way. If only the Tower could see fit to invest its total concentration upon him, it could make him over from the ground up and perhaps salvage something of the disaster he had brought down upon them.

Please, Dom silently prayed to the livid insects in his brain, *please fix me so I can do what I have to do*.

Over a hill and down through tangled brush that lashed at his broken arm in a fond reminder of how naïve he'd been about pain only minutes before, he came out onto the meadow. Over fallow fields and tumbleweeds, Dom seemed to sleepwalk, but he was quite aware of every creeping thing that invaded him. It was as if a million, billion little wings lifted him just a few inches off the ground and bore him to the open doors of the big house, where two men stood, waiting, apparently, for him.

One of them he recognized right away as the towtruck driver. His inbred weasel eyes were still swollen shut, and his face and neck were pocked with *Das Kapital* in pus-oozing Braille. His love-bombed, cult-groupie grin was screwed on tighter than his *Snap-On Tools* meshback trucker cap, or his grip on the hogleg twelve-gauge he pointed at the other man on the porch.

This other one wore a beekeeper's hood, heavy gloves and a canvas suit, like an old-time deep-sea diver, that admitted no egress to the legions of bees that warily orbited him. In one hand, he held a smoke gun—a canister of slow-burning fuel that drooled heavy, cloying smoke, which got the bees stoned.

"I have come to deliver terms," said the beekeeper. It was impossible to judge how solid he was in the baggy suit, but his voice was old, crusty and weak, crackly and thin, like it came down a hair-clotted, phlegm-choked tube.

Dom could smash him down, or at least hobble him, make him show the proper respect, but no orders came. He stood there with a broken arm, bone-deep dog bites, third-degree burns and angry bees boring into his tear ducts, but the next words out of his mouth were flat and foreign to him. "You are an agitator from outside. You are not of the Proletariat. We do not recognize your authority."

Not even the voice that came out of Dom's mouth was his own. It was harsher, deeper, thickly accented. He sounded Russian. What the hell? The intrusion was like finding a hand on your ass in the street, but at least the bees in his brain had settled down.

"I do not represent your workers." The beekeeper waved his smoke at Dom, like the Pope with his censer. "The consensus outside is that this has spiraled out of control. The collateral cost of containment is way beyond acceptable. Not to put too fine a point on it, Dr. Grodenko, but we just don't think we can learn anything more from you."

Dom's answer was a long time coming. There was simply no way into the visitor's head. Fuzzy images of cartoon characters and dinosaurs and a Whopper with fries and a drink and some kind of colorful toy were all that Dom felt. Palpable waves of sheer will pushed out of the house, into and through the lightning rod he had become . . .

But it just dissolved around the beekeeper, like a hurricane converging and petering out as a dust devil over his hooded head. The Tower could barely contain its fury, and the effort threatened to make Dom swallow his tongue. "We have not begun to show you what we are capable of."

The beekeeper shrugged in sympathy. "That is exactly what they fear. The centrist factions are all for pushing on with some key policy changes, but we believe that such changes would destabilize the colony. That's why we recommended aborting the experiment."

"We need more workers."

"Out of the question. You're facing a full tactical purge, Arkady. This isn't about how many disappearances we can manage, anymore. This is terminal."

"We are one."

"Not from what our eyes on the ground tell us. You are many, with many problems. We're past arguing, *tovarisch*, but you still have a chance to survive this."

"We will not leave the Colony . . ."

"It's over. It was a beautiful dream, Arkady, but it's time to wake up. We have a very attractive relocation package, but it isn't a family plan. You can go—"

"We will not go to a lab to be studied . . . dissected . . ."

"Now, Arkady, it's not like that at all. Face facts, we'll be lucky to reboot the experiment at a later date, but you're not entirely without blame here. If you'd only—"

The towtruck driver raised his shotgun and blew the beekeeper's heart out his back. He rocked back on his heels and dropped the smoke pot, but otherwise seemed not too perturbed by the whole thing. "That was petty, reckless and stupid," gasped the beekeeper, "even for you, Arkady."

Dom, quite without his own volition, bent and tore off the hood. The beekeeper tottered around in a half-circle and fell down.

Fuck me, Dom said, or would have, if he had any control over his mouth.

The beekeeper, in a very meaningful way, was Dom's perfect foil, another puppet for the puppet show. His face, relaxed in death, was pinched and withered beyond its years. Eyes half-lidded, almost buried under thick epicanthic folds; pug nose, squishy, slack mouth with the tip of the tongue peeking out. Dom was no doctor, but he knew Downs Syndrome when he saw it. The poor, dead mongoloid had a headset wired into his jug ears, gnarly scars slicing his skull up like a pie, and a speaker dangling in front of his mouth, from which the crusty old spook voice still chattered. "If this is really the state of things, I'm afraid there's nothing more we can do for you, Arkady."

Dom dragged the body out into the field and dropped it. It still chattered at him as he walked away, but the Tower didn't let him hear what it had to say.

A few minutes later, a helicopter touched down with combat zone efficiency. Two men in biohazard suits, covered by two more with Pancor automatic shotguns, collected the body and just as quickly took off.

Inside the stifling, lightless sweatbox of the great hall, they came together. Their numbers were pitiful, but Dom felt the fitful spark of what the Colony had been and might be again, what it meant to each of them, and felt it redouble and burn brighter as they linked hands and radiated it into each other.

"We are at war," said the guttural, utterly imperious voice that came out of him and the towtruck driver and everybody else, but nobody said jinx, and nobody was buying anyone a soda.

With who? Dom wondered, not expecting an answer.

But an answer came. "With all who are not us," it said. "To face them, we must be one, not many. The body must be healed. The Colony will be united. The anarchists' cancerous counterrevolutionary head will be purged, and the Colony will thrive."

"Death to the anarchists," said the towtruck driver. "Death to the many," said Sheriff Bialecki.

"Long live the one," they all said together.

CHAPTER 27

WATCHING THEM WORK, Andrew wondered what it would be like, to live without a head.

A human brain used twenty percent of the body's resting energy. An agile, socially adept tool-using chimpanzee's brain eats up only about nine percent. He remembered picking this up from a late-night cram session for an introductory anthropology class. Another fact squeezed out for a test and forgotten, until now.

The body could work very efficiently indeed, without much of the cerebral cortex, and if the conserved energies were redirected, how much more efficient of a worker he could become was limited only by the imagination of the planner.

Intelligent design, my ass . . .

He belched and gagged, spat out honey-tinged bile. How long had it been since he'd eaten real food?

The brains of the workers and soldiers of the colony had not simply rotted off, but had drastically atrophied and been reabsorbed into the spine. The sensory organs, likewise, had shrunk with the redistribution of resources, but not totally vanished.

Workers could see quite well with the augmentation of the swarms of drones that followed them. In the right light, he could see the glistening spots around their mouths that seemed to serve as eyes, and the flesh-flowers splayed out like tiny, eager satellite dishes. As small as their brains were, some rudimentary telepathy connected them to the insects, feeding them scattershot stimuli from the bees and each other and, above all, from their leader.

Andrew couldn't argue with its efficiency. In a stable, empty world, such colonies would flourish, reproduce and spread, but it would be a silent hegemony, the only sounds the buzz of relayed commands and the clamor of endless toil. The only words, the only inspiration, would have to come from the head.

With all the citizens of the colony feeding their perceptions into, and taking their orders from, the head as a single body, they could invent only what the leader imagined, adapt only to threats the leader perceived. There would be no dissent, but neither would there be music.

The bees, the honey, the shadowy minds behind the scheme to shape human evolution—they had not asked for any of it. The Colony could have evolved to suit any environment, if the leader had only surrendered himself to it, but he had remained aloof. The changes that wracked the workers and left them mute and near-headless automatons had all sprung from the perverse ambitions of the man who ruled it.

Andrew now saw his role. Grafting Andrew to itself, it sought to connect to him and make itself his new body, but it could never overcome the trauma of the original decapitation. There had to be a reckoning.

How had it happened? How could the body of the Colony, so thoroughly dominated by Grodenko, throw off his absolute biological control?

"God, how do you turn it off?" He had only asked himself if the workers were better off without their minds, and triggered an avalanche of useless analysis. He had to tiptoe in his own head for fear of stirring the hive.

In just a couple hours, twenty workers had cleared the heaps of timber and rusty machinery from the sawmill floor, and built ladders and battering rams out of the longest, stoutest beams. They only worked when Andrew remained close by. He felt his brain guiding them, feeding orders, observations. He had never taken a shop class or built anything more complex than a paper airplane, but he seemed to know everything they needed to do the job. It must have come from Dean, who had a workshop in his garage and made all his kids' furniture. He wondered what else of Dean's was stuffed up there.

The other sixteen were in the tunnels, digging out the blockages to the cellar of the big house. The soldiers scouted the big house. They had observed no movement after the helicopter came and went. It was a mixed blessing that he could no longer tell which one of the bee-filtered mosaic of impressions came from Dean.

Trying to force it all out of his mind, he pulled focus to the one silk purse he'd managed to make out of this sow's ear. At last, after a lifetime of failure, he'd finally found a musical instrument he could play.

Holding his hands out like a conductor, he raised his left on the beat while massaging the timbre with his right. A winged armada flawlessly executed the repeated chord change. He had only to think the notes to make the bees reproduce them, but he enjoyed playing conductor. In the midst of all this, it gave him peace.

"What're you doing?" Sprague asked.

"Check it out," Andrew said, and put them through the portion of the "How To Disappear Completely" that he'd worked out so far. He'd tried to get them to do some Pixies songs for Laura, but they had tempo issues. "You like it? It's Radiohead."

"Never heard of him," Sprague sniffed. "You need to quit fooling around. We've got a war coming."

"How did you do it?" Andrew demanded. "Why?"

Sprague poked at the fire, watching the disturbed strands of smoke float up through the sundered roof of the sawmill. "Do what?"

"You know what I mean. The bees."

"I guess you puzzled out there's more to me than I let on. Everything I told you was the truth. The big house was my home. It made me what I am."

"You didn't just come to watch. You brought them here."

Sprague produced a green apple from his pocket. He took out his dentures, buffed them on his coat. "There are outsiders, some powerful, who sincerely care about the big problems, the ones too big for most folks to see, let alone come to grips with. They know the fix is in, because they're the ones who phoned it in, but they also know we're all boiling in the same pot. They had this solution in their hands, and they were going to try it with or without any help from me. When it went astray, I took steps to fix it. Grodenko was the wrong man, but the one who wants power the most almost always is."

"Who's the right man now, Sprague? Me, or my brainwashed brother . . . or you?" Andrew got up and walked back to the cells.

May lay spooned between a hulking, gray-bearded biker and a rail-thin but arrestingly nubile blonde in a tube top. It looked like amateur Internet porn, if you could overlook the shit and honey-vomit everywhere, and the harsh changes rippling through their bodies so violently they all trembled together, like time-lapse footage of animal corpses decomposing.

Were they better off than before? None of them volunteered for this shit. As they slept, worms of transforming energy burrowed through them, remaking them according to the inscrutable master plan of the colony . . . or was it just his big, busy brain that scrambled their brains and their bodies and siphoned off whatever they used to call their minds?

May awakened and reached out for him. She wore a sly come-hither smirk that still pulled his strings, even with her eyes rolled back in her head.

The others were becoming workers, their sexual features withering away like overripe fruit, but May's allure had been turbocharged. Her bloated breasts spilled off her slim form like udders, yearning to be milked. Her flanks and hips had a voluptuous new heft to them, while her swollen ass displayed a crimson rainbow stain, like a baboon in estrus. Despite and because of this, she was a perverted cartoon of her sister.

When she crawled over the bodies, the heady, hothouse stench of her made his eyes water. She reeked of Dean, an ammoniac stamp of ownership that he sprayed on her even after his unit dropped off. She reveled in the degradation; at least he had finally claimed her as his own.

What had she wanted, from her life? Certainly not this; but the avid sheen in her eyes, like a starved dog in the moments before it turns on its owner, showed no regrets.

"You should mate with her," Sprague said. He finished his apple and tossed the core into a compost pile.

The longer Andrew looked at her, the more his imagination made her into Laura. "What the hell makes you think that's any business of yours?"

"It would be good for the Colony. She's fertile, and your seed would insure that a next generation—"

"There isn't going to be any next generation! There isn't going to be a next weekend! It's out of control, and those fucking black helicopter guys were probably pretty pissed when their guy got blown away."

"They wouldn't let their own get close to Grodenko. He'd squeeze the poor bastard flat and find out what they're really up to, or turn him. No, it was only a cutout, with just enough brains to ring the doorbell . . . "

"Who are those guys, Sprague? Are they your friends with their eyes on the big picture? CIA? KGB? Microsoft? Go ahead, old man! Tell me another story!"

Andrew advanced on Sprague, but the hermit scuttled backwards until he slammed into the wall. Something about it was so spastic, so involuntary, that Andrew cut short a giggle when it dawned on him that he was pushing the old man with his mind.

He didn't need to ask, anymore.

Sprague resisted at first, but when Andrew asked harder, all of it came in a gush of state secrets and layered lies. It took seconds to rip the memories out, but swarms of minutes passed as the bees in his bonnet unpacked them like nesting dolls filled with toxic waste. In the end, he didn't know if it was just another artful line of bullshit, but it was more than he ever wanted to know about Sprague, about bees, about the colony, and about America.

"Jesus fucking Christ," was all he could say.

Sprague couldn't even manage that much. The shock of the interrogation looked to have caused a seizure, perhaps even a mild stroke. Strings of spit dangled from his twitching lips. Still crucified on the wall, the tired old radical sagged on the psychic nails Andrew had driven into him, and wept.

"There's no other way to end this, is there? We can't just leave. We have to go in there. *I* have to go in there, and face him."

Sprague could not speak, but he palsied a nod.

"They're just going to sit back and watch? They don't care if more people get killed or sucked into this mess, so long as they can keep a lid on it?"

Sprague shook his head. Through his tears, the old man showed Andrew something he'd never seen on any other human face, when it looked at him: true fear.

He let the old man sink into a ball at his feet.

He shouldn't feel good about what he did, but at least he wasn't helpless. Now, instead of just running from one crisis to the next, he could make things happen. "And then what? When we've done . . . whatever we have to do . . . what will your fancy friends with the big picture do, then?"

Through his trembling hands, the mute old man

peeked out at him, but no matter how he probed, pried and squeezed, Sprague would not tell him, because he did not know.

CHAPTER 28

WHEN THE SKY turned black and the full moon rose like God's own fool's gold, they attacked.

From his cell in the sawmill, Andrew watched. The larval workers from the cells massed around him in a trance, armed with hammers, clubs and an old police revolver. He didn't feel much safer for their protection, since their bones were still as soft as ear cartilage.

Bees alit on his head and flew off in constant flurries; every incoming insect was a message in a bottle, while every outbound bee was a bullet of psychochemical command aimed at the vestigial brain of a Colony worker. The symphony of command flowed out of him like prenatal reflexes, and lucky for him that it did, for inside his teeming, pupating hive-mind, Andrew felt as if he'd been buried alive.

This isn't real/It's happening too fast/We are a monster/a God/Laura's coming/She doesn't love you

The workers formed up at the edge of the meadow, in teams around the ladders and rams, bearing huge slings and piles of stones. A soldier led each team, but they were his fingers. Motionless, silent but for the volleys of bees all about them, they waited for him to close them into a fist.

A straggling worker bee with tattered wings arrived and showed him that under the ground, they had cleared the tunnel opening into the cellar, and encountered no resistance.

We are doomed/We are destiny/It doesn't matter/ Nothing matters/She is coming/She doesn't love you/NOW

He forced the order out through the network of bees and felt it lighting up every head in his pitiful people's army. At once, as one, they began to move.

He felt the sawmill settle all around him as the ground shook. Almost before they entered the meadow, the swarm-network shook with the dumb cries of his workers dying.

Through a splintered shutter on a second-floor window flanking the front door, Dom watched the woods. The dumb fucking apes lurked in the shadows about two hundred yards away, well spread out but still easy to pick off, if only the tower would let him.

The Remington deer rifle didn't have the rapid-fire fudge factor of the AK, but he could sight them up as big as life and bright as day on the nifty starlight scope. He could even tell which one was Dean.

Leading a team of four workers carrying a sick-ass battering ram with a four-foot radial saw blade set into its knocking end, Dominic's twin stood at attention, ramrod-stiff and staring fixedly at the big house. No doubt he was playing Sousa marches and a John Wayne pep speech full-blast in his head, right now. Getting psyched.

Dom was *already* psyched. He flexed his broken arm in its splint of rusty iron bars and gauze, savoring the twinge of pain like white-hot solder running up his arm into his heart. He could see it gathering out there. All he waited for was for the Tower to release the trigger lock on his body, and let the magic happen.

Yes, he only joined the Army for a steady paycheck, and to spite the family, which had always turned out sailors. He hated the Army, but tonight, he could honestly say that he loved war. All it took was the right cause, and the right enemy.

The floor vibrated with a thunderous, rolling tocsin of blows. The tunnels. The striking workers must have hit the booby trap they set up with the volatile ether and shit from the meth kitchen. It was on, now . . .

The crosseyed hillbilly kid watched at the next window, a scoped .22 propping up his stooped shoulder. When Dom asked him if he was ready to kill some monsters, he just stared at his own nose like it was telling a dumb, endless joke.

Oh well . . . As a wise man once said, you went to war with the army that you had, not the one you wish you had.

Movement in the trees. Movement in the air . . . oh shit. A rock bigger than Dom's head smashed into the window. The rusty bars and shutters crumbled like rotten bread. The shattered rock parted his hair and sailed into the great hall. Goddamn it, they must have scopes on their slingshots.

Grabbing his rifle and crawling to the next window, Dom heard and felt more rocks crashing into the big house. The barred roof rang like tolling bells. The walls shivered and shed bricks as brittle mortar gave way under the concerted onslaught.

He heard a random fusillade of gunfire from the other colonists at the windows, but the rock bombardment only intensified. It was weird, this artillery coming down with no explosions, no screams. It made the battle seem somehow like a war between machines and animals, and in every way that mattered, it was. When the chaos opened up, he felt the Tower's restraining force, like the finger of a hesitant chess player on his head, abruptly and totally vanish. The Tower was under heavy attack.

The fields were crawling with running monsters, but at this height, they were merely targets. Free at last, Dom propped his rifle on a windowsill and started shooting.

Dean led the charge across the meadow.

There was no cover in the fields. The weeds came up to their knees, and all the sheds within a hundred yards of the big house had been flattened. The running workers spread out into four arrows, two with ladders flanking the monolithic house, while Dean's team and the one carrying their shield raced for the front door. The shield team took the lead and angled their broad, flat raft of sheet-metal faced planks to catch the brunt of the fire, but Dean's team lagged behind, and the bullets punched through the shield with little resistance.

Bullets sang off the huge rusty blade of the ram and smacked the tough hides of the workers, but none of them cried out. None balked or flinched the way even fearless men did, in the face of battle. The Proletariat fought for its life. The bullets were only slivers, and did not slow them, yet.

They did falter when they shared the blast of transmitted pain from the tunnel, felt the flames and crushing earth and shared the deaths as keenly as the severing of their own limbs, but Dean rallied them and redoubled the pace. He pushed the workers forward on their shorter, stumpy legs, uttered heated exhortations that came out as wordless, breathless, growls.

Somewhere high up in the big house, a scab taunted them over his rifle. The voice nettled Dean, though he couldn't recognize it or make sense of the words. If the enemy still had to use words, it meant they were desperate and undisciplined.

A meteor shower pummeled the façade of the big house. One shooter was hit and silenced, but the loud one kept laughing and jeering as he punched holes in Dean's team. Somehow, he knew the scab sniper was talking to him, which was strange, because who was he? Only a soldier . . . an enemy.

Forty yards from the house, the battering ram foundered and tipped up at the sky as one of the workers fell down with its left knee blown out by a rifle shot. The others struggled to take up the slack, but they bogged down, pallbearers stumbling into a lead-laced hurricane. The wounded worker hopped after the ram, but couldn't catch up. Dean stepped into the gap and grabbed the pegs in the butt end of the ten-foot sledge of charred hardwood.

A bullet slammed into the ram beside his head. "I see you, sailor-boy!"

The shield team reached the door minus two workers, who lay sprawled on the ground, nearly tripping him. With his own wounded workers scrambling to keep up, Dean steered the ram in under the shield and stumbled up the litter-strewn stairs. Shattered rocks, bricks and bullets rained down on the shield.

Dean locked arms with his brothers and kicked off the top step to drive the ram forward with all his weight and power. The workers lost their footing, but went down thrusting. The ram smashed into the door like a bobsled dropped from the moon. It would have gone through Mount Rushmore like it was Jell-O, and it sure enough cracked the huge oak doors from lintel to threshold.

The iron hinges tore away from the granite frame, but the doors did not budge. The saw blade hacked a slot in the wood and stuck fast. This would've been a good idea if the doors weren't reinforced, as the workers could surely have pulled it apart after the first blow. But the scabs had built a solid rampart of earth and stone against the door, that spilled out through the narrow gap.

Above his head, someone was singing. The echoing, taunting voice inspired a primal fury. Before he had a name or a body of his own, he had this enemy. And tonight, his enemy sang, *"You keep a-knockin' but you can't come in . . ."*

A humming roar like a sandstorm built all around them, and the world was filled with bees.

Fire burned. Bullets stung and blasted flesh. Bees stung, pumping hateful chemical propaganda into the divided Proletarian body.

His body.

Out there on the battlefield, his body was failing. It was dying.

Andrew fought it with all his might, spying out of all those roving insect eyes, reaching in and spiking all those stunted brains with hope and urgency, but from where he sat in a cell at the back of the sawmill, he could do nothing but feel more intensely their many wounds, their sad, silent deaths.

Through his half-lidded eyes, he could see Sprague kneeling before him, gnarled hands steepled, but not praying. Willing. Andrew vaguely felt some tenuous force trying to pour out of the wild, palsied old hermit, but he could not share his strength or his hope with the Colony. Neither could he know how badly it really went.

When Andrew closed his eyes, he could see everything that they saw, filtered through the whirling, maddening compound eye of the hive. Sprague only cultivated nine hives from the one he stole, and their numbers were badly depleted. An average hive could produce fifty thousand females and drones in the summer. They had scarcely that many left, total. The surviving workers would go blind on the battlefield.

"They're all dying," Andrew moaned, drowning in their pain. "Do something!"

"If you're going to lead them, you'd better learn to step over blood." Sprague smacked him in the mouth. "Save them! Don't come crying to me, get in there and lead them!"

Andrew closed his eyes and reached out. The network was scattered and rarefied. His thoughts leaped from one conducting bee to the next like a weak radio signal across the ionosphere, but the reception was spotty.

Garbled, yet the dire tone of the news was unmistakable.

The doors were barricaded and heavily defended. The team with the ram had been slaughtered. The survivors had abandoned the frontal assault to join the ladder teams, who were locked in a bloody stalemate with armed defenders, harried by bees and badly mauled by the rocks that flew back at them twice as hard as they threw them. He sensed the besieged Head Of State, glowing like a negative sun in Andrew's mind's eye, shining down beams of crackling angry will from the Tower.

In the tunnel, workers battled to dig out their buried comrades while bullets and buckshot peppered their hides. One soldier crawled over the rubble and into the cellar. The scabs cut it down, though only after it had gutted three of them with its berserker claws. Strange, to feel relief that it wasn't Dean.

He had to dig in and fight against a floodtide of terror that threatened to wash him away in his own head. Here, he was helpless, protected only by Sprague and his zombie harem—but out there, he was only a rider, running them faint-heartedly for fear of feeling it when they died.

His fear sent him hopping around the sawmill when he should buckle down, sweep all his insecurities into a hole, and bury them, but he could not do it. He *was* his fear, and even if he knew it, he still shrank from the greater terror of losing himself, of becoming nothing more than an organ in a giant, mindless body.

So did Grodenko, and it ruined the Colony. He ruled absolutely, but he could not fulfill his end of the bargain, shut out the light of his ego and join them. He hated them for submitting, and feared them for changing to become his ideal subjects, because he hated himself. The more powerful he became, the more he stripped from those who elevated him, until they were nothing but tools, and he a tin god disgusted with their mute, blind worship.

Knowing this did nothing to save them.

Andrew opened his eyes. "We have to go out there. Now."

"It's not safe." Sprague shifted his unsteady weight. His knurled birdclaws cradled his shriveled skull, as if he could hold anything back from Andrew.

Andrew rose up and walked out of the cell, across the mossy flagstones and out into the night. As if dragged by wires streaming out of his mind, four of the unfinished workers rose and shambled after him. May crept up and touched his shoulder, nakedly eager, but he took no notice. *If you're going to lead, you have to learn to step over blood.*

The sounds of the battle at the big house welled up on the wind. When frantic bees alit on him, he focused too hard at first, burning them out like tiny fuses to flutter in his wake. The picture he fed them, a portrait in light and scent-memory, was of Laura. *Find her*, he told them. *Sting her, just once . . . and make her wait.*

Dom fell back when the action moved to the roof and spilled into the big house. He was out of bullets, anyway.

The gun gave him a false sense of lethality in this fracas. Three workers lay prone on the field, crippled and lowing like unmilked cows, still dragging their hulks through the weeds towards the big house. Unless you hit them at a critical joint or right down their yawning gobs, the workers' padded hides stopped the bullets cold. You could empty your gun into one and hardly give him a charley horse. The bees only distracted them, never stung a lick of sense into them. There had to be a better way.

His mind swam in a miasma of cordite, sweat and blood. Blood was dangerous; it pushed the words right out of his brain. He could think only in red pictures, and shaking it off with words only made them worse. Dean. The Tower, victorious astride the whole world, scraping the stars. Mama. Dean.

There he was. Dom heard him yelling red rage outside. The bees must be stinging him. The pain and the crossfire of chemical propaganda must be pumping his brain fit to pop. Good.

Through a side window, he saw the shadow of a ladder propped against the house. Gunfire, clouds of bees and falling bricks roared. Muzzle flashes lit up a climbing soldier like cheap dinner-theater lightning, but didn't stop his rush, up the ladder and out of sight. If he had bullets, Dom could have shot him, but he couldn't stop the mindless killing machines, any more than he could lay to rest the scarlet undertow inside his head.

The Tower. Mama. Dean. The blizzard of red pictures shredded his mind. He wanted to tear himself into three Doms and go see to them all.

How did this turn from a shooting gallery into a meat grinder? Dean's fingerprints were all over this strategy. Dean and Andy, that two-faced little worm. When Dom saw him again, he would not be so conflicted.

The tread of heavy running footsteps rumbled overhead. Dom ran through the great hall and took the stairs three at a time.

Someone rushed him at the top landing, crazy bloodshot eyes spitting sock-puppet lunacy as he passed. "Ain't this a party?" Dom narrowly avoided taking the towtruck driver's head off. The mullethead scurried up and down the corridor, popping buckshot off through the bars like the sky itself had besieged them.

The iron cage of the roof rang with rocks, ricocheting

bullets and stampeding feet. He saw a pair of workers kneeling at the base of the watchtower, prying bars apart like sugarcane stalks. The mullethead peppered them, pumped and dry-fired. "God damn, I'm out! You got any shells?"

Dom looked up and dodged a shower of bricks. A soldier clumsily scaled the side of the Tower. The Sheriff staggered across the bars of the roof, emptying three speedloaders into its back, but the soldier climbed to the open cage at the peak and reached in through the bars to capture the flag. *Game over*, Dom thought, but then the headless soldier flew back off the tower like a flicked bottle cap.

Flipping end over end, back arched in rigid paralysis, the soldier flew thirty feet before it crashed through the rust-gutted bars. Dom and the trucker ran to where it lay on the concrete floor. It did not move, but Dom took an iron bar and drove it through the traitor's hyperventilating thorax before it could recover. Forcing it in through the ribs until it hit a spongy resistance that gave way with an audible pop, and a sluice of bright, bubbling blood from the hole in its neck.

The Tower was soft. It would not kill these traitors, not even to defend itself. It fell to Dom to save the Colony.

Three days ago, he would only have killed to save his own life, and would not have risked his life for anything you could name. Yet here he was. Sure, it was the strangest reversal in his life, but hardly the worst.

He leapt up to catch the ragged ends of the hole in the roof through which the soldier fell. The bars came away in his hands. No orders came from the tower. What the hell was going on, up there?

Something heavy dropped through the roof, down the hall, by the stairs. The towtruck driver whirled and clicked his empty shotgun. "God damn, I'm out! You got any shells?"

Sheriff Bialecki had fallen through the rusty bars and broken his neck. Bees bombarded him with pheromone cheerleading—*get up, Comrade, get up, for the Tower*—but for all his hard-bitten country grit, the sheriff wasn't going anywhere. Flopping around in sweeping circles with a dislocated arm against his back, seeming to chase himself across the floor, the broken lawman reminded Dom of Shemp, his favorite Stooge. But this wasn't funny—

In a blur, someone dropped on the trucker and punched out his throat, then turned to smile at Dom.

A red picture danced and burned out of his mind. Dean. The look in his eye was so dead, it might have been painted on, but he was more alive than Dom had ever seen him. Splashed with blood from dozens of wounds, crawling with stinging bees, he turned his nose to the wind like a wolf, and ran away from the Tower, to the stairs.

Dom smelled it, too, and knew where he was going. He ran after his brother, roaring a primal challenge and exulting that now, at last, it would happen.

"Mama!" he shouted. "I'm coming!"

CHAPTER 29

THE BIG HOUSE was a dynamo of misery, betrayal, madness and confusion. Its stones oozed human suffering, leakage from batteries charged with misguided desire to perfect the bungled and the botched, then left to ferment in decades of neglect. As a sanatorium, it had been stained by the torture of the mad to bring them to reason. As a commune, it had been fired by the frustration of men and women who had lost the human race, chasing an impossible dream. The first commune had burned through like a fever, leaving no survivors but Sprague, who flew like a seed on the wind to bring back more naïve human food for the house in the woods. The second colony brought the seething psychic residue to a rolling boil. The drowning giant they became had reached out and dragged his family down after it.

Andrew saw no signs of life as he crossed the field, but he heard much. Guns discharged, bullets pinged and screamed off brick and concrete, and men, almost certainly scabs, screamed as they died. His workers died in silence.

They went around to the back door. The stairs and porch had been ripped away, leaving the door marooned ten feet off the ground. Workers boosted him up to it, but it was locked. Andrew despaired of getting in, when the door simply shook in its frame, and swung wide open. Was it good that he was invited?

Inside, the air hummed with charged ions, and machines throbbed inside the walls. No one challenged him as he followed the thread of bodiless violence through the maze of service corridors to the great hall. Once he heard stomping and shouting that sounded like Dom, but as he crossed the dark ocean of the great hall and found the stairs outlined in smoke-filtered starlight, he saw no one.

Running up the stairs as if someone shoved at his back, he stepped over a dying redneck in overalls and a trucker cap. Blue of face, with eyes like softboiled eggs, the towtruck driver pointed a shotgun at him. Andrew cowered, but the gun clicked empty, and the driver wheezed and died staring at Andrew, his eyes filling with blood.

Down the hall, a mob of workers—his workers—idled at the base of the tower. They stepped aside when Andrew approached. The door was heavy iron, like a bank vault or a submarine hatch, but they had pulled it out of the brick wall with their bare hands. Shredded to the bone, those huge, broken human shovels brushed red calligraphy on his back as he passed among them.

A tight spiral staircase of rusty iron curled up on itself before him. The silence was palpable, but deceptive. Behind it, a ponderous, galvanic tension grated in the dark, as if every stick and stone of the big house longed to leap out and pound him to paste. But some equally powerful force held it back.

"You're lonely, aren't you?" Andrew's voice cracked, but the clotted, charged air, dense as the ocean floor, soaked and amplified it, all ears. "Nobody but yourself to argue with all the time. I'll bet you're just dying for somebody to talk to, who can talk back, for a change."

The tower shivered. A choral, keening whine of stressed metal pierced his ears. Bolts spun in their mounts in the spinal column transfixing the tower, upon which the spiral staircase, like an articulated fossil, spontaneously and explosively decomposed.

The uneasy step beneath his foot buckled and cracked. He jumped over it and ran just ahead of the remaining stairs collapsing underfoot, to sprawl out on the top landing with a relieved gasp.

He reflexively cradled his head and wrapped his limbs around his vulnerable guts, but nothing stirred in the dark. The walls were a barred cage open to the air, the roof a cap of slate and steel. The warped wooden floor was littered with broken bars and bits of rock, and shiny black with blood.

A hushed but unnerving hum, as of millions of tiny fans whirring, stirred the syrupy summer night air. A bowel-squeezing thickness to the atmosphere, an eminence, an enormity, hung poised over his head like an electrified anvil.

And breathing. Slow, sussurrant wheezing breath and the tidal smack and slither of the ocean of flesh that sucked it in.

The darkness just before him was a shroud thicker than the shadow of the conical roof, darker than drowning in motor oil. The faint starlight avoided it like a sensible cop detours around a bad neighborhood at midnight.

"So, your majesty," Andrew said, "you want to talk, or what?"

The darkness rolled back like a live thing and lay bare what waited right under his nose. "Usurper!"

Speechless, he saw it. Unbelief paralyzed him. He let his guard down. Glowing black beams of force he could only see with his eyes closed shoved him backwards like a bouncer, a typhoon, a Mack truck.

Feet flapping in the wind, Andrew slammed into the bars. Corroded iron bit into his back, crumbled under his weight and dangled him over empty space.

He threw out his arms, caught the bars and felt a sickening lurch as they tore out of the roof and floor like balsa wood.

He was going to fall. He would plummet thirty feet to the barred roof below, and probably go right through that, as well. He could grab nothing stable to catch himself. His center of gravity wobbled crazily. His heels hung out over empty space.

He grabbed for the only thing he could reach. By the naked, newborn force of his overheated hive-mind, he threw out a ray of pure desperation and hooked the colossal anchor of Grodenko, who loomed up out of the empty dark behind Andrew's eyelids like a third rail. The contact burned his mind like dreams of drowning in lava, but he clung fast, pulled himself bodily forward by the fleeting suggestion of a tether, and toppled away from the void.

Andrew felt his mental grasp brushed away as if he'd come at Grodenko with a feather, but he had saved himself. He knew he had neither the strength, the mental acuity, nor the will, to dictate terms to the bodiless head of the Proletariat.

"Listen, Arkady Ilyich Grodenko, cut it out! I thought you wanted to talk!"

The outburst seemed to disarm Grodenko for the moment, but Andrew took a while to steel himself, before he could look the deposed leader in the eye. It took another long stretch of hard studying to find one.

Arkady Grodenko had always been, physically and mentally, a huge, overpowering man. Raised on Communist Party doctrine and schooled by the elite inner circle of the Soviet empire, he thrived in a climate of total authority, and fully expected that, one day, he would run it.

When the glory-fire of the Revolution guttered and died out in the 90's, he wandered in the Siberian wilderness, nursing a bitter grudge and vowing one day to restore that fire, to lead the workers into a brighter future, but first and last, to *lead*. In his heart, this was his birthright. In the incubator of the Colony, all that bottled, raging ego had burst forth and turned Grodenko inside out. He must have always looked like this, inside, just as his followers had always been, in a very real sense, practically headless.

If Grodenko still had a body, it was dwarfed and crushed beneath his head, which was the size of a golfcart. The baggy, furrowed folds of the gigantic face that scowled at him hid whatever play of emotion went on behind it, but ropy tendrils of soft, pallid tissue restlessly thrashed like restless intestines straining the turgid, boneless sac of the cranium.

Shot through with wriggling blood vessels and squirming nerves, agitating endlessly like the skin of a scrotum pouch, the head had outgrown its skull long ago, for the whorled convolutions beneath the translucent scalp, the quivering, blubbery texture of grilled blood, were the folds of an enormous, naked brain.

A human brain weighs about three pounds. Grodenko's brain looked to weigh at least four hundred. And the whole of it was sheathed in bees.

Columns and clumps of swarming drones jutted out from the pulsating brain-sac, which was encrusted with waxen honeycombs laden with millions of larvae. By the rich, sour stink of royal jelly, Andrew knew what Grodenko was about. Fearful even of the bees' disloyalty, he hoarded the queens of a hundred hives inside his monstrous body, tying his safety to the hives' survival, and making of himself an obscene bee factory.

"Listen, man . . . Dr. Grodenko . . . I know what you're going through . . . I mean, nobody knows what it's like, man, but I just want to say . . . Fuck this! I don't want your job! Any of it! You can keep it!"

Grodenko knotted his brow and lashed around in his web of nerves. Like the face of some god of gigantic deep-sea predators, every line of his inscrutable form spoke of malicious contempt. Andrew saw how spontaneous limbs coalesced out of ghostly vapor rising like steam off the pulsating brain. Like phantom hands, they coagulated into fluid, then ectoplasmic flesh, as the leader got upset.

Several taproot cables, as thick as railroad ties, sprouted from Grodenko's brain stem, down through holes in the floor of the tower. His overgrown nervous system must run through the whole of the big house like telephone lines, monitoring every corner of the valley and broadcasting his commands and providing for the future of the Colony . . . Andrew noticed a translucent tube among the bundles that seemed to convey a trickle of cloudy white fluid, and seemed to sprout from somewhere south of Grodenko's brain.

Andrew gave thanks that, despite everything else this fucking hellish weekend had wrought, his unit had not dropped off yet. In the hive, male drones have no stingers, and no work ethic whatsoever. They idly consume honey and groom themselves for their only duty, to fertilize the queen on her mating flight. Disposable, the drone has his sex organs ripped out in the midair consummation of his life's purpose. But as the Good Book said, Men are not bees.

The leader reserved the sole right to procreate, in the world as Grodenko had reinvented it. This looked like a lousy place for a harem, and Grodenko plainly didn't jog up and down the stairs too often. Andrew really wished he could turn his brain off.

"My family and I never asked to have a dog in this fucking fight," Andrew shouted, "and all I want is out! But those fuckers out there, they dragged us into this, and people are dead, and your utopian Colony is killing itself, and the cold-blooded cocksuckers who set this whole thing up are going to kill us all, because they're pissed at you, too. Stop and think about that, Arkady. Just ask yourself, because I bet you never really have, before . . . Why is everybody so pissed at *you*?"

"Traitors," Grodenko spat, but the feverish collage of images that blew through Andrew's mind revealed shades of conflict in the knee-jerk judgment. Billions of tiny pheromone arrows pricked him, commanding him to kneel and submit.

"No, man . . . The Proletariat walked out on you, but they never gave up on the idea of a perfect society. It was . . . " Andrew took a deep breath, braced himself against another psychic assault, and continued. "It was *you*, wasn't it, who betrayed the idea."

The mountain before him vibrated, but did not move to crush him. The air crackled with the overloaded mental voltage of Grodenko's anger but somehow, he held it in check. Andrew's mind was firing its own arrows, psychochemical persuasion that cut through the alkaline miasma of the colony chairman's lair.

"It's not your fault. You didn't set out to make it like this, did you? Nobody really ever factored in the big changes, the ones that shaped who and what we are."

Andrew modulated his tone as if to stave off an avalanche, but as his mouth ran away with him, the ominous throbbing tapered to an idle purr. Grodenko's piggish eyes drooped, lulled by the sweet nectar of coherent thoughts from outside his own brain.

"I may have flunked biology, but I know beehives don't have kings, and it's not so great to be the queen, either. She lays eggs all day, and only leaves the hive once to mate, and once to swarm. I don't think God drew blueprints and planned it all out, but it's worked for millions of years.

"But who runs the hive? Bees don't have elections, but somehow, every bee does her job. The laws are wired into each and every one of them. The whole hive runs the hive, and sacrifices any single bee who gums up the works, even the queen. If you want to turn people into bees, you have to let go of being human, first."

That last remark seemed to provoke a belch of

cognitive indigestion in Grodenko, but Andrew raised his arms and threw every subliminal cue he could conceive at the gigantic brain. *You could crush me at any time with little or no effort*, he projected beneath his words, and in the meek, church-mouse scent of his sweat. *I'm no threat to you. You could crush me, but you can only do it once . . . Listen!*

"Our bodies pretty much stopped changing a hundred thousand years ago because of our technology, but the pressure on our minds, and on our ability to cooperate in groups, is only speeding up. We kid ourselves that we have a plan, but all we've ever made, was the result of blindly adapting to the world and flattering ourselves. If we don't start planning how we're going to change, we're doomed, but we're not ready, are we?

"No one man can make a plan for the ideal society, let alone the ideal species. The Soviet model fell apart after turning the workers' paradise into a prison and killing more people than Hitler. The dream was a good one, and it didn't fail. People did.

"A bright, charismatic guy named Arkady Grodenko took the heart and soul out of these people, but he didn't give his own. He tried to stay outside it. He made changes to suit his ego and crushed all dissent, to make his perfect society. He tried to rule them, like every other asshole who ever put on a crown. He had a perfect family. But he broke it."

A guttural rumble shuddered through the tower, like a deluge of shit choking up cheap plumbing. Grodenko's psychic fist unclenched and deflated over Andrew's head. *"I . . . have failed . . ."*

"Let them in. All you have to do is let them back in. Stop ruling them, and join them. They are not *your* body. You are their brain, but you're not their mind. Those voices of dissent aren't a sickness. They're the healthy dialogue that goes on in every mind. It's a new mind, trying to be born. Listen to it, and it'll show you what to do."

Grodenko trembled. A cloud of bees rose from his brow like black steam and dissipated on the warm evening breeze. Those horrible, buried eyes rolled up in their sockets. The whole, huge, abortive mass shuddered and made a sound as if it were swallowing its tongue.

Was it really that easy? Andrew almost turned to walk away.

"They were . . . wise . . . to choose you." Grodenko's shapeless mass contorted, wracked by seizures. Slowly, tiny buds of ectoplasm extruded out of his body, like tender new growth after a postwinter thaw. They reached out for Andrew. *"You have showed us our error . . . "*

"Oh no," Andrew said, "I just . . . From outside, it all looks simpler, than when you're . . . caught up in it." He took a step back, hands raised. The stairs were gone.

"We are pleased with you . . . join us." The tendrils swelled into undulating coils thicker than Andrew's calves. Weightless, gliding like smoke from burning plastic, they enfolded Andrew. Perhaps most unsettling of all, they floated, relaxed, awaiting his surrender, when their charged potential could utterly, effortlessly crush and engulf him.

Showing its true power with creeping gentleness, the head of the Colony coaxed him closer and made its eyes bulge out of its monolithic face to stare into his naked soul. Its voice was the chorus of over sixty men and women, the mute workers, soldiers, nurses and scabs it had taken into itself, and now set free. *"We would become . . . a new mind . . . WE . . . NEED . . . YOU."*

"No, I can't . . . I already have a family . . . " Andrew struggled to suppress the broiling self-doubt he felt oozing out of his pores to undo his lies.

What did he have? Laura turned her back on him, but she was here, somewhere. Without her, he would have wilted into the collective and gratefully been swallowed whole. To be a part of something larger, to be surrounded by a family that loved and understood him, needed him . . .

"JOIN US," the Colony growled. Grodenko was already gone, a forgotten nightmare. Andrew could have pulled away from the imperious Russian, even if it meant throwing himself from the tower. But the common will of the Colony had aligned itself inside that monstrous body, and it directed all of its authority upon him, now.

He felt the brittle, rusty bars at his back again. The half-real plasma tendrils rasped like cats' tongues at his exposed skin. His hands passed through them when he tried to brush them away, but he could feel their force growing harder to deny, pulling him back from the edge.

Images ransacked his brain, so powerful they blotted out his sight: Laura, Dom, Dean, Mom and Andrew, together in their new family. All wounds healed, all hatred forgotten, joined closer than ever in the loving bosom of the Colony. Dean and Dom would be its arms, defending them against the outside world; Laura and Mom would make children, adding to their numbers and, someday, birthing whole new colonies to go forth and thrive. And Andrew would watch and guide it all from the tower, fused with the head of the Proletariat as the most valued voice of the hive: its conscience.

No. She was out there, waiting for him. "I can't. My wife is looking for me . . . "

"SHE WILL JOIN US . . . " The Colony's raw will took hold of Andrew and lifted him off his feet. Helpless, he closed his eyes and went limp. No use fighting, nothing left to fight for.

What was there in Andrew Carruthers, that merited all this fuss? No great shakes at anything he loved, no will to do what he should; nothing at all, really, but a smart mouth and a lot of harmless lies, half-believed, until now. But as a part of something larger, he could count, at long last, for something. To live in utopia . . .

The ghostly plasma coiling around him went rigid, then shattered like breakaway glass. Andrew fell to the

CODY GOODFELLOW

floor on his ass, rolled over, but found his legs quite unable to lift him up.

The brain writhed in agony, a gibbering babel of voices, a tornado of languages, all unhinged with an infant animal's pain and terror. Andrew crawled back towards the stairwell, numb with shock and recoiling from the sudden withdrawal of the warm, soft family-dream.

The Colony reached out for him again, but it seemed to fight with something he could not see, to shrink into a puddle on the floor even as it dragged itself towards Andrew. Beneath it, the fleshy cables that bored through the floor pulsed red and stretched thin, then snapped back. Someone, somewhere at the other end of that rambling network of imperial flesh was ripping it out by the roots.

Andrew dove down the collapsing stairwell. The wounded howl of the Colony scarred his ears and propelled him through the hail of debris from the disintegrating tower. He had to get out, he had to find Laura . . . but he knew who was tearing the Colony apart, and he knew that if it cost him his life, he must try to stop them.

326

CHAPTER 30

THEY WERE FINALLY coming for her.

After all this time alone, they were finally coming.

Of family, this much, she knew, was true. They never forgot, never forgave, but they always came back. And no matter how they had ruined her body and tied her down, wrung the juice out of her soul and stolen the best years of her life and flown away hating her, so long as there was meat on her bones, she would love them. She had poured her life into them, and all she had ever wanted, all she lived for, now, was to get a little of it back.

She heard them coming, but she could be dreaming, again. There wasn't much to do, besides eat and sleep. The other thing she'd been promised hadn't quite worked out the way she'd hoped, but it was still love, of a sort, and she had a chance to start fresh with a new family.

She almost regretted that the old one had come back, now. Dean and Dom were too much alike, not to hate each other. She knew in her gut that the new family could not fit them both.

Dean was a caricature of his father: stiff, humorless—tough as nails, yet so easy to manipulate. She had tried, maybe a little too hard, to break the cycle, but he wasn't ready for her kind of love, and retreated even deeper into his insecure robot routine. She supposed it was her fault, but you could beat yourself up about something your whole life, and get nothing but a bruised ego.

Dom was something else—he was everything his father could have been. He inherited her sense of humor and her survival skills, and an independent streak she could have admired, if it didn't cut him off from her. If only he'd been the one with the broken arm, how different it all might have been. She might not have had to keep May a secret, and the poor girl wouldn't have grown up such a mess.

Dom could adapt and overcome and go along to get along, but she knew that, deep down, under all the programming, he hated her, and she would never quite get a handle on him. Dom was his dog's master; there was no getting around it.

The food cravings were always worst right after she woke up. She fumbled in the dark for snacks before she remembered that there was no proper food, not even dietetic shit. Her next meal bubbled and churned into her out of the tubes in the walls. Her hand tangled in the rubbery hoses that transfixed her bloated abdomen. Were they part of her, or were they communal property? The difference grew more meaningless by the day. *She* was communal property, a state-run factory, and she was stuffed to the rib-rafters with the most precious product of all.

She reached for her remote, but couldn't find it. No bed, either. Oh, she could see it, but she floated ten feet above it, nestled up against the groin-vaulted ceiling of the cellar like a mother spider in its nursery nest.

She noticed, only now, the acrid reek throughout her living room. Overlapping odors of panic and disaster and blood gibbered at her, and the stranger aromas of explosives and scorched dust wafted through the galleries of the cellar on unfamiliar currents.

Something was wrong.

She was missing Letterman. The show had gone to shit after he moved to CBS, but even his fossilized gags offered the comfort of familiarity. "Where's the goddamned clicker?" she moaned.

None of her nurses came. She began to worry. The creepy, sexless busybodies pampered and protected her morning, noon and night, and she was almost eager to push out the first litter prematurely, just to keep them too busy to bother her.

"Hello? One of you goldbricking assholes better answer me! I'm getting upset—"

A nurse hobbled into view from one of the tunnels. It dragged a foot behind it, leaving a trail of blood across her living room rug. Mom held her tongue as the nurse bowed to the TV and switched it on, then tuned in the CBS affiliate in Sacramento. They were just about to do the Top 10 List.

At least something around here still works, she thought, and drifted off to sleep.

Dean bounced down the stairs and rolled across the great hall with his twin brother wrapped in his arms. Trapped in a rib-cracking embrace, they could only kick each other in their featureless groins, butt skulls and bite each other's faces. Dom's teeth met with a jarring click in the meat of Dean's nose, grinding skin and cartilage, but Dean was trying to get at Dom's throat with his own toothless, but chisel-edged jaws, so he barely noticed.

Even now, Dom was bigger, stronger, but Dean dug deeper into himself. His anger was pure, and he had fed it and kept it burning bright and bathed in it every night. In a recurring dream he'd had since puberty, he killed Dom, skinned him and ate him, then ran through the jungle in his brother's tattooed hide, free and whole at last. Though his overtaxed muscles tore loose from his bones like overtuned guitar strings, he clung to his brother and strove to give worse than he got.

The floor groaned under them where they stopped rolling and found their feet, rising in a wobbly boxers' clench.

Dom tore off Dean's nose and spat it in his eyes. Most of his teeth, yellow, brittle corn niblets, came out with it.

"You know," Dom grunted, "I used to have this crazy dream where I ate you, but now I know it was wrong. You taste like shit."

Dean shoved Dom back, almost toppled on him when he unexpectedly folded and retreated. "Dominic," he gasped, "tonight, you are going to hell."

"Doubt it," Dom replied, "but it's on my way, if you need a lift."

With a savage grace worthy of the pro wrestlers they were imitating when he broke Dean's arm back in the day, Dom pivoted and whipsawed Dean ass-first into a wall. Dean went right through pine paneling and granite and trays of honeycomb, fetching up against solid brick. Brittle blobs of sloppy mortar gouged his shattered ribcage. Hundreds of bees stinging him barely registered as he tried to find his legs and pull himself out of the ravaged hive.

Dizzy, blacking out, he welcomed Dom coming to help hold him up. He wrapped his arms around his twin as Dom slammed into him, driving them both through the antique brick wall.

Dean was conscious only of rushing air and the stink of mold and sweat mingled with potpourri, vanilla, pumpkin pie and the rank, oily perfume of smegma.

Dean remembered the friction burns on Mom's inner thighs, blisters like pearls under her skin, the prickly heat rash when she got big with their daughter. Throughout the long, hot pregnancy, they kept Mom in a shack across the fields from the communal house, and they never let her bathe. The odor of his mother seeped out of everything overripe, everything wrong, in his world, and he showered three times a day to suppress it.

Strange, the things that went through your mind when you were plummeting to your doom.

The bottom, when it came, was not the end. They landed on stairs and rolled down three flights of them in a snarling, throttling knot. Though Dean limped and leaked blood like a sieve, his head was clear enough to see his brother and charge him, but his feet slipped, snarled in a shaggy area rug. He tripped over a glass-topped coffee table, and rolled to a stop, picking glass out of his knees and Dom's teeth out of his face, and taking inventory. It dawned on him, in a wash of frustrated fear, where he was.

All his hard work was undone, yet again.

He was back in Mom's living room.

The tired old Magnavox console TV etched the cluttered ensemble with its blue battery-acid glow. Scented candles threw off weak dribbles of red-gold light, and wafted pungent faux-food perfumed smoke into the dank, stifling war of odors. The absent walls were defined by bookshelves stuffed with romance and true crime paperbacks and the stuffed cadavers of her favorite pets.

Beyond the living room, the furnishings of the bedrooms, garage and bathroom—no toilet or sink, just a bucket—had all been unpacked and lovingly reassembled in the shadowy void of the dungeon. The bare, theatrical unreality of it galled him even more than the undoing of all his work. He put it all away, boxed it up and loaded it to be delivered out of his life, and it just exploded out and trapped him again, over and over—

These thoughts coiled tighter round Dean's broken brain, so Dom got nary a rise out of him when he knocked a wall system over on his back. The shelves battered and dumped books on him, but only broke him by painful stages out of his reverie.

Dean kicked the shelves away and whirled to look for Dom just as a flying bookend smashed the TV screen. The tube popped like a champagne magnum, spraying sparks and leaving the dazzling purple darkness reeking of ozone.

Dean's throat and sinuses closed up in revulsion. The

darkness was stifling, steeped in *her*. And when he *heard* her . . .

Mom screamed, "You boys stop it! This is not a goddamned wrestling arena! You're wrecking all my nice things! Oh God, why do I try . . . "

Dean lurched across the living room and into her recreated bedroom, shrugging off the impact of the other bookend tagging the side of his head. She was here, all along. After the wreckage of her old family cast her out, she'd simply wormed her way into a new one. She was a scab, a breeder of scabs, the hateful maker of a self-hating monster split into two bodies to destroy itself.

Roaring red, wordless rage, he lunged for the bed, hands clenched into murdering talons. The bed was empty. The cheap frame legs buckled and broke under his weight. The sheets shredded in his hands like tissue.

Somewhere he couldn't reach, she cooed, "Dean, you came back! My son, my boy, oh, you'll never know how I missed you . . . " The voice came from directly overhead.

In the dull red gloom of the candles, he saw her floating just beneath the rafters. She made an unlikely angel, appallingly bloated, her belly a waxy, translucent sac dangling down past her swollen, gangrenous ankles. She was pregnant again, knocked up as never before. Her turgid abdomen wriggled between her twitching legs like a sleeping bag stuffed with puppies.

She reached out to him with boneless, flopping tentacles flushed with dead, black blood. Fleshy tubes and hoses penetrated her every orifice, pumping gouts of honey down her throat and sinuses so her voice was disfigured and bleary, her speech slurred with viscous blasts of honey. Thicker tubes, quivering sluggishly, impaled her nether parts, pumping out solid waste and sluicing the tenements of her many-chambered womb with semen and enzyme-rich broth to tailor the growth of the next generation.

In spite of all this—or because of it—Dean was drawn

to lock in on her imploring gaze, which had not changed at all. Into those warm brown eyes, he could fall forever and never hit bottom. The first thing he saw when he slithered out of the womb, the eyes of the goddess of his world, those eyes to whom he'd posed his first, wordless question, in the form of wailing. *Why?*

There were still no answers, but only the corrosive acid bath of her love, only the hunger to keep him with her, loving her always until she had him stuffed and mounted. Her heart was a refuge from pain and questions, but it was no home.

All his rage, all his betrayal, all his misguided self-loathing, came out in a single word as he leapt up to destroy her. "SCAB!"

Dom came down on top of him, threw an arm around his neck and wrapped him in a sleeper hold. They fell off the bed and rolled. Dean got his hands up through Dom's arms and tore off an ear.

And still, he heard her voice. "Dean, my darling boy, my treasure, my only true love, fight him! You're my favorite, you always were. You know I chose you! I sent him away so we could be together, as a mother and son who truly love one another . . . I'm so sorry I let them take you away, but now we can be together with a new family . . . fight him! Kill him!"

The words buzzed in his brain and he fought harder, even as Dom redoubled his efforts to choke the life out of him. Dean brought his elbow down into Dom's slate-hard gut, clawed at his barely healed broken arm, and broke the hold.

Looking at his twin as he gasped for breath on all fours beside him, Dean saw the same glazed fascination in Dom's eyes that made him ignore his wounds and think only of tearing his brother's head off. He knew Dom must be hearing the same twisted song of persuasion.

"The old head is finished. His hold is broken. You can

be the Daddy, now. There was no man in the whole wide world strong enough for me, so I had to make you myself. You know nobody else could know you inside and out, and still love you . . . not like me . . . "

Dean and Dom clashed again, pushing, tugging, twisting, smashing furniture to splinters and writhing in mirror shards. Dom's fists played the anvil chorus on his head, but he tore something out of his twin's throat that blinded him with hot red blood. Still, Dom growled and beat on him, his fury unabated.

"She . . . did this . . . to us . . . " Dean tried to scream. "Dom . . . she doesn't care . . . who wins . . . I don't want it . . . want her . . . do you?"

Dom slammed his head into the floor. Dean's vision blurred. He felt Dom climb off him, then a foot planted on his chest, heard choked sobs as he tried to breathe. "You want *him*?" Dominic roared. "You love *him* the most? I stole for you! I would have killed for you! You threw me away like trash . . . "

Dom staggered back and sat on an overturned nightstand. Mom sagged in her webs like a punctured weather balloon. A small crowd gathered around the twins—stunted, unripe girl nurses—and tried to repair the damaged room.

"You never listened, Dominic. You were selfish and lazy, and you always made trouble. I loved you because you reminded me of myself . . . but you could never take care of a family, because you only look out for yourself." Mom's boneless arms caressed her pendulous udders, coaxing hot honey-milk from rigid nipples.

If you looked past the forced-feeding tubes and the monstrous, lolling grub worm of her belly, she was still the doe-eyed, velvet-skinned archetype of sex that haunted their first, shameful wet dreams. "Are you man enough, now, little boy? I know what you wanted. I know what you were looking for all your life! Can you claim it, now? Can you?"

"Get up," Dom wheezed. He took hold of Dean by his close-cropped hair. Jagged nails dug into his scalp, but Dean was too weak to resist. Dom pulled Dean upright and braced his arms on his shoulder. "You . . . bitch," he snarled, "you never knew me!"

Putting all his weight on Dean, he climbed his brother and sprang up at Mom. Dean flopped back on the flagstone floor and screamed at his broken collarbone.

Dom caught Mom by a fistful of her abdomen. Hanging from it, he wrung a warbling shriek from her as the quilted skin began to tear, but Dom reached up and ripped out hoses. Some of them tore out of her mouth and nose while others, anchored into her uterus, crushed like straws or came slithering out of holes in the ceiling. Shit and piss rained down, and gouts of half-digested honey so sweet he burned to lick it off the floor.

Mom tumbled out of her harness and fell on Dean. Her ant-queen abdomen split open and dumped gushers of plasma and wriggling, half-formed human grubs across the floor. The nurses limped over to try to retrieve them, but Dom shoved them aside and stomped the larvae flat in his red berserker fury.

Mom lay prone atop Dean, split wide open and screaming, without a trace of irony, "Look what you've done, you rotten son of a bitch! You ruin everything I care about, everything else I have in this world!"

Dom gathered up the trailing, twitching hoses that hung from the ceiling and gave them a good, stout yank. "You like fucking my mom? You want to make babies with my mother? *Come down here and fuck her, then, Daddy!*"

Bricks, splintered timbers, honey, semen, shit and scalding hormone soup pelted them. The house gave a long, low groan like the last tired sigh of a suicide.

"Mama," Dean whispered, "I'm so sorry . . ."

"I'm sorry too, baby," Mom answered. With all the undulating grace of a wounded elephant seal, she rolled over and smothered his face in her plentiful bosom. "I'm sorry I didn't scrape you ungrateful bastards out of me when I had the chance."

Dean couldn't turn his head or break free to get a breath. His beaklike jaws snapped in the blubber of her suffocating dugs, sucking wads of fat and rancid milk in, with no breath to expel it. He was drowning in her.

She cooed lustily, as if he was turning her on, as if this reunion of mother and child had restored all her stolen youth. Blood and milk gushed up his nose and into his lungs and washed him away to a place where even dreams couldn't find him.

CHAPTER 31

DOWN FROM THE watchtower and all through the gallery to the stairs, Andrew swam in bees. To him, they said nothing at all, but Colony workers, soldiers and scabs lay on the floor everywhere, transfixed by stingers and trembling before a new wave of programming.

Grodenko was overthrown, but the Colony lived. True communism had been achieved at last. The workers seemed more than a little overwhelmed. Many of those the bees crawled on, scab and striker alike, were cold and dead. Bodies choked the staircase. Andrew had to leap over them. He skidded on a river delta of blood at the foot of the stairs, landing on his ass. Nobody laughed. A Colony soldier knelt beside a dying, disemboweled scab, gingerly packing her entrails back into their yawning cavity like a child with a broken toy. Andrew saluted the new regime.

A rolling, thunderous clamor shivered the whole house. Waves of clanging concussion bowed the high ceiling of the great hall. Andrew supposed the panopticon watchtower must have collapsed.

Across the great hall, a huge hole gaped in the center of a wall mural beside an open door revealing descending stairs. A resounding bellow echoed up from the cellars. The walls of the house rippled and shook as the colonial infrastructure of nerves and viscera was yanked like the emergency brake on a train. Andrew recognized the shouting voice. He ran for the stairs.

The cellar was larger than any medieval dungeon, and illuminated by only a few scattered candles. It was still way too much light.

Dom hung from the rafters by a braided strand of hoses, jerking them like Quasimodo ringing the bells of Notre Dame.

Mom lay splayed out face-down on the flagstone floor, a deposed and disemboweled queen, wailing and swatting at the helping hands of her retinue of nurses. The wreckage of her burst belly lay strewn like a bloody bridal train across the floor and over her tattered bed. Her slime-trail was littered with gobbets of crushed fetuses, some of which mewled and struggled to crawl back to their blasted womb. Mom wept, but consoled herself by seizing and eating the scraps of her unborn brood.

Andrew covered his eyes and screamed, "Stop!"

Mom fixed on Andrew and tried to lift herself on her rubbery forelimbs. Grunting like a woman in labor, she slid off the body she'd been crushing. Dean didn't appear to be breathing.

"You must be Andrew, my new son." Mom shambled across the flagstones towards him on all fours, manifestly eager. Her shredded belly left a snail-trail behind her. Andrew tried not to look.

All at once, the hoses Dom yanked ripped free and dropped him to the floor, buried in coils of flesh and masonry.

Mom came too close to ignore. Her tentacles reached out and waves of bees crawled out of her matted hair and launched at him. "Laura tried to keep you a secret, but I like you, already. Come give your new mommy a big kiss."

Andrew tripped over something and fell hard on his ass. Dom guffawed, but he might have been laughing at his reflection in the big shard of mirror he picked up and gripped like a dagger.

"I'll bet everyone told you a lot of crazy stories about

me," Mom purred. "Almost none of them are true, I promise."

Andrew tried to push her away with his mind, but it was like pushing at quicksand. He crawled backwards until he found a wall. He tried to stand, but the bricks were too slimy, and slipped free of disintegrating mortar and hit his tender skull. He sagged sideways as Mom crawled up onto him and cornered him with her gaze.

"We're going to make a new family here, and you'll want to stay close. Dom and Dean are useful, but we need someone like you, someone with brains. We can be happy, Andrew. You want to be part of my happy family, don't you?"

Mom leaned in to plant a kiss on him, when her head snapped back. Her eyes bulged out like deviled eggs. Someone dragged her off him. A thin bullwhip of translucent raw nerve stood taut like a leash from the base of Mom's skull. Andrew followed it into the dark with his exhausted eyes as it reeled her in.

The moribund head of the Colony smashed through Mom's ruined household like a bulldozer carried by thousands of snakes. The united survivors, loyalists and scabs alike, limped or marched in after it and gathered round their battered brain. The nerve-leash dragged Mom out onto the open floor, where she lay tense yet paralyzed, like a kitten hanging by the scruff of its neck.

A curious assortment of eyes studied Andrew, perhaps measuring him for the same treatment. Swarms of bees took off from the hives in its whorled brain folds to sting and probe the twins, stopping Dom within inches of driving the mirror-shard into his brother's throat.

Dean opened his eyes and sat up, shaky but no more aware of his damage than any other animal machine would be. The instant his eyes focused, Dean's mutilated flesh seemed to melt like boiling wax. He lunged at Dom, who caught him in a weary boxers' clench and plunged the mirror shard into his brother's back. They staggered in circles, trying to throttle each other, and there they melted together, fluid features fused in a crude, brutish Janus mask facing forwards and backwards, a four-legged beast thrashing itself senseless.

Something rippled through every other citizen of the Colony, a tidal command that Andrew felt only as an intangible force that lifted, then left him behind as it passed through the cellar, like a swell in the ocean.

The Colony drew into a knot around Mom. At first, Andrew thought it was to protect her from the brothers, but they rose and joined the inner circle pressing in until it blocked her from sight. Inside the tightening gauntlet of bodies, Mom howled, "You bastards! You stupid, blind chauvinistic assholes! Not a single stiff dick between you, but you're still stupid fucking men! I'm the queen! You can't make new life! You couldn't bear the pain and the sacrifice, but you think you can judge me? Without me, there's no future! Without me, you're all dead!"

Though severed from this Colony, Andrew still knew what was happening. The queen is the heart and life of the hive, but when she fails or betrays her subjects—by producing too few eggs, or even as a scapegoat in the face of disaster—a new chemical imperative spreads, and the hive is driven to commit regicide. No one knows where or how the mandate for a coup originates and spreads, but the queen is not the hive, and her survival means nothing, if she cannot serve it.

Within minutes, the entire hive clusters upon the queen as they do to protect her during a swarm or in winter hibernation, but now linking limbs and squeezing until they crush her to death. No single bee plays Brutus, but all act as one to murder their mother. Beekeepers call this aberrant behavior "balling the queen."

Andrew couldn't see her, but he heard her pleas and curses dwindle to gurgling groans under the combined weight of the Colony linked into one enormous, crushing muscle. They grunted and strained and stamped for endless, ugly minutes until at last, there was only the collective gasp and wheeze of the exhausted, motherless Colony, and the C-sharp flutter of agitated wings.

After a long, pregnant pause, the mound of workers, soldiers, nurses and scabs broke apart and sleepwalked away from the trampled remains of their queen. Andrew had only met her minutes ago, and he allowed that whatever she'd done to her children, she wasn't herself when she came after him. She had tainted every life she touched with her poisoned ego, but she brought Laura into the world, so Andrew could not feel relief at her death.

Strange, but the strongest feeling that welled up in him now was fear for the Colony. When a hive balls its queen, they swiftly hatch and groom a successor; but the new queen does not always adapt. The Colony's nursery was empty. Mom had proved surprisingly fertile, but she could never truly become a queen bee.

The nurses swept in and dipped their dainty hands into the steaming juices oozing from Mom's crushed husk. Turning, they scanned the ranks of colonists. When the roving black eyespots lingered on Andrew, he pressed against the wall and wished for the strength to run, the will to give a shit, but they passed on, searching until some secret sign stopped them.

Taking up dripping slabs of royal carrion in their slim but sturdy arms, the nurses surrounded and crowned the new queen by smearing the regally scented womb-flesh over every exposed inch of her skin, while another of them slid a feeding tube into her mouth and down her unresisting throat. Through it all, May trembled with tired exaltation. Through it all, the hulking fusion of Dom and Dean only stared into space.

Across the crowded cellar, Andrew and the giant brain stared at each other. A Colony could never have two heads.

No communication passed by mouth or mind. Andrew silently tried and failed to appeal to the solar ego that confronted him, but he sensed that the Colony now saw him with fifty or more minds, not one.

Even those who died in this senseless war looked out of its eyes with a weird, sad wisdom no individual human could grasp. It—they—pitied him. The Colony considered not whether or how it could kill him, but if it could show mercy without endangering itself.

Without warning, streamers of ectoplasm burst from the dorsal folds of the brain to lock onto the spine of each and every colonist. Grodenko's cyclopean bulk seemed to subside, as if the critical tension of the egomaniacal tyrant had at last totally dissipated. The taut cords binding him to the Colony trembled mildly, as fluid pumped out of the brain poured into their bodies.

In this endless, silent ritual, the human barriers to a perfect communal union were finally swept away. Grodenko's brain deflated amid roiling cyclones of bees abandoning their cranial hives, as the colonists absorbed him. It was simple necessity, for they could never travel with the huge burden of the centralized mind. With the liquid consciousness of the human hive distributed among them, they could at least have a chance to escape, and any one of them could reproduce and settle a new colony.

When Grodenko's body was a flaccid mound of empty skin, the colony fixed its collective gaze on Andrew. In the fused voice of dozens, it said, "WE WILL SWARM."

"I know." Andrew slowly rose and walked sideways along the wall. "This tunnel goes the furthest into the forest. I'll go first . . . scout it out for you."

He looked one last time at Dom and Dean. It was hard to pick them out of the crowd of bloated, blank-eyed colonists. In their fused, straining faces, he saw only no echoes of Laura, the family resemblance all but erased from their newly consolidated body. He owed them nothing, but they were his only family, and for a while, he had been part of the Colony. He had helped heal it, and so he could not but feel a momentary pang of loss as he turned and ran away.

Nobody stopped him as he raced blindly up the black tunnel. Roots and rocks scraped his head, so he doubted the Colony meant to use it as an escape route. It was older, probably dating back to the first commune, or even the house's original incarnation as an asylum. There were other tunnels, but this one had recently been chalked with a series of arrows, pointed inward.

He emerged into gray half-light. Ground mist flowed and clotted around rocks and fallen trees and hummocks of ferns.

When a stooped, shadowy shape lurched at him out of the trees, he was not surprised at all. "Hey, Sprague."

"Are they coming?" The old man cracked his gnarled knuckles and cocked the hammers on his shotgun.

"What are you going to do, Sprague, shoot them all?"

"Kill the head, and the body will die . . . but you were the new head. You're the one they chose. You failed them . . . "

"It's over. Grodenko's joined them. There is no head, anymore. They are one, now."

"We'll see about that. Just call them out."

"You know, I was wondering . . . All the workers and the soldiers went on strike, but the nurses stayed to take care of the new breeder. What happened to the old queen?"

Sprague emitted a stalling hum as he tried to figure where Andrew was headed. "She wouldn't come with the striking workers . . . too tied to Grodenko. The soldiers killed her, to stop her making scabs . . . "

The order to ball the old queen was anything but

natural, its origin anything but mysterious. "Just a machine, was she? A baby factory?"

"Nature can be cruel sometimes, boy, harder than men at their worst. This is the new nature . . . "

"It was *your* strike, Sprague! You stole the bees! You reprogrammed them! She was just a machine to make more colonists, but they were all just tools, to you. Just like animals, down on the farm: when they fail, you shoot them, eat them and plug in a new one, right? Just like them . . . " He waved at the sunken, fern-furred hollow all around them, at the rows of low moguls that were not rocks.

"You shut your fucking mouth," Sprague bristled, but there was nothing left to deny. Andrew had learned the whole, ugly truth when he struck the old hermit down, but only now did it unpack itself and become real.

"They failed the ideal of the commune. They failed you. But they never really left, did they?"

Sprague raised the shotgun, but his thumb would not cock the hammers. The air thrummed with angry, vengeful wings. He couldn't shoot Andrew, any more than he could lie to him. He popped sweat-rivets, trying gamely but in vain to do both. "Sturtevant was a tyrant . . . just like Grodenko . . . Dunlap and his cronies wanted to break up the colony, if they couldn't take it over. If the commune broke up . . . the dream was going to die . . . "

"Bullshit! Sturtevant was just like Grodenko. But he didn't poison them. He didn't bury them out here. He was going to pack up and leave or get a new batch of serfs to lord over, but you were born into the colony. It was all you ever knew, and when they were going to abandon it, you killed them."

Sprague threw down the shotgun as if it burned him. His shoulders dropped, and Andrew could almost hear the weight slide off them—the lies, the secrets . . . "I guess it's easy to judge from up on that throne, where I put you. How did it feel, boy? Being part of a perfect family, with one heart, one soul, one purpose? It felt good, didn't? You felt strong, didn't you? No doubt, no weakness, no loneliness, no lies . . . " He pushed and slapped at the air like he felt hands all over him, reaching out of the past. "Makes you feel so big and smart, you think you read me like a book, so you know what I went through . . . but if you'd lived it, you'd show a little more respect."

"I do know. I saw it in your head, old man, looked at it through your eyes. It's not too hard to judge, if you're not the one trying to escape the guilt. You poisoned their last breakfast together. You must've been all of, what, ten years old? I know you told yourself you weren't going to kill them. Just make them too sick to leave. But they died and you lived, and you went out into the world and had a really tough time, and you came back, and you didn't learn a goddamned thing, did you?"

From deep inside the beaten man, a low groan began to leak out, like an antique hand-cranked air raid siren. "No, no, no." Stamping his feet, he made ready to charge off into the woods or throw himself at Andrew, but his tired old body betrayed him, and he fell down on a bed of moss with his head in his hands.

"You can't make them share," Andrew said. "You can't make them obey, and you can't make them stay. You can love them and share with them and hope they love you back, but you can't control them, or they stop being alive." Andrew knelt over Sprague, uncertain if he was even breathing. "You got your wish. The Colony is going to survive. They're swarming. They're going somewhere far away, to try again."

Sprague looked up, yellow eyes wide. "They can't." His breath hitched, and he looked like he might have another seizure. You were supposed to test someone for a stroke: ask them their name, and what day it was, and the days of the week backwards. Though he foamed at the mouth, the tremor seemed to impose in him an awful lucidity. "The bees . . . carry a virus. If they get out, it'll wipe out all the other bees. Government'll come . . . kill everyone . . . "

Andrew tried to reach into Sprague to pull out the truth, but it was like trying to find a number in a wet phone book. It was all mush running together, circling the drain, and Andrew had to struggle to get out before the undertow sucked him down with it.

Sprague whimpered, "I don't want to go . . . alone . . . "

Andrew pried the dead man's grip from his mind and backed away, suddenly feeling like an intruder in that unmarked graveyard. Nothing clawed its way out of the earth to claim old man Sprague. They didn't have to.

Turning to go, Andrew smelled something on the wind—a bitter tang of smoke. He climbed the ridge the tunnel burrowed into and, hiding in a stand of pines, looked down into the meadow.

Fire engulfed the toppled watchtower and the roof of the house, and every so often, rockets of flaming debris shot out of the inferno to land and kindle satellite fires in the tinder-dry forest all around. The flames walked across the field like a ghostly scarecrow army, gorging recklessly on the meager fuel of wild grass and sheds before burning out; but a few fiery missiles reached his side of the forest and began to dine on the arid pines and firs on the hillside below his vantage point.

He watched the house burn for a while, looking for some sign of life. He reached out, but could feel only the flickers of scattered bees relaying the last orders of the Colony. It was as if they had switched channels, because he got nothing but garbled bits of coded nonsense.

Cut off from the Colony, he felt a weird dragging inertia pulling him down. It was as if he was finally succumbing to shock, now that he could, but he was also suffering withdrawals from the nurturing broadcast warmth of the collective.

A helicopter buzzed low over the house. Its whispering

rotors ripped spiral tatters out of the huge pillar of smoke rising from the roof.

Andrew could see a man in a biohazard suit hanging out the door with a huge, belt-fed machine gun. He raked the rooftop with a brilliant sleet of tracer rounds for a few moments while the helicopter lazily rode the updrafts from the fire like a gigantic bumblebee.

Out of the fire, the wreckage of the watchtower rose up like a colossus and shook its rusty iron fist at the spies. For just a moment, the burning house awakened and catapulted the iron golem headfirst into the whirling blades.

In the air, the missile diffused into a shotgun spray of bars and bricks. The helicopter wheeled around to take the barrage on its port side—windshield shattered, door gunner flapping alongside like a leaky yoyo—then plunged sideways to the east and out of the valley with its tail almost vertical, leaving its own trail of black smoke like blood in murky water, over the mountains and out of sight.

Who did that? He wondered. There was nobody else left in the woods. An empty shadow of his anger at the chopper, so suddenly quenched, floated like a smoke ring in the empty hive of his mind. *Did I see that? Did I do that?*

The heat from the fire began to warm his cheeks and singe his eyebrows. The convection from the furious devouring of the nearest trees sent a hot, ember-heavy wind racing up the slope. Tiny red fireflies alit and pollinated the yellow leaves all around him with Halloween blossoms.

Morning would unleash catastrophic fires, bee plagues and a swarming posthuman colony on the land, but Andrew had nowhere better to go.

A bee landed on his ear and danced. Unlike all the others, this one communicated something he could understand, something that undid all the pain and suffering of the night, of the whole godforsaken trip.

She is here, the thrumming wings whispered.

She waits.

CHAPTER 32

SMOKE OBSCURED THE paths between the trees. Fat white flakes of ash drifted on the sulfur-yellow breeze.

Andrew lost his way in the woods. The trail he thought would lead to Mom's cabin brought him back to May's trailer. He got tangled in berry thorns and had to turn back when he tried to get out onto the road. He heard rumbling engines like fire trucks nearby, but in the baffled atmosphere of the smoke, he couldn't tell where they came from, or where they went, or if they were even real.

His mental map of the area was fragmented, like memories of a loved one confronted with the tarted-up husk of the real thing in an open coffin. The forest was a ghost of itself, and all he could feel when he tried to touch it, was that it didn't want to let him leave.

Dark, toxic doubt seeped into his gutshot soul. He really didn't have anywhere to hurry to, after all. Why rush to be judged and found guilty, yet again? This fire was for him. Better to just lie down and wait—

Something else that came up in counseling bubbled up out of memory to validate his gloom. It was a question the therapist posed at one of their last sessions: do you love Laura despite her faults, or *for* them, because her crippling neuroses validate your own?

The therapist never helped him answer the question, never got to the point of helping them pull it together. She went on leave for a month, and never called them back to schedule another appointment, never sent them a bill for any of the months of counseling they'd already had. It was a tacit admission, Andrew thought at the time, that the whole exercise had been bullshit, and the therapist had nothing to say because there was no solution. Laura's demand for a divorce had taken him completely by surprise because he had thought they planned to limp on through life together.

Had he ever really loved Laura, or just needed her, and would he ever know the difference?

When he closed his eyes, he could see her, and his heart beat faster. Wherever she was, wherever she went, was his only home. Wasn't that love? If it wasn't, he had nothing. He was less than nothing.

He would make a commitment. He would dig in and give all he had to make her happy. Wasn't that what they meant, when people talked about making a marriage work?

What if the Colony still needed him? What if his desertion killed them all? When Grodenko had reached out to engulf him, he'd thought of Laura, and recoiled. Now, he regretted his haste. They wanted him; they needed him, and he rejected their love out of the childish longing to cling to something already dead and buried. Maybe the bee lied to him, if it had spoken to him at all. Wasn't that the problem of any dictatorship, that the leader heard only what he wanted to?

A long, conversational growl startled him. A shadow crouched on the ridge ahead. The sight of it struck Andrew thoughtless. Out of the perfect blackness, the wildfires danced in a pair of lambent golden eyes.

The shadow shook off a coat of ash and padded down the ridge. Those diabolical eyes flashed and cut through the yellow murk, that coughing bark dripped animal mockery as it led him out of the fire.

It was Toshiro. The dog regarded him for only a moment, and then turned and bolted out of sight. Andrew made himself climb the ridge, and followed the echoing barks down a smoke-choked slope.

When he could not see or hear Toshiro, he stumbled out into a clearing and saw Mom's cabin. Her black Cadillac sat in the driveway with its rear end crushed like a beer can. Beside it, with its driver's side door hanging open and the interior dome light glowing, was a green Dodge Dart Swinger with bumper stickers spreading like herpes up the trunk and rear window, just like Mom's.

Laura.

He stopped in the gravel driveway and checked himself in the dusty rearview mirror on Laura's car. His haggard eyes jabbed at him out of an emaciated, rubbery mask caked with filth. His hair had fallen out and his brain bulged through the burst sutures of his skull like a second head. Laura had once said she loved him for who he was, not how he looked, after an argument about the cost of a prescription acne treatment. He hoped she really meant it.

Anxiety sparked inside him like whipping short-circuits. He could smooth things out. He could take control of the situation, assert his natural dominance and command her . . . but then he would become what he'd rejected in the Colony. She had to want him. He knew that she had only come out of guilt and worry, but he had to hope that something inside her would awaken when she saw him again.

The door hung open, but he could see only darkness inside. If she had any sense, she would have fled at the first whiff of smoke, and maybe she had. Maybe her car wouldn't start, or someone had disabled it to keep her from leaving. All the maybes were driving him crazy.

Moving as if he wore a deep-sea diver's suit, Andrew trudged on up the steps to the porch. To step over the threshold now was, just like the first time, like breaking through a membrane. His mouth, when it finally opened, only let out a stuttering croak. "Laura?"

The entry hall was littered with chunks of sheetrock where something had crashed through the wall, but he saw small, pointy-toed bootprints in the gypsum dust. They went in, but none came out.

Andrew held his breath and walked into the empty house. "Laura!" he called out, but the only answer was the bright, tight empty-house echo of his voice.

Laura lay on the floor in the middle of the room. Dead bees lay in a halo around her like spent shell casings. Andrew stopped and fought the sinking feeling that he was, like always, just five minutes too late.

His hands dithered at his sides. He'd have to explain about the ring and how he'd lost it, but it wouldn't matter, now, they didn't need empty symbols, they'd be truly bound together. But symbols were important, they told you things you couldn't see otherwise. He'd lost the ring because he was a loser, and now he'd lost her—

She stirred when he approached, peering at him through squinted eyes. Her expression was oddly neutral, the way it always was when he saw her wake up, as if she had to take a moment to orient herself and remind herself which life, which body, she found herself in. It was always a moment of delicious unease, watching that unfamiliar face regard him in sleepy puzzlement, always broken a moment later by her warm smile and a kiss. But then she would look away, and that far-off stranger's face would try to remember the dream she'd been chasing when she woke up next to him.

She looked at him now, and that moment of non-recognition went on and on. Her eyes widened, and she made a sound that was beneath words, but became the seed of a scream.

"It's me!" he tried not to scream. "It's Andrew, baby. I'm here. I'm okay. I know I look like a mess, but—"

"Andrew?" She sounded fuzzy, disconnected, as if she were recovering from anesthesia after major surgery. As if the name was not even a word, but just a noise to her, with no meaning, no love—

He could make her love him. He could bind her to him like never before, just by willing it. He ordered the bees to make her stay, to wait for him. But he did not order her to love him.

Would it be wrong? Did he have any control over his love for her? If he could turn it off as easily as she apparently could, none of this would ever have happened.

"I came as fast as I could," he said in a rush, the old excuse routine, but she just kept staring through him. "Laura, I tried to call you, to warn you about what was happening up here. It—your Mom, and your brothers . . . But I . . . I'm really glad you're here, baby. I love you so fucking much . . . "

He could not hold back any longer. He reached out for her. Laura pressed herself flat against the floor as if she could bury herself and escape him, but still she made no sound.

Refugees pressed against the sliding glass door in the living room, shuffled in over the broken glass, stepping over the incongruous refrigerator door on the patio. Andrew recognized some from from the sawmill, but the others must have come from Utopia. Half-naked, dripping honey and less wholesome secretions, the orphaned draftees had begun to truly change.

Which side are you on, my people?

It was far too late for any of them to go back to their old lives. Slack-jawed and glassy-eyed, they filed into the empty room and gathered around him and his wife.

They had no choice, any more than he did. But what did free will have to do with love, or family?

An exhausted squadron of bees flitted in the open doorway behind him and alit on his neck. He felt the unmistakable tread of royalty dancing among the hairs on the back of his neck—a renegade queen, calling her swarm.

Laura tried to get up. Andrew gathered her into his arms. He hated them for taking away his chance to talk with her, to work it out, to give her the choice to love him. He hated them as one hates his fists or his face, when they decide one's fate. He could not even ask her once, just to know, because they were a part of him. He feared what they might do to her if they aroused his anger, even for an instant.

"You're going to feel a little sting," he told her, "but after, you'll feel a whole lot better about everything. I promise."

Andrew held Laura closer as the bees settled on her because he couldn't bear to look into her eyes. The only thing worse than seeing her fearful reproach would be seeing them go dead and flat like Dean's.

He held her all through the shaking and seizures as the venom took hold. Finally, in a weak, but inflected voice, she said, "What do you want to do?"

He thought about that. The first rays of sunlight pierced the windows and played over the barren expanse of shag carpet and the ragged family that gathered around them.

"We need to get away from here," he told her, lifting her up and steering her towards the door. "I want to try again. I want to love you, treasure you, make you my queen. I want . . . to start a family."

Which side are you on?

The humming of the bees clumsily rendered the Pixies' "Havalina," the song they danced to at their wedding.

He held her close and whispered in her ear, "I got this."

Her smile was a vending machine dispensing candy. The moment stretched into minutes as she waited for him to tell her what to say next.

If men were angels, no government would be necessary. If angels were to govern men, neither external nor internal controls on government would be necessary. In framing a government which is to be administered by men over men, the great difficulty lies in this: you must first enable the government to control the governed; and in the next place oblige it to control itself.

—James Madison, Federalist Paper 51

"Must the citizen ever for a moment, or in the least degree, resign his conscience to the legislator? Why has every man a conscience, then? I think that we should be men first, and subjects afterward. It is not desirable to cultivate a respect for the law, so much as for the right. The only obligation which I have a right to assume is to do at any time what I think right.

—Henry David Thoreau

ABOUT THE AUTHOR

CODY GOODFELLOW has written nine novels and five collections of short stories, and edits the hyperpulp zine *Forbidden Futures*. His writing has been favored with three Wonderland Book Awards. His comics work has been featured in *Mystery Meat, Creepy, Slow Death Zero* and *Skin Crawl*. As an actor, he has appeared in numerous short films, TV shows, music videos by Anthrax and Beck, and a Days Inn commercial. He also wrote, co-produced and scored the Lovecraftian hygiene films *Baby Got Bass* and *Stay At Home Dad*, which can be viewed on YouTube. He "lives" in San Diego, California.

SPOOKY TALES FROM GHOULISH BOOKS

☐ **BELOW | Laurel Hightower**
ISBN: 978-1-943720-69-9 $12.95
A creature feature about a recently divorced woman trying to survive a road trip through the mountains of West Virginia.

☐ **MAGGOTS SCREAMING! | Max Booth III**
ISBN: 978-1-943720-68-2 $18.95
On a hot summer weekend in San Antonio, Texas, a father and son bond after discovering three impossible corpses buried in their back yard.

☐ **LEECH | John C. Foster**
ISBN: 978-1-943720-70-5 $14.95
Horror / noir mashup about a top secret government agency's most dangerous employee. Doppelgangers, demigods, and revenants, oh my!

☐ **RABBITS IN THE GARDEN | Jessica McHugh**
ISBN: 978-1-943720-73-6 $16.95
13-year-old Avery Norton is a crazed killer—according to the staff at Taunton Asylum, anyway. But as she struggles to prove her innocence in the aftermath of gruesome murders spanning the 1950s, Avery discovers there's a darker force keeping her locked away . . . which she calls "Mom."

☐ **PERFECT UNION | Cody Goodfellow**
ISBN: 978-1-943720-74-3 $18.95
Three brothers searching the wilderness for their mother instead find a utopian cult that seeks to reinvent society, family . . . humanity

☐ **SOFT PLACES | Betty Rocksteady**
ISBN: 978-1-943720-75-0 $14.95
A novella/graphic novel hybrid about a seemingly psychotic woman who suffers a mysterious head injury.

☐HARES IN THE HEDGEROW | Jessica McHugh

ISBN: 978-1-943720-76-7 $21.95

15 years after the events in *Rabbits in the Garden*, Avery Norton is a ghost. 16-year-old Sophie Dillon doesn't know anything about the alleged murderer, yet she's haunted nightly by the same dark urges, which send her on a journey to uncover her past with the Norton family and to embrace the future with her spiritual family, the Choir of the Lamb. But Sophie's devotions can't protect her from the ghosts waiting in the wings. After all, she's the one they've been waiting for.

Not all titles available for immediate shipping. All credit card purchases must be made online at GhoulishBooks.com. Shipping is 5.80 for one book and an additional dollar for each additional book. Contact us for international shipping prices. All checks and money orders should be made payable to Perpetual Motion Machine Publishing.

Ghoulish Books
PO Box 1104
Cibolo, TX 78108

Ship to:

Name _____

Address _____

City_____ State_____ Zip _____

Phone Number _____

Book Total: $_____

Shipping Total: $_____

Grand Total: $_____

Patreon:
www.patreon.com/pmmpublishing

Website:
www.PerpetualPublishing.com

Facebook:
www.facebook.com/PerpetualPublishing

Twitter:
@PMMPublishing

Newsletter:
www.PMMPNews.com

Email Us:
Contact@PerpetualPublishing.com